PENNY JORDAN

has been writing for more than twenty-five years and has an outstanding record—more than 165 novels published, including the phenomenally successful *A Perfect Family, To Love, Honour And Betray, The Perfect Sinner* and *Power Play*, which hit the *Sunday Times* and *New York Times* bestseller lists. She says she hopes to go on writing until she has passed the 200 mark—and maybe even the 250 mark.

Although Penny was born in Preston, Lancashire, U.K., where she spent her childhood, she moved to Cheshire as a teenager, and has continued to live there. Following the death of her husband, she moved to the small traditional Cheshire market town on which she based her Crighton books.

She lives with her Birman cat, Posh, who tries to assist with her writing by sitting on the newspapers and magazines Penny reads to provide her with ideas she can adapt for her fictional books.

Penny is a member and supporter of the Romantic Novelists' Association and the Romance Writers of America—two organizations dedicated to providing support for both published and yet-to-be-published authors.

PENNY JORDAN

Mistletoe Brides

TORONTO NEW YORK LONDON
AMSTERDAM PARIS SYDNEY HAMBURG
STOCKHOLM ATHENS TOKYO MILAN MADRID
PRAGUE WARSAW BUDAPEST AUCKLAND

Recycling programs for this product may not exist in your area.

ISBN-13: 978-0-373-68839-5

MISTLETOE BRIDES

TABLE OF CONTENTS

THE CHRISTMAS BRIDE

PROLOGUE

'IT'S A TOTAL NIGHTMARE, it just couldn't be any worse.'

'Spending Christmas in a castle in Spain is a nightmare?'

Tilly gave a reluctant smile as she heard the wry note in her friend and flatmate's voice.

'Okay. On the face of it, it may sound good,' she agreed. 'But, Sally, the reality is that it will be a nightmare. Or rather a series of on-going nightmares,' she pronounced darkly.

'Such as?'

Tilly shook her head ruefully. 'You want a list? Fine! One, my mother is about to get married to a man she's so crazily in love with she's sends me e-mails that sound as though she's living on adrenalin and sex. Two, the man she's marrying is a multi-millionaire—no, a billionaire—'

'You have a funny idea of what constitutes a nightmare,' Sally interrupted.

'I haven't finished yet,' Tilly said. 'Art—that's ma's billion-aire—is American, and has very strong ideas about Family Life.'

'Meaning?'

'Patience. I *am* getting there. Ma's got this guilt thing that it's her fault that I'm anti-men and marriage, because she and Dad split up.'

'And is it?'

'Well, let's just say the fact that she's been married and di-vorced four times already doesn't exactly incline me to look upon marriage with optimism.'

'Four times?'

'Ma loves falling in love. And getting engaged. And getting married. This time Ma has decided she wants to be married at the stroke of midnight on New Year's Eve in a Spanish castle. So Art is transporting his entire family to spend Christmas and New Year in Spain to witness the ceremony—at his expense. We're all going to stay at the castle so that we can get to know one another properly "as a family". Because, according to Ma, Art can't think of a more Family Time than Christmas.'

'Sounds good so far.'

'Well, here's the bit that is not so good. Art's family comprises his super-perfect daughters from his first marriage, along with their husbands and their offspring.'

'And?'

'And Ma, for reasons best known to herself, has told Art that I'm engaged to be married. And of course Art has insisted that I join the happy family party at the castle, along with my fiancé.'

'But you haven't got a fiancé. You haven't even got a boyfriend.'

'Exactly. I have pointed this out to my mother, but she's pulling out all the high-drama stops. She says she's afraid Art's daughters are going to persuade him not to marry her, and that if I turn up *sans* fiancé it will add fuel to their argument that as a family we are not cut out for long-term, reliable marriages. She should really have gone on the stage.' Tilly looked at her friend. 'I know this sounds crazy, but the truth is I'm worried about her. If Art's daughters are against the marriage, then she won't stand a chance. Ma isn't a schemer. She just can't help falling in love.'

'It sounds more like you're the parent and she's the child.'

'Well, Ma does like to imply that she was little more than a child when she ran off with my father and had me. Although she was twenty-one at the time, and the reason she ran off with Dad was that she was already engaged to someone else. Who she then married after she realised she had made a mistake in marrying my dad.' Tilly was smiling as she spoke, but there was a weary resignation in her tone. 'I feel I should be there for her, but I just don't want her to blame me if things go wrong because I didn't turn up with a fiancé.'

'Well, you know what to do, don't you?'

'What?'

'Hire an escort.'

'What?'

'There's no need to look like that. I'm not talking about a "when would you like the massage" type escort. I'm talking about the genuine no-strings, no-sex, perfectly respectable and socially acceptable paid-for social escort.'

Sally could see that Tilly was looking both curious and wary. 'Come on, pass me the telephone directory. Let's sort it out now.'

'You could always lend me Charlie,' Tilly suggested.

'Let you take my fiancé away to some Spanish castle for the most emotionally loaded holiday of the year for loved-up couples?' Sally gave a vehement shake of her head. 'No way! I'm not letting him miss the seasonal avalanche of advertisements for happy couples with their noses pressed up against jewellers' windows.' Sally balanced the telephone book on her lap. 'Okay, let's try this one first. Pass me the phone.'

'Sally, I don't…'

'Trust me. This is the perfect answer. You're doing this for your mother, remember!'

'WILL I DO *WHAT*?' Silas Stanway stared at his young half-brother in disbelief.

'Well, I can't do it. Not in a wheelchair, with my arm and leg in plaster,' Joe pointed out. 'And it seems mean to let the poor girl down,' he added virtuously, before admitting, 'I need the money I'll be paid for this, Silas, and it's giving me some terrific contacts.'

'Working as a male escort?' Beneath the light tone of mockery Silas felt both shock and distaste. Another indication of the cultural gap that existed between him, a man of thirty plus, and his barely twenty-one-year-old sibling—the result of his father's second marriage—for whom Silas felt a mixture of brotherly love and, since their father's death, almost paternal concern.

'Loads of actors do it,' Joe defended himself. 'And this agency is *respectable*. It's not one of those where the women you escort are going to come on to you for sex. Mind you, from what I've heard they're willing to pay very well if you do, and it can be a real turn-on in a sort of Mrs Robinson way. At least that's what I've heard,' he amended hastily, when he saw the way his half-brother was looking at him. 'It's only for a few days,' he wheedled. 'Look, here's the invite. Private jet out to Spain, luxury living in a castle, and all at the expense of the bridegroom. I was really looking forward to it. Come on, be a sport.'

Silas looked uninterestedly at the invitation Joe had handed to him, and then frowned when he saw the name of the bridegroom-to-be. 'This is an invitation to Art Johnson the oil tycoon's wedding?' he demanded flatly.

'Yeah, that's right,' Joe said with exaggerated patience. 'Art Johnson the Third. The girl I'm escorting is the daughter of the woman he's going to marry.'

Silas's eyes narrowed. 'Why does she need an escort?'

'Dunno.' Joe gave a dismissive shrug. 'She probably just hasn't got a boyfriend and doesn't want to show up at the wedding looking like a loser. It's a woman thing; happens all the time,' Joe informed him airily. 'Apparently she rang the agency and told them she wanted someone young, hunky and sexy, Oh, and not gay.'

'And that doesn't tell you *anything?*' Silas asked witheringly.

'Yeah, it tells me she wants the kind of escort she can show off.'

'Have you met her?'

'No. I did e-mail her to suggest we meet up beforehand to set up some kind of background story, but she said she was too busy. She said we could discuss everything during the flight. The bridegroom is organising the private jet. All I have to do is get in a taxi, with my suitcase and passport, and collect her from her place on the way to the airport. Easy-peasy. Or at least it would have been if this hadn't happened during that rugby match.' Joe grimaced at his plaster casts.

Silas listened to his half-brother's disclosures with growing contempt for the woman who was 'hiring' him. The more he heard, the less inclined he was to believe Joe's naïve assertion that his escort duties were to be strictly non-sexual. Ordinarily he would not only have given Joe a pithy definition of exactly what he thought of the woman, he would also have added a warning not to do any more agency work and a flat refusal to step into his brother's shoes.

Normally. If the bridegroom in question had not been Art Johnson. He had been trying to contact Art Johnson for the last six months for inside information about the late legendary oil tycoon Jay Byerly. Jay Byerly had, during his lifetime, straddled both the oil industry and the political scene like a colossus.

As an investigative journalist for one of the country's most prestigious broadsheets, Silas was used to interviewees being reluctant to talk to him. But this time he was investigating for a book he was writing about the sometimes slippery relationships within the oil industry. And Jay Byerly was rumoured to have once used his connections to hush up an oil-related near-ecological disaster nearly thirty years ago. Until recently Art Johnson had been a prime mover in oil, and he had been mentored by Jay Byerly in his early days.

So far every attempt Silas had made to get anywhere near Art Johnson had been met with a complete rebuff. Supposedly semi-retired from the oil business now, having handed over the company to be run by his sons-in-law, it was widely accepted that Art still controlled the business—and its political connections—from behind the scenes.

Silas wasn't the kind of man who liked being forced to give up on anything, but he had begun to think that this time he had no choice.

Now it seemed fate had stepped in on his side.

'Okay,' he told his half-brother. 'I'll do it.'

'Wow, Silas—'

'On one condition.'

'Okay, I'll split the fee with you. And if she does turn out to be a complete dog—'

'That condition being that you don't do any more escorting.'

'Hey, Silas, come on. The money's good,' Joe protested, but then he saw Silas's expression and shook his head. 'Okay... I guess I can always go back to bar work.'

'Right. Run through the arrangements with me again.'

CHAPTER ONE

THERE WAS NO WAY THIS was going to work. No way she was ever going to be able to persuade anyone that a hired escort was her partner for real, Tilly decided grimly. But why should she care? Given free choice, she wouldn't even be going to the wedding. Her mother hadn't picked a decent partner yet, and Tilly had no faith in her having done so this time. And as for Art's family... Tilly tried to picture her fun-loving, rule-breaking, shock-inducing mother living happily within the kind of family set-up she had described to Tilly in her e-mails, and failed.

The marriage would not last five minutes. In fact it would, in Tilly's opinion, be better if it never took place at all—even if her mother was adamant that she was finally truly in love.

She was a fool for letting herself be dragged into her mother's life to act the part of the happily engaged daughter. But, as always where anything involving her mother was concerned, it was always easier to give in than to object.

The only thing Tilly had ever been able to hold out about against her mother was her own determination never to fall in love or marry.

'But, darling, how can you say that?' her mother had protested when Tilly had told her of her resolve. 'Everyone wants to meet someone and fall in love with them. It's basic human instinct.'

'What if I find out that I'm not in love with them any more, or they aren't in love with me?'

'Well, then you find someone else.'

'Only to marry again, and then again when that doesn't work out? No, thanks, Ma.'

Mother and daughter they might be, and they might even share the same physical characteristics, but sisters under the skin they were most definitely not.

No? Who was she kidding? Wasn't it true that deep down she longed to meet her soul mate, to find that special someone to whom she'd feel able to give herself completely, with whom she'd feel able to remove all those barriers she had erected to protect herself from the pain of loving the wrong man? A man strong enough to believe in their love and to demolish all her own doubts, noble enough to command not just her love but her respect, human enough to show her his own vulnerability—oh, and of course he must be sexy, gorgeous, and have the right kind of sense of humour. The kind of man that came by the dozen and could be found almost anywhere then, really, she derided herself. Just as well she had never been foolish enough to tell anyone about him. What would she say? *Oh, and by the way, here's a description of my wish for Christmas...*

Get a grip, she warned herself sternly. He—her 'fiancé', and most definitely *not* soulmate—would be here any minute. Tilly frowned. She had e-mailed him last night to explain in exact detail what his role would involve, and to say that he would be required to pose convincingly as her fiancé in public. And only in public. No matter how many times Sally had assured her that she had nothing to worry about, and that hiring an escort was a perfectly reasonable and respectable thing to do, Tilly was not totally convinced.

Luckily, because she hadn't taken any time off during the summer, getting a month's leave from her job now had not been a problem. However, she could just imagine what the reaction of the young and sometimes impossibly louche male trainee bankers who worked under her would be if they knew what she was doing.

Other women in her situation might think of themselves as being let loose in a sweet shop at having so many testosterone-charged young men around. Tilly, however, tended to end up mothering her trainees more than anything else.

She tensed when she heard the doorbell ring, even though she had been waiting for it. It was too late now to wish she had taken Sally up on her offer to go into work later, so that she could vet the escort agency's choice.

The doorbell was still ringing. Stepping over her suitcase, Tilly went to open the door, tugging it inwards with what she had intended to be one smooth, I'm-the-one-in-control-here movement.

But her intention was sabotaged by the avalanche of female, hormone-driven reactions that paralysed her, causing her to grip hold of the half-open door.

The man in front of her wasn't just good-looking, she recognised with a small gulp of shock. He was… He was… She had to close her eyes and count to ten before she dared to open them again. Tiny feathery flicks of sensual heat were whipping against her nerve-endings, driving her body into a fever of what could only be lust. This man didn't just possess outstanding male good looks, he also possessed that hard-edged look of dangerous male sexuality that every woman recognised the minute she saw it. Tilly couldn't stop looking at him. He was dark-haired and tall—over six feet, she guessed—with powerfully broad shoulders and ice-blue eyes fringed with jet-black lashes. And right now he was looking at her with a kind of frowning impatience, edged with cool, male confidence, that said he certainly wasn't as awestruck by her appearance as she was by his.

'Matilda Aspinall?' he asked curtly.

'No…I mean, yes—only everyone calls me Tilly.' For heaven's sake, she sounded like a gauche teenager, not an almost thirty-year-old woman capable of running her own department in one of the most male-dominated City environments there was.

'Silas Stanway,' he introduced himself.

'*Silas?*' Tilly repeated uncertainly. 'But in your e-mails I thought—'

'I use my middle name for my e-mail correspondence,' Silas informed her coolly. It wasn't entirely untrue. He *did* use his middle name, along with his mother's maiden name as his pen-name. 'We'd better get a move on. The taxi driver wasn't too keen on stopping on double yellows. Is that your case?'

'Yes. But I can manage it myself,' Tilly told him.

Ignoring her attempts to do exactly that, he reached past her and hefted the case out of the narrow hallway as easily as though it weighed next to nothing.

'Got everything else?' he asked. 'Passport, travel documentation, keys, money…'

Tilly could feel an unfamiliar burn starting to heat her face. An equally unfamiliar sensation had invaded her body. A mixture of confusion and startlingly intense physical desire combined with disbelieving shock. Why was she not experiencing irritation that he should take charge? Why was she experiencing this unbelievably weird and alien sense of being tempted to mirror her own mother's behaviour and come over all helpless?

Was it because it was Christmas, that well-known emotional trap, baited and all ready to spring and humiliate any woman unfortunate enough to have to celebrate it without a loving partner? Christmas, according to the modern mythology of the great god of advertising, meant happy families seated around log fires in impossibly large and over-decorated drawing rooms. Or, for those who had not yet reached that stage, at the very least the loved-up coupledom of freezing cold play snow fights, interrupted by red-hot passionate kisses, the woman's hand on the man's arm revealing the icy glitter of a diamond engagement ring.

But, no matter how gaudily materialism wrapped up Christmas, the real reason people invested so much in it, both financially and emotionally, was surely because at heart, within everyone, there was still that child waking up on Christmas morning, hoping to receive the most perfect present—which the adult world surely translated as the gift of love, unquestioning, unstinting, freely given and equally freely received. A gift shared and celebrated, tinsel-wrapped in hope, with a momentary suspension of the harsh reality of the destruction that could follow.

She knew all about that, of course. So why, *why*, deep down inside was she being foolish enough to yearn to wake up on her own Christmas morning to that impossibly perfect gift? *She* was the one who was in charge, Tilly tried to remind herself firmly. Not him. And if he had really been her fiancé there was no way she would have allowed him to behave in such a high-handed manner, not even bothering to kiss her...

Kiss her?

Tilly stood in the hall and stared wildly at him, while her heart did the tango inside her chest.

'Is something wrong?'

Those ice-blue eyes didn't miss much, Tilly decided. 'No, everything's fine.' She flashed him her best "I'm the boss" professional smile and stepped through the door.

'Keys?' This woman didn't need an escort, she needed a carer, Silas decided grimly as he watched Tilly hunt feverishly through her bag for her keys and then struggle to insert them into the lock. It was just as well that Joe *wasn't* the one accompanying her. The pair of them wouldn't have got as far as Heathrow without one of them realising they had forgotten something.

What was puzzling him, though, was why on earth she had felt it necessary to hire a man. With those looks and that figure he would have expected her to be fighting men off, not paying them to escort her. Normally his own taste ran to tall, slim soignée brunettes of the French persuasion—that was to say women of intelligence who played the game of woman-to-man relationships like grand chess masters. But his hormones, lacking the discretion of his brain, were suddenly putting up a good argument for five foot six, gold and honey streaked hair, greenish-gold eyes, full soft pink lips, and a deliciously curvy hourglass figure.

He had, Silas decided, done Joe more than one favour in standing in for him. His impressionable sibling wouldn't have stood a chance of treating this as a professional exercise. Not, of course, that Silas was tempted. And even if he had been there was too much at stake from his own professional point of view for him to risk getting physically involved with Matilda. Matilda! Who on earth had been responsible for giving such a beauty the name Matilda?

What was the matter with her? Tilly wondered feverishly. She was twenty-eight years old, mature, responsible, sensible, and she just did not behave like this around men, or react to them as she did to this man. It wasn't the man who was causing her uncharacteristic behaviour, she reassured herself. It was the situation. Uncomfortably she remembered that sharp, hot, sweetly erotic surge of desire she had felt earlier. Her body still ached a little with it, and that ache intensified every time her female radar picked up the invisible forcefield of male pheromones surrounding Silas. Her body seemed to be reacting to them like metal to a magnet.

She grimaced as she looked up at the December grey-clouded sky. It had started to rain and the pavement was wet. Wet, and treacherously slippery if you happened to be wearing new shoes with leather soles, Tilly recognised as she suddenly started to lose her balance.

Silas caught her just before she cannoned into the open taxi door. Tilly could feel the strength of his grip through the soft fabric of the sleeve of her coat and the jumper she was wearing beneath it. She could also feel its warmth...*his* warmth, she recognised, and suddenly found it hard to breathe normally. Who would have thought that such a subtle scent of cologne— so subtle, in fact, that she had to stop herself from leaning closer so she could smell it better—could make her feel this dizzy?

She looked up at Silas, intending to thank him for saving her from a fall. He was looking back down at her. Tilly blinked and felt her gaze slip helplessly down the chiselled perfection of his straight nose to his mouth. Her own, she discovered, had gone uncomfortably dry. So dry that she was tempted to run the tip of her tongue along her lips.

'I 'aven't got all day, mate...'

The impatient voice of the taxi driver brought Tilly back to reality. Thanking Silas, she clambered into the taxi while he held the door open for her before joining her.

Joe would never have been able to deal with a woman like this, Silas decided grimly as the taxi set off. Hell, after the way she had just been looking at his mouth, he was struggling with the kind of physical reaction that hadn't caught him so off-guard since he had left his teens behind. In the welcome shadowy interior of the cab he moved discreetly, to allow his suit jacket to conceal the tell-tale tightness of the fabric of his chinos.

'Why don't I take charge of the passports and travel documentation?' he suggested to Tilly. 'After all, if I'm supposed to be your escort—'

'My fiancé,' Tilly corrected him.

'Your *what*?'

'You did get my e-mail, didn't you?' she asked uncertainly. 'The one I sent you explaining the situation, and the role you would be required to play?'

For the first time Silas noticed that she was wearing a solitaire diamond ring on the third finger of her left hand.

'My understanding was that I was simply to be your escort,' he told her coolly. 'If that's changed...'

There was a look in his eyes that Tilly wasn't sure she liked. A cynical world-weary look that held neither respect nor liking for her. What exactly was a man like this doing working for an escort agency anyway? she wondered. He looked as though he ought to be running a company, or...or climbing mountains—not hiring himself out to escort women.

'You will be my escort, but you will also be my fiancé. That is the whole purpose of us going to Spain.'

'Really? I understood the purpose was for us to attend a wedding.'

She hadn't mistaken that cynicism, Tilly realised. 'We *will* be attending a wedding. My mother's. Unfortunately my mother has told her husband-to-be that I am engaged—don't ask me why; I'm not sure I know the answer myself. All I do know is that, according to her, it's imperative that I turn up with a fiancé.'

'I see.' And he did. Only too well. He had been right to suspect that there was a seedy side to this whole escort situation. His mouth compressed and, seeing it, Tilly began to wish that the agency had sent her someone else. She didn't think she was up to coping with a man like this as her fake fiancé.

'What else was in this e-mail that I ought to know about?'

Tilly's chin lifted. 'Nothing. My mother, of course, knows the truth, and naturally I've told her that we will have to have separate rooms.'

'Naturally?' Silas quirked an eyebrow. 'Surely there is nothing *natural* about an engaged couple sleeping apart?'

Tilly suspected there would certainly be no sleeping apart from a woman he was really involved with. Immediately, intimate images she hadn't known she was capable of creating filled her head, causing her to look out of the taxi's window just in case Silas saw in her eyes exactly what she was thinking.

'What we do in private is our business,' she told him quickly.

'I should hope so,' he agreed, *sotto voce*. 'Personally, I've never seen the appeal of voyeurism.'

Tilly's head turned almost of its own accord, the colour sweeping up over her throat with betraying heat.

'Which terminal do you want, gov?' the taxi driver asked.

'We're flying out in a privately owned plane. Here's where we need to go.' Tilly fumbled for the documents, almost dropping them when Silas reached out and took them from her, his fingers touching hers. She was behaving like a complete idiot, she chided herself, as Silas leaned forward to give the taxi driver directions—and, what was more, behaving like an idiot who was completely out of her depth.

Probably because she *felt* completely out of her depth. Silas just wasn't what she had been expecting. For a start she had assumed he would be younger, more like the boys at work than a man quite obviously in his thirties, and then there was his raw sexuality. She just wasn't used to that kind of thing. It was almost a physical presence in the cab with them.

How on earth was she going to get through nearly four weeks of pretending that he was her fiancé? How on earth was she going to be able to convince anyone, and especially Art's daughters, that they were a couple when they were sleeping in separate rooms? This just wasn't a man who *did* separate rooms, and no woman worthy of the name would want to sleep apart from him if they were really lovers. Anxiously she clung to her mother's warning that her husband-to-be was very moralistic. They could say that they were occupying separate rooms out of respect for his views, couldn't they?

'We're here,' Silas said as the taxi jerked to a halt. 'You can explain to me exactly what is going on once we're on board.'

She could explain to him?

But there was no point arguing as he had already turned away to speak with the taxi driver.

CHAPTER TWO

THE ONLY OTHER OCCASION when Tilly had travelled in a private jet had been in the company of half a dozen of her male colleagues, and the plane had been owned by one of bank's wealthiest clients. She hadn't dreamed then that the next time she would be driven up to the gangway of such a jet, where a steward and stewardess were waiting to relieve them of their luggage and usher them up into luxurious comfort, the jet would be owned by her stepfather-to-be.

Tilly wasn't quite sure why she found it necessary to draw attention to her large and fake solitaire 'engagement ring' by playing with it when she saw the way the stewardess was smiling at Silas. It certainly seemed to focus both the other girl's and Silas's attention on her, though.

'Ms Aspinall.' The male steward's voice was as soothing as his look was flattering. 'No need to ask if you travel a lot.' He signalled to someone to take their luggage on board. 'Everyone in the know travels light and buys on arrival—especially when they're flying to somewhere like Madrid.'

Tilly hoped her answering smile didn't look as false as it felt. The reason she was 'travelling light', as he had put it, was quite simply because she had assumed that this castle her mother's new man had hired came complete with a washing machine. The demands of her working life meant that she rarely shopped. A couple of times a year she restocked her working wardrobe with more Armani suits and plain white shirts.

But, bullied by Sally, she had allowed herself to be dragged down Knightsbridge to Harvey Nicks, in order to find a less businesslike outfit for the wedding, and a dress for Christmas day. The jeans she was wearing today were her standard week-end wear, even if they were slightly less well fitting than usual, thanks to her anxiety over her mother's decision to marry again.

Once inside the jet she settled herself in her seat, trying not to give in to her increasing urge to look at her new 'fiancé,' who seemed very much at home in the world of the super-rich for someone who needed to boost his income by hiring himself out as an escort.

Jason, the steward, offered them champagne. Tilly didn't drink very much, but she accepted the glass he was holding out to her, hoping that it might help ease the tension caused by her unwanted awareness of Silas's potent sexuality. Silas, on the other hand, shook his head.

'I prefer not to drink alcohol when I'm flying,' he told Jason. 'I'll have some water instead.'

Why did she suddenly feel that drinking one glass of cham-pagne had turned her into a potential alcoholic who couldn't pass up on the chance to have a drink? Rebelliously she took a quick gulp of the fizzing bubbles, and then tried not to pull a face when she realised how dry the champagne was.

They were taxiing down the runway already, the jet lifting easily and smoothly into the grey sky. Tilly wasn't a keen flyer, and she could feel her stomach tensing with nervous energy as she waited for the plane to level off. Silas, on the other hand, looked coolly unmoved as he reached for a copy of the *Economist*.

'Right, you'd better tell me what's going on,' he said, flick-ing through the pages of the magazine. 'I was informed that you wanted an escort to accompany you to your mother's wedding.'

'Yes, that's right—I do,' Tilly agreed. 'An escort who is my fiancé—I did explain it all to you in the e-mail I sent,' she in-sisted defensively when she saw the way he was looking at her.

'E-mails are notoriously unreliable.' But not, perhaps, as un-reliable at passing on information as his dear brother, Silas ac-knowledged grimly. 'You'd better explain again.'

Tilly glanced over her shoulder to make sure they were alone in the cabin. This was her mother's new man's plane, staffed by his employees. 'My mother's husband-to-be is an American. He has very strong ideas about family life and…and family relationships. He has two daughters from his first marriage, both married with children, and my mother…' She paused and took a deep breath. Why on earth should she be finding this so discomfiting? As though somehow she were on trial and had to prove herself? She was the one hiring Silas, the one in charge, not the other way around.

'My mother feels that Art's daughters aren't entirely happy about their marriage.'

Silas's eyebrows lifted. 'Why not? You've just said that they're both married with children. Surely they should be happy to see their father find happiness?'

'Well, yes… But the thing is…'

Tilly chewed anxiously on her bottom lip—a small action which automatically drew Silas's attention to her mouth. How adept the female sex was at focusing male attention on it, Silas thought cynically. Mind you, with a mouth as full and soft-looking as hers, Tilly hardly needed to employ such tired old tricks to get a man to look at it and wonder how it would feel beneath his own. His imagination had been there already, and gone further. Much further, in fact, he admitted reluctantly.

How did she put this, Tilly wondered, without being disloyal to her mother? 'My mother doesn't think that Art's daughters feel she will make him happy.'

'Why not?'

'Well, he's a widower, and Ma is a divorcée.'

Silas gave a small brusque shrug. 'So your mother made a mistake? It's hardly unusual in this day and age.'

'No…but…'

'But?'

'But Ma has made rather more than just one mistake,' Tilly informed him cautiously.

'You mean she's been married more than once?'

'Yes.'

'How much more than once?'

'Well, four times, actually. She can't help it.' Tilly defended her mother quickly when she saw Silas's expression. 'She just falls in love so easily, you see, and men fall in love with her, and then—'

'And then she divorces them, and starts over with a bigger bank balance and a richer man?'

Tilly was shocked. 'No! She's not like that. Ma would never marry just for money.'

Silas registered the 'just' and said cynically, 'But she finds it easier to love a rich man than one who is poor?'

'You're just like Art's daughters and their husbands. You're criticising my mother without knowing her. She loves Art. Or at least she believes she does. I know it sounds illogical, but Ma *is* illogical at times. She's afraid that Art's daughters will be even more antagonistic towards her if they know that I'm single. Art was boasting to her about his daughters and their marriages, and Ma lost the plot a bit and told him that I was engaged.'

It was such a ridiculous story that it had to be true, Silas decided. 'And you don't know any single available men you could have asked to help you out?'

Of course she did. She knew any number of them. But none whom she felt she could rely on to act the part convincingly enough.

'No, not really.' How easily the fib slipped from her lips. She was obviously more her mother's daughter than she had known, she admitted guiltily. But Silas knew nothing of her personal and professional circumstances—or the fact that she would have rather walked barefoot over hot coals than let the boisterous and youthful sexual predators who made up her staff know about her lack of a sexual partner. Even if it was by choice. As far as Tilly was concerned it was a small and harmless deceit—she wasn't to know that Silas, in between flying in and out of the country to complete an assignment in Brussels after his meeting with Joe, had done as much background-checking on her as he could, and thus knew exactly what her professional circumstances were.

No available men in her life? Silas was hard put to it to bite back the cynical retort he longed to make and ask why she didn't use her status as the head of her own department to provide herself with a fake fiancé from one of the ten-plus young men who worked under her.

On the other hand, for reasons he was not prepared to investigate too closely, it brought him a certain sense of relief to know that he had found her out as a liar and therefore not to be trusted. And he certainly wasn't going to be taken in by that pseudo-concern she had expressed for a mother who sounded as though she was more than a match for any number of protective daughters and their husbands.

Not, of course, that Art's daughters were exactly your run-of-the-mill average daughters. Silas had learned all about them when he had done his initial search on their father. They had learned their politics and their financial know-how at their father's knee, and while they adopted a Southern Belle manner in public, in private they were not just steel magnolias but steel magnolias with chariot spikes attached to their wheels.

More than one person had been eager to relate to him some of the urban mythology surrounding the family, about the way Art's daughters had targeted their husbands-to-be: disposing of a couple of fiancés, and at least one illegitimate child, plus a handful of quashed drink-driving and drug charges on their way to the altar.

If one thing was certain it was that they would not tolerate their father marrying a woman they themselves had not sourced and checked out.

'Okay, so your mother is afraid that her potential stepdaughters might persuade their father not to go ahead with the wedding. But I still don't understand how you turning up with a fiancé can have any effect on that.'

'Neither can I, really, but my mother was getting herself in such a state it just seemed easier to give in and go along with what she wanted.'

'Easier, but surely not entirely advisable? I should have thought a calm, analytical discussion—'

'You don't know my mother. She doesn't *do* calm or analytical,' Tilly said, before adding protectively, 'I'm making her sound like a drama queen, but she isn't. She's just a person who lives in and on her emotions. My guess is that she simply got carried away with trying to compete with Art in the perfect daughter stakes. I've told her that I've managed to find someone to pose as my supposed fiancé, but I haven't told her about using the agency,' she warned. 'She'll probably assume that I already knew you.'

'Or that we're past lovers?'

Tilly was aghast. She shook her heed vehemently. 'No, she won't think that. She knows that I—'

'That you what? Took a vow of chastity?'

For some reason the drawling cynicism in his voice hurt. 'She knows that I don't have any intention of ever getting married.'

'Because you don't believe in marriage?'

Tilly gave him a level look and replied coolly, 'No, because I don't believe in divorce.'

'Interesting.'

'Not really. I daresay any number of children with divorced parents feel the same way. Why are you asking me so many questions? You sound more like a…a barrister than an actor. I thought actors liked talking about themselves, not asking questions.'

'I can assure you that I am most definitely *not* a barrister. And surely actors need to study others in order to play their roles effectively?'

Not a barrister. But she was astute enough to have recognised his instinctive need to probe and cross-question, Silas recognised.

What was it about the quality of a certain kind of silence that made a person feel so acutely uncomfortable? Tilly wondered as she hunted feverishly for a safer topic of conversation. Or in this instance was it the man himself who was making her feel so acutely conscious of things about herself and her attitude to life? Things she didn't really want to think about.

'I was a bit worried that the agency wouldn't be able to find someone suitable who was prepared to work over Christmas,' she offered, holding out a conversational olive branch as brightly as she could in an attempt to establish the proper kind of employer—her—and employee—him—relations. Not that it was true, of course. The truth was that she would have been delighted if Sally's plan to provide her with a fiancé had proved impossible to carry through.

'If that's a supposedly subtle attempt to find out if I have a partner, the answer is no, I don't. And as for working over Christmas, any number of people do it.'

Tilly had to swallow the hot ball of outrage that had lodged in her throat. She could almost visualise the small smouldering pile of charcoal that had been her olive branch.

'I was not asking if you had a partner. I was simply trying to make polite conversation,' she told him.

'More champers?'

Tilly smiled up at Jason in relief, welcoming his interruption of a conversation that was leading deeper and deeper into far too personal and dangerous territory. Far too personal and dangerous for *her*, that was.

'We'll be landing in ten minutes,' Jason warned them. 'There'll be a car and driver waiting for you, of course.'

Tilly smiled, but less warmly.

'What's wrong?' Silas asked her.

'Nothing. Well, not really.' She gave a small shrug as Jason moved out of earshot. 'I know I should be enjoying this luxury, and of course in a way I am, but it still makes me feel guilty when I think about how many people there are struggling just to feed themselves.'

'A banker who wants to save the world?' Silas mocked her.

Immediately Tilly tensed. 'How did you know that? About me being a banker?'

Silently Silas cursed himself for his small slip. 'I don't know. The agency must have told me, I suppose,' he said dismissively.

'Sometimes it's easier to change things from the inside than from the outside,' Tilly explained after a slight pause.

'Indeed. But something tells me that it would take one hell of a lot of inner change to get the City types to think about saving the planet. Or were you thinking of some kind of inducement to help them? A new Porsche, perhaps?'

'Toys for boys goes with the territory, but they grow out of them—usually about the same time as their first child is born,' Tilly told him lightly.

The jet had started its descent, and Jason's return to the cabin brought their conversation to an end.

CHAPTER THREE

SNOW IN SPAIN. WHO KNEW? She supposed *she* ought to have done, Tilly admitted, as she huddled deeper into her coat, grateful for the warmth inside the large four-wheel drive that had been waiting at the airport to transport them up to the castle.

Silas had fired some rapid words in Spanish to their driver at the start of their journey, but had made no attempt to engage her in conversation, and the long, muscular arm he had stretched out across the back of the seat they were sharing was hardly likely to give anyone the impression that they were besotted with one another.

The castle was up in the mountains, beyond the ancient town of Segovia. Tilly had viewed the e-mail attachment her mother had sent, showing a perfect fairy-tale castle against a backdrop of crisp white snow, but foolishly she hadn't taken on board that the snow as well as the castle was a reality. Now, with the afternoon light fading, the landscape outside the car windows looked more hostile than beautiful.

It didn't help when Silas suddenly drawled, 'I hope you've packed your thermals.'

'No, I haven't,' she was forced to reply. 'But the castle is bound to be centrally heated.'

The now-familiar lift of dark eyebrows made her stomach lurch with anxiety.

'You think so?'

'I know so. My mother hates the cold, and she would never tolerate staying anywhere that wasn't properly heated.'

'Well, she's *your* mother, but my experience is that most owners of ancient castles hate spending money on heating them—especially when they are hiring them out to other people. Maybe on this occasion, since your mother, like us, has love to keep her warm, she won't feel the cold.'

Tilly gave him a look of smouldering antipathy. 'That wasn't funny.'

'It wasn't meant to be. Have you given any real thought as to just how intimately we'll have to interact with each other, given that we're going to be part of a very small and potentially very explosive private house party?'

'We won't have to interact intimately at all,' Tilly protested, hot-faced. 'People will accept that we're an engaged couple because we'll have told them we are. We won't be expected to indulge in public displays of physical passion to prove that we're engaged. Besides, I'm wearing a ring.'

She was totally unprepared for the sudden movement he made, reaching for her hand and taking possession of it. His fingers gripped her wrist, his thumb placed flat against her pulse so that it was impossible for her to hide the frantic way it was jumping and racing.

'What are you doing?' she demanded crossly, when he removed her fake ring with one deft movement.

'You don't really imagine that *this* is going to deceive the daughters of a billionaire, do you?' he taunted, shaking his head as he put it in his pocket. 'They'll know straight away it's a fake, and it's only a small step from knowing your ring is a fake to guessing our relationship is fake.'

Tilly couldn't conceal her dismay. His confidence had overpowered her own belief in the effectiveness of her small ploy.

'But I've *got* to wear a ring,' she told him. 'We're supposed to be engaged, and it's as her properly engaged daughter that my mother wants to parade me in front of Art and his daughters.'

'Try this.'

Tilly couldn't believe her eyes when Silas reached into his jacket pocket and removed a small shabby jeweller's box.

Uncertainly she took it from him. He couldn't possibly have *bought* a ring.

'Here, give it to me.' he told her impatiently, after he'd

watched her struggle with the catch, and flicked it open so easily that she felt a complete fool. Warily she looked at the ring inside the box, her eyes widening in awe. The gold band might be slightly worn, but the rectangular emerald surrounded by perfect, glittering white diamonds was obviously very expensive and very real.

'Where—? How—?' she began.

'It was my mother's,' Silas answered laconically.

Immediately Tilly closed the box and tried to hand it back to him.

'What's wrong?'

'I can't wear your mother's ring.'

'Why not? It's certainly a hell of a lot more convincing than that piece of cheap tat you were wearing.'

'But it's your *mother's*.'

'It's a family ring, not her engagement ring. She didn't leave it to me with strict instructions to place it only on the finger of *the* woman, if that's what you're thinking. She wasn't sentimental, and I daresay she had stopped believing in Cinderella and her slipper a long time before she died.'

'Do you always carry it round with you?' Tilly asked him. Her question was uncertain, and delivered in an emotional whisper.

Silas looked at her. He couldn't remember the last time he had met a woman who was as absurdly sentimental as this one appeared to be. Silas didn't *do* sentimentality. He considered it to be a cloying, unpleasant emotion that no person of sound judgement should ever indulge in.

'Hardly,' he told her crisply. 'It just happens that I recently had it revalued for insurance purposes, and I collected it from the jewellers on my way over to you. I was on my way to the bank to put it in my safety deposit box, but the traffic was horrendous and we couldn't miss the flight. If one were to assess the odds, I should imagine it will be safer on your finger that it would be in my pocket.'

He sounded as though he was telling the truth, and he certainly did not look the sentimental type, Tilly acknowledged.

'Give me your hand again.' He took hold of it as he spoke, re-opening the box and obviously intending to slide the ring onto her finger. Immediately she tried to stop him, shaking her head.

'No, you mustn't do that,' she said. A small icy finger of pre-sentiment touched her spine, making her shiver. She could see the mix of derision and impatience in the look he was giving her, and although inwardly she felt humiliated by his obvious contempt, she still stood her ground.

'What's wrong now? Worried that you're breaking some fearful taboo or something?' he demanded sarcastically.

'I don't like the idea of you putting the ring on. It seems wrong, somehow,' Tilly admitted.

'Oh, I see. My putting my ring on your engagement finger when we aren't engaged is wrong, but pretending that we are engaged when we aren't is perfectly all right?'

'It's the symbolism of it,' Tilly tried to explain. 'There's something about a man putting a ring on a woman's finger... It might sound illogical to you—'

'It does, and it is.' Silas stopped her impatiently, taking hold of her hand again and slipping the ring onto her finger.

Tilly had told herself that it couldn't possibly fit, but extraordinarily it did—and perfectly. So perfectly that it might have been made for her—or meant for her? What on earth had put that kind of foolish thought into her head?

'There, it's done. And nothing dramatic has happened.'

Not to him, maybe, Tilly acknowledged, but something *had* happened to her. The worn gold felt soft and heavy on her finger, and inside her chest her heart felt as constricted as though the ring had been slipped around it. When she looked down at her hand the diamonds flashed fire. Or was it the tears gathering in her own eyes that were responsible for the myriad rainbow display of colours she could see?

This wasn't how a ring like this should be given and worn, and yet somehow just by wearing it she felt as though she had committed to something. Some message, some instinctive female awareness the ring was communicating to her. A sense of pain and foreboding filled her, but it was too late now. Silas's ring was on her finger, and they were coming into Segovia, the lights from the town illuminating the interior of the car.

'What was she like?' Tilly asked softly, the question instinctive and unstoppable.

'Who?'

'Your mother.'

Silas wasn't going to answer her, but somehow he heard himself saying quietly and truthfully, 'She was a conservationist, wise and loving, and full of life. She died when I was eight. She was in a protest. Some violence broke out and my mother fell and hit her head. She died almost immediately.'

Tilly could feel the weight of the silence that followed his almost dispassionate words. Almost dispassionate, but not quite. She had sensed, even if she had not actually heard, the emotion behind them. She looked down at the ring and touched it gently, in tribute to the woman to whom it had belonged.

Silas had no idea why he had told Tilly about his mother. He rarely thought about her death these days. He was very fond of his stepmother, who had shown him understanding and kindness, and who had always respected his relationship with his father, and he certainly loved Joe. Damn all over-emotional, sentimental women. A wise man kept them out of his life, and didn't make the mistake of getting involved with them in any way. There was only one reason he was here with Tilly now, and that was quite simply because she was providing him with the opportunity to get close to Art. And if that meant that he was using her, then he wasn't going to feel guilty about that. She, after all, was equally guilty of using him.

'I HADN'T EXPECTED THE CASTLE to be quite so remote,' Tilly admitted, nearly half an hour after they had driven through Segovia, with its picturesque buildings draped in pretty Christmas decorations. 'Nor that it would be so high up in the mountains.'

They had already passed through the ski centres of Valdesqui and Navacerrada, looking as festive as a Christmas card, and although the snow-covered scenery outside the car was stunningly beautiful in the clearness of the early-evening moonlight, Tilly was surprised that her mother, who loved sunshine and heat, had chosen such a cold place for her wedding.

They turned off the main road onto a narrow track that wound up the steep mountainside, past fir trees thick with snow, towards the white-dusted, fairytale castle perched at its summit, lights shining welcomingly from its many tall, narrow windows. The castle was cleverly floodlit, heightening the impression that it had come straight out of a fairy story, and the surrounding snow was bathed in an almost iridescent pale pink glow

'It's beautiful,' Tilly murmured appreciatively. Silas glanced at her, about to tell her cynically that it looked like something dreamed up by a Hollywood studio. But then he saw the way the moonlight filling the car illuminated her face, dusting her skin with silvery light and betraying her quickened breathing.

Extraordinarily and unbelievably his mind switched track, and suddenly he was asking himself if he held her under him and kissed her, with a man's fierce need for a woman's body, would that pulse in her throat jump and burn the way the pulse in her wrist had done when he had held her hand? And would that pulse then run like a cord to the stiffening peak of her breast when he circled the place where the smooth pale flesh gave way to the soft pink aureole? Would that too swell in erotic response to his touch, a moan of pleasure suppressed deep in her throat causing her pulse to jump higher, while he rolled her nipple between his thumb and forefinger, savouring each further intimacy, knowing what her small restless movement meant? Knowing, too, that she would be wet and hungry for him—

Abruptly Silas blocked off his thoughts. It startled him to discover just how far and how fast they had travelled on their own erotic journey without his permission. He wasn't given to fantasising about sex with a woman he was in a relationship with, never mind one who was virtually a complete stranger to him. He didn't need to fantasise about sex, since it was always on offer to him should he want it. But, just as he was revolted by the thought of eating junk food, so, equally, he was turned off by the idea of indulging in junk sex. Which was probably why he was feeling like this now, with an erection so hard and swollen that it actually felt painful. He had been so busy working these last few months that he hadn't had time to get involved in a relationship. The ex with whom he occasionally had mutually enjoyable release sex had decided to get married, and he couldn't really remember the last time he had spent so much time in close proximity to a woman in a non-sexual way. And *that*, no doubt, was why his body was reacting like a hormone junkie who had the promise of a massive fix.

Their driver turned the four-wheel drive into the inner courtyard of the castle, coming to a stop outside the impressive iron-studded wooden doors.

Tilly smiled at the driver as he held open her door for her and helped her out. The courtyard had been cleared of snow, but she could still smell it on the early-evening air, and there was a shine on the courtyard floor that warned her the stones underfoot would be icy.

The huge double doors had been flung open, and Tilly goggled to see two fully liveried footmen stepping outside. Liveried footmen! She was so taken aback she forgot to watch where she was walking, and gasped with shock as she stepped onto a patch of ice and started to lose her balance.

Hard, sure hands gripped her arms, dragging her back against the safety of an equally hard male body.

And there she stood, her back pressed tightly into Silas's body, his arms wrapped securely around her, as her mother and the man Tilly presumed must be her mother's new fiancé stood in the open doorway, watching them. Her reaction was instinctive and disastrous. She turned her head to look at Silas, intending to demand that he release her, but when she realised how close she was to his mouth all she could do was look at it instead, while the hot pulse of lust inside her became a positive volcano of female desire. She lifted her hand—surely not because she had actually intended to touch him, to trace the outline of that firmly shaped male mouth with its sensually full bottom lip? Surely she had not actually intended to do that? No, of course not. She simply wasn't that kind of woman. How could she be when she had spent the better part of her young adult life training herself not to be? All she had wanted to do was to push her hair back off her face. And that was what she would have done too, if Silas hadn't caught hold of her hand.

The hand on which she was wearing his mother's ring. A hard knot of emotions filled her chest cavity and blocked her throat. An overwhelming sense of sadness and love and hope.

'Silas…' Her lips framed his name and her eyes filled with soft warm tears.

What the hell was a going on? Silas wondered in disbelief. One minute he was reacting instinctively to save an idiotic female from falling over; the next he was holding her in his arms and getting an emotional message he couldn't block, feeling as if he was experiencing something of such importance that it could be the pivot on which the whole of his future life would turn.

He watched as Tilly's lips framed his name, and felt the aching drag of his own sexual need to bend his head to hers and to explore the shape and texture of her mouth. Not just once, but over and over again, until it was imprinted on his senses for ever. So that he could recall its memory within a heartbeat. So that he could hold it to him for always.

Silas tensed as he heard the sharp ring of an inner warning bell.

This was not a direction in which he wanted to go. This kind of emotional intensity, this kind of emotional dependency, was not for him. And certainly not with a woman like this. Tilly had lied to him once already. He did not for one moment believe the sob story of concerned and loving daughter she had used when describing her mother's marriage history. Logic told him that there had to be some darker and far more selfish reason for what she was doing. As yet he hadn't unearthed it—but then he hadn't tried very hard, had he? After all, he had his own secret agenda. He might not have discovered her hidden motive, but that didn't mean it didn't exist. For now he was content to play along with her game, and the role she had cast for him, because it suited his own purposes. But this looking at her mouth and feeling that he'd stepped into another dimension where emotion and instinct held sway rather than hard-headed logic and knowledge had to be parcelled up and locked away somewhere.

In the few seconds it had taken for him to catalogue his uncharacteristic reaction, Tilly's face had started to glow a soft pink.

'Darling...'

Abruptly Tilly wrenched her unwilling gaze from Silas's mouth to focus on her mother.

Physically, Annabelle Lucas looked very much like her daughter, although where Tilly downplayed her femininity, Annabelle cosseted and projected hers. Slightly shorter than Tilly, she had the same hourglass figure, and the same honey and butter-coloured hair. However, where Tilly rarely wore make-up, other than a hint of eyeshadow and mascara and a slick of lipgloss, Annabelle delighted in 'prettifying' herself, as she called it. Tilly favoured understated businesslike suits, and casual clothes when she wasn't working; Annabelle dressed in floaty, feminine creations.

Tilly tried to wriggle out of Silas's grip, but instead of letting her go he bent his mouth to her ear and warned, 'We're supposed to be a deliriously loved-up, newly engaged couple, remember?'

Tilly tried to ignore the effect the warmth of his breath against her ear was having on her.

'We don't have to put on an act for my mother,' she protested. But she knew her argument was as weak as her trembling knees.

The arch look her mother gave them as she hurried over to them in a cloud of her favourite perfume made Tilly want to grit her teeth, but there was nothing she could say or do—not with her mother's new fiancé within earshot.

'Art, come and say hello to my wonderful daughter, Tilly, and her gorgeous fiancé.'

Her mother was kissing Silas with rather too much enthusiasm, Tilly decided sourly.

'How sweet, Tilly, that you can't bear to let go of him.'

Tilly heard her mother laughing. Red-faced, she tried to snatch her hand back from Silas's arm, but for some reason he covered it with his own, refusing to let her go.

'Silas Stanway,' Silas introduced himself, extending his hand to Art, but still, Tilly noticed dizzily, managing to keep her tucked up against him. She could have used more force to pull away, but slipping on the ice and ending up on her bottom was hardly the best way to make a good impression in front of her stepfather-to-be, she decided.

Her mother really must have been wearing rose-tinted glosses when she had fallen in love with Art, Tilly acknowledged, relieved to have her hand shaken rather than having to submit to a kiss. Fittingly for such a fairy-tale-looking castle, he did actually look remarkably toad-like, with his square build and jowly face. Even his unblinking stare had something unnervingly toadish about it.

He was obviously a man of few words, and, perhaps because of this, her mother seemed to have gone in to verbal overdrive, behaving like an over-animated actress, clapping her hands, widening her eyes and exclaiming theatrically, 'This is all so perfect! My darling Art is like a magician, making everything so wonderful for me—and all the more wonderful now that you're here, Tilly.' Tears filled her eyes, somehow managing not to spill over and spoil her make-up. 'I'm just so very happy. I've always wanted to be part of a big happy family. Do you remember, darling, how you used to tell me that all you wanted for Christmas was a big sister? So sweet. And now here I am, getting not just the most perfect husband but two gorgeous new daughters and their adorable children.'

If only her father were here to witness this, and to share this moment of almost black humour with her, Tilly thought wryly, as she wondered how her mother had managed to mentally banish the various sets of stepfamilies she had collected via her previous marriages.

Her mother beamed, and turned away to lead them back into the house. Silas bent his head and demanded, 'What was that look for?'

Too disconcerted to prevaricate, Tilly whispered grimly, 'Ma already has enough darling ex-steps and their offspring to fill her side of any church you could name.'

'Somehow I don't think that Art would want to know that.'

'You don't like him, do you?' Tilly said, with a shrewd guess of her own.

'Do you?'

'Hurry up, you two. You'll have plenty of time for whispering to each other later, and it's cold with the door open.'

The first thing Tilly saw as she stepped into the hallway was an enormous Christmas tree, its dark green foliage a perfect foil for the artistically hung Christmas tree decorations in shades of pale green, pink and blue, to tone with the hallway's painted panelling. Suddenly Tilly was six years old again, standing between her parents and gazing up with eyes filled with shining wonder at the Christmas tree in Harrods toy department.

That had been before she had understood that when her father complained about her mother's spending habits, and the circle of friends from which he was excluded, he wasn't 'just teasing'. And that the 'uncle' her mother had been so desperate for her to like was destined to replace her father in her mother's life. That Christmas she had been so totally, innocently happy, unaware that within a year she would know that happiness was as fragile and as easily broken as the pretty glass baubles she had gazed at with such delight.

Christmas—season of love and goodwill and more marital break-ups than any other time of year. A sensible woman would take to her heels at her first sighting of a Christmas tree and not come back until the bleakness of January had brought everyone to their senses.

'What time is dinner, Ma?' Tilly asked her mother prosaically, determined to set the tone of her enforced visit from the start. 'Only, I could do with going up to my room and getting changed first.'

Behind Art's back Annabelle made a small moue, and then said in an over-bright voice. 'Oh, I am sorry, darling, but we won't be having a formal dinner. Art doesn't like eating late, and then of course we have to consider the children. The girls are such devoted mothers, they wouldn't dream of breaking their routines. Art is quite right. It makes more sense for us to eat in our own rooms. So much more comfortable than dressing up and sitting down for a five-course dinner in the dining room.'

Tilly, who knew how much her mother adored dressing up for dinner, even when she was eating alone at home, opened her mouth to ask what was going on and then closed it again.

Her heart started to sink. She knew that she wasn't imagining the desperation she could hear in her mother's voice.

'Isn't this the most gorgeous, magical place you have ever seen?' Annabelle was saying in an artificially bright voice, as she indicated the huge octagonal hall, decorated in its sugared almond colours, from which a delicate, intricately carved marble staircase seemed to float upwards.

'It is beautiful, Ma,' Tilly agreed. 'But rather cold.'

Immediately her mother gave small pout. 'Darling, don't be such a spoilsport. There is heating, but... With the children being used to living in a controlled-temperature environment they really do need to have the benefit of what heating there is in *their* suites, even if that means that some of the other rooms have to go without.' Annabelle was heading for the stairs. 'I've put you and Silas in the same room, just like you asked me to do.'

So he had been right, Silas decided grimly. So much for this just being an innocent, escort-duties-only commission! However, before he could say anything, Art had begun to study him, frowning.

'You look familiar... Have we met somewhere before?'

Silas felt his stomach muscles clench. 'Not so far as I know,' he responded truthfully. Art had turned down all his attempts to get an interview with him, but that didn't mean Art hadn't seen his photograph somewhere, or perhaps requested information about him. And if he had...

'So what exactly is it you do?' Art persisted.

'Silas is an actor,' Tilly answered firmly for him, pre-empting the criticism she sensed was coming by adding determinedly, 'And a very good one.' She gave her mother a look which she hoped she would correctly interpret as *I need to talk to you urgently about this bedroom situation*, but to her dismay her mother was refusing to make eye contact. In fact, now that she looked at her mother more closely, Tilly could see how tense and on edge she was beneath her too-bright smile, how desperate she was for everyone's approval of the castle. And of herself? Was it because of this insecurity within her mother that she had always kept the gates to her own emotions firmly padlocked? Because she was afraid of becoming like her mother?

As had happened so many times in the past when she sensed that her mother was unhappy, Tilly felt her protective instinct kick in. Leaving Silas's side, she moved over to Annabelle, linking her arm with her mother's in a gesture of daughter-to-mother solidarity.

'An actor. How exciting!' Annabelle exclaimed. 'That's probably why you think Silas's face is familiar, Artie, you must have seen him in something.'

'I doubt it. It don't waste my time watching people play at make-believe.' Art gave a snort of derision.

How could her mother be in love with a man like this? Tilly wondered despairingly. Her original misgivings about the marriage were growing by the second.

She gave her mother's arm a small squeeze. 'Why don't you take me upstairs and show me the room?' she suggested lightly, adding, 'I'm sure that Silas and Art can entertain one another while we indulge in some mother-and-daughter gossip.' She knew she was taking a risk, throwing Art and Silas together without being there herself to make sure Silas didn't say the wrong thing, but right now her need to ensure they had separate rooms took precedence over everything else. 'I haven't even seen your dress yet,' she reminded her mother.

'Oh, darling, it's so beautiful,' Annabelle enthused, the tension immediately leaving her face to be replaced by a glow of excitement. 'It's Vera Wang. You know, she does all the celebrity wedding gowns. Her people swore at first that she couldn't fit me in, but Art persuaded them to relent. It's just such a pity that I didn't think to get you to come to New York at the same time, so that we could have looked for something for you. Art's grandchildren are going to be our attendants, of course. We've agreed that they'll be wearing Southern Belles and Beaux outfits, so…sweet. And it would be lovely if your Silas would give me away…'

Suddenly Tilly wanted to cry—very badly. Here was her mother, trying desperately to put a brave face on the fact that while Art had his daughters and grandchildren to provide him with family support and fill the traditional wedding roles, Annabelle had to rely on her daughter and a man who was being paid to escort her.

Swallowing hard, Tilly sniffed back the tears that were threatening to fall.

'Dad would probably have given you away if you'd asked him.'

Immediately her mother looked anxiously at Art. 'I did think of your father,' she admitted. 'But Art's daughters can't see how it's possible to maintain a platonic relationship with an ex-husband, and Art feels…well, he thinks… Well, Art agrees with them.'

The retort Tilly was longing to make had to be smothered in her throat when she saw her mother's *please don't* look.

What the hell had he got himself into? Silas wondered angrily as he watched the two women walk up the stairs arm-in-arm. Whatever was going on, mother and daughter were both in on it—and deep in it too, right up to their pretty little necks. He was being used, and not just for the escort duties he was being paid for. Annabelle had let the cat out of the bag with regard to Tilly's sexual expectations. No woman asked to share a room with a man unless she expected sex to be on the agenda. Tilly had lied to him when she had claimed they would be having separate rooms, and if it wasn't for the fact that he needed information from Art he would be calling a cab right now, to take him straight back down to the airport in Madrid. Because he didn't want to have sex with a woman he had just spent the last few hours acknowledging had a mind-blowingly intense erotic effect on his body.

Who was he kidding? Okay, so he *did* want to have sex with her—but on his terms, not hers. And he certainly wasn't going to let her get away with lying to him—even if she *had* surprised him with her determination to show Art she wasn't going to let him put Silas down for being an actor. That *had* surprised him, Silas admitted. The last woman to protect him from someone's unflattering opinion had been his mother, and he had been all of five.

Tilly was gutsy; he had to give her that. But that didn't mean he was going to let her get away with manoeuvring him into her bed. There was no real danger to him in being plunged into this kind of situation. He could handle it. But what if it had been Joe she had tricked into sharing her bed? The young idiot was green enough to have had sex with her without any thought for the possible consequences: to his health, to the fate of any child that might be conceived, to anything other than giving in to a young heterosexual male's natural reaction to being in bed with a sexually attractive woman who had invited him there.

Whereas he, of course, wouldn't be facing any of those problems? Okay, he would be facing one of them, since he wasn't in the habit of travelling everywhere with a packet of condoms. Would Tilly have thought to deal with that kind of necessity? She was certainly old enough and no doubt experienced enough to be as aware of the risks as he was himself, he decided cynically as he turned to follow his uncommunicative host into the bar.

CHAPTER FOUR

'HERE IS YOUR ROOM, DARLING. It's lovely, isn't it…?'

Annabelle had thrown open the door into a room on the second floor of the castle.

More because she wanted to make sure they weren't overheard than because she was genuinely interested in her accommodation, Tilly stepped past her and into the room.

It was large, certainly. Large, and cold, and very obviously an attic room, decorated in faded cabbage rose wallpaper, and scented with the unmistakable odour of damp.

'It's got its own bathroom. With the most fabbie real Edwardian bath.'

The determined brightness in her mother's voice made Tilly's spirits plummet. Annabelle looked so vulnerable, getting angry with her felt like being unkind to a child.

Very gently Tilly took hold of her mother's hands and led her across to the large double bed, pulling her down until they were both seated on it, facing one another.

'Ma, what is going on?' she asked, as calmly as she could. 'You know that Silas and I aren't really engaged. We don't even know each other. He's just someone I've hired to pretend to be my fiancé. You *know* that. We were supposed to have separate rooms. I've *told* him that we are having separate rooms. You *assured* me that we would be having separate rooms. So what's gone wrong?'

Tears filled her mother's eyes. 'Oh, Tilly darling, please don't be cross with me. It isn't my fault. I *had* planned to put you and Silas—he is gorgeous, by the way, and he would be just perfect for you—in the most heavenly pair of interconnecting rooms.

More like a suite, really, both with their own bathrooms and the most divine little sitting room, but then Art's daughters arrived and everything went horribly wrong.'

Tilly waited while her mother paused to blow her nose and clear her throat. 'You see, I hadn't realised that Susan-Jane and Cissie-Rose would want to have their children sleeping on the same floor with them, or that they would expect to have connecting rooms. But of course once Susan-Jane had explained that she and Cissie-Rose need to be close by, and how it made much more sense for them to have the suite I'd earmarked for you and Silas...

'She said that the children's nannies, and the personal assistants to Dwight and Bill—that's their husbands, of course—would also have to be on the same floor, because Dwight and Bill frequently work late at night. They have to be in touch with Head Office at all times, and having to come all this way has caused them so much disruption. I felt so guilty about that—especially when Cissie-Rose told me that the children had been upset because they wouldn't be spending Christmas at home. I don't know how it happened, but somehow or other it turned out so that they practically took up the whole of the first floor, apart from the suite Art and I are sharing, and that meant the only rooms left were up here on the second floor.'

Inwardly Tilly counted to ten. Something was telling her that her relationship with her new stepsisters-to-be was not going to be one made in heaven, she thought grimly.

'Okay, but there must be more than one room up here, Ma. I mean, there's only one bed in here—'

'Darling, I know, and I am truly sorry. But I'm sure that Silas will behave like a perfect gentleman. I mean, a man like him doesn't need to go around persuading women to have sex with him, does he? Do you know what I think?' she said brightly. 'I think that he'll probably be glad of the opportunity to be with a woman who isn't coming on to him.'

'Ma, let's stick to the point. How many rooms are there on this floor?'

'Oodles,' Annabelle told her promptly. 'But there's been a

problem with the roof, apparently, and most of them are damp, and the ones that aren't are already occupied by the staff. Strictly speaking we aren't supposed to be using any of the rooms up here, according to the contract the Count's legal people gave us, but when I spoke to the *major-domo* and explained the problem he was really sweet about it, and everyone has worked so hard to get this room ready for you. I'd hate for them to think that we aren't grateful.'

Tilly wrapped her arms around her cold body. 'Ma, it's freezing in here.'

'Yes. I'm sorry about that. The Count's PA did explain to us how the heating system worked, and that we weren't to turn up any of the radiators because if we did it would mean that some others wouldn't work. And I did try to explain this to Art's daughters, but I can see their point about the children needing to be kept warm.'

Tilly could hear a strange noise in her ears. It took her several seconds to realise that it was the sound of her teeth grinding in suppressed frustration.

'Ma—'

'Please don't be difficult about this, darling. I so want everything to go well, and for all of you to get on. Art's daughters have been so sweet—offering to help me once Art and I are married, explaining to me how their social circle works. They've even warned me that some of Art's late wife's friends will be hostile to me, and that some of the men might behave towards me in a flirtatious way because of the way that I look, and because I've been married before. It's kind of them, really.'

'Is it? It sounds more to me as though they're trying to undermine you,' Tilly told her mother shrewdly, and then wished that she hadn't been so blunt when she saw the hurt look on her mother's face.

'Darling, don't say that. You're going to love them, I know. Now, why don't I leave you to unpack, while I go down to the kitchen and organise evening meals for everyone?'

'Some hot water bottles might be a good idea as well,' Tilly suggested dryly.

After her mother had gone she examined the room and its adjoining bathroom. The bath was, as her mother had said, truly Edwardian. Of massive proportions, it stood in the middle of a linoleum-covered floor in a room that was so cold Tilly was shivering even though she was still wearing her coat. There was also a shower, and a separate lavatory.

She heard the outer door reopening, and hurried back into the bedroom, saying despairingly, 'Ma. I don't— Oh, it's you.' She came to an abrupt halt as she saw Silas standing just inside the door, holding it open for a young man carrying their luggage.

She had to wait for him to put it down and leave before she could speak. 'I'm really sorry about this. My mother seems to have allowed Art's daughters to bully her into letting them take the two-bedroom suite she had earmarked for us, and this appears to be the only room that's left.'

'And presumably the only bed?' Silas asked silkily.

'I don't like this any more than you do,' Tilly assured him. 'But there's nothing I can do except offer to sleep on the floor.'

'And of course you're fully prepared to do that?'

'Actually, yes, I am,' Tilly said. She didn't like the tone he was using, and she didn't like the way he was looking at her either. If she had thought the bedroom and the icy-cold bathroom were cold enough to chill her blood, they were nothing compared to the coldness of the look Silas was giving her.

'Do you make a habit of this?' It infuriated Silas that she didn't seem to think he had the intelligence to see through what she was doing.

'Do I make a habit of what?' Tilly demanded, perplexed.

'Hiring men to have sex with you.'

Tilly was glad she had the bed behind her to sink down onto. His accusation hadn't just shocked her, it had also blocked her chest with a huge lump of indigestible and unwanted emotional vulnerability—and pain. *Pain?* Because a man she didn't know was misjudging her? Why should that cause her to feel like this? She had only just met Silas. He meant nothing whatsoever to her, and yet here she was reacting to his unpleasant remarks with the kind of hurt feelings and sense of betrayal that were more appropriate for a long-standing and far more intimate relationship. Was that it? Did she secretly *want* to have sex with him? Had he somehow sensed that, even though she hadn't been aware of it herself? Was *that* the reason for his accusation, and her own emotional reaction to it?

This time when Tilly shivered it wasn't just because she was cold. She didn't like what was happening. She had never wanted to do any of this in the first place—not coming here, not hiring herself an escort, and most certainly not sharing a bed with Silas. She took a deep breath.

'I do not hire men to have sex with me. I don't need to.' Well, it was true, wasn't it? 'I've already made it perfectly clear to you why I need an escort, and if you thought I was lying or had some ulterior motive then surely it was up to you to refuse the commission. You don't strike me as the kind of man who would allow himself to be put in a situation you don't want,' she told him shrewdly.

Her reaction wasn't what Silas had been expecting. He had assumed that she would use his accusation as an excuse to lay her cards on the table. At which point he had intended to make it plain that, while he was prepared to act as her fiancé in public, making use of the intimacy provided by their shared accommodation was most definitely not on the agenda.

The nature of his profession meant that Silas was immediately and instinctively suspicious of everyone's motives. As far as he was concerned, everyone had something to hide, something they were prepared to sell, and something they were prepared to buy. He himself wanted to hide the fact that he was using his position as a fake fiancé to get closer to Art, but he was only prepared to sell his time, not his body. He was also a man who hated being wrong-footed and forced to accept that he had made an error of judgement—especially by a woman he had no reason whatsoever to respect.

'I thought your explanation owed more to imagination than truth,' he told her uncompromisingly. 'As far as I am concerned, and in view of what has transpired, I was right to question the validity of what you were telling me. Not, I must say, that I admire your taste in sexual boltholes,' he added disparagingly. 'Apart from anything else, it's freezing. Are those radiators on?' He walked over to one of them and put his hand against it.

'Apparently Art's daughters have messed up the delicate balance of radiator temperature and fair heating for all,' Tilly told him tiredly. 'Or at least I think that's what my mother was trying to tell me.'

Somehow Tilly managed to answer his mundane question with an equally mundane answer, even though her heart was pumping so much blood through her veins she could actually feel the adrenaline surge. There was no way she was going to let his insults go unchallenged.

'You don't have to stay here, you know,' she told him. 'There's nothing to stop you leaving if you want. I certainly won't be trying.' She tried to put as much withering scorn into her words as she could.

Silas gave her a derisory look. 'We've only just arrived, and we're supposed to be engaged. I can hardly walk out now.'

'Why not?' Tilly demanded, in a brittle voice that betrayed her tension. 'Engaged couples do quarrel and break up. It happens all the time. In fact, I think it's a very good idea.'

She could feel the comfort of her own relief at the thought of him leaving. He was having an effect on her she really did not like or want. It—*he*—had made her feel uncomfortable and on edge even before he had accused her of lying to him. There was no way she wanted to spend a week sharing a room with a man who thought she was gagging for sex with him and about to pounce on him at any minute. She might be being a tad old-fashioned, but the truth was that she much preferred the traditional scenario in which *she* was the one imagining that he might pounce on *her*. Not that she wanted him to do so, of course. Not for one minute.

'In fact,' she continued fiercely, 'I think it would be an excellent idea if I went down right now to find my mother and tell her that the engagement is off.'

'Wouldn't that be somewhat counter-productive? I thought the whole idea of this was to help your mother.' The conversation and Tilly's behaviour were taking a direction Silas hadn't expected, and one he did not want. Tilly was quite obviously working herself up into a mood of moral outrage and, worse, she was throwing out the kind of challenges he had no intention of taking up.

It wasn't like him to misjudge a situation, and it irked him that he might have here. But Tilly was behaving in a way he considered out of character for the slot he had mentally fitted her into. He despised women who insisted on playing games, and normally he wouldn't have tolerated an assumed 'injured innocent' act, but right now he had too much at stake to risk her carrying out her threat. Much as he disliked having to admit it, he recognised that it night have been wiser for him to have played along with her pretence for a bit longer before letting her know that he had guessed what she was planning. He couldn't allow this new situation to accelerate.

He might not mind walking out on Tilly, but if he did he would also be walking out on his chance to talk to Art. He had already sown the seeds for what he hoped would become more informative confidences once Art had let down his guard a bit more.

He walked over to the bed and eyed it assessingly. At least it was large enough for him to ensure that Tilly kept her distance from him.

He was standing next to her when they both heard Annabelle calling out from the other side of the door. 'It's only us, darlings!'

'That's my mother now,' Tilly told him unnecessarily. 'I've made up my mind. There's no way I want to continue with this charade now, after the accusations you've just made. I'm going to tell her that we've had a row, that our engagement is over and that you're leaving.'

She was making to remove the ring he had given her as she spoke, and Silas could tell that she meant what she was saying. The door was already opening. He thought quickly, and then acted with even greater speed.

It shocked Tilly how silently and lethally fast Silas moved, dropping down onto the bed next to her and imprisoning her in his arms as he rolled her torso down under his own and then covered her mouth with his.

Tilly tried to push him away, but he was holding her too tightly, one muscular leg thrown over her in what was surely one of the most intimate embraces a fully clad couple could perform—even if he was only adopting it to keep her pinned beneath the weight of his body. Pinned in such a way that she was shockingly aware of the physical differences between them—his hardness pressed to her softness, his body dominating and unyielding, while, to her outraged horror, her own was soft and accommodating, as though her flesh welcomed the possessive maleness of his.

While she tried to grapple with her own confused reactions he started to kiss her. Not gently, but fiercely and possessively, and with an added edge of almost dangerous urgency, as though there was nothing he wanted more than to have her mouth under his, as though at any moment now he would strip the clothes from their bodies so that her only covering would be him, and then… Somehow or other his free hand was cupping her breast, the hard pad of his thumb resting against her hard nipple.

This couldn't be happening. It certainly *should* not be happening. Incredulously she struggled to resist him, distantly aware of her mother's amused, 'Whoops! Sorree…' and then the immediate closing of the bedroom door.

He could let Tilly go now. Silas knew that. The danger was over. No way could she tell her mother now that they had quarrelled and that he was leaving after what she had just witnessed. But the bedroom was bitingly cold, and the rounded warmth of Tilly's breast fitted into his hand as though it had been made for him. It surprised him to discover just how much he wanted to go on cupping it, and just how strong his urge was to caress the hard thrust of her nipple slowly and thoroughly, until she responded to his touch with her own urgency, arching up into his hands, wanting him to peel back the layers of her clothing until they could both see her arousal. He could certainly feel his own. He slid his other hand up into Tilly's hair, lifting his mouth briefly from hers, watching as her eyes opened, her gaze soft and clouded. He traced the shape of her mouth with small, teasingly light kisses that mirrored the delicate touch of his fingertips on her breast.

Tilly was hazily aware that what she was doing was very dangerous—that *Silas* was very dangerous. But the room was so cold that it seemed to be numbing her ability to respond and react in a normal way. And Silas felt so warm, lying on top of her, even if he *was* tormenting her with those tiny kisses that were compelling her to arch up to him, wanting something much more intimate. She shuddered with pleasure when he spread his fingers against her scalp and held her head while he plundered her mouth with the intimate thrust of his tongue, over and over again, until she was shuddering in the grip of the most intense physical longing she had ever experienced.

The shock of her own sexual arousal was enough to bring her to her senses and make her push Silas away. She was trembling from head to foot and felt foolishly close to tears. What she was feeling made her feel both vulnerable and confused. She didn't even know how it had happened—or why.

'You had no right to do that,' she told him, almost tearfully.

'I thought it was what you wanted.'

'*What?* How could you think that? I'd just told you that I wanted you to leave.'

Silas looked into her flushed, mutinous face and a sensation, an emotion he couldn't recognise, speared through the armour-plating of his cynicism. He lifted his hand to his chest, as though he could actually feel the sharp, unfamiliar pain as a physical reality, and then let it drop to his side as he pushed the feeling back out of the way.

'And I've just shown you that I don't want to,' he responded softly. 'In fact…right now I don't even think I want to leave this room.' A corrosive inner voice, no doubt prompted by his conscience, was demanding if not a retraction then at least an explanation of this outright lie. But he had a job to do, a truth to find, and he needed real, hard facts. As far as Silas was concerned it was his ethical duty to get those facts, and that came before any duty he might have to maintaining the same degree of truth within this current aspect of his personal life.

As ugly and unpleasant as it sounded, Tilly was using him— and he was using her. Both of them could claim that they were being forced into doing so in order to benefit others, of course. And that made it acceptable? Maybe not, but it certainly made it necessary, Silas told himself harshly.

Tilly's mouth had gone dry. She couldn't bring herself to look at him. Her heart was pounding so heavily she wanted to press her hand against her chest to calm it.

'If you're trying to imply that you...' She picked her words as carefully as she could, but they still literally stuck it her throat. 'That you want me, then I don't believe you,' she finally managed to say. 'It's less than ten minutes since you were warning me off and accusing me of hiring you for sex,' she reminded him.

'Ten minutes ago I hadn't kissed you or touched you,' Silas told her meaningfully. 'Ten minutes ago I hadn't been so turned on by the way your body was responding to my touch that right now I can't think beyond taking that response to its natural conclusion—to our mutual benefit.'

To Silas's chagrin his own words were conjuring up the most erotic images inside his head, and his body was responding powerfully to them. So powerfully that it was making it clear to him that, no matter what his brain might have to say, his body was more than willing to have sex with Tilly.

The room might still be icy cold, but suddenly Tilly felt far too hot. He had to be lying to her, and she had better remember that. Instead of... Instead of what? Wanting him to be telling the truth? Wanting him to mean what he was saying? Wanting him to want her? Was she crazy? This kind of thing was her mother's emotional territory, not hers. She knew better. Didn't she? She started to shiver. She didn't want to stay here in this room with Silas any longer—a room that she could have sworn now smelled subtly of their mutual arousal, and his deceit, and her own foolish longing. She wanted to go back downstairs, where she would be safer—and warmer.

'It's your own fault that I kissed you, you know,' Silas told her.

Tilly had had enough. 'Look, I've already told you, I did *not* hire you to have sex with me,' she insisted fiercely.

'I didn't mean that.' Silas was smiling so tenderly at her that her insides twisted with need. 'I meant that it's your fault because when you offered me the chance to leave I knew that I couldn't, and that in turn told me how much I want you.'

Tilly stared at him. It really wasn't fair of fate to inflict this on her. It was almost Christmas, for heaven's sake, and she was very vulnerable. Silas had touched a note, a chord deep within her, that she badly wanted to ignore. It would be far too dangerous to let herself believe that he meant what he had said, and even more dangerous to admit how much she *wanted* him to have meant it.

'We've only just met,' she reminded him. 'We hardly know each other...' She was almost stuttering, she realised, as she squirmed inwardly at the sound of her own ridiculous words.

'So? Isn't fate giving us an opportunity to remedy that?' He smiled at her again, and Tilly felt her heart literally flip over inside her chest as though it were a pancake. 'She's even ensured that we'll be sharing a room, and a bed, and she's provided the added incentive of the need to share our body heat just to keep warm.'

Tilly could feel not just her face but her whole body suddenly growing hot as she curled her toes into her shoes and looked helplessly down at the bed. Things like this just did not happen to me. She wasn't that sort of person. She was too sensible, too cautious, too wary...too damn dull! She looked at Silas.

'We are engaged, after all. Who knows what might happen, or where fate might lead us?' As he spoke he reached out, sliding his fingers between her own so that they were intimately held together. 'Why don't we just let her take us where she wishes?' he suggested sexily.

'No, no, *no*! I don't want to hear any more.' Tilly put her hands over her ears in despair. 'I'm going downstairs.'

'Then I'm coming with you,' Silas said promptly. He wasn't going to give her the opportunity to end their 'engagement' in his absence.

CHAPTER FIVE

'OH, THERE YOU ARE, DARLINGS. Oh, Tilly, you haven't even changed for dinner.' There was a reproachful note in her mother's voice that made Tilly's stomach muscles clench defensively, but she stood her ground.

'But you said it had been arranged that we'd all be eating in our rooms,' she reminded her mother, as calmly as she could.

'Oh, well, yes, I did say that. But I must have misunderstood the girls, because they've both come down dressed for dinner. Tilly, why don't you pop back up to your room and get changed into something pretty and formal? You'll have time, because the chef says that it will be another half-hour before everything will be ready.'

It was becoming increasingly plain to Tilly that Art's daughters were determined to behave as selfishly and make life as difficult for her mother as they could.

'I haven't unpacked yet, Ma,' she reminded her mother. 'And it's freezing in our room.'

'Oh, darling, please don't be such a crosspatch. What on earth will Art's girls think?'

'I daresay I might be sweeter if I had a warm bedroom,' Tilly couldn't help responding. 'And what exactly do you mean—something pretty and formal?'

'Well, the girls are both wearing the most gorgeous vintage Halston gowns. I've told them how good-looking you are, Silas, and I think they want to have a look at you,' Annabelle confided, adding blithely, 'It's dinner jackets for the men, of course—and wait until you see the drawing room and the dining room, Tilly. They are gorgeous—pure Versailles.'

Tilly had finally had enough, and she was sure that her sudden flash of temper didn't have anything to do with the thought of other women appreciating Silas's sexy masculinity. 'I don't care how gorgeous they are,' she snapped at her mother. 'I am not going back upstairs to that icebox of a room to get changed. Not, of course, that I'm not dying to show off my own vintage Oxfam.' She relented almost immediately when she saw her mother's chastened expression, going over to her to hug her tenderly, and apologising. 'I'm sorry, Ma.' How could she explain to her mother that it wasn't the cold bedroom she was dreading so much as her own desire to succumb to Silas's sexual overtures once they were in it?

'No, it's my fault, darling. I am really sorry about that dreadful room. What must Silas think of me?'

'What Silas thinks is that you've given him the perfect excuse for sharing his body warmth with his fiancée,' Silas answered promptly.

As her mother turned away Tilly shook her head at Silas and mouthed silently, *Ma knows our engagement is* fake*, remember?*

'Tilly, why don't you come to my room with me and let me find you something to borrow,' Annabelle offered.

'Yes, you go with your mother, Tee, and I'll nip up and change into my DJ,' Silas suggested.

Tee. No one had ever called her Tee before, and Tilly discovered it made her feel slightly giddy, dizzy with a dangerous sort of fizzing delight, that Silas should be the one to do so. Just as though they were really a couple, and Tee was his special pet name for her.

'YOU AND ART HAVE SEPARATE rooms?' Tilly queried several minutes later, as she surveyed the feminine fabric-festooned bedroom her mother was occupying.

'Art didn't think it was right that we should share, especially not with his girls and their children being here. We aren't like you modern young ones, you know, Tilly. Here, put this on. It's a bit big for me, but I think it will fit you perfectly.'

Tilly took the sliver of amber silk chiffon her mother had just removed from the wall of mirror-fronted closets and surveyed it doubtfully.

She looked at the label and then shook her head. 'Isn't this the designer who designs those outrageously sexy things that film stars' wives wear?' she asked her mother accusingly.

'Darling, it was summer when I bought it in Saint-Tropez—everyone was wearing his stuff, and I just fell in love with it. In fact, I nearly wore it the night I met Art. But then I changed my mind.'

Tilly held the dress up in front of herself and looked at her reflection in the mirror. 'This isn't a dress,' she protested. 'It's half a dozen strips of material *pretending* to be a dress.'

'Sweetheart, that's the whole secret of his style—it's all in the cut. You wait and see when you put it on. You can use my bathroom.' She was already bustling Tilly towards the opulent marble and gold-ornamented chamber that masqueraded as a bathroom. 'Oh, and why don't you put a bit more make-up on? And perhaps smooth on some of this wonderful body cream I use?'

Very determinedly, Tilly closed the door between them.

She showered first, very quickly, and then used some of the cream her mother had mentioned because her skin felt dry. It was scented, as well as gold-coloured, and she couldn't help sniffing it appreciatively as she stroked it onto her bare skin.

Now for the dress...

'TILLY? WHAT ARE YOU DOING...? Aren't you ready yet?' Annabelle knocked anxiously on the bathroom door, and when there was no response she turned the handle, relieved to discover that the door wasn't locked.

Tilly was standing in the middle of the bathroom, wearing the designer dress and staring at her reflection in the mirror.

'Oh, my!' Annabelle breathed.

'Oh, my God, don't you mean?' Tilly corrected her grimly. 'Ma, I can't possibly wear this.'

'Why not? You look gorgeous.'

'Just look at me. I'm spilling out of it everywhere. I look like a...a hooker,' Tilly said through gritted teeth.

'Sorry to interrupt you both, but Art sent me up to find out where you are. He said to tell you that his stomach thinks his throat's been cut.'

'Silas.' Annabelle beamed. 'You're just the person we need. Come and tell Tilly to stop being so silly. She looks gorgeous in this dress, but she says it makes her look like a hooker.'

Tilly's face burned as Silas stepped into view and stood studying her in silence. He had changed into a dinner suit, and her heart did its pancake trick again. How unfair it was that men should look so wonderful in their evening clothes.

'Tilly's quite right,' he announced uncompromisingly, adding softly, as her face burned with chagrin, 'and yet totally wrong. She looks like a classy, very expensive kept woman—or an equally classy and very expensive rich man's wife.' He crooked his arm. 'May I have the pleasure of escorting you both down to dinner? Because if I don't I'd better warn you that Art is going to be on his way up here, and his mood isn't good.'

Silas was smiling, but it shocked Tilly to see how apprehensive her mother suddenly looked. If they'd been on their own she would have asked her outright if she was as afraid of Art as she looked—as well as insisting that her mother loan her something else to wear. Right now, though, her concern for her mother disturbed her far more than her own self-conscious discomfort at wearing a dress that was way too revealing for her own personal taste.

Her disquiet was still with her five minutes later, when she watched Annabelle hurry over to where Art was waiting impatiently for them by the drawing room door, apologise prettily to her fiancé and reach up to kiss his cheek—or rather his jowl, Tilly thought grimly, as she tried to control her own growing unease about her mother's marriage plans.

TILLY TRIED TO LOOK DISCREETLY at her watch, heaving a small sigh of relief when she saw that it was almost midnight. Tonight had to have been the worst evening of her life. How could her mother even *think* about joining a family so appallingly dysfunctional and so arrogantly oblivious to it?

Art's daughters, Susan-Jane and Cissie-Rose, were stick-thin and must, Tilly imagined, take after their mother. There was nothing of their father's heavy squareness about them. Their husbands, though, were both unpleasantly overweight. Art's daughters were, according to Tilly's mother, 'Southern Belles.' If so, they were certainly Southern Belles who had been left out in the sun so long that all humanity had been burned out of them, Tilly decided, as she listened to them deliberately and cruelly trying to destroy her mother with their innuendos and subtle put-downs.

At one point during the evening, when she had been obliged to listen politely yet again to Cissie-Rose praising herself to the skies for the high quality of her hands-on mothering, and complaining about the children's nanny daring to ask for time off over Christmas so that she could visit her own family, Tilly had longed to turn round and tell her what she thought of her. But of course she hadn't, knowing how horrified her mother would have been.

For such an apparently clean-living family, they seemed to consume an incredible amount of alcohol. Although very little food had passed what Tilly suspected were the artificially inflated and certainly perfectly glossed lips of Art's 'girls', as he referred to them. Predictably, they had expressed horror and then sympathy when Tilly had tucked into her own meal with gusto, shuddering with distaste at her appetite.

'Dwight would probably take a stick to me if I put on so much as an ounce—wouldn't you honey?' Cissie-Rose had observed.

'No guy likes an overweight gal. Ain't that the truth, Silas?' Dwight had drunkenly roped Silas into the conversation.

'Oh, you mustn't tease Silas, Dwighty,' Cissie-Rose had told her husband in her soft baby whisper of a voice. 'He and Tilly are newly engaged, and of course right now he thinks she's wonderful. I can remember how romantic it was when *we* first got engaged. Although I must say, Tilly, I was shocked when Daddy told us about the way you and Silas were carryin' on earlier.'

'T'ain't right, doing that kind of thing in a house where there's young 'uns around,' Dwight had put in.

'Which begs the point that presumably young 'un number one was sent away somewhere when young 'un number two was conceived?' Silas had murmured indiscreetly to Tilly, on the pretext of filling her wine glass.

She had desperately wanted to laugh, only too glad of the light relief his dry comment had provided, but she hadn't allowed herself. He had no business linking the two of them together in private intimate conversation of the kind only good friends or lovers exchanged.

Tilly didn't think she'd ever seen two men drink as much as Art and Dwight. Art's other son-in-law—Susan-Jane's husband, Bill, a quiet man with a warm smile, hadn't drunk as much as the other two—although Tilly suspected from the amount of attention he was paying her that either he and Susan-Jane had had a quarrel before coming down for dinner, or he was a serial flirt who didn't care how much he humiliated his wife by paying attention to another woman.

Tilly tried not to show what she was feeling when she watched Art down yet another whiskey sour, but she was relieved to see that Silas wasn't joining the other men in what seemed to be some sort of contest to see who could mix the strongest drink.

In truth, the only good thing about being downstairs was the warmth—and the excellent food. Had her room been more comfortable, and had she had it to herself, she would have escaped to it long ago, Tilly admitted as she tried and failed to smother a yawn.

'Darling, you look worn out,' Annabelle exclaimed with maternal concern. 'Art, I think we should call it a night…'

'You can call it what the hell you like, honey, but me and the boys are callin' for another jug of liquor—ain't that right, boys?'

Tilly's heart ached for her mother when she saw her anguished look.

'The staff must have had a long day, with everyone arriving. It would be considerate, perhaps, to let them clear away and get to bed?' Silas spoke quietly, but with such firm authority that everyone turned to look at him.

'Who the hell needs to be considerate to the staff? They're paid to look after us.' Dwight's face was red with resentment as he glared at Silas.

Tilly discovered that she was holding her breath, and her stomach muscles were cramped with tension. But Silas had the advantage, since he had already stood up and was moving to her chair to pull it out for her.

'You're right. I apologise if I overstepped the mark.' Silas ignored Dwight to address his apology direct to Art. 'It was only a thought.'

'And a good one Silas,' Tilly heard her mother saying heroically. 'I'm tired myself, Artie, do let's all go to bed.'

Tilly wasn't at all sure that Art would have complied if a flustered young girl hadn't come hurrying in to the room to tell Cissie-Rose that one of her children had been sick and was asking for her.

'Oh, my poor baby!' Cissie-Rose exclaimed theatrically. 'I knew coming here was gonna make her sick. I told you—you know that I did.'

'Come on. Let's make our escape now, whilst we can,' Silas muttered to Tilly.

She was tired enough to give in, going over to her mother first to give her a quick kiss, and then saying a general good-night, while Art's daughters were still protesting in high-pitched whiny voices about the disruption to their children's routine.

'Does your mother know what she's letting herself in for?' Silas demanded as they headed for the stairs.

'I don't know,' Tilly was forced to admit. Her own concern betrayed her into adding, 'She says she's in love with Art, but I don't see how she can be.'

By the time they reached the second floor her skin had broken out in goosebumps, and she was so cold that her longing to crawl into bed to try and get warm was overwhelming her apprehension about sharing it with Silas.

'Do you suppose there'll be any hot water up here?' she asked Silas as he opened the bedroom door for her.

'Potentially,' Silas answered her dryly. 'There's an electrically heated shower in the bathroom, although my experience of it so far suggests that it isn't totally efficient.'

'Meaning what?' Tilly asked him suspiciously.

'Meaning lukewarm is probably as good as it's going to get,' he replied. 'At least the bed should be warm, though. I went down to the kitchen earlier and borrowed a kettle and a couple of hot water bottles.'

Tilly's eyes widened, and then blurred with tired tears. Somehow he wasn't the type she had imagined doing something so domestic and so thoughtful.

He would be a fool to start feeling sorry for Tilly, Silas warned himself, hardening his heart against her obvious misery. His only purpose in being here was to get his story. And that was exactly what he intended to do, no matter what methods he had to use to do so.

'I don't think I can bear a week of this.' Tilly was too tired to care about how vulnerable her admission might make her seem. 'I hate the cold, and I hate even more the thought of not being able to have a decent hot shower whenever I want.'

Silas looked at her. 'If that's a hint that you're expecting me to be a gentleman and offer to let you use the shower first, I've got a better idea.'

'You mean I should use my mother's bathroom?' Tilly asked absently, as she stepped into the lamp-lit bedroom that looked cosier and felt slightly warmer than she had expected.

'No, I was going to say that it would make sense for us to share the shower, to make the best use of what hot water it provides.'

Was he serious? He couldn't be, could he? She looked at him, and then wished she hadn't as her body reacted to the intimacy of discovering that he was looking right back at her.

'It's warmer in here than I was expecting.' She gave him a too-bright smile to match the light tone of her voice. Anything— just as long as she didn't have to respond to the suggestion that they share a shower. Already her senses were working overtime, bombarding her with erotic messages and images.

'That's because I bribed one of the maids to find us a plug-in electric radiator.' He had closed the door and was looking at her in a way that made her heart bounce about inside her chest like a tennis ball hit by a pro. 'Now, about that shower...'

Tilly shook her head, trying to cling on to her normal, firm common sense, and to react to what he was saying as though it had been said by one of her young subordinates. The kindly but firm maternal voice of authority she used on them would surely make it plain to Silas that she wasn't expecting what he thought, as well as controlling her own dangerous longing.

'Silas, I've already told you, you've got it all wrong. You don't have to have sex with me.'

The effect of her words wasn't what she had hoped for. Instead of obediently backing off, Silas stopped leaning casually against the wall and straightened up to his full height. Such a small movement, barely more than a single step, but in terms of meaningful body language it sent her a message that had her muscles cramping with sexual tension.

'Well, that certainly isn't what my body is telling me,' he announced silkily. 'It's telling me that right now there is nothing I need or want more than to take you to bed and make love to you slowly and thoroughly and completely.'

Tilly was beyond words. She could only shake her head.

He smiled at her, and her resistance melted under the heat of the look in his eyes.

'This is crazy.' Was that quavering, somehow betraying, yearning voice really hers? 'I mean, we've only just met. We don't know one another. We're *strangers.*'

'Is there a law that says strangers can't become lovers?' He was walking very purposefully towards her now, and she felt positively light-headed with shocked excitement.

The only reason he was doing this was as a form of insurance against her threatening to break off their engagement and forcing him to leave, Silas told himself. If he could keep her happy in bed she would get what she wanted, whether she knew it or not, and he, with any luck, would get his information. The fact that he was so strongly physically attracted to Tilly wasn't what was motivating him at all. This was simply something that it was necessary for him to do.

Very necessary.

If only she was the sort of person who could just live for the moment and enjoy what that moment was offering, Tilly acknowledged giddily. If only she didn't have these crazy hang-ups about love and sex working together. If only she was able to separate them as others could. If only she didn't have even more inhibiting hang-ups about permanency and commitment, and a fear that they simply did not exist. She closed her eyes. What was wrong with her? She wanted Silas sexually so much. So why not indulge in that wanting? Why not simply offer herself up to him now? Why not slide her arms around his neck, press her body eagerly against his and lift her face for his kiss…?

Why not? Because she could not. She simply couldn't cold-bloodedly have sex with a man just because physically he turned her on. Cold-bloodedly? She was so hot for him that it hurt!

Silas was used to playing a waiting game. So why the hell did he feel so impatient now that he was tempted to cross the distance that separated them and show Tilly what they would have instead of waiting for her to agree to it?

'I'm sorry. I can't do it.' The words burst out from Tilly in a flurried tremble, causing Silas to check in mid-step and stare at Tilly in disbelief. 'It's true that I do… That is…you… Physically I *am* attracted to you,' she managed to say primly, whilst her stomach went hollow with the intensity of her body's disappointment. 'But I don't want to have sex with you.'

It surprised Silas that she was prepared to go to such lengths to show him that he had originally misjudged the situation, but what surprised him even more was how gut-wrenchingly savagely deprived he felt. The intensity of his disappointment was a measure of just how much he wanted her—and that was far too much, he decided grimly.

'If that's your decision then that's your decision,' he told her flatly. If she expected him to coax and plead she had the wrong man. Because he had no intention of doing so.

CHAPTER SIX

TILLY BLINKED IN THE DARKNESS, luxuriating in the bed's delicious warmth. She had no idea what had woken her, unless somehow the sound of Silas's breathing had penetrated her sleep.

She was, she realised, thirsty. She remembered there was a bottle of water on the small table in front of the window. Sliding out of bed as carefully as she could so that she wouldn't disturb Silas, she made her way towards the window. Enough light was coming in through the thin curtain to guide her. She held her breath and watched Silas apprehensively, in case the sound of her uncapping the bottle woke him.

Silas was already awake, and had been awake from the second Tilly had moved and murmured in her sleep. The bed was large enough for them to sleep apart, but at some stage while she slept Tilly had moved closer to him, so that she had been sleeping almost curled into him.

As she drank her water, Tilly pulled back the curtain slightly to look out through the window, her eyes rounding with delight when she realised that it was snowing: huge, fat flakes whirling down from the moonlit sky. A childhood sense of excitement and joy she had forgotten it was possible to feel filled her, and she leaned closer to the window to watch the snow. How could something so delicate and so beautiful to watch from the safety and warmth inside also be so deadly? She was already beginning to shiver in her thin and flimsy vest, but somehow she couldn't drag herself away from the magic of watching the snow fall.

Silas studied Tilly's unguarded expression as she watched the snow. She looked as joyful and excited as a child might have done. Something that felt like a heavy stone trap door being shifted by a long-unused mechanism seemed to be happening inside his chest. Both the movement and the sensation of something touching what was raw and unprotected within him physically hurt. He badly wanted to turn over and ignore Tilly, to push back the heavy door he had locked against his own emotions. But for some reason he couldn't.

She really was cold now, Tilly admitted as she left the window to make her way carefully back to her side of the bed. The far side—which meant that she had to skirt very quietly past the end of the bed so that she didn't wake Silas.

The bed felt welcomingly warm as she slid back into it, but her feet were freezing, and as she snuggled down beneath the duvet the delicious heat coming off Silas's sleeping body acted like a magnet to her cold toes. The dip in the bed made her feel as though she was trying to go to sleep on a slope—a cold, snow-covered slope that was all the more inhospitable because of the warmth that she knew lay waiting for her if she just let her body roll a little bit closer to Silas.

She relaxed and let herself roll, luxuriating for several blissful seconds in an almost purring enjoyment of the solid wall of warm male flesh she was now lying against. Her feet seemed of their own accord to find the perfect toasty resting place on Silas's lovely warm bare calves. *Bare?* She had already been in bed when Silas had emerged from the bathroom, and of course she hadn't looked to see what he was or wasn't wearing, and she certainly wasn't going to start doing a hands-on body-check now.

Snow falling from a midnight sky, and the pleasure of exploring Silas's body with every single one of her senses divided into every individual delight they could bring. What could possibly be more perfect? She would start by looking at him, enjoying the security of the moonlit semi-darkness as she allowed her eager gaze to move over the hundreds of subtle variations of light and shadow. She would lie here doing that until it slowly got light enough to see the contours clearly.

That was if she could wait that long before she touched him. It would be a special sort of sensual heaven and hell to touch him in the darkness without previously knowing his body, to use her fingertips to guide her and to relay every nuance of his flesh, its texture firm and taut where it padded his muscles, sleek and cool over the length and strength of his bones, deliciously male-scented and erotic in the vulnerable hollows of his throat, the inside of his elbows, behind his knees.

Her own flesh seemed to be vibrating in a hymn of sensuality that was beyond her own hearing. She could feel it growing and expanding within her, deepening and tightening, filling her senses until it spilled over and flooded every bit of her.

Silas, who had been lying wide awake, gritting his teeth against his own aching desire, heard her soft moan and the accompanying acceleration of her breathing. It was too much for his self-control. He turned over, reaching for her, covering her mouth with his own before she could object and kissing her with so much skilled sensuality that she didn't even want to.

She reached up and wrapped her arms around him, trembling under the forceful pressure of her need for him as he gathered her up against himself. He *was* naked, she recognised, submitting to the starburst of heated pleasure that the knowledge brought.

When and how had she learned to open her legs just enough to be able to feel the delight of the space she had created accommodating the hard strength of his erection as he slid her down against it? His hands were sliding beneath the waist of her thin cut-offs so that he could cup her buttocks and press her more deeply against it, moving her rhythmically as he did so. Up and then down the thickness of his flesh, just a little, just enough to make her want to cry out in fierce recognition of her own aching frustration every time the movement sensitised her growing ache for a deeper intimacy.

She tried to focus away from the clamouring demands of her clitoris and to concentrate instead on the slow, explorative thrust of his tongue against her own. Only it wasn't slow any more, and she didn't know if the urgent movements galvanising her body were the result of what he was doing to her or the cause of it. She could feel the hot, tight, piercingly erotic ache of her nipples as her movements brought them into contact with his naked chest. She wanted him to touch them, to caress them, to soothe their hard need with the comfort of his kiss and then to inflame it again with the hotter, harder lash of his tongue and the rake of his teeth. She wanted him to slide her body free of her sleepwear and then explore each and every part of it while she gave herself up to the pleasure of that intimacy.

'You're going to have to provide the condom; I didn't think to bring any with me.'

Tilly stared up into Silas's face and gulped. 'Neither did I,' she told him. 'I'm a woman. They aren't the kind of thing I usually carry around with me.'

'But presumably, like me, you don't have unprotected sex?'

It was a question rather than a statement.

'I don't have sex, full stop,' Tilly admitted honestly.

She sounded so self-conscious that Silas knew immediately that she was telling the truth. He reached out and switched on the bedside lamp, keeping a firm grip on her arm when she would have squirmed away.

'It isn't that I have any problem with having sex,' Tilly assured him. 'The problem has been meeting the right kind of partner.'

Silas arched one dark eyebrow in disbelief.

'You work in the City. You're in charge of a department of testosterone-fuelled young males.'

'Exactly,' Tilly agreed vehemently, adding in exasperation when he continued to look slightly aloof and disinclined to believe her, 'Don't you see? If I started dating one of them, then it would be bound to be discussed by the others, and then they'd all...'

'Want to take you to bed?' Silas suggested, and then wished he hadn't when he was suddenly savaged by the most unexpected raw male jealousy.

'Hardly. But in order to maintain my authority over them I have to ensure that they respect me. They wouldn't do that if they thought they could have sex with me.' She gave a small shrug. 'It sounds brutal I know, but it's the truth. The City has a very macho image, and the young men working there are keen to uphold that image. They're pushing the boundaries all the time. They're like pack animals—if you show a weakness they'll sense blood and go in for the kill. If I want to date a man it has to be someone outside the City, and the hours I work make that almost impossible.'

Silas knew what she was saying was true. 'Hence your decision to include some recreational sex in the deal you set up when you hired an escort?' he suggested.

Tilly stiffened in angry outrage. 'How many times do I have to tell you that there was no such decision—either by me or for me?'

'You haven't had sex in a very long time, to judge from the way you were responding to me. It makes sense that you should think of getting a double deal for the price of one.'

Tilly's face had started to burn with the heat of her emotions. 'I *do* not and *would* not pay for sex. I've already told you that. And if that had been my intention you can be sure that I would have taken steps to ensure that I was properly protected. I don't use *any* kind of contraception,' she told him fiercely. 'Never mind carry condoms with me just in case.'

Silas could hear the emotional tears thickening her voice. If she was telling the truth then his accusations weren't just in bad taste and unfair, they were also cruel. Her need must have been very great indeed to make her respond to him as intensely as she had.

'Okay, I was out of order. You'll have to put my lack of subtlety down to the fact that I'm frustrated and disappointed as hell that we can't take this to its natural conclusion.'

Tilly gave a muffled sound and let him draw her back against his body and hold her there, with her head tucked into his shoulder.

'It's been a long time for me as well,' he told her quietly. He felt her sudden shocked movement. 'No, I'm not lying. It's the truth. Contrary to the impression I'm probably giving right now, I don't go in for impulsive spur-of-the-moment sex. My own work means that finding the right kind of partner isn't easy.'

Tilly assumed he meant that because he was an actor the opportunities were many, but so were the risks. As Sally had once graphically said to her, every time she slept with a new man she felt totally put off by the thought that she was also in part sleeping with all his previous partners—and their partners too.

'Perhaps I'm not thinking laterally enough,' Silas murmured.

'About finding a sexual partner?'

'No, about having the satisfaction of giving you the pleasure and fulfilment I want to give you. After all, we don't need a condom to achieve that.'

Tilly's heart somersaulted, and then slammed into her chest wall. She didn't know now whether to feel shocked or excited, and ended up feeling a mix of both, tinged with wary resoluteness.

'If you're saying that because you *still* think I hired you with the ulterior motive of having sex with you—' she began.

But Silas didn't let her finish her objection, putting his fingers to her lips instead to silence her, and then bending his head to her ear to tell her meaningfully, 'Right now I ache like hell with frustration, and, like I said, it's the best way I can think of to go at least part-way towards getting rid of that.'

'By satisfying *me*?'

Silas could hear the disbelief in her voice. 'I don't know what kind of men you've known, but I can't believe they haven't shown you how much pleasure a man can get from bringing his partner to fulfilment. From seeing it in her eyes, feeling it in her kiss, from witnessing that he's satisfied her.'

'There haven't been *men*,' Tilly felt obliged to admit. 'Just one man. It was when we were at university, and I felt I should...'

She'd only had *one* previous lover? Silas was caught off-guard by the wave of unexpected tenderness that surged through him. And even more startled by the ease with which he could accept the truth of what she had said.

He started to pull her down against him, his hands shaping her body, but Tilly resisted.

'What's wrong?' he asked. 'Don't you want me to?'

'Yes,' Tilly told him honestly, pausing before she said, even more honestly, in a small breathless rush of words, 'But I want our first time together to *be* together.'

It seemed a long time during which she had to bear his silent scrutiny before Silas reacted to what she had said, but when he did it wasn't with words. Instead he cupped her face, brushing the soft quiver of her lips over and over again with the pad of his thumb before bending his head to kiss her so intimately that she was afraid that she might actually orgasm after all.

When he finally lifted his mouth from hers it made her shiver in delicious awareness of his arousal to hear the thick roughness in his voice when he said, 'I wonder if you know how much I was tempted to break all my own rules on health and irresponsibility? But, while I might have broken them for myself, I don't have the right to expect you to break your own rules for me. Another time we'll have to organise things better.'

Not the most romantic words in the world, perhaps, but to Tilly they had a meaning and depth to them that went beyond the lightweight glitter of mere romance. 'What are the plans for today?' Silas asked.

'I'm not sure,' Tilly admitted. 'But if it's possible I wouldn't mind going back into that town we came through on the way here. I feel I ought to get the children a small Christmas present each.'

Silas hesitated for a second. From his own point of view it made sense for him to spend as much time as he could with Art, and yet he felt strangely reluctant to pass up on the opportunity to have Tilly to himself and get to know her better.

'I'll see if I can find out the best way for us to get into town, if you like,' he offered. After all, they were here for a week. Plenty of time for him to get close to Art later.

CHAPTER SEVEN

'DARLING. I HOPE YOU WON'T BE offended, but I'm afraid you and Silas are going to have to entertain yourselves today, because the florist is coming out from Madrid to see me this morning, and then this afternoon I need to finalise the menu with the chef.'

'Don't worry about us, Annabelle,' Silas answered, before Tilly could say anything. 'Art, I hope you don't mind,' he continued. 'Before we joined you for breakfast I took the liberty of having a word with the chap who is in charge of your fleet of vehicles here to ask if there was any possibility of us borrowing a car and driving down into Segovia. We had to leave London in a bit of a rush and we both still have some essential Christmas shopping to do. Martin said it was okay with him if I borrowed one of the four-wheel drives so long as you had no objections.'

'Of course he doesn't—do you, sweetheart?' Annabelle smiled, looking relieved. 'You are so lucky, Tilly, to have such a thoughtful fiancé. Art hates going shopping.'

'Maybe Silas doesn't mind because *he* isn't a billionaire.'

Tilly felt a rush of anger on her mother's behalf as Art's younger daughter dropped the venom-tipped words onto the now-silent air of the room where they had eaten breakfast. It was no wonder her husband was looking embarrassed and shame-faced, Tilly decided, feeling sorry for him.

However, it was Silas who took up the gauntlet on her mother's behalf, saying coolly, 'I daresay the experience of bringing up two daughters has made Art wise enough to see through predatory females.'

The insult was delivered so lightly and easily that it was almost like a fine needle plunged into the heart, Tilly decided.

You knew you'd received a mortal wound, but you couldn't see how or where. That it *had* been delivered, though, was obvious in the sudden red flush on Susan-Jane's face.

When Tilly had woken up alone in the attic bedroom that morning, she had been torn between hurrying to get showered, dressed and out of the room before Silas returned, because she felt so embarrassed about the previous night, and an equally strong impulse to remain hidden under the bedclothes, because she wasn't sure she could face Silas at all. In the event he had behaved so naturally towards her that it had been unexpectedly easy to return his good-morning kiss when he had come into the dining room several seconds behind her, smelling of cold air and explaining that he had been outside.

Now, of course, she knew why. Just as she knew what the nature of the essential shopping he had referred to was.

For a man who was perilously close to being an out-of-work actor, he possessed a rare degree of self-confidence. In fact the lack of flamboyance in his manner, allied with the cool purposefulness he displayed, seemed to Tilly to be closer to the behaviour of the top handful of her clients—wealthy, self-assured men, some of whom had inherited their wealth and some of whom had made it from scratch, but all of whom were the kind of men who didn't need to prove anything to anyone, and to whom other men seemed to automatically defer.

'I've told Martin that we should be ready to leave at about eleven,' Silas told Tilly. He glanced at his watch, which looked simple and robust but, as Tilly well knew from the boys on her team, was an expensive and highly covetable Rolex. 'That gives us just over half an hour to get ready. Is that enough time? Or shall I—?'

'Half an hour is fine,' Tilly assured him.

She was just about to push back her chair and go up to the bedroom to get her coat when Cissie-Rose suddenly announced, 'I was planning to take the kids into Segovia myself today. They're so bored, cooped up here. Since you're driving in, Silas, we may as well come with you, so that Daddy will still have the other SUV here if he needs to go out.'

'You could be spoiling Silas and Tilly's fun if you do that,' her husband chuckled.

'Oh, don't be silly. Silas won't mind. After all, it's not as if he's still courtin' Tilly. I mean, Tilly and Silas are practically living together—even though they aren't legally married yet.'

For bitchiness, Art's daughters would take some beating, Tilly decided, as Silas stood up to pull her chair out for her. She tried to imagine how she might be feeling right now if she and Silas *were* newly engaged and passionately in love, desperate for some time alone. Oddly enough it wasn't hard at all for her to conjure up exactly what she would feel. In fact it wasn't very much different from what she *was* feeling, she admitted. Which meant *what*, exactly? Because she and Silas *weren't* engaged, and they *weren't* in love. But something was happening between them, and she couldn't pretend that it wasn't. Last night, for instance… The ache last night's interrupted lovemaking had left behind, like a tamped-down fire, smouldering beneath the surface, suddenly burst into fresh life.

All the way up the stairs, too conscious of Silas, walking alongside her, Tilly struggled to smother her aching desire. It overwhelmed her that she should feel like this for a man she barely knew. Inside herself a monumental tug of war seemed to be taking place, between her head and her heart. She knew as surely as she knew her own name that she was someone who could only touch the heights of her own sensuality when her physical desire was equalled by her emotional commitment. Loveless sex had no appeal at all for her, which was why she had always held back from allowing herself to get involved with anyone. Up until now.

So what had happened to make things so different? Silas had happened, that was what! Silas, an out-of-work actor, who hired himself out as an escort. She, with all she knew about the vulnerability of love, was actually admitting that she was close to committing the insanity of falling in love with a man engaged in just about the most relationship-unfriendly career there was. She was kidding, right? She was simply testing herself—seeing how far she could stretch her self-imposed boundaries; she wasn't

seriously falling in love with a man she had only just met. She
couldn't be.

They had reached their bedroom door. Silas opened it for her.

'Thanks for saying what you did to Cissie-Rose. I wanted to
say something myself, but I know if I had it wouldn't have been
anything like such a masterly put-down.'

Silas gave a dismissive shrug. 'It was obvious when she tried
to make a dig about your mother being motivated by money that
that is *exactly* what motivates her. There's something profoundly
ugly and depressing about the pathetic need the sons and daughters of the very wealthy often seem to have, to ring-fence their
parents' assets and stick a "mine all mine" label on them.' He
gave another shrug. 'Mind you, I suppose if you've been brought
up to think that everything can be bought, including your own
love, the thought of anyone else getting their hands on your parents' money is threatening. Makes me glad my own father was
just comfortably off.'

Yes, she could see him in the social background described
by the brief sketch he had just drawn. Good school, and a good
university too, she judged shrewdly. The kind of background she
would normally have expected to lead to a career in the City, or
the law. 'Is there a tradition of acting in your family?' she asked
curiously.

'Like the Redgraves, you mean?' He shook his head. 'No.'

His half-brother's desire to act had surprised them all, and it
had been Silas who had had to act as a bridge between Joe and
their father in Joe's early teenage years, when he had first decided he wanted to act.

'Disappointed that I'm not connected to theatre aristocracy?'
he asked dryly.

It was Tilly's turn to shake her head. 'No, not at all. It's just
that I find it hard to imagine you as an actor, somehow. You
don't seem the type.'

'No? So what type do I seem, then?' This was dangerous
territory, but he couldn't resist asking her—even as he was inwardly deriding himself for his predictable male vanity.

'Something big in the City—not a City-boy type. Something

else, perhaps in one of the controlling bodies, a sort of overlooking and critical role.'

Her perspicacity reminded him that he was not dealing with a woman of Art's daughters' ilk. Tilly didn't only have far more humanity than them, she also had far more intelligence. Intelligence in a lover when you were keeping something hidden from them was not exactly an asset, he warned himself. But it was too late for him to backtrack now. Last night he had made Tilly the kind of promises—verbally as well as non-verbally—that were likely to cause him an awful lot of problems.

'Is it my imagination, or is this room actually slightly warmer?' Tilly asked.

She was glad of an excuse to change the subject and get away from the personal. Not that she didn't want to find out as much about Silas's background and his way of life as she could—she did. In fact she craved details about him. But that in itself was enough to make her want to take to her heels and put as much distance between them as she could. She was involved in a tug of war, with her head pulling in one direction and her heart in another.

'I had a word with the Count's PA,' Silas said. 'Apparently the Count won't be too pleased if he finds out his instructions with regard to the necessity of keeping all the rooms equally heated have been ignored. Even the insurance on this place is dependent on certain conditions—one of which is keeping all the rooms equally heated. I doubt that even Art, with all his billions, would be too happy if he were landed with a bill for the renovation work on one damaged castle.'

'Art's daughters aren't going to be very pleased.'

'Probably not, but they are free to take up their argument with the PA if they wish to.' He paused, and then asked dryly, 'I know it's none of my business, but does your mother have *any* idea of what she's taking on?'

'My mother prefers to only see what she wants to see, and right now what she wants to see is that Art is a wonderful man and his daughters are going to be loving stepdaughters to her.

She's so unworldly. I can't help worrying about her,' Tilly admitted.

'So who does the worrying about you?'

'No one,' Tilly answered promptly. 'No one needs to worry about me. I'm not like my mother. The way she falls in love and then falls out of it again would leave me too disillusioned to keep on looking for Mr Right, but she seems to be able to pick herself up and start all over again.'

Silas could hear the underlying troubled note in Tilly's voice. It was his opinion that her mother was rather shallow, but the more he saw of Annabelle the less inclined he was to think of her as being avaricious or manipulative. 'How old were you when your mother fell out of love with your father?'

The unexpectedness of his own abrupt question startled Silas as much as it did Tilly.

'I was six when they divorced, and from what they've both told me the marriage had been in trouble for some time. I think Dad tried to stay the course because of me, but Ma had had enough.' Tilly opened the wardrobe and removed her coat and boots.

'You're going to need something a bit sturdier than those,' Silas warned her. 'Martin told me that they're expecting a fresh fall of snow later today.'

'I don't have anything else,' Tilly admitted ruefully. 'I shall have to see what I can buy while we're out. It didn't register properly with me that the weather was going to be like this.'

'If we had really come here as a newly engaged couple I daresay we'd have been only too happy to use the snow as an excuse to stay up here in bed. And no doubt we would have come prepared,' Silas said.

Tilly could feel her face turning pink, and the surge of longing that gripped her body was so intense that it made her give a small, low gasp of protest. She placed her hand flat to her lower body, in an attempt to quell the pulse of raw need that had kicked into life.

She could see from Silas's expression that he knew exactly what she was feeling. When he stepped towards her, she protested shakily, 'No.' But she didn't make any attempt to step back or to avoid him when he cupped her shoulder with one hand and slid the other into the small hollow of lower back, determinedly propelling her towards him.

'That look says you ache for me in the same way I do for you.' Even the warmth of his breath as he murmured the words against her ear was a form of caress and arousal, making her quiver with pleasure and exhale on a small, shuddering breath, desperate to turn her face to his so that his mouth would be closer to her own.

What was it about this particular woman that made him behave in ways that ran counter to all his plans? Silas wondered grimly. This agonisingly sharp and relentlessly demanding stab of need burning through him wasn't what he had intended at all. It had to be something in the small quiver within her body that alerted him to her physical susceptibility to him that was responsible for this fierce, male, *driven* urge within him, pushing him to cover her mouth with his own, rather than any independent desire of his own. It had to be. Otherwise... Otherwise, what? Otherwise he would be getting himself into a situation that he couldn't control?

'We'd better go downstairs before Martin thinks we've changed our minds and we don't want the car any more.'

She was glad that he wasn't taking things any further, Tilly told herself firmly, when Silas released her and started to step back.

'Don't do that!' Silas groaned, almost dragging her back into his arms.

'Don't do what?' Tilly protested.

'Don't look at me as though all you want is the feel of my mouth on yours,' Silas told her harshly.

'I wasn't—' Tilly began to object, but it was too late. Silas had imprisoned her face between his hands and he was bending towards her, his kiss silencing her.

Long after she should have been asleep the night before she had lain awake, desperately trying to tell herself that Silas's kisses couldn't possibly have been as wonderful as she was now thinking. She had derided herself for being bewitched by a potent combination of her own physical desire, the moonlight outside on the snow and the proximity of Christmas. She had told herself sternly that if Silas had kissed her, say, in her own flat in London, she probably wouldn't have been affected by him at all. But here she was, being swept up under last night's magical spell all over again—and if anything this time his effect on her was even more intense. If he chose to pick her up and carry her over to the waiting bed now, she knew that she wouldn't want to stop him.

An intense ache pulsed deep in the core of her sexuality. She wanted him so badly she felt shocked, almost drugged, by the overwhelming strength of her need. Panic flared inside her, causing her to push Silas away. She didn't want to feel like this about any man, and especially *his* kind of man.

The minute he released her she headed for the door. When he reached it ahead of her she held her breath, half fearful and half hopeful that he would lean against it, barring her exit, but instead he opened it for her, simply saying, 'Don't forget your coat.'

'RIGHT, KIDS, YOU GET IN the back with Matilda. You won't mind if I sit in front with you, Silas, will you? Only I get so carsick if I sit in the back.'

Not a word of apology to *her*, Tilly seethed, as Cissie-Rose appropriated the passenger seat of the large four-wheel drive. Unlike her, Cissie-Rose seemed to have arrived in Spain well equipped for the snow, Tilly realised, as she looked a little enviously at her expensive winter sports-style outfit.

'I want a window seat.'

'So do I.' Cissie-Rose's children were already clambering into the back seat.

'You'll have to sit in the middle, Tilly,' Cissie-Rose instructed—for all the world as though she were some kind of servant, Tilly thought crossly.

'One of the children will have to sit in the middle. Not Tilly,' Silas intervened, in the kind of voice that said there would be no argument. 'They can take turns to have the window seat—one when we drive out and the other when we drive back.'

'*Maria* always sits in the middle,' the elder of Cissie-Rose's sons piped up.

'Maybe she does. But Tilly is not Maria.'

'Goodness, what a fuss you're making, Tilly,' Cissie-Rose said spitefully, and so blatantly untruthfully that Tilly was too taken aback to retaliate.

'Call this an SUV?' the older boy commented derogatively. 'You should see our SUVs back home.'

'Fix my seat belt for me,' the other commanded Tilly in a disagreeable voice.

She was just leaning forward to help him when Silas stopped her. '*Please will you help me with my seat belt, Tilly?* That's what I think you meant to say, isn't it?'

Tilly couldn't help feeling a bit sorry for the two boys. They were only young, and it was obvious their mother was the type of woman who treated her sons as useful bargaining tools—to be fussed over when it suited her, and then be dismissed and kept out of her way when it didn't.

For the entire length of the time it took them to drive into Segovia Cissie-Rose focused her attention on Silas—to such a degree that she and the children might just as well not have been there, Tilly decided, more upset on behalf of the children than for herself. After all, Silas had already shown her that he had no interest in Cissie-Rose, and without knowing quite how it had happened Tilly discovered that she was actually allowing herself to trust him. That would make her dangerously vulnerable, an inner voice warned her, but Tilly chose to ignore it. In fact she was choosing to ignore a lot of warnings from her inner protective voice since she had met Silas.

The boys, once they realised Tilly wasn't the kind of person who could be cowed or spoken to in the way they were used to speaking to Maria, the young girl Cissie-Rose hired to look after them, began to respect her calm firmness and even responded to it. Tilly liked children, and she enjoyed enlivening the journey for the boys, teaching them some simple travel games and talking to them about their sports and hobbies.

To Silas, forced to endure the unwanted intimacy of Cissie-Rose's deliberate and unsubtle touches to his arm and occasionally his thigh, as she underlined various points of an unutterably boring monologue, the snatches of giggles reaching him from the back seat felt like longed-for sips of clean, cold water after the cloying taste of cheap corked wine. He could only marvel at the miraculous way in which Tilly was drawing out Cissie-Rose's two young sons. Something about her calm, matter-of-fact way of talking to them touched a chord in his own memory. Inside his head he could almost hear the echo of his own mother's voice, and with it his own responding laughter.

No child should have to grow up without a mother. He had been lucky in his stepmother, he knew that, and he genuinely loved her, but listening to Tilly had brought to life an old pain. He flicked the switch on the steering column that controlled the radio, increasing the volume so that it blotted out the laughter and chatter from the back seat. Immediately Cissie-Rose gave him an approving smile, and wetted her already over-glossed lips with the tip of her tongue. When he failed to respond she leaned towards him, very deliberately placing one manicured hand high up on his thigh.

'I am so glad you did that,' she told him huskily. 'Tilly's voice is quite shrill, isn't it? I suppose it must be her English accent. It was beginning to make my head ache. How long have you known one another, did you say?'

'I didn't,' Silas answered her coolly.

'She's a very lucky young woman to have landed a man like you in her bed.'

'The luck's all mine,' Silas responded.

Cissie-Rose was coming on to him strongly, and he recognised that if he encouraged her she might provide him with a shortcut to the information he needed. But his immediate rejection of the idea was so intense it was almost as if he was recoiling physically and emotionally from the thought of sharing the kind of intimacy he had begun with Tilly with anyone else.

A physical and an *emotional* recoil? Just what exactly did that mean? If he carried on like this he would soon be telling himself he felt guilty about what he was doing, and he couldn't afford that kind of self-indulgent luxury.

Even when they had reached town and parked the car, Cissie-Rose was still trying to claim Silas's attention, leaving Tilly to help her two sons out of the car, checking that they were well wrapped up against the icy cold wind whipping down Segovia's narrow streets.

The ground underfoot was covered in snow and ice, and—predictably—Cissie-Rose clutched at Silas's arm. The two boys positioned themselves either side of Tilly, clinging to her so trustingly that she didn't have the heart to say anything.

Silas looked grimly at Tilly's bent head and wondered why she had this ability to make him feel emotions he didn't want to feel, and how she managed to activate a protective, almost possessive male instinct in him that no other woman had ever touched. It certainly wasn't what he wanted to feel. Yet, watching her now with the two boys, he was conscious of a sharp sense of irritation that they were there, fuelling his need to have her to himself.

'Tilly and I have rather a lot to do, so we might as well split up, Cissie-Rose, and let you and the boys get on with your shopping. How long do you think you'll need?' he asked, lifting his arm to check his watch so that Cissie-Rose was forced to remove her hand from it.

'Oh! I thought we could all shop together,' she protested. 'It would be so much more fun that way. Tilly and I could do some girly stuff, and you guys could go have a soda or something, and then we could all meet up for lunch.'

This was Cissie-Rose in smiling 'good mom' mode, Tilly recognised, as the boys looked uncertainly at their mother.

'You're okay with that, aren't you, you guys?' Cissie-Rose appealed to her sons. 'Or would you prefer to stay with Tilly.'

Witch! Tilly thought with uncharacteristic venom. Tails you win, heads I lose.

'We want to stay with Tilly,' the two boys chanted together.

Immediately Silas shook his head. 'Sorry, boys, but I'm afraid you can't.'

The vehemence in his voice made Tilly curl her toes in excited reaction to the intimacy his determination to have her to himself suggested. 'Tilly and I have some Christmas shopping to do. And she *is* my fiancé.' The look he was giving her made her face burn, and Cissie-Rose's expression changed to one of acid venom as she glared at Silas.

She would make a bad enemy, Tilly realised when she saw the look in her eyes.

Silas didn't seem too concerned, though. Ignoring Cissie-Rose's obvious hostility to his suggestion, he continued calmly. 'I don't want to linger in town, Cissie-Rose. The weather forecast they gave out on the way over didn't sound very good.'

'Oh. I see. Well, okay, then.'

It was obvious that Cissie-Rose did not think it was anything like okay at all, Tilly realised, feeling uncomfortable as she saw the furious look the other woman was giving her.

'Look, why don't we meet back here in, say, a couple of hours?' Silas suggested. 'Here's a spare key for the car in case you get back before us. That way you won't have to stand around waiting in the cold. And I'll give you my mobile number just in case you need it. Ready, Tee?'

Tilly disengaged herself from the boys and hurried towards him, hating herself for being so grateful both for the supporting arm he slid round her and the warmth of the smile he gave her.

'It's okay. You can let go of me,' she told him slightly breathlessly five minutes later. 'Cissie-Rose can't see us now.'

'You are my fiancé; we're passionately in love. We're hardly going to walk feet apart from one another, are we? And you never know—we could bump into Cissie-Rose anywhere. It is only a small town. Besides,' Silas told her softly, 'I don't want to let go of you.'

Was it necessary for him to go to these lengths? He had established himself now as Tilly's fiancé. And after last night... After last night, what? It was because of last night that he had been left with this ache that had somehow taken on a life force of its own. This ache that right now…

What was Silas thinking? Tilly wondered. What was making him look so distant and yet at the same time, now that he had turned his head to look at her, so hungry for her?

When he reached for her Tilly didn't even try to resist. He turned her around to face him in the shelter of an overhanging building, where no one could see them, and then pressed her back against the wall, covering her body with the warmth of his own.

He whispered into the softness of her parting lips, 'I know there are any number of reasons why I shouldn't be doing this, but right now I don't want to know about them. Right now, right here, what I want, *all* I want, is you, Tilly.'

Why was he doing this when he didn't have to? Why ask himself questions that he couldn't answer? Silas answered himself as he gave in to the need that had been aching through him since last night and bent his head to kiss Tilly.

This wasn't a sensible thing for her to be doing, Tilly warned herself. But suddenly being sensible wasn't what she wanted. What she wanted was… What she wanted was Silas, she admitted. And she stopped thinking and worrying and judging, and simply gave herself over to feeling, as they clung together, kissing like two desire-drugged teenagers, oblivious to everything and everyone else.

What followed should have been an anticlimax. Instead it was the start of the most wonderful few hours Tilly had ever had.

The small town was picture-perfect, with its honey-coloured stone houses covered in pristine snow—which, thankfully, had been swept off the streets. Silas insisted on keeping her arm tucked through his. And when at one point he simply stopped walking and looked at her, she could feel her cheeks turning pink in response to the look in his eyes.

'Don't do that,' she protested.

'Don't do what?'

'Look at me like that.'

'You mean like I want to kiss you again?'

'This is crazy,' Tilly said, shaking her head.

'Isn't that what people are supposed to say when they start to fall in love?'

Silas could see the shock in her eyes. He could feel that same shock running through his own body. What the hell was he doing, dragging love into the situation? He felt as though he had suddenly become two people whose behaviour was totally alien to each other—one of whom was saying that he never played emotional games with women, that he despised men who did, so why the hell was he using a word like "love", while the other demanded to know who had said anything about playing games? It was as though he was at war with himself. He tried to shake off the feeling that they had somehow strayed into a maze and come up against a blank wall.

'There's a coffee shop over there. Shall we go in and have a drink?' Anything to try and get himself back to normal.

Tilly nodded her head in relief. Now that she was free of the spell the intimacy of Silas's sexuality seemed to cast over her, she was shakily aware of how vulnerable she was. Things were moving far too fast for her. She wasn't used to this kind of situation. And somehow she couldn't quite get her head round accepting that Silas could actually *mean* what he was saying. It was too much too soon. But she wanted him. She couldn't deny that.

She drank the coffee Silas ordered for them both, and tried to focus on the people hurrying up and down the street outside the window rather than on Silas, as she secretly wanted to do. In fact right now what she wanted more than anything else was just to be able to look at him, to absorb every tiny physical detail while she tried to come to terms with what was happening.

Silas watched her. He felt as though he could almost read her thoughts. She didn't know whether to believe he was being honest with her. He could sense it in every small action she made. She wanted him; he knew that. But he could see that she was dubious about accepting the immediacy of the situation.

They had both finished their coffee. Silas stood up. 'I'll be back in a minute,' he said, nodding his head in the direction of a pharmacy on the other side of the street.

Tilly didn't catch on immediately, but when she saw the green cross over the building her face burned, and she made an incoherent sound of assent, using Silas's absence to go to the ladies' room to comb her hair and replace the lipstick he had kissed off earlier. By the time she emerged, Silas had returned and was waiting for her.

'I think I'd better buy your mother a small Christmas gift, but I'm going to need you to advise me,' he said, steering her in the direction of a small gift shop with a mouthwatering window display. To Tilly's relief he didn't say a word about his visit to the pharmacy.

The gift shop proved to be a treasure trove of the unusual and the enticing, and Tilly found presents for each of the children. It was only when the small ornamental jewellery box Silas had bought for her mother was being giftwrapped that Tilly looked at her watch and realised that it was almost two hours since they had left the car park.

'We ought to be heading back,' she warned Silas.

'Yes, I know. Not that I'm particularly looking forward to the return trip with Cissie-Rose. She can sit in the back this time—car sickness or not,' he told Tilly, before adding in a warmer tone, 'I thought you handled the boys very well, by the way. You obviously like children.'

'Yes. And it's just as well, really. My father remarried and has a second younger family, and all my mother's exes have children—most of whom also have children of their own now.'

'The ramifications of the modern extended family can be quite complicated,' Silas observed as he took the package from the shop assistant.

As they stepped out in the street, Tilly gave a small gasp of delight. 'It's snowing!' she exclaimed.

'Martin warned me that heavy snow had been forecast.'

This time it was Tilly who automatically slipped her arm through his as they headed for the car park.

A clock was just striking the hour when they reached it,

making their way through the parked vehicles to where Silas had left the four-wheel drive.

But when they got to where it should have been there was only an empty space that the snow was just beginning to cover.

CHAPTER EIGHT

'SILAS, SOMEONE MUST HAVE stolen the car,' Tilly exclaimed, shocked.

'I doubt that.' There was a grimness in his voice that made Tilly look uncertainly at him. His mobile had started to ring and he removed it from his pocket, flicking it on, while Tilly moved discreetly out of earshot so as not to seem as though she were listening in.

'That was Cissie-Rose,' Silas announced, coming over to her. 'Apparently she'd had enough of Segovia, and the boys were cold and tired, so she decided to take the car and drive back without us.'

Tilly's face revealed her shocked disbelief.

'You mean she's left us here with no way of getting back to the castle?'

'I mean exactly that,' Silas agreed curtly.

'But why on earth would she do that?'

Silas suspected that he knew the answer. Cissie-Rose had made it plain that she was offended because he hadn't responded to her sexual overtures on the drive to Segovia, and this, he suspected, was her way of paying him back for his refusal to play along. This development was a complication he hadn't allowed for, he admitted. From the point of view of achieving his purpose in coming to Spain, it made sense to cool things down with Tilly. He could continue to play the role of her fiancé while at the same time discreetly making use of Cissie-Rose's none-too-subtle hint that she was open to a flirtation with him, since Cissie-Rose would undoubtedly provide him with a more direct route to Art's confidences than Tilly. With his research at stake he wasn't in a position to allow himself the luxury of moral scruples. He had a duty to reveal the truth.

But no duty to live it?

If he had to choose between vindicating those who had worked to reveal the truth about Jay Byerly and sacrificing Tilly's good opinion of him, he had to choose the greater need. And what about Tilly herself. What about her need and her feelings?

Silas could feel anger with himself boiling up inside him. He was dragging issues into the equation that did not need to be there. He and Tilly were sexually attracted to one another. There was no logical or moral reason why, as two consenting adults, they shouldn't be free to explore that mutual sexual attraction, and no reason either why they should not enjoy a shared relationship. It didn't need to affect his original purpose in coming here.

And it could be over as quickly as it had started. Was that what he hoped for and wanted? Because he didn't want to have to see the look in Tilly's eyes if she discovered the truth?

There was no point in telling her. His original decision had been made before he had met her, and had nothing whatsoever to do with her. Semantics, Silas warned himself. And they weren't enough to take away the acid sour taste of growing dislike of his dishonesty.

Tilly looked up at the sky, from which snow was falling increasingly heavily and fast. Icy prickles of anxiety skidded down her spine. She was pretty sure that Cissie-Rose had acted out of spite and selfishness, but she didn't want to run her down in front of Silas and end up sounding catty and judgemental. Besides, she had more important things to worry about than complaining about what Cissie-Rose had done. Like worrying about how on earth they were now going to get back to the castle.

'Perhaps we should ring the castle and ask if someone could come and collect us?' she suggested to Silas.

He shook his head. 'It will be much simpler if we try and organise a car from this end. I noticed a car-hire place earlier.'

Half an hour later, there was a grim look on Silas's face as he was told that the earliest anyone could provide them with a car would be the following day.

The snow was now falling thick and fast.

'There's nothing else for it, I'm afraid,' he told Tilly. 'We're going to have to spend the night here in town. I noticed a couple of hotels when we were walking round.'

What Silas said made good sense, but Tilly's heart had sunk further with every word. She too had noticed the hotels as they'd walked past them. Both of them had looked very exclusive, and would therefore be expensive. Knowing she was on a limited budget, she had deliberately left her credit card at the castle, in case she was tempted to use it, and all she had in her bag was a small amount of currency that would be nowhere near enough to pay for even one hotel room, never mind two and the cost of a hire car.

'It does make sense to stay here,' she agreed. 'But I'm afraid we're going to have to find somewhere inexpensive, Silas. You see, I didn't bring my credit card with me…'

Silas could see how uncomfortable and worried she was. 'It's my fault we've been stranded here,' he told her calmly. 'I suppose I should have guessed that Cissie-Rose might play this kind of trick on us. Don't worry about the cost of the hotel and the car hire. I'll pay for them.'

'You can't do that,' Tilly objected. 'Both those hotels looked dreadfully expensive. It wouldn't be fair. They could cost you more than I've paid the agency…'

'It's okay. Calm down. The agency always give us emergency cover money. I daresay they'll reclaim it from you once we get back home,' he fibbed, adding briskly, 'Look, we either book in somewhere or we hang around for hours in the hope that Martin can be called in from his half-day off to come and collect us.'

His reference to Martin being on his half-day off had the effect on Tilly's conscience he had known it would. Immediately she shook her head and protested, 'Oh, no, we can't do that. It wouldn't be fair.'

'And it won't be fair to us either, if we stand here and freeze to death—will it?' he said, taking hold of her arm and firmly turning her round in the direction of the town.

'It's going to look very odd if we book in without any luggage,' Tilly warned him.

'Not in these weather conditions. They're probably used to travellers getting stranded.'

Ten minutes later they were standing in the snow outside one of the hotels Tilly had noticed. It looked even more exclusive close up than she had thought when she'd seen it earlier.

'We can't book in here,' she protested to Silas.

'Of course we can,' he said, ignoring her inclination to hang back and nodding his head in acknowledgement of the uniformed doorman holding open the door for them.

Although he had a relatively well-paid job, Silas wasn't dependent on it financially. His maternal grandparents had been wealthy, and Silas, as their only grandchild, had inherited the bulk of it. Ordinarily he chose to live on what he earned, but he was perfectly comfortable in the kind of moneyed surroundings they were now entering—as Tilly noted when she stood back while he approached the reception desk.

Within five minutes he had returned to her side, explaining, 'They're pretty fully booked, because of the time of year, but they can give us a suite and they'll sort out a hire car for us for the morning.'

'A suite? But that will cost the earth!' Tilly protested.

'It's all they had left,' Silas told her grimly. 'We'd better go up and make sure it's okay. Then, since we won't be returning to the castle until tomorrow morning, I think that we might as well find somewhere to have a late lunch and explore the rest of the town.'

He didn't want to admit even in his most private thoughts how torn he was between the sheer urgency of his physical desire for Tilly and the cautionary voice inside him that was warning him that if he had any sense he would keep Tilly at arm's length, instead of increasing the intimacy between them—for her sake as well as his. *Her* sake? When exactly had he started to care about wanting to protect her?

Tilly nodded her head in approval of Silas's plan. The lift had arrived, and Silas stood back to allow her to precede him into it, his hand resting against her waist in the kind of discreet but very proprietorial gesture powerful men tended to use towards their partners. She could feel an almost sensual warmth spreading out from where he was touching her to envelop virtually the whole of her body. It made her want to move closer to him, so that she could absorb even more of it. In fact it made her want to do things she would normally have a run a mile rather than do…such as lifting her face for his kiss the second the lift doors closed.

How could it have happened that she had become so desperate for his touch that she felt like this? She had grown used to thinking of herself as the kind of woman who scorned such things as passionate embraces in lifts. But now she felt achingly disappointed because Silas was not making any move towards her at all.

Getting into the lift with Tilly instead of using the stairs had been a serious misjudgement, Silas admitted. The small enclosed space meant he was standing close enough to Tilly to be surrounded by the woman-scent of her skin and hair. They drew him to her with the irresistible pull nature had expressly designed them to have. Standing this close to her made him want to stand even closer still, and to do far more than just stand with her. He wanted to take her and lay her down beneath him, so that he could explore and savour every delicious inch of her, starting with the toes he had watched her curl up in sexual reaction to him, and moving all the way up to her mouth.

The lift jolted to a halt, its doors opening. Tilly stepped out into an elegant corridor and waited for Silas to join her.

'We're in here,' he told her, indicating a door to their right and going to open it.

Silas had said he'd booked them a suite, and she had assumed this meant they would have two bedrooms and their own bathroom, Tilly thought as she stood in the middle of the smart sitting room of the suite. She said uncertainly, 'There's only one bedroom.'

'I know, but, as I said, this suite was all they had left. And, after all, it isn't as though we aren't already sharing a bed.' Something about the words 'already sharing a bed' had an effect on her emotions Tilly wasn't sure she was ready for. They made them sound so intimate, so partnered—almost as though they were not just having a relationship but were already a couple.

'If you aren't happy with this we could always try the other hotel,' Silas offered.

Tilly shook her head. 'That would be silly. We might not get in.'

Ordinarily she would have been thrilled to be staying somewhere so upmarket and elegant. The building in which the hotel was housed was centuries old, but somehow the designers had managed to complement the age of the building by teaming it with the very best in modern design, rather than create a discordant mismatch.

Their suite comprised a sitting room, a bedroom, a state-of-the-art limestone bathroom, and a separate dressing room. While the bedroom overlooked the street, the sitting room overlooked a private courtyard garden to the rear of the hotel, which Tilly guessed would be used as an outdoor dining area in summer but which right now was covered in inches of snow.

'I just wish I had the clothes with me to do this place justice,' Tilly admitted ruefully.

At least she was wearing her good winter coat and her equally good leather boots. She'd become a fan of careful investment dressing with her first job in the City, even though her mother frequently complained that her choice of immaculately tailored suits was dull and unsexy. The black coat she was wearing today was cut simply, and her leather boots were neat-fitting and smart, just like the knee-length skirt she had on underneath the coat, and the plain cashmere sweater she was wearing with it. Thank heavens she had decided at the last minute this morning, after mentally reviewing the impression she had gained of the town the day before, not to wear jeans.

'I really ought to ring my mother and explain what's happened,' she told Silas.

'Why don't I ring Art instead?' he suggested.

Tilly looked at him. She had a good idea that he wanted to speak to Art and make his feelings about Cissie-Rose's behaviour very clear.

'There's no point in making a fuss about what's happened. Cissie-Rose will have calmed down by the time she gets back to the castle, and I don't want Ma to get herself upset.'

'You mean you think we should let Cissie-Rose get away with it?' Silas shook his head. 'No. When we tolerate that kind of behaviour in others, we allow them to continue with it. She needs to know that what she did is not acceptable.'

'I know what you're saying, but it's obvious that Art adores his daughters.' And equally obvious—to her at least—that her mother was living in mortal fear that they might somehow persuade their father not to marry her. So, no matter how much she might agree with Silas, her concern for her mother made her want to protect her. 'I do agree in principle,' she acknowledged. 'But since we're all going to be spending the next week together at the castle, I think on this occasion it makes sense to turn the other cheek, so to speak.'

'Giving in to Cissie-Rose won't prevent her from trying to oust your mother from her father's life, you know.'

Tilly wasn't quite quick enough to conceal from him how much his awareness of her private thoughts had caught her off-guard.

'Did you really think I wouldn't guess why you wanted Cissie-Rose spared the repercussions of her nastiness? It wasn't hard to work out what you were thinking. After all, Cissie-Rose hasn't given you any valid reason to want to protect *her*.'

'I feel so sorry for her sons. She uses them like...'

'Bargaining counters?' Silas supplied astutely.

'Well, I wouldn't have put it as directly as that. I meant more that she uses them to highlight and underline her own role as a good mother.'

'Oh, yes, she does that all right. But you can bet your City bonus that should the need arise she would have no compunction whatsoever about reminding Art where the future lies and who it lies with—and that won't be your mother.'

'You don't think that Art will marry Ma, do you?' Tilly said.

'He'd be doing her a favour if he didn't,' Silas responded harshly. 'I assumed at first that your mother was marrying him for the financial status and privileges marriage to him would give her, but it's obvious that she doesn't have the—'

'Careful,' Tilly warned him. 'Especially if you were thinking of using words such as *intelligence, nous* or *astuteness.*'

'You're right. It wouldn't be fair to use any of them in connection with your mother,' Silas responded, with such a straight face that it took Tilly several seconds to recognise that he was deliberately teasing her.

'Oh, you,' she protested, picking up one of the cushions from the sofa and throwing it at him.

He caught it easily, but when he threw it back down on the sofa he said menacingly, 'Right...' and began to walk purposefully towards her.

Tilly did what came naturally, and took to her heels.

Silas, as she had known he would, caught her in seconds and with ease, turning her round in his arms to face him as she laughed and pretended to protest.

This wasn't what he had allowed for at all, Silas acknowledged as he felt the heavy slam of his heart in his chest wall and the flood of awareness it brought with it. 'This is completely crazy—you know that, don't you?' he heard himself saying thickly.

'What's crazy?' Tilly asked.

'Us. What's happening between us. *This,*' Silas answered.

Tilly knew that he was going to kiss her, and she knew too how much she wanted him to. So much that she was already standing on tiptoe so that she could wrap her arms around his neck to speed up the process.

Beneath his mouth she gave a soft sound of pleasure when he slid his hands inside her coat and then pulled her top free of her skirt, so that he was touching her bare skin. His hands were warm, their strength somehow underlining her own female weakness. She wanted to give herself over completely to his touch and his hold, and to know that he would keep her safe within that hold for ever. His hands moved further up her back, slowly caressing her skin, his thumbs probing the line of her bra, making her shudder in recognition of just how much she wanted to feel his hands cupping her breasts, stimulating her already tightening nipples with the urgent tugging demand of his fingers. In fact her desire was so great she had to stop herself from reaching out and guiding his hand to her breast.

Silas, though, had no such inhibitions, and openly moved against her so that she could feel his arousal. He wanted her as much as she did him.

Or did he? Was he just pretending to want her because he thought it was what she wanted? Was the kindness and the intimacy he was showing her nothing more than a cynical act? He had accused her of hiring him for sex. She had vehemently denied it. But what if he hadn't believed her?

Frantically, Tilly started to push him away.

Silas's immediate and very male reaction was to keep her where she was. He was already strongly aroused, and his body and his experience were both telling him that she wanted him just as much as he did her. But he could also see the agitation and panic in her eyes, and he knew it was *that* he had to respond to, not his own desire. Unwillingly, he let her go.

It was her old fear of getting out of her emotional depth as much as the current situation that had led to her blind, panicky decision to put an end to the growing intimacy of Silas's caresses, Tilly admitted. She shivered slightly, already missing the physical warmth of Silas's body. The trouble was that she simply wasn't used to this kind of sexual intimacy and intensity. And it scared her. Or rather her increasing hunger for Silas scared her. She had fought so hard against the danger of falling in love and giving herself to someone, of allowing herself to be vulnerable to them emotionally. And yet now here she was, virtually ready to throw away all that effort, ready to ignore everything she had warned herself about, to break down all the protective barriers she had set in place to guard herself simply because of Silas. A man she had only known a matter of days. Known? She didn't know him, did she?

'Are you going to tell me what's wrong, or do I have to guess?'

The formidable determination in Silas's voice made her whirl round to look at him.

'There isn't anything—' she began.

But he cut ruthlessly through the platitudes she would have mouthed, shaking his head and stating curtly, 'Of course there's something. You're no Cissie-Rose, Tilly. You aren't the game-playing type. You want me.'

'Yes,' she agreed, as lightly as she could. 'But, since I'm already heavily in debt to you for the cost of this suite, I didn't think it was a good idea to put even more pressure on my bank account by letting you think— Silas!' she protested shakily.

He had crossed the distance separating them so quickly that she had barely seen him move, never mind had time to take evasive action. And now he was holding her arms in an almost painful grip, looking at her as though he wanted to physically shake her, and with such a blaze of passion in his eyes...

'If you are actually daring to suggest what I think you are...'

She had never seen such anger in a man's eyes—and yet oddly, instead of frightening her, it actually empowered her.

'You were the one who accused me of wanting to hire a man for sex,' she reminded him fiercely.

'You're making excuses,' Silas said dismissively. 'I consider myself to be a pretty good judge of character, and I've spent enough time with you now to know that my first assumption was incorrect. You didn't push me away because you thought I'd be demanding payment from you, Tilly. We both know that.' Abruptly his eyes narrowed, and he continued softly, 'Or was it perhaps that you were afraid that the payment I might demand would be something other than money?'

What was he doing? Silas asked himself. Why hadn't he let Tilly just walk away from him? Because he wanted her so badly that he couldn't? And what exactly did *that* mean?

First he had been forced to deal with questions that came perilously close to admitting to a feeling of guilt, and now this. This feeling that he wanted to protect both Tilly and their burgeoning relationship from being damaged by the truth about why he was here.

Silas was getting far too close to the truth. Tilly wriggled uncomfortably in his grip, torn between a longing to lay her vulnerabilities bare to him and tell him how she felt and her deeply rooted habit of protecting her feelings from others.

'The situation we're in is promoting intimacy between us faster than I'm used to, so I suppose that I *do* feel a bit wary about it—and about you,' Tilly told him, covering her real feelings with careful half-truths, and hoping that he'd challenge her again.

Why was he doing this? Silas asked himself irritably. His behaviour was totally unfamiliar and irrational. He had agreed to stand in for Joe simply because acting as Tilly's fictional fiancé would give him the chance to get closer to Art Johnson, but now he was behaving as though the person he was most interested in getting closer to was Tilly herself. This kind of behaviour just wasn't him.

It wasn't that he was against committed relationships. It was simply that he hadn't as yet come up with any logical reason why he should want to be involved in one. He had always known that if the time ever came when he really believed he loved a woman he would want their commitment to one another to be exclusive and lead to marriage, but he had also decided that he didn't really believe that kind of love existed. So far he had been perfectly happy to substitute good-quality sexual relationships for the muddled emotional mess-ups that others called 'love', and he had never had any reason to want to push those relationships onto his sexual partners. In fact if anything he had always held off a little, and allowed them to be the ones to invite him to pursue them.

So what the hell was happening to him now? Because Tilly most certainly was not inviting him to do any such thing, and yet all he could think about was not just getting her into his bed and keeping her there but... But what? Getting her into his *life* and keeping her there?

Silas reminded himself again that his first duty was to his writing. He was too intelligent not to recognise that his determination to reveal the hidden scandal of the environmental damage caused by Jay Byerly's oil company had its roots in his childhood, his desire to support the cause his mother had espoused and in supporting had lost her life.

Millions of children suffered far worse childhood traumas than his own. He had been wanted. He had been loved. By both his parents. Those parents had been committed to one another and to him. And his father had done everything he could to ensure that the tragedy of his mother's death strengthened his own commitment to Silas rather than weakened it. When his father had remarried, nearly ten years after his mother's death, his introduction to his stepmother had been handled wisely and compassionately. Silas admired and liked his stepmother, and he genuinely loved his half-brother. He had no reason to feel hard done by in life.

But the loss of his mother had hurt. So how must Tilly feel, watching her mother enter into one bad relationship after another? Tilly! How had she crept into his chain of thought? What the hell was happening to him?

'There is only one reason I would ever take a woman to bed,' he told Tilly harshly, as he pushed aside his inner thoughts and feelings. 'And that is my desire for her and hers for me.'

If only she was the kind of woman who had the courage to go up to him now and suggest boldly and openly that taking her to bed was exactly what he should do—and sooner rather than later. But she wasn't. And she was afraid to trust the overexcited eager need inside her that was trying to push her out of her relationship comfort zone. She had got so used to protecting her emotions that her sense of self and self-judgement no longer seemed to be working properly.

But she couldn't just walk away from a situation she had helped to create and pretend it wasn't happening. That was rank dishonesty, and if there was one thing she prided herself on and looked for in others it was total and complete honesty.

She took a deep breath, and then said to Silas, 'I know I gave you the impression that…that sex between us was something that could be on the agenda if it was what we both wanted. But…'

'But?'

'What happened last night wasn't…isn't… I just don't *do* casual sex,' she told him truthfully. 'Last night I got a bit carried away by the heat of the moment, so to speak, but now that we've both had time to reflect…'

'You've changed your mind?' Silas finished for her.

'I haven't changed my mind about finding you sexually attractive,' Tilly felt obliged to admit. 'But I have changed my mind about how sensible it would be to go ahead.'

She wanted him so badly, and yet at the same time she was afraid of taking the step that would take her from her emotionally secure present into a future that couldn't be guaranteed. Perhaps it was old-fashioned, but for her giving her body couldn't happen without giving something of herself emotionally. Modern men didn't always want that. She certainly didn't want to burden Silas with something he didn't want, and she didn't want to burden herself with an emotional commitment to a man who couldn't return it. It might be illogical, but she felt that by holding back sexually she was protecting herself emotionally.

Tilly was handing him the perfect get-out from his own unwanted temptation, and he would be a fool not to take it. So why was Silas even thinking about hesitating? Guilt wasn't a condition he liked experiencing. Neither were the feelings gripping him right now. Silas told himself that it wasn't too late for him to draw back and tell himself that he didn't really feel what he was feeling.

'My thoughts exactly,' he told her tersely. 'After all, one should never mix business with pleasure.'

Tilly felt his words like a physical blow, but she told herself that it was a good, clean blow she herself had invited, and that what didn't kill a person made them stronger. And she wanted to be strong to fight the very dangerous and intoxicating mix of emotions and desires Silas aroused in her.

'I'll give Art a ring to explain what's happened, and then I suggest we go and eat and explore the rest of the town.'

Why was she looking at him like that? Making him want to go to her and hold her and tell her... Tell her what? That he had lied to her?

His guilt lay so heavily on his conscience that it felt like a physical weight.

Tilly nodded her head. She was willing to agree to anything that meant she would be safe from the intimacy of being alone with him and the effect both it and he had on her.

It was his frustration at not being able to get on with his research that was fuelling his mood now, Silas tried to tell himself. Not Tilly, or how he felt about her.

CHAPTER NINE

TILLY LOOKED UNCERTAINLY at her reflection in the shop mirror. Not because she was in any doubt about the dress she was trying on—she had known the moment she had seen it in the window that it would be perfect for her, and it was. No, her doubts were coming from the guilty conscience that made her remember that even though her mother might have apologised to her over the phone for what Cissie-Rose had done, and urged her to treat herself to 'something pretty' for which she would pay, Tilly knew that on her return to London she would have to find the money to pay back their hotel bill.

And if that wasn't enough to put her off the admittedly very reasonable cost of the little black dress that was clinging so lovingly to her curves, then she only had to point out to herself that she did not live the kind of lifestyle that actually required the wearing of little black dresses. But perhaps if she had one, another inner voice persuaded, she might accept more invitations where she could wear it.

She had seen the dress in the window of a small shop close to the hotel when she and Silas had walked past it earlier, on their way to find somewhere to have a late lunch. Afterwards she had made an excuse to slip away from Silas to have a closer look at it, telling him that she needed to buy a few personal items because of their overnight stay.

'It is perfect on you,' the sales assistant told her with a small smile. 'It's a dress that requires a woman to have curves. Its designer is Spanish, and it is a new range we have only just started to carry.'

It was just as well the other woman's English was better than her own Spanish, Tilly acknowledged, as she smoothed the fine-knit black jersey over the curve of her hip. The dress might be fitted, but it was also elegant, without any hint of tartiness or flamboyance. It was, in fact, the kind of dress one might spend a lifetime looking for and not find.

'With the right jewellery or a scarf it could be so versatile. See…' the shop assistant coaxed, bringing a chunky-looking costume jewellery necklace of black beads, glass drops and cream pearls tied with black silk ribbon and slipping it around Tilly's neck to show her what she meant. Then, putting the necklace on one side, she tied a brightly coloured silk scarf around Tilly's waist in the same way Tilly had noticed the elegant assistants in Sloane Street's Hermès shop wearing their scarves.

She needed something to wear for dinner at the hotel tonight, Tilly told herself, weakening.

Silas, who had been standing on the other side of the road watching her, reached into his pocket for his wallet. He had spent enough time on shopping missions with both his stepmother and his lovers to be able to recognise when a woman and an outfit were made for one another. If Tilly didn't go ahead and buy herself that dress in which she looked so intoxicatingly desirable then he would buy it for her. Even if he had to do so surreptitiously. He was, after all, her fiancé.

But why did he want her to have it? Because of the look of dazed disbelief he could see so plainly in her reflection as she stared at herself in the mirror, or because of what he was doing? Angrily he pushed aside his inner questioning of his motives. He had no option other than to use Tilly as the key to the locked door of Art Johnson's confidence.

'I'll take it,' Tilly told the waiting shop assistant.

'And the shoes?' the girl asked with a smile, indicating the pretty black satin evening shoes she had persuaded Tilly to try on with the dress.

Tilly looked down and then nodded her head, trying to control the almost dizzying sense of euphoria that was speeding through her. She had never thought of herself as the kind of woman who got excited about buying new clothes—but then she had never thought of herself as the kind of woman who got excited about the thought of having sex with a man she barely knew either, before Silas had come into her life.

Silas! He would be wondering where on earth she was. They had agreed to meet back at the restaurant where they had had lunch, and she still had another purchase to make. She gestured towards the pretty underwear set on display—a matching bra and boy-cut shorts in soft black and pale baby pink.

'It's another new range,' the saleswoman told her approvingly. 'It's been one of our most popular sellers.'

'GOT EVERYTHING YOU WANTED?' Silas asked calmly when she met him outside the restaurant, as if she hadn't been half an hour longer than she'd said she'd be.

Silas had obviously been shopping himself, she noted, because he was carrying a very masculine-looking carrier bag.

'I didn't think the *maître d'* would be too pleased with me if I turned up for dinner tonight in chinos and a polo shirt,' he informed Tilly easily.

'I thought the same thing. Not about you. I meant about me,' Tilly said hurriedly. 'Well, I mean, I thought I'd better buy myself something to wear for dinner.' She was gabbling like a person on speed. Why? Surely not because just for a second, when she had watched the sales assistant packing up the rather more sexily cut bra than she would normally have chosen to wear and its accompanying briefs, she had had a sudden mental image of Silas removing her new dress to reveal them? And that, of course, was *not* the reason she had changed her mind about buying a pair of tights and had opted for hold-ups instead, was it?

It had stopped snowing while she had been in the shop, but now it had started again, falling so quickly and so thickly that she knew Silas was right when he told her to hold on to him. She still refused. 'I'll be perfectly all right.' What she really meant was that she would rather risk losing her balance in the snow than lose her heart in the intimacy of being physically close to him.

'Okay. Are you ready to go back to the hotel?' he asked. 'Or...?'

'I think we'd better, otherwise we're going to end up looking like walking snowmen.' She gave a small shiver, and then gasped as a crowd of young people came hurrying round the corner. One of them accidentally bumped into her, and Silas reacted immediately, grabbing her with both hands to keep her upright while she regained her balance.

Each time she was close to him the feelings she remembered from the time before came back—and more strongly, so that now her heart was racing, thudding clumsily into her chest wall and then bouncing off it, as though his body was a magnet to which it was helplessly drawn.

She lifted her head to thank him, but her gaze got as far as his mouth and then refused to go any further. It also refused to allow any of her other senses to override it. She was, Tilly recognised distantly, totally unable to do anything other than focus helplessly on Silas's mouth and long for the feel of it possessing her own. She had made her decision back in the suite. Had she? Was she sure about that? Given a second chance, would she make the same decision? Wasn't she already regretting the opportunity she had let slip from her through a fear that no longer seemed important compared with her desire? How had it come to this? That she should be so bewitched by the shape and cut of a pair of male lips to the extent that she yearned with everything in herself to reach out and touch them with her fingertip, to trace the shape of them and store it inside her memory.

The way Tilly was looking at him was making Silas aware of himself as a man in ways and with nuances he hadn't known were possible, he acknowledged. If she reached out and touched his mouth now, as she looked as though she was about to do, he knew that the touch of her fingertips against his lips would end up with the intimate caress of his mouth against the lips of her sex, by way of a hundred different kisses and touches, until his tongue probed for the hard bead of her clitoris so that he could bring her to orgasm and watch her pleasure filling her. He also knew that he couldn't let that happen. Not now that he had begun

she had been tempted by the lamb for which the area was famous, and she had not been disappointed. She was beginning to feel slightly light-headed, though. The wine—her second glass—was obviously stronger than she had realised. Or was it Silas who was having such a dramatic effect on her? It was far too dangerous to take that line of thought any further. It would be safer to focus instead on the conversation Silas had instigated, even if right now recklessly she would much rather have been... What? In bed, with Silas making love to her? She shuddered so intensely that she had to put down her glass of wine.

'Cold?' Silas asked, frowning.

Hot was more like the truth, Tilly thought giddily. Hot for him, for his touch, his kiss, his body...

'If Art ever asks for my financial advice or input I'll be delighted to help him,' she told Silas, as lightly as she could. The truth was she suspected that Art, to judge from the interaction between the members of his family, probably had the kind of business ethics she most deplored. But her mother loved him, or at least believed that she did, and for her mother's sake she knew she would keep her own private opinions as exactly that.

'But you don't think that he will?' Silas knew that he was probing and pushing too hard—so hard, in fact, that it was almost as though he wanted to provoke an argument with Tilly. To offset the effect of seeing her in that dress that somehow managed to be both prim and incredibly sexy at the same time. He tried to ease his lower body into a more comfortable position. The table might be doing a good job of hiding the unwanted erection that was aching through him, but that didn't make its presence any easier for him to endure.

'You seem an unlikely candidate for ethical conservation,' he told Tilly abruptly, deciding to stop pushing her for a response to his earlier question.

Was there something in the air that was causing Silas to behave towards her so antagonistically? Tilly wondered miserably. Or was this simply his way of warning her that he wanted her to keep her distance from him?

'If that's some kind of dig at my mother,' she said, giving

up on her earlier attempts to pretend that she wasn't aware that he was trying to needle her, 'just because she's fallen in love with Art it doesn't mean that she agrees with his opinions. As a matter of fact, my mother met my father at a fundraising event for Save the Children.' She wasn't going to tell him that her mother had attended the event thinking it was a charity ball. 'My father is a very committed conservationist; he and my step-mother run a small organic farm in Dorset.'

He could see her against that kind of background, Silas recognised. Free-range hens, a quartet of unruly children, and probably a couple of even more unruly goats. What locked his heart muscle, though, was that he could see those children with a mixture of their shared colouring and features. Him? With four children? He frowned at his wine glass. He was skating on very thin ice now, and what lay beneath it was deep and dark and had the potential to change his whole world. Was that what he wanted? Because if it wasn't he needed to banish those kind of thoughts right now, and put something in their place that would remind him of all the reasons why he needed to keep Tilly out of his life. Like how guilty he was going to feel when he saw the look in her eyes if she learned the truth. He couldn't afford that kind of emotional involvement with Tilly.

'FINISHED?'

Tilly nodded her head. She had been toying with the last dregs of the coffee they had been served half an hour ago for so long that she was not really surprised by Silas's question. But she was unnerved by it. By it and by him, she admitted as she got to her feet on legs that suddenly seemed unfamiliar and shaky.

With every step she took out of the restaurant and along the corridor to the lift, the shakiness and the mixture of longing and apprehension that accompanied it grew. In a few minutes she would be alone with Silas in their suite. And then she would be alone with him in its bed... And then...

Tilly had to have one of the smallest waists he had ever seen, Silas decided as he tried to distract his thoughts from what was really on his mind by mentally measuring it with his hands. And then, far more erotically, mentally allowing those hands to slide slowly down to the curve of her hips and up over her back, so that he could tug down the zip of her dress and encourage the fullness of her breasts to spill into his hands.

She and Silas were inside the lift. Tilly could hardly breathe she felt so on edge.

'I have to say that I find it hard to understand how someone who purports to be so keen on environmental ethics doesn't feel more inclined to take issue with the mindset of a man like Art Johnson—especially when her mother is going to marry him. Or does the fact that he is a billionaire excuse him?'

The lift had stopped, and Silas was getting out. Tilly was in shock from the unexpectedness and savagery of his verbal attack on her. She could feel the hot burn of tears at the backs of her eyes.

'No, it doesn't,' she told him fiercely as he opened the suite door for her. Walking past him, she went over to the window, unable to trust herself to look at him in case he saw how much his words had hurt her. 'I may not agree with his business ethics, but I have to think of my mother.' She spoke with her back to Silas, biting hard on the inside of her bottom lip as she felt the betraying tears escape and fill her eyes.

It had been hard for her the previous evening, not to speak out against some of the things that Art and his family had said, but she had warned herself that arguing with them would not change the way they thought, and could potentially make things even more difficult for her mother. She could end up being hurt.

But now *she* was the one being hurt, and the shock of discovering just how easily and lethally Silas's critical comments could hurt her was making it very difficult for her to find her normal calm resistance to the negative opinions of others. The problem was that Silas wasn't 'others'. Somehow he had managed to stride over the subtle defences she'd thought she had so securely in place and put himself in a position where she was vulnerable to him. Far too vulnerable. As her reaction now was proving.

Silas could see Tilly's reflection in the window. The sight

of the tears she was battling to suppress caused him a physical pain that felt like a giant fist hammering into his heart. His reaction to her tears rocked his belief system on its axis, throwing up a whole new and unfamiliar emotional landscape within himself. He inspected it cautiously, whilst his heart hammered against his ribs. He scarcely recognised himself in what he had become. And he certainly didn't recognise the intensity of the emotions battling it out inside him. His guilt, his pain for Tilly's own pain, were raw open wounds into which he had poured acid. How could he have changed so dramatically and swiftly? He felt as though something beyond his own control had blasted a pathway within him, along which were travelling emotions and truths that only days ago had been wholly alien to the way he felt and thought.

He strode over to where Tilly was standing, driven there by him. She was so engrossed in trying to control her unwanted emotions that she didn't even realise he was there until she felt Silas's hand on her arm.

She stiffened immediately, in proud rejection of what she felt must be his pitying contempt for her vulnerability, and tried to turn away from him. But it was too late. He was turning her towards him. She'd thought she had herself under control, but a single tear betrayed her, rolling down her set face. She heard the muffled explosive sound Silas made, but she was battling too desperately to control her emotions to interpret it.

When he reached out and touched her face with his fingertips, catching the tear, she flinched and started to push him away, telling him fiercely, 'Don't patronise me. Just leave me alone.'

'Patronise you?' Silas groaned.

'Don't pity me, then, or feel sorry for me.'

'If I feel sorry for you it's because I'm burdening you with the weight of my need for you, Tilly.'

Tilly could hear his voice thicken with a mixture of pain and angry self-contempt that was so raw it made her throat ache. She looked up at him and saw the tension in his face. She could feel it too in the pressure of his hands on her arms, drawing her towards him.

'I want you with a compulsion I don't understand. You make me feel emotions I don't recognise. Being with you feels like walking through a landscape that is so alien to me I have no way of negotiating it, no inbuilt compass—nothing other than the need itself. You've made me a stranger to myself, Tilly. You've found something within me I didn't know was there.'

'I haven't done anything—' Tilly started to protest, but Silas stopped her, stealing the denial from her lips, tasting the *oh, please, yes* concealed within the *no* along with the salt of her tears as he kissed her and went on kissing her, until she was clinging to him, tears spilling from her open eyes, leaving them clear for him to read the emotions that were filling them.

'You know what's happening to us, don't you?' Silas demanded against her mouth as he kissed away the final tear.

What? Tilly wanted to beg him, but she was afraid to ask the question in case it spoiled the magic that had transported her to this new world, and broke the spell that was binding them together. So instead she whispered passionately to him. 'Show me! Don't tell me about it, Silas. Show it to me.'

CHAPTER ELEVEN

A HEARTBEAT LATER—or was it a lifetime?—Silas was undressing her in between fiercely possessive and demanding kisses, and she was undressing him. The room was full of the sound of rustling clothes, soft sighs and hungry kisses, as fabric slithered and slipped to the floor, and eager hands moved over even more eager flesh.

Somehow Silas had managed to remove all of his own clothes, as well as most of hers. Now, as he held her against him and slid his hands from her waist down over her hips, past her bottom and then up again under the fluted legs of her pretty new briefs, to cup her warm flesh and press her into his body, her own hand was free to give in to the unfamiliarly wanton demands of her emotions and explore the shape and texture of his rigid erection.

'Don't—' Tilly heard him protest thickly. But it was too late for him to deny the effect her touch was having on him. She had felt it in the savagely intense shudder of pleasure that had gripped and convulsed him.

His reaction gave her the courage to explore more intimately and to give way to the erotic urgings of her own senses. It both excited and aroused her to see and feel him responding so helplessly to her, so possessed by desire and need that he couldn't control the visibly physical pleasure she was giving him.

She could feel the heavy slam of his heart against her own body, its arousal mirrored by the uneven sound of his breathing in her ear as he held her and caressed her with growing passion. But when he stroked a shockingly erotic caressing fingertip down her back, beyond the base of her spine, it was her turn to moan in fevered arousal and melt into him.

Immediately she curled her hand around him, wanting to reciprocate the pleasure he was giving her, but Silas stopped her, telling her hotly, 'I can't let you do that. If I do…' She felt him shudder, and then shuddered herself when he told her, 'I want you so damn much that I can't trust myself not to come too soon if you touch me.'

'That works both ways,' Tilly protested breathlessly, squirming with heated pleasure under his exploratory touch, shocked by her own verbal boldness and yet at the same time acknowledging how much it meant to her to be able to be so open and natural with him about her sexual responsiveness.

How tame her imaginings in the shop as she had bought the new underwear seemed now, compared to the reality of what Silas's touch was actually doing to her. And as for her not touching him. How could she not when her need to do so was growing by the heartbeat? When she ached so badly to stroke her fingertips along the full length of his erection? She wanted to know every single nuance of the texture of its flesh. She wanted to explore the inviting slick suppleness of its pulse-racing male rhythm beneath her caress. She wanted…

She shuddered wildly under the erotic influence of her own thoughts, and then more wildly still when Silas stroked slowly all the way up her spine. His tongue-tip prised her lips apart and she admitted it eagerly, giving herself over completely to the thrusting passion of his kiss. His hand cupped her breast, and the heat inside her exploded in a firework display of shimmering pleasure. She caught his hand and pressed it fiercely against her breast as she moved rhythmically against him, every single part of her gripped by and focused on her longing for him.

Somehow, at some deep level, he had known it would be like this between them, Silas admitted as he lost the battle to control his response to Tilly's arousal. What she was doing to him was causing what felt like a huge unstoppable wave of aching intensity and need to power through him. He knew that he was helplessly unable to stop himself from succumbing to it and to her. He knew that he didn't even want to stop himself. And he knew that both of them were going to be overwhelmed by it, swept along together with only each other to cling to as the full power of what was happening to them possessed them. It was too late to stop it now, even if he wanted to. The openly urgent rhythmic movement of Tilly's body against his own was driving him over the edge of his self control.

'I want you,' he cried out in a raw voice. 'I want you more than I have ever wanted any other woman or will ever want any other woman ever again.' He heard the words, thick and half-crazed with emotion, being dragged from his throat, and he knew that they were true. He could see shock, delight and yearning in Tilly's eyes. He took her mouth in a kiss of fierce, consuming possession, picking her up and carrying her over to the bed.

Tilly moaned when Silas put her down, unable to bear even for a handful of seconds not to have him touching her or to be touching him.

She could see him kneeling over her, and she watched as he bent his head and traced a line of kisses down her body. His hands cupped and held her hips, and she shuddered when he anointed her hipbones in turn with slow, tender kisses and then moved lower. She could feel his fingers sliding through her ready wetness as he deliberately parted the outer lips of her sex. She could see him looking at her as he touched her.

Her flesh was flushed and swollen with arousal, making Silas ache to taste her, to feel the sharp shudders of her orgasm against his mouth. He wanted to slide his fingers through the wetness of her sex, between the fullness of the labia, and then part them so that he could stroke his tongue along the path made by his fingertip. He wanted to take the small responsive bead of her clitoris and caress it until he had brought her to the edge he had already reached, and then he wanted to slide slowly and deeply the full length of her, so that he was filling her, and she was holding him, and her flesh was taking him and using him for its pleasure, making that pleasure his own.

What he wanted, he recognised, was a degree of intimacy

with her, a connection with her, a *completeness* with her that was outside any sexual experience he had ever had previously, or imagined he could want. Because what was happening for him wasn't something he only wanted to experience on a sexual level. What he wanted from her went way beyond that into a realm he had always thought more akin to make-believe and fiction than reality.

Tilly gave a small aching moan. Silas bent his head and parted her labia, stroking his tongue-tip the full length of her sex.

It was more than Tilly could stand. She cried out and dug her nails into his shoulders, clinging desperately to the edge of her own self-control.

'No,' she told him fiercely. 'Not yet. Not until you're inside me. That's how I want it to be, Silas.' Determined tears sprang into her eyes as she looked at him. 'It has to be both of us. I want *you*, Silas,' she insisted. 'I want you *inside* me. I want that so much.'

She felt him move, heard the brief rustle of a wrapper being opened and then discarded, and then blissfully he was holding her, kissing her, sliding his hands down to her hips and lifting her. Hungrily Tilly wrapped her legs around him, arching up eagerly to meet his first slow, sweet thrust into her.

Silas shuddered as he felt her muscles grip and hold him. Even this was a new kind of pleasure. Where he had previously known experience, with Tilly there was freshness, an untutored naturalness that was so much more erotic. Her body welcomed him joyfully and eagerly, offering all its pleasures to him, wanting him to take them, wanting him to thrust deeper and harder until he fitted her so well that they might almost have been one flesh.

Was *this* what love was? Silas wondered. Was *this* why he had always refused to believe in it before? Because he had been waiting for Tilly?

She cried out his name, her flesh gripping him, pulsing fiercely.

Through the fierce contractions of her orgasm Tilly felt Silas's final deep thrust as he joined her in the soaring ecstasy that was binding them both together and taking them to infinity.

SILAS MOVED AWAY FROM the window and looked towards the bed. It was nearly two o'clock in the morning, but he hadn't been able to sleep. He hadn't been able to do anything since they had made love except go over and over inside his head the now familiar journey that had led from his first meeting with Tilly to this. He felt as though his whole life had suddenly veered off course and gone out of his control. How was it possible for him to have changed so much so quickly? How was it possible for him to feel so differently?

He made his way back to the bed. Not being within touching distance of Tilly made him feel as though a part of him was missing, that he was somehow incomplete.

As he slid back the duvet he realised that she was awake.

'You know what's going on, don't you?'

'I think so, and it isn't something I wanted to happen,' Tilly answered, trying to make her voice sound light and careless but hearing it crack as easily as he'd cracked apart the protective casing she had put around her heart.

'Falling in love wasn't exactly on my agenda either,' Silas told her dryly.

'Perhaps if we try really hard we can stop it.'

There was enough light from the moon for her to see the cynically amused look Silas was giving her. 'Like we've already tried once tonight, you mean?' he derided, causing Tilly to give a small shiver.

'Silas, I don't want to love you. I don't want to love anyone. Loving someone means being hurt when they stop loving you.'

'I won't stop loving you, Tilly. I couldn't.' It was, Silas recognised, the truth.

'This is crazy,' Tilly whispered, but she knew that her protests meant nothing and that her own emotions were overwhelming her.

'Love is crazy. It's well known that it's a form of madness.'

'Maybe it's just the sex?' she suggested. 'I mean…'

Silas shook his head.

'No, it isn't just the sex,' he assured her. 'You can trust me on that.'

'There can't be love without trust. And honesty,' Tilly whispered solemnly.

This was all so new to her, and so very precious and vulnerable. Acknowledging her feelings felt like holding a new baby. Her heart did a slow high-dive. A baby. Silas's baby.

Trust and honesty. Silas reached for Tilly. He was going to have to tell her the truth about himself, and his reason for taking Joe's place.

But not tonight. Not now, when all he wanted to do was hold her and kiss her and feel the responsive silky heat of her body, taking him and holding him, while he showed her his love.

TILLY GLANCED ANXIOUSLY at Silas. He had hardly spoken to her as he drove them back to the castle, and whatever he was thinking his thoughts didn't look as though they were happy ones.

'Second thoughts?' she asked him lightly.

'About the wisdom of returning to the castle? Yes. About us? No,' Silas answered her truthfully. 'What about you?'

'I rather think I've made it obvious how I feel.' They had made love again before breakfast, and now her body ached heavily and pleasurably with an unfamiliar, satisfied lassitude. She touched the comfortable weight of the ring on her left hand and then coloured self-consciously when she saw the gleam in Silas's eyes.

'I wish we could go back to London and get to know one another properly, instead of having to go back to the castle,' Tilly admitted. 'And I can't help worrying about my mother. It's obvious that Art's family doesn't want him to marry her.'

'My guess is that if they don't manage to break them up before they marry, they'll make her life hell afterwards. To be honest, I'm surprised she can't see that for herself.'

'Ma only sees what she wants to see,' Tilly told him. 'She can be very naïve like that. I just don't want her to be hurt. When her last marriage broke up she was desperately unhappy. It was the first time she hadn't been the one to end things. If Art decides not to go ahead with the wedding, I don't know what it will do to her. Ma's one of those women who doesn't feel she's a viable human being unless she's got a man in her life.' Tilly smiled ruefully. 'That's probably more than you want to know. I'm sorry. But this is the first time I've felt close enough to someone to be able to be talk honestly about how I feel without thinking I'm being disloyal.'

'What about your father?'

'Oh, I love Dad, of course. But he disapproves of Ma, and they don't see eye to eye. I'd feel I was letting her down if I told him how much I worry about her, and why. They were so unsuited—but that's the trouble about falling in love, isn't it? You don't always know until it's too late that you aren't compatible. And sometimes even when you are it isn't enough.'

'Sometimes a couple meet and are fortunate enough to recognise that what they share goes far beyond mere compatibility,' Silas told her. 'Like soul mates.'

Tilly felt a fine thrill of the most intense emotion she had ever experienced run through her as he turned to look at her.

It moved her beyond words that Silas should say such a thing to her, almost as though he already knew how vitally important it was to her that the love growing between them should be perfect in every way.

And yet the closer they got to the castle the more she sensed that Silas seemed to be distancing himself from her, retreating to a place where he didn't want her to follow him. His answers to her efforts to make conversation became terse and unencouraging, giving her the message that he preferred the privacy of his own silence to any attempt to create a more intimate mood between them.

She told herself that she was being over-sensitive, and that what to her felt like a distancing tactic was probably nothing more than a desire to concentrate on his driving.

The closer they got to the castle the more Silas recognised the dual agenda he would now be operating under. From the outset he had been totally clear to himself about his purpose in stepping into Joe's shoes. He had told himself that deceiving a young woman he didn't know, while regrettable, would be justified by the exposure that would be the end result of his research. But he hadn't anticipated then that the impossible would happen and he would fall in love with Tilly.

Now that he had, his deceit had taken on a much more personal turn. He was now in effect lying by default to the woman he loved. He was lying to her about his real identity, the real nature of his work, the fact that he was using her as a cover to screen his own agenda.

For each and every one of those lies he had an explanation he believed she would understand and accept—after all, he had not set out with the deliberate intention of deceiving *her*. But the highly emotionally charged atmosphere of the castle, where they would be surrounded by Art and his family, was not, in Silas's opinion, the best place for him to admit totally what he had done, or his reasons—even though normally his first priority would have been to tell her the truth. For that he felt he—they—needed real privacy, and the security of being able to discuss the issue without any onlookers.

Knowing Tilly as he believed he did know her now, he couldn't ignore the instinct that told him that if his suspicions about Art's involvement in Jay Byerly's underhand dealings were confirmed, Tilly would at the very least want to warn her mother about the true nature of the man she was planning to marry. And if she did that, Silas thought it entirely likely that Annabelle would go straight to Art and beg him to deny the accusations being levelled against him.

Silas knew the last thing his publishers would want was to be threatened with a lawsuit by some expensive lawyer before his book was even written. And he certainly had no intention of putting himself in a position where the truths he had already worked so long to make public were silenced before they had been heard.

Tilly would, of course, be hurt, and no doubt angry when he told her the truth on their return to London, but he felt sure that once he had explained the reasons he had not been able to confide in her she would understand and forgive him. But while logically it made sense not to say anything to Tilly yet, loving her as he did meant that he wanted to share his every thought and feeling with her. It was for her own sake that he could not do it, he reminded himself. She was already doing enough worrying about her mother, a woman who in Silas's opinion ought to recognise how truly fortunate she was to have such a wonderful daughter.

Something was on Silas's mind, Tilly decided. In another few minutes they would be reaching the castle and the opportunity to ask him would be gone. She took a deep breath and said quietly, 'You look rather preoccupied. Is something wrong?'

Her awareness of his concern caused Silas to turn his head and look at her, and to go on looking at her. 'Yes,' he told her truthfully, adding, not quite so truthfully, 'The closer we get to the castle the more I wish I could snatch you up and take you somewhere we could really be on our own. There's so much I want to learn about you, Tilly. So much I want to know about you and so much I want you to know about me. And, selfishly, I want you all to myself so that we can do that. I've never thought of myself as a possessive man, but now I'm beginning to realise how little I really know myself—because where you are concerned I feel very unwilling to share you with anyone else.'

'Don't say any more,' Tilly begged. 'Otherwise I'll be pleading with you to turn around and drive back to the hotel.'

'The first thing I intend to do when we reach the castle is take you upstairs to our room and make love to you,' Silas told her thickly.

'I rather think that we'll be called upon to explain ourselves to Cissie-Rose first, and apologise for putting her to the trouble of having to drive back alone,' Tilly warned him wryly. 'She won't be happy to see us together, Silas.' That was the closest Tilly felt she wanted to go in telling Silas that she was aware that Cissie-Rose's interest in him was sexual and predatory.

'We don't owe her any explanations. She chose to leave in a strop and abandon us because I'd shown her that I wasn't interested in what she was offering.'

Tilly heard the hardness in his voice and winced a little.

Silas saw her small movement and shook his head. 'Don't waste your sympathy on her, Tilly. She doesn't deserve it.'

'I can't blame her for wanting you when I want you so much myself,' Tilly told him honestly.

Silas drove in to the courtyard, turning to look at her as he stopped the four-wheel drive to say softly, 'Promise me something, Tilly?'

Something? Her heart was so filled with love and happiness she wanted to promise him *everything*. 'What?' she asked instead.

'Promise me that you'll always be as honest and open with me as you are now. I love it when you tell me that you want me. And, just as soon as we get the chance, I intend to show you just how much.'

'YES, POOR TILLY NEEDS TO GO and lie down. She started with a headache on the way back—didn't you, darling?'

Tilly shot Silas a reproving look, but he was too busy convincing her mother that she wasn't going to be well enough to emerge from their bedroom for at least a couple of hours.

'Well, I'm sure that Art and the boys won't mind keeping you company in the bar, Silas,' Annabelle told him, before turning to Tilly to say reproachfully, 'I wanted to show you my dress and the sketches Lucy has done for the flowers. Perhaps if you just took a couple of aspirin you wouldn't need to lie down…?'

Tilly wavered. She was so used to answering her mother's needs when she was with her, and Annabelle was looking at her like a disappointed child deprived of a special treat, making her feel wretchedly guilty. But Silas had reached for her hand and was very discreetly, but very sensually, caressing the pulse-point on the inside of her wrist. Her desire for him was turning her bones and her conscience to jelly.

She looked at her mother and lifted her free hand to her forehead. 'Silas is right, Ma.' she told her. 'I really do need to lie down.'

Five minutes later, when Silas locked the door to their room and leaned on it for good measure, taking her in his arms and drawing her very deliberately into the cradle of his hips so that she could feel his arousal, Tilly shook her head at him.

'I don't believe I've just done that. I've never lied to my mother before…'

'When there's a conflict of interests I'm delighted that you opted to choose me,' Silas teased her.

Tilly didn't respond to his smile as readily as he had expected. 'Loving someone shouldn't mean abandoning your own moral code. Telling my mother I had a headache when I haven't…'

'What would you have preferred to do? Tell her that we wanted to make love?'

Tilly exhaled in defeat. 'No,' she admitted. 'But it still doesn't make me feel good.'

'Maybe this will, though.'

Silas was teasing her with small, unsatisfying kisses that made her reach up for him and pull his head down to hers…

'YOU REMEMBER THAT TV SHOW *Dallas?* Well, I'm telling you that was nothing compared with the reality of how the oil business was in my father's time. I started working in the family business straight out of school. My father said that was the best way to learn.' Art reached for his drink and emptied his glass, demanding, 'Come on Dwight, I thought you were playing bartender. Set them up again, will you?'

It was almost dinnertime, and to judge from his slurred voice and red face Silas suspected that Art had been drinking for the best part of the afternoon. He had greeted them affably enough when they had finally come downstairs dressed for dinner, and had then begun reminiscing about the early days of his family's oil business. Silas, sensing that this might be the breakthrough he needed, had encouraged him to keep talking by asking him judicially timed questions. He suspected from the bored expressions on the faces of Art's sons-in-law that they had heard all Art's stories before.

'I imagine you must have known all the big players in the old oil world?' Silas suggested casually.

'Sure did,' Art agreed boastfully. 'I knew 'em all.'

'Even Jay Byerly?'

'Yep. He was some guy, was Jay. He had a handle on just about everything that was goin' on.'

'I know that the shareholders voted him off the board of his own company in the end, but no one ever said why.' While they had been talking Silas had filled up Art's glass, making sure that he didn't fill up his own.

'For goodness' sake, no one wants to hear all those old stories all over again. Poor Annabelle will be so bored she'll change her mind about wanting to marry you if you don't change the subject,' Cissie-Rose exclaimed with acid sweetness, sweeping into the room in a dress that was more suitable for a full-scale diplomatic reception rather than what was supposed to be a quiet family dinner. 'You really mustn't encourage him, Silas,' she added, giving Silas and Tilly the kind of posed and patently artificial smile that showed off her excellent teeth and the cold enmity in her eyes. 'Are you really sure you're over your headache, Tilly?' she asked. 'Only, if you don't mind my saying so, you really don't look well. There's nothing like a headache for making a person look run-down.'

'Annabelle, why don't you girls go and talk wedding talk in one of the other rooms?' Art suggested.

Tilly suspected that he had been enjoying basking in the attention of Silas's good-mannered social questions, and that he wasn't very pleased about Cissie-Rose's interruption. Although he wasn't exactly slurring his words, he had had what to Tilly seemed to be rather a lot to drink. Her doubts about the wisdom of her mother marrying him were growing by the hour.

'Silas is just being polite, Dad. Why on earth should he be interested in what happened over thirty years ago? Unless, of course, someone's thinking of making a film of Jay's life and you're hoping to be invited to try for the lead part, Silas.'

Cissie-Rose's claws were definitely unsheathed now, Tilly recognised. The other woman's cattiness made her want to place herself physically in front of Silas to protect him. Although the thought of Silas needing anyone defending him, least of all her, made her smile to herself.

'Ignore her, Silas,' Art instructed, giving his daughter a baleful look. 'You're right. There was a scandal Jay was involved in that threatened to blow him and the business sky-high. Luckily a few of the big old boys called in some of their debts and managed to get it all quietened down. Jay had been buying up oil leases and then—'

'Daddy, I don't think you should say any more,' Cissie-Rose interrupted her father sharply. 'It's all in the past now, anyway. Annabelle, I have to say that those sketches you were showing me for the flowers are just so pretty.'

It wasn't worth pushing Art any further, Silas decided. There would still be plenty of opportunity for him to pick up their conversation between now and the wedding on New Year's Eve. All he had to do was to make sure he mixed Art a jugful of extra-strong whiskey sour.

CHAPTER TWELVE

'CHRISTMAS EVE AND I'VE already had the best present I could ever have,' Tilly told Silas emotionally.

They were in their bedroom getting ready for dinner, having spent the afternoon outside in the snowy garden playing with the children. Or rather Tilly had played with them while Silas had watched.

'It's kind of you to be so patient with Art, Silas. His face positively lights up when you walk in and let him tell his stories. He must be exaggerating some of them, though.' Tilly gave a small shiver. 'It seems wrong that men like Art should have had that kind of power and abused it the way they did.'

'Things are different now,' Silas agreed. 'But as for Art exaggerating what happened in the past…' He paused, all too aware of what he knew that Tilly did not. 'If anything,' he told her heavily, 'I suspect that Art is using rather a lot of whitewash to conceal some of what went on. Of course most of those who perpetrated the worst of the crimes are no longer around, but that doesn't mean the world doesn't need to know about them.'

'I'm so lucky to have met you,' Tilly said spontaneously. As he looked at her Silas felt his heart turn over inside his chest slowly and achingly as his love for her overwhelmed him. He reached for her hand, entwining his fingers with hers. He still found it hard at times to come to terms with the speed with which his life had changed so dramatically. And all because of one person.

'You're a saint for putting up with everything the way you have.'

'A saint! That's the last thing I am. In fact…' He had to tell her the truth, Silas decided, even though he knew that in doing so he would be subjecting her to divided loyalties. He was finding the deceit that he knew lay between them increasingly burdensome, plus he wanted to share his work with her now that he recognised that she was the most vital and important part of his life. Not involving her in what he was thinking and planning somehow felt like being deprived of the ability to work the way he wanted to do. He wanted her input and her support. He wanted her to know, to understand, and to accept what he was doing and why. He wanted, Silas recognised, to lay not just his heart but his very soul at her feet, so that she could know his every strength and vulnerability.

'Tilly, there's something—' he began, and then had to stop when there was a brief knock on their bedroom door and they both heard Tilly's mother calling out anxiously.

'Are you ready yet?'

'Almost,' Tilly answered, giving Silas a rueful look as she slipped from his arms and went reluctantly to open the door.

'Oh, you must hurry, then—because Cissie-Rose has just rung through to our room to say she wants us all downstairs now, because she's got something important to say. Do you think she could possibly be expecting another baby, Tilly? Wouldn't that be lovely? Oh, you both look fine. Come on, we may as well go down together. Art's already down...'

'You said we'd have the buffet at seven,' Tilly reminded her. 'It's not even six yet.' She had been looking forward to having some private time with Silas before they had to join the others, but it was obvious that her mother wasn't going to leave without them.

He would tell Tilly later, when they came back up to their room, Silas promised himself. Preferably in bed, when he was holding her in his arms.

The familiar ache of his body for hers began to speed through him.

As they descended the stairs Tilly could hear the sound of familiar Christmas carols filling the hallway.

'I remembered to bring a CD of carols with me,' Annabelle

told Tilly proudly. 'You used to love them so much when you were a little girl.'

The children were all in one of the smaller salons, watching television and trying to guess what Santa would be bringing them.

'There you are, Silas.' Art's voice boomed out. 'You're already a couple of drinks down on us.'

Tilly shook her head when Dwight offered to make her a drink, knowing from previous experience how strong it would be.

'So what's this news Cissie-Rose has for us, Dwight?' Annabelle asked excitedly. 'And where is she?'

'She's upstairs, taking a call.'

'If I know Cissie she's probably checking up on Hal to make sure he's got the wording of our pre-nup right,' Art joked.

Tilly looked anxiously at her mother, worrying about how she might be taking this less than romantic comment from her husband-to-be.

'Sorry to have to keep you all waiting, but I just wanted to make sure I had all my facts right before I came down.' Cissie-Rose paused dramatically in the doorway, and then slowly made her way over to Tilly. 'That's a mighty pretty engagement ring you're wearing, Tilly. Pity that neither it nor your engagement is real, though. In fact there isn't much that *is* real about you—is there, Silas? You see, Silas here isn't Tilly's fiancé at all. Are you, Silas?'

White-faced, Tilly reached for Silas's hand and drew on the warm comfort of its reassuring grip. This was awful—dreadful. And she could hardly bear to look at her mother. There was no doubt in Tilly's mind that this was Cissie-Rose's revenge on them for Silas's rejection. But Tilly still had no idea how on earth she had found out about them.

'Tilly thinks that Silas is an out-of-work actor she hired to come here and pretend to be her fiancé, so that we'd think she was a clean-living girl who was about to get married. Poor Tilly,' Cissie mocked, giving her a malicious smile. 'I really do feel sorry for you. Look at you, clinging on to him. How sweet. But

I'm afraid there's worse to come. Isn't there, *Silas*? You see, Silas has been deceiving us all about the true purpose of his being here.'

'You don't understand,' Tilly protested fiercely. 'Yes, I admit that I originally hired Silas as an escort to accompany me here. But since we've been here...' She turned to Silas and gave him an anxious, pleading look that twisted his heart with pain.

'Since you've been here *what*?' Cissie-Rose taunted her triumphantly. 'He's taken you to bed and told you he wants you? Poor Tilly. I'm afraid it is *you* who don't understand. Because if that is the case then he's been lying to you as well as to us, and he's made a complete fool of you. There's only one thing he wants—only one reason he's come here—and it's got nothing to do with wanting you, has it, Silas? Or should I call you James? You see, everyone, this is *James* Silas Connaught.'

Tilly, who was battling to take in what Cissie-Rose was saying, saw the swift look of recognition Art and Dwight were exchanging, and something as cold as death started to creep through her veins like poison.

'Yes,' Cissie-Rose confirmed. 'The journalist who has been trying to get an interview with Dad for the best part of a year. That's right, isn't it, Silas? He must have thought it was his lucky day when you gave him the opportunity to use you, Tilly. *Of course* he took you to bed. He's known for being a journalist who always gets his story—aren't you, Silas?'

'No, that's not true. It can't be! There's been some mistake,' Tilly protested, white-faced. 'Please tell me this isn't true,' Tilly begged, turning to face Silas.

'Yes, there has been a *very* big mistake.' Cissie-Rose laughed unkindly. 'And you're the one who's made it, Tilly. Of course I saw right through you in a minute, *Silas*,' she said. 'Which is why I've had Dad's lawyers doing some digging on you.'

'Silas?' Tilly begged. Why wasn't he denying what Cissie-Rose had said?

'Tilly, I can explain everything,' Silas told her fiercely.

Tilly stared at him. Where was the denial she had expected to hear? She couldn't bear to see what she was seeing in Silas's eyes. She wanted to run and hide herself away from the pain of it. She could feel herself starting to tremble violently inside. Nausea gripped her stomach, and a pain like none she had ever previously known tore at her.

'How could you? *How could you?*' She was still holding onto Silas's hand, but now she released it, not caring what anyone else might think as she ran towards the door and headed for the stairs.

She had to escape from their mockery and contempt. She had to escape from her own pain and humiliation. But most of all she had to escape from Silas. She wanted to lock herself away somewhere private and dark while she tried to come to terms with what she had just learned. She would have defended Silas against all accusations Cissie-Rose had made against him, just as she would have given him her trust and her belief unquestioningly if he had denied what Cissie-Rose had said. But instead he had shown her with his plea, and more tellingly with the look in his eyes, that everything Cissie-Rose had accused him of was true.

She could hardly think or reason logically for the pain that was swamping her. What a fool she had been—to believe his lies about falling in love with her. And no wonder he had been so keen to talk with Art. A mirthless smile twisted her mouth. How ironic it was that she had been stupid enough, dense enough, besotted enough to praise him for his kindness. The pain tightened its grip, raking her emotions raw.

Silas caught up with her outside their bedroom door, refusing to let go of her when she tried to drag her wrist free of his imprisoning grip, bundling her inside the room and closing the door, enclosing them in what was for Tilly its tainted and treacherous intimacy.

'Let go of me,' she demanded.

'Not yet. Not until you've listened to me. I know you're upset, and I understand how you must feel—'

'How dare you say that to me? You know nothing. If you did you would never... You used me. You lied to me. You pretended to care about me when all the time—'

'Tilly, no!'

'So it's not true? You're not this James Connaught?'

Silas's mouth compressed. Why the hell hadn't he followed his own instinct and his heart and told Tilly the truth earlier? 'I *do* write as James Connaught, yes.'

'And you also moonlight as an out-of-work-actor, hiring yourself out as an escort?'

The bitterness in Tilly's voice made him want to hold her as tightly as he could, until he had absorbed her pain into himself.

'No,' he told her quietly. 'It was my half-brother Joe who was supposed to come here with you. He asked me to stand in for him because he'd had an accident. At first I refused, but then when he mentioned Art—'

'You changed your mind.'

It wasn't in Silas's nature to lie, especially not to someone who was as important to him as Tilly. 'Yes.'

'And when you accused me of hiring you for sex you were just testing the water, were you? Seeing how far you'd have to go to get what you wanted?'

'That had nothing to do with my hope that I could get closer to Art. I was concerned for Joe. He's young and impressionable, and I wasn't convinced that the outfit he was working for was as above board as he claimed.'

Silas took a deep breath. What he had to say to her now was going to be the hardest thing he had ever had to say. He knew his honesty was going to hurt her, but the truth had to be told, so that they could move on from today.

'That first night here, when you threatened to end our "engagement", I did think in terms of establishing a relationship with you to ensure that I stayed.'

'You used me,' Tilly accused him, her voice flat and devoid of the emotion she was desperately afraid might overwhelm her. 'You deliberately lied to me, pretended that you were falling in love with me, when all the time I meant nothing to you.'

'No, that's not true.'

'You're right,' Tilly agreed. 'The fact that I was falling in love with you *was* quite important to you. After all, it made everything so much easier for you, didn't it?'

'That's not what I meant and you know it. You can't really believe that I would lie to you about loving you?'

'Why not? You've lied to me about everything else, haven't you? If you'd really cared about me, Silas, you would have told me the truth.'

'I intended to.'

Tilly laughed mirthlessly. 'When? After you'd got your story?'

'I should have told you. I admit that. But I felt… I didn't want to risk spoiling what was happening between us.'

Tilly could hardly bear to listen to him. The rawness in his voice made her eyes sting with fierce tears. He sounded so genuine, but of course he wasn't.

'As a matter of fact, I was about to tell you earlier—just before your mother interrupted us.'

Tilly frowned, her heart missing a heavy beat as it clung desperately to the fragile hope of his words. She remembered that he had been on the verge of saying something to her. She ached with longing to be able to believe him, but she wasn't going to let herself give in to that weakness. Not a second time. Her was using her, manipulating her vulnerable emotions, just as he had done all along.

'If you had really loved me you would have been honest with me right from the start.'

'Life is not like that, Tilly. I didn't know I was going to fall in love with you. I didn't even realise at first that was what I was doing. By the time I did, it was too late. You'd already accepted me as what you believed I was. And, rightly or wrongly, I felt that our love was still too new and too fragile to bear the weight of the kind of revelations I would have had to make. But that doesn't mean that I didn't plan to tell you everything. I did. I love you, Tilly, and you love me. Surely that love—our love— deserves a chance?'

Tilly gave him a cynical look. 'You really think you can go on lying to me, don't you? I may have been stupid enough to fall for your lies the first time round, Silas, but I'm not stupid enough to fall for them again now. You don't love me. And as for me loving you—the man I thought I loved doesn't exist, does he? You've still got the hire car here. I think the best thing you can do now is pack your things and leave. There's nothing here for you now.'

Silas felt the shock of her rejection slicing through him, snapping the chain with which he had been leashing his own emotions. 'Nothing? Then what exactly is *this*, then?' he demanded.

He was still holding her wrist, and so he was able to catch her off balance enough to drag her into his arms and then cover the furious protest she made with the fierce heat of his mouth.

She wanted to resist him. She fought to do so. But something stronger than pride or pain was wrenching control of her responses from her, so that instead of closing into a tight, hard line against him her lips were opening under his, to return the full fury of his anguished passion. Somehow it was as though this was the only way she could show him the damage he had done—by violating the memory of what he had told her was love but what she now who knew was a lie.

This was all they had shared. Not love, not tenderness, and most certainly not the kind of almost spiritual emotional bond she had so stupidly deluded herself into thinking they had. Just this ferally savage physical need, poisoned with bitterness and deceit. Let it have its way, then; let it take her. Let it take them both and destroy itself as it did so, Tilly decided furiously.

Somehow he would break down Tilly's anger and resistance. Somehow he would find the right way to show her that their love was strong enough to survive the damage he had inflicted on it and on her. He had to find it. Because he couldn't endure the thought of losing her, Silas acknowledged as he tried to gentle the fierceness of his need and bring tenderness back into their intimacy.

He wanted to take Tilly and show her everything he felt—his remorse and regret, his pain and despair, his sorrow that he had hurt her and his reasons for having done so. He wanted to hold her in his arms, body to body, skin to skin, and to kiss the tears from her eyes. He wanted to beg for her forgiveness and to heal the wounds he had inflicted with the salve of his true love. He wanted to wipe away everything that had gone wrong and give them a fresh start. But most of all he wanted her to know that his love for her was hers for ever.

And this wasn't the way to show her that, Silas warned himself as he fought against succumbing to the drug of his own need. If he took her now, like this, when she was acting out of anger and bitterness, he would be damaging them both. He knew that, and yet at the same time he ached to take the chance that somehow he could mend things between them by showing her physically how much she meant to him.

The fire was dying out of her anger now, leaving behind a void that was filling with pain. Tilly shivered in Silas's hold.

'Tilly...'

'Just go, Silas. Please, just go.'

CHAPTER THIRTEEN

'SILAS RANG AGAIN this morning.'

Tilly heard her father's words but she didn't give any sign. It was over two months since she had last seen Silas. Two months during which he had attempted with relentless determination to make contact with her, and she had refused to let him with equal determination.

He had even tracked her down here, to her father's farm in Dorset, where she had come for a much-needed break not so much from her job as from Silas himself, and the ghost of their love.

'He's sent you this,' her father continued, holding out to her a large A4-sized parcel. 'It's the typescript for his book. He asked me to tell you that he wants you to be the first to read it.'

Tilly's mouth compressed. Somehow or other Silas seemed to have managed to persuade her father to act as his supporter, even though she had told her father what he had done.

'Tilly, I know what he did was very wrong, but why don't you give him a chance to explain and make amends?'

'Why should I?'

'Do you really need me to tell you that?' Her father asked dryly. 'You still love him, no matter how much you might try to convince yourself that you don't, and from what he's said to me he certainly loves you.'

'It's because of what he did that Art broke off his engagement to Ma,' Tilly pointed out.

Her father raised his eyebrows. 'If you ask me, your mother had a lucky escape. *She* certainly seems to think so. And she hasn't lost much time in finding someone to replace Art, has she?'

Tilly gave a small uncomfortable wriggle. It was true that her mother was now blissfully in love with a new man—and, although Tilly wasn't about to say so to her father, Annabelle too had been doing her utmost to persuade Tilly to give Silas a second chance.

'We're going out now,' her father said. 'See you later.'

TILLY WAS TRYING VERY HARD not to look at the manuscript on the table in front of her. She didn't even know why she had removed the packaging. But she had, and now, like Pandora with the lid of the box lifted, she was unable to control her own curiosity to see what lay inside.

Pinned to the first page of the manuscript was a letter addressed to her. She wasn't going to read it. She was going to tear it up, as she had all the other letters Silas had sent her. But somehow her fingers weren't obeying her brain, because the letter was open and unfolded, and Silas's firm, masculine handwriting was dancing on the page in front of her through the sudden surge of tears filming her eyes.

How could she still love a man who had already shown her so devastatingly that his career would always come first and that in order for it to do so he was prepared to lie to her? What kind of future would they have if she gave in and let Silas back into her life? Did she really need to ask herself that? It would be a future in which she and their children could never completely trust in Silas's love and honesty; a future in which they could never totally rely on him to be there for them. The future, in fact, that she had always feared.

Her fingers trembled as she held the letter. Why bother to add to her own pain by reading it? But it was too late.

I won't write to you yet again of my love for you. Love is, or should be, two halves of one whole, Tilly. I know my own half for what it is, but only you know yours. I had thought—mistakenly, perhaps—that your half matched mine in its absoluteness and constancy. Perhaps the message you want to send me via your silence is not that you refuse to forgive me or accept my explanations for my errors, but rather that you yourself have had second thoughts and have welcomed the chance to act on them.

As she read what he had written Tilly could hear him speaking the words as clearly as though he were standing next to her. She closed her eyes and let the pain take her.

Silas.

She still loved him. She knew that. Just as she knew that she always would. She opened her eyes and continued to read.

If that is so, then that is your right, and I cannot persuade you otherwise, but so far as my own feelings are concerned my love for you exists as truly as it always has done and always will. Meeting you has had a profound effect on me in more ways than one. If you read this manuscript then I hope you will see and understand.

Tilly turned over the first page. On the second there was a brief dedication which read *For my mother*.

She read for so long that her body felt stiff and cramped, but she was so engrossed in what she was reading that she hadn't been able to drag herself away, Tilly admitted.

She had expected Silas's book to be about the oil industry—which in some respects it was. But only some. What it told was the story of his mother, and those like her, who had crusaded against the tyranny of materialism over human life and the environment. What she'd read compelled her to go on reading, and moved her immensely. Now she had almost reached the end, and as she turned the final page of the penultimate chapter she found an envelope pinned to the manuscript.

It was addressed to her.

Inside she found a brief note, and another envelope.

If you have read this far then you will know by now
that I decided against writing about Jay Byerly and have
written instead about my mother's life and work. I made
that decision because of you, Tilly. I was wrong not to tell
you right from the first who I was and why I took Joe's
place. I love you, and I'd like the chance to prove my love
to you if you will give it to me. In the envelope is a ticket.
If you choose to give me a chance then please use it. If you
choose not to—if you don't, after all, love me enough to
accept me with my faults and flaws—then I won't bother
you again.

Did Silas really dare to question her love for him? Angrily,
Tilly opened the second envelope. It contained an air ticket to
Madrid.

Very carefully she put it to one side, and went back to the
manuscript. When she read Silas's spare description of his mother's death in an accident that should never have happened, and
would never have happened if it hadn't been for the actions
of Jay Byerly, Tilly had to stop reading because her tears had
blurred the print so badly.

At the end of the chapter Silas had written:

The very best gift my mother gave me was her love for
me; the legacy she left me was to learn to grow enough to
understand that love achieves more than bitterness or resentment. It was her love for her fellow man that prompted
her to give so much to others, and it is my love for one
very special person that has led me to write about the love
that motivated my mother rather than my own bitterness
at the manner of her death.

And then, underneath:

You are that woman, Tilly. Just as my mother's ring
fitted you perfectly, I would like to think that in one way
she was responsible for bringing you, the woman who fits

me so perfectly, into my life and my heart. Both of them
are empty without you.

She was a fool for doing this. It was crazy. No, Tilly corrected
herself as she walked through the Arrivals hall and blinked in
the sharp Spanish spring sunshine. *She* was crazy. What was the
point of doing this? It was over between her and Silas. So over
that there hadn't been a single night since they had been apart
when she had not fallen asleep thinking about him, nor a single
day that hadn't been shadowed by her bitterness and pain? Just
how over was that, exactly? Tilly derided herself.

She could see a small plump Spaniard, holding up a placard
bearing her name.

'I am José,' he informed her cheerfully. 'I am your driver.
You have just the one bag?'

'Just the one,' Tilly agreed. She had no idea what Silas was
planning, and even less why she should be travelling like this—
on trust and hope and something that came perilously close to
the love she had spent the last few weeks furiously denying existed.

There was no snow in Madrid, but as they began to climb
Tilly could see where it still lay across the mountains, and she
could see too where their route was taking them. Her heart thud-
ded into her chest wall, and she gave in to the ache inside her
that contained longing as well as pain.

It was no real surprise when they finally reached Segovia,
and José brought the car to a halt outside the hotel where she
had stayed with Silas.

A smiling receptionist welcomed her, and in no time at all
she was being shown up to the familiar suite.

The only thing that did surprise her was that it was empty and
there was no sign of Silas. Surprised her or disappointed her?

She looked out of the window and down into the street below.
On some impulse she didn't want to answer to she had brought
with her the black dress she had bought here. She heard the outer
door to the suite open and she turned round.

Silas! The bones in his face were surely more prominent, and he wore something in the aura he carried with him that looked like shadowed pain.

'All this is a bit dramatic, isn't it?' she asked, striving to sound cool and self-possessed.

'It wasn't intended to be.'

'No? Then what *was* it intended to be?' she challenged him.

'A hope that although it isn't possible to physically turn back time, I can at least show you how much I wish that I could do so.'

It had been here that they had finally made love, and she had given herself to him in love and in hope and with trust and belief. And now, with him standing here in front of her, her body and her emotions were filled with the memory of all that they had shared before reality had destroyed her dreams.

'When would you turn back time to? The moment you rejected Cissie-Rose's advances? After all, she could have helped you so much more than I did.'

'She could have. But by that stage you had become far more important to me than my book—even though I didn't have the wit to admit that to myself. No. I'd turn it back to the time before we made love, when I held you in my arms, knowing that we would do so. To when I should have told you the truth but was too afraid of spoiling things between us. Perhaps I sensed then more strongly than you did yourself that you already had doubts about your own feelings.'

Tilly couldn't answer him. While his challenge to her in his letter had shocked and angered her, she was honest enough to know that there was an element of truth in it.

'I'd spent so long planning to reveal Jay Byerly and his coterie of associates for what they were because of my mother that I felt honour-bound to stick to my plan—even though I knew I would have to deceive you. I couldn't see then that I would honour my mother's memory far more positively by writing about what she believed in rather than denouncing those who had stood against those beliefs. I hope I have done her justice.'

'You have,' Tilly told him softly. 'No one could read your

book and not be moved by it, Silas. If you had told me from the first...'

'I'd planned to tell you once we were back in London, when you wouldn't be under so much pressure from conflicting interests.'

'What about your own conflict of interests?' Tilly asked him quietly. 'How can you expect me ever to feel that the emotional security of our relationship and our children will be safe in your hands, Silas, when I've already witnessed you lying to me for the sake of your ambitions?'

'It wasn't like that. I had committed to that ambition before I met you and fell in love with you, and I had already abandoned my commitment to it because of my love for you—even though I didn't get the opportunity to tell you that. You and our four children will always come first with me, Tilly.'

'Our *what*?'

Tilly watched, fascinated, to see a faint tide of colour creeping along Silas's jawline.

'That was when I knew how much you meant to me. When you told me about your father's farm and out of nowhere I started visualising you living in the country with four children—our children.'

'I've always thought that four children would be the ideal family,' Tilly told him shakily.

'You'll have to marry me to get them. And you'll have to love me and let me love you—and them—for always.'

Just being with him and listening to him was melting away all her stubborn resistance. Reading Silas's book had already filled her with a tide of emotion that had swept away everything that had dammed up her love and turned it sour and bitter with anger and resentment. And now...

'Silas...' she began unsteadily.

'Don't look at me like that,' he warned her. 'Because if you do, then I will have to do this...'

How could she ever have convinced herself that she could live without him, when here in his arms was the only place she really wanted to be?

'Silas,' she said again, but this time she was whispering his name eagerly and happily against his lips, and letting him take the aching sigh of her breath from her as he kissed her.

AN HOUR LATER, LYING CURLED UP next to Silas in the warmth of the bed where he had just shown her how much he missed her, and promised her that their future together would be everything she wanted it to be, Silas lifted Tilly's left hand to his lips, kissing the finger on which he had replaced his mother's ring.

'Just promise me one thing?' he said.

'What?' Tilly asked.

'That you won't tell me that you want to get married on New Year's Eve in a castle in Spain. Because there is no way I can bear to wait that long.'

'Neither can I,' Tilly admitted, laughing. And then she stopped laughing as Silas bent his head to kiss her.

* * * * *

CHRISTMAS EVE WEDDING

CHAPTER ONE

A LITTLE HESITANTLY Jaz pressed the button for the lift to take her to her hotel bedroom. She was alone in the dimly lit foyer apart from the man who was also waiting for the lift. Tall, broad-shouldered, and subtly exuding an aura of very male sexual energy. Being alone with him sent a frisson of dangerous nervous excitement skittering over her skin.

Had he moved just that little bit closer to her whilst they waited, blocking her exit and hiding her from the view of anyone walking past the lift bay so that only he knew she was there, or was she imagining it? Like she had 'imagined' that look he had just given her body...her breasts...

And had he noticed the treacherous reaction of her body to his sexually predatory glance? The taut peaking of her breasts, the sudden soft gasp of her indrawn breath. Could he tell that recklessly she was in danger of actually becoming physically excited, not just by his presence but also by her own thoughts?

There was an awesome sexuality about him that made her tremble inside with arousal and guilt.

Was it possible he guessed what she was thinking? Was that why he had moved closer to her?

Colouring up self-consciously, Jaz looked away from him, determined to focus her thoughts elsewhere. She pondered on what had brought her to this hotel in New Orleans in the first place.

On the other side of the city her godfather would be going through the final details of the sale of his exclusive and innovative English department store to the American family who had been so eager to buy it, to add to their own equally prestigious and larger chain of American stores. They needed the store to give them an entrée into the British market.

She knew that her own job as the store's display co-ordinator and window designer was totally secure, but it had been a struggle for her, and a test of her determination and resolve to prove herself and succeed in her chosen career.

Her parents, loving and caring though they most certainly were, had initially been shocked and disbelieving when their only child had been unable to share their commitment to the farm she'd grown up on, and had instead insisted on making her own way in the world.

They had been very reluctant to accept her decision to go to art college, and Jaz knew that it was really thanks to the intervention of her godfather, Uncle John, that her parents had finally taken her seriously. Thanks to him too that she now had the wonderful job she did have.

It was no secret that her parents still harboured the hope that she would fall in love with someone who shared their own lifestyle and ambitions, but Jaz was fiercely determined never to fall in love with a man who could not understand and did not share her feelings. She felt that the right to express the artistic side of her nature had been hard-won, and because of that it was doubly precious to her. She was ambitious for her talent, for its expression, and for the freedom to use it to its maximum capacity, and she knew how impossible that would be if she were to marry a man like her father, kind, loving and generous though he was.

To further validate her ability she had recently been headhunted by a top London store, but she had chosen to remain loyal to her godfather and to the unique and acclaimed store which had originally been begun by his grandfather.

Now in his late seventies, her godfather had been for some time looking for a worthy successor who would nurture the store's prestigious profile, and although at first he had been dubious about selling out to new owners on the other side of the Atlantic, a visit to New Orleans to see the way the Dubois family ran their business—a trip on which he had invited Jaz to go with him—had convinced him that they shared his own objectives and standards. Since he had no direct heirs to pass the business onto, he had decided that the best way to preserve the traditions of the store was to sell it to the like-minded Dubois family, a decision Jaz herself fully endorsed.

As the lift arrived and the doors slid open Jaz's thoughts were snapped back into the present. She couldn't help snatching an indiscreet look at the man waiting to step into it with her, her heart bumping against her ribs as she acknowledged the buzz of sexual excitement she had felt the moment she had seen him. Was it the fact that she was out of her own environment, a stranger in a different country, that was encouraging her to behave so recklessly? Or was it something about the man himself that was making her touch the tip of her tongue to her lips as she stared boldly at him, her female senses registering his sexy maleness?

Just the thought of being alone in the lift with him was filling her mind with all manner of forbidden erotic scenarios. A wanton inspection of his body verified just how completely male he was. A soft, dangerous lick of excitement ran over her as her senses reacted to the way he was looking at her, silently responding to the fact that she had looked at him for just that little bit too long, challenging him in a way that was wholly female to show her that he was equally wholly male.

'Seen something you like, hon?' he asked her as the lift door closed, trapping Jaz inside the intimate space with him.

Apprehension curled feather-soft down her spine. She knew that what she was doing was totally out of character, but for some reason she didn't care. There was something about him that brought the secret ache deep within her body to a wire-sharp intensity that could not be ignored.

Refusing to back down, she met his amused look head-on, tossing her head as she replied huskily, 'I might have done.' She had been warned before her visit that New Orleans was home to a very dangerous type of sexually attractive man—men who never refused to gamble against fate or to take up a challenge. And she held her breath now, wondering how he would respond.

She couldn't resist glancing into the mirrored wall to her side to take another peek at him.

His shirt was unbuttoned at the throat, exposing an exciting 'V' of male flesh. Impulsively she took a step towards him. She wondered how it would feel to caress that flesh with her lips, to taste and tease it until he had no option but to reach for her and—

She could feel her body melting with arousal. Everything about him tormented her senses in ways she had never imagined. Just looking at him made her want him. She could feel her face burning, her heart racing at the explicitness of her own thoughts and fantasies. She felt shocked by them.

Her heart thumping, she continued to study him. Over six foot, with very thick rich brown hair just touched with honey-gold where the fierce heat of the sun had lightened it. In the close confines of the lift she could smell the cool expensive tang of his skin. Everything about him looked expensive. From his clothes and his haircut to his elegantly discreet watch. Everything apart from his hands which for some reason, whilst immaculately clean, were slightly callused. Her stomach lifted and clenched with female excitement at the thought of those hands, so tellingly male, pressed against the soft femininity of her own skin.

She had started to breathe too fast, betrayingly fast, she recognised as his glance locked on her mouth.

'Go ahead,' she heard him urging her shockingly. 'Go ahead, hon, and do what you want to do. And you do want to, don't you?' he guessed, his voice dropping until it was a low sexy murmur, as rawly sensual as though he had actually caressed the most sensitive parts of her body with the rough male heat of his tongue.

Somehow she had actually put one hand against his chest! His skin was warm and tanned, with tiny lines fanning out from his eyes. His eyes…

Her breath locked in her chest and another wave of sensual dizziness filled her. She had never, ever seen eyes so blue before. It was a denser, deeper, stronger blue than the bluest sky she had ever seen, the colour so intense that she felt her own golden-brown eyes must look totally insignificant in comparison.

'I can't,' she responded shakily, too lost in her own desire to conceal what she was feeling from him. 'Not here.' Her voice faltered and fell to a husky whisper. 'Not in the lift.' But as she spoke her gaze went betrayingly to where his jeans were now visibly straining against the tautness of his arousal.

'Liar!' he taunted her softly. 'I could take you here and now. And if you want me to prove it—' His hand was already reaching for the buckle of his belt.

Jaz felt dizzy with the aching intensity of her fevered longing. Impulsively she moved even closer to him, and then stopped.

The knowing smile that accompanied the look he was giving her brought a deep flush of colour to Jaz's skin.

He had the whitest, strongest teeth, and it was hard not to imagine him biting them into her skin with deliberate sensuality. A fierce, shocked shiver ran through her at the explicitness of her own thoughts, and she moved a little uncomfortably, shifting her weight from one foot to the other.

'Careful, hon,' she heard him warning her. 'If you keep on looking at me that way I guess I'm just going to have to give you what those big eyes of yours are asking me for. In fact...'

Jaz shook her head and tried to deny what he was saying, but it was too late for her to say or do anything. He had moved so quickly, so light-footedly for such a big man, and he had somehow imprisoned her against the back of the lift, his hands planted firmly either side of her as he lowered his head until his lips were resting on hers.

The feeling of being surrounded by him, by the heat of his body, the weight of it that was almost resting on her, the scent of it that filled the air around her, was so intensely erotic that she felt almost as though he had laid her bare and actually touched her. She shuddered as he placed his hand on her breast, caressing it through the fine silk of the dress she was wearing. He bent his head and she turned her own to one side, then cried out in protest as she felt his lips caressing her nipple through the fine silk.

Swooningly Jaz closed her eyes. She ought not to be doing this. It was so dangerous. Common sense told her that. But her hand had already gone to his groin, seeking, stroking, needing the hot hard feel of him to prove to her that she was not alone in the savage almost frightening urgency of her need. The sensation of him swelling fiercely beneath her touch soothed her fractured ego, just as the sudden rough acceleration of his breathing brought her a swift feminine surge of triumph. She was not alone. He wanted her as much as she wanted him!

The lift shuddered to a halt and the door opened. Immediately she pushed past him.

They stepped out of the lift together, Jaz aware that her face was burning hotly and that her legs felt so weak they were barely able to support her. What if they had remained in the lift for longer? Would he…? Would she…?

As she turned away from him she heard him saying softly to her, 'Let's go to your room.'

Helplessly she stared at him. He was a man totally outside all her previous experience—which she had to admit was less than worthy of any kind of comparison. She had always led an unfashionably sedate kind of life, compared with the lives of her peers. Her battle to prove to her parents how important her chosen career path was to her had not left her with time to indulge in the sexual experimentation of other girls her age.

But it was a life which suited her and which she had always been very happy with. Sexual adventures of the kind that involved kissing tall, dark, handsome men in lifts were not something that had ever remotely interested her—or if they had she was certainly not prepared to admit it publicly, she hastily amended, as she wordlessly led the way to her hotel bedroom with her head held high but her heart thumping frantically in a mixture of excitement and apprehension.

It was only when they reached the door that qualms of conscience made her hesitate. She turned to him as she searched in her bag for her key.

'I don't think—' she began, but he had taken her bag from

unresisting fingers and was reaching out to draw her into his arms. In the same movement he slid open the door.

'What is it that you don't think, hon?' he asked her with male emphasis. 'That you don't want this?'

Jaz's whole body shook in the hard embrace of his arms as he bent his head and kissed her, a long, slow, lingering kiss that melted her bones and her will-power. They were inside the room, now and he had closed and locked the door, all without letting go of her, and now in the soft darkness he was still kissing her. Though what he was doing to her mouth was more, much more than merely kissing it. What he was doing was…

Jaz shuddered convulsively as his hands touched her body lightly, delicately, knowingly… This man knew women… He knew them very, very well. She could feel it in his touch…feel it in him. His tongue caressed her lips, as though he sensed and wanted to soothe her fears, circling them slowly and carefully, until the delicate pressure of his tongue-tip became not soothing but frustrating, tormenting…making her want…

The darkness seemed to increase her awareness of him, of the hot, musky male scent of his body. It made her doubly aware of the feel of his skin against her as she felt the roughened rasp of his jaw on her cheek, and the corresponding texture of his jacket sleeve against her bare arm. She was almost intoxicated by the cool fresh hint of cologne he was wearing.

In her mind's eye she could see him in a very different environment from that of her hotel room—the Bourbon court had been exited from France to New Orleans, and it didn't take much imagination on Jaz's part to picture him at Versailles at the height of the Sun King's reign. How well he would have fitted into that sophisticated and splendid milieu; his sexuality would have driven the court ladies into swooning fits of desire—would have had much the same effect on them as it was having on her right now!

He was like no other man she had ever met, dangerous and exciting, and she was drawn to him in a way that both shocked and thrilled her.

His teasing kiss was beginning to aggravate her. He was

treating her like a girl, not a woman—not like the woman she knew she could be with him. All fire and passion, need and hunger. A woman to whom nothing else mattered more than her man, the feelings and desires they were generating and creating between them. Her made her feel… He made her feel alive, primitive, sensual—all woman! His woman!

Reaching up, she wrapped her arms around him, boldly tangling her tongue with his, drawing him into a kiss of fierce passion.

'Uh-huh, so that's what you want, is it?' he demanded thickly against her mouth as he responded to her. 'Well, in that case, hon—'

Jaz gasped as he picked her up as easily, as though she were a child, making his way sure-footedly towards the bed like a mountain cat.

As he laid her down he was already undressing her, and she made no move to stop him. She had known the moment they stepped into the lift together that this was going to happen. Had wanted it to happen. As it had happened with this man so many times since she'd arrived in New Orleans. She positively longed for Caid's now familiar touch.

Moonlight streamed in through the unclosed curtains, silvering her exposed breasts. She gasped in pleasure as he touched them, running the slightly coarse pad of his fingertip round the exquisitely sensitive flesh surrounding each pouting nub.

Excitement, as hot and sweet as melting chocolate, filled her with shocked pleasure. Her body arched like a bow as she offered her breasts to him in the silent heat of the shadowy room, its stillness broken only by the raw tempo of their aroused breathing.

This was what she had been imagining them doing in the lift—she'd been picturing their naked bodies entwined in the still heat of the Louisiana night.

Fiercely she reached for him, her fingers tugging at buttons and fastenings, not stopping until she was able to touch the hot skin that held the muscled tautness of his naked body.

Just touching him unleashed within her a driven hunger she

was half afraid to recognise. It was far, far outside the boundaries of her normal emotions. A reckless and alien, dangerous and wild wantonness that refused to be controlled or tamed.

As he reached for her, covering her body in fierce, rawly sensual kisses, she sobbed beneath the onslaught of her own response—which was immediate, feral and unstoppable.

Passionately they clung together, stroking, touching kissing, devouring one another in their mutual driving need. In the moonlight Jaz could see the scratches she had scorched across his back, and in the morning she knew her own body would bear the small bruise-marks of his hotly male demands on her, his desire for her. Then perhaps she would wonder at her own behaviour, but right now her thoughts were elsewhere.

'Ready, hon?' he demanded as he gathered her closer, so close that she could feel the heavy thud of his heart as though it were beating within her own body.

Wordlessly she answered him with her body, lifting her legs to wrap them tightly around him as he thrust into her.

The sensation of him filling her, stretching her, made her shake with almost unbearable pleasure.

Each movement of his body within hers, each powerful thrust, increased the frenzy of need that was taking her higher, filling her senses with the immensity of what was happening. And then abruptly the fierce, breath-catching ascent was over, and she was cresting the topmost wave of her own pleasure, surfing its heights, awed by the power of what she was experiencing. She cried out unknowingly, clinging to the body covering her own, feeling the male release within her; her body accepting the satisfaction of knowing it had given him completion whilst her exhausted senses relaxed.

CAID LEANED UP ON ONE ELBOW and gently tickled the impossibly delicate curve of Jaz's jaw with his fingertips. She was so tiny, so fragile, and yet at the same time so breathtakingly strong, this Englishwoman who had walked so unexpectedly into his life and his heart.

He had had his doubts—one hell of a lot of them, if he was

honest—and with good reason. But then he had overheard her godfather talking to his mother about her background, and Caid had started to relax. Knowing that she came from farming stock—that she had been raised in a country environment and that her role within the store was simply a temporary one she had taken on to show her independence until she was ready to settle down and return to her roots—was all he had needed to lower his guard and stop fighting his feelings for her.

Which was just as well, because there was no way he could stop loving her now. No way he would ever contemplate settling down with a girl who did not share his deep love of country living and his determination that their children would be raised on his ranch, with their mother there for them, instead of travelling all over the world in the way his own mother had done. She had never been there when he had most needed her, and his parents finally divorced when his father had grown tired of his mother's constant absences, her single-minded devotion to the family store. Caid had never been in any doubt that the store mattered more to his mother than he did. She had always been frank about the fact that his conception had been an accident.

As a young boy Caid had been badly hurt by his mother's open admission of her lack of maternalism. As a teenager that hurt had turned to bitter resentment and as Caid had continued to grow his resentment had become an iron-hard determination to protect his own children from the same fate. Like many people who'd experienced a lonely and painful childhood, Caid had a very strong desire to have his own family and create the kind of closeknit unit he felt he had missed out on.

One of the most painful episodes of his childhood had been the time when his mother had not even been able to be there for him when his father—her ex-husband—had been killed in a road accident.

Caid had been eleven at the time, and he had never forgotten just how it had felt to be taken to the mortuary to identify his father... How alone, how afraid and how angry with his mother he had felt.

He had made a vow then that there was no way anything like that was ever going to happen to his kids. No way!

Consequently he had been very wary of becoming emotionally involved, despite the number of women who had tried to coax and tempt him into falling in love with them.

Until now… Until Jaz.

He had walked into the restaurant where the family, including his mother, was having dinner with Jaz and her godfather, and the moment he had set eyes on her he had known!

He had known too, from Jaz's dazed expression and self-conscious pink-cheeked colour, that she was equally intensely aware of him.

It hadn't taken him long to skilfully detach her from the others, on the pretext of showing her the view of the Mississippi from the upper floor of the restaurant, and even less time to let her know how attracted he was to her.

That his behaviour had been somewhat out of character was, he recognised, an indication of just how strong his feelings for her were.

Ironically, he had almost not met Jaz at all.

Although Caid had now established a workable and accepting adult relationship with his mother, one of the legacies from his childhood was his intense dislike of the family business. Had he been able to do so he would have preferred to have nothing whatsoever to do with the stores at all. However, that simply wasn't possible. His maternal grandfather had left him a large portfolio of shares in the family business, which he held in trust, and as a further complication his mother had put emotional pressure on him to take on the role of the business financial adviser, following the completion of his Masters in Business Studies, claiming that if he didn't she would never be able to believe he had forgiven her for his childhood.

Rather than become involved in painful wrangling Caid had given in, and of course the family had insisted that he further his role as financial adviser on their proposed purchase of the English store his mother was so keen to acquire—to add to the portfolio of highly individual and specialised stores already operating in Boston, Aspen and New Orleans.

Unlike the rest of his mother's family, Caid's first love was the land, the ranch he had bought for himself and was steadily building up, financed by the money he earned as a much sought-after financial consultant.

But he had come to New Orleans, protesting all the way like a roped steer, and thank heavens his mother had persevered, insisted on his presence. Because if she hadn't...

The sexy smile curling his mouth deepened as Jaz opened her eyes.

'Mmm, that sure was another wonderful night we spent together, ma'am,' he teased her softly.

As he had known she would, Jaz started to blush. It fascinated him, this delicate English colour of hers that betrayed her every emotion, and made him feel he wanted to wrap her up and protect her.

'You'd better go,' Jaz told him unsteadily. 'You know we both agreed that we wanted to keep this...us...to ourselves for now, and my godfather will be expecting me to have breakfast with him. Your mother has arranged for us to visit her warehouse this morning.'

Jaz gave a small soft gasp as Caid leaned forward and covered her mouth with his own, kissing her into silence, and from silence into sweetly hot fresh desire.

'Are you sure you want me to leave?' he asked, breathing the words against the sensitivity of her passionately kissed mouth whilst his hand pushed aside the bedclothes to mould round her breast.

As she struggled to keep her head and behave sensibly Jaz breathed in the intoxicating warm man-scent of Caid's skin and knew she was fighting a lost cause.

Much better simply to give in, she acknowledged giddily as Caid started to kiss her again, gathering her up in his arms and rolling her swiftly beneath him.

'Oh!' Just the feel of his naked flesh against her own was enough to prompt Jaz's soft betraying gasp, swiftly followed by a second and much more drawn out murmur of female pleasure as Caid made his intentions—and his hungry desire for her—very clear.

In terms of days they had known each other for very little time, but in terms of longing and love it felt to Jaz that they had known one another for ever.

'A month ago I never dreamed that I'd be doing anything like this,' she gasped as Caid's hand stroked her body.

'I should hope you didn't,' he growled mock-angrily.

'After all, a month ago we hadn't met.'

Immediately Jaz's eyes filmed with tears.

'Hon... What is it? What's wrong? What did I say?' Caid demanded urgently, cupping her face with his hands, his expression turning from one of amusement to anxious male concern.

'Nothing,' Jaz assured him. 'It's just that... Oh, Caid... If I hadn't come to New Orleans—! If we hadn't met—! If...I hadn't known...'

'You did come to New Orleans. We did meet, and you do know. We both know,' Caid emphasised rawly. 'I know, Jaz, that we were made to be together, that you are perfect for me. Perfect,' he repeated meaningfully, glancing down the length of her body and then looking deep into her eyes.

Jaz could feel her toes curling as she looked at him. The way she felt about him still totally bemused and awed her. She had never thought of herself as the kind of woman who fell head over heels in love at first sight, who behaved so rashly that nothing would have stopped her sharing Caid's bed or his life once he had told her how much he wanted her there.

It still made her feel giddy with happiness to know that Caid, who was surely the epitome of everything she had ever imagined she could possibly want in a man, had fallen in love with her. Caid was exactly the kind of man she had always secretly hoped she might meet: sophisticated, virile, sexy. A man who shared her world, who understood how important it was for her to be able to give free rein to her artistic nature; a man whose background meant that he would know instinctively why she preferred to stroke the sensual silkiness of rich velvet than to rub down the hindquarters of a horse. And why she could spend hours, days, wandering in delight through an art gallery, whilst the delights of a cattle market left her cold.

'Will you be joining us this morning?' Jaz asked him.

Caid shook his head and Jaz tried to conceal her disappointment. As excited as she was at the thought of seeing behind the scenes of the store, so to speak, she knew it would have been an even more wonderfully fulfilling experience if Caid had been there with her.

She knew that his mother had overall control of all the buying for the stores, and that she travelled the world seeking out new and different merchandise to tempt their discerning customers, but it was through Caid's eyes that she wanted to see the Aladdin's cave she suspected the warehouse would be—in Caid's presence that she wanted to explore a part of the world he had made it clear they were going to share.

'We can meet up this afternoon at the house,' Caid said once they were both dressed. 'You and I have talking to do and plans to make,' he told her meaningfully.

'Uncle John and I are flying home tomorrow,' Jaz reminded him.

'Exactly,' Caid acknowledged. 'Which is all the more reason for you and I to make those plans.'

CHAPTER TWO

JAZ SMILED EXCITEDLY as she hurried towards the luxurious house in the centre of the French Quarter of New Orleans, where Caid was staying for the duration of his visit.

He had given her his spare key to the house the same night he had declared his love for her—a week to the day after they had first met—and now, as she turned it gently in the lock and opened the door to step inside the house's hallway, Jaz wondered how on earth she was going to cope tomorrow morning when she was due to fly home—without him!

Already, secretly, she had fantasised about the life they would live together—the children she hoped they would one day have. A boy, a miniature Caid, patterned on his father, and a girl, to fill the home they would share. Suddenly it struck her that she did not know where Caid's permanent home actually was!

Not that it mattered, she assured herself. After all, she knew all the really important things about him… Like the fact that he slept on his right-hand side and that he was such a light sleeper that if she so much as brushed the lightest of kisses against his skin he was immediately awake—even if on one occasion he had fooled her into thinking he wasn't, and she had betrayed herself, giving in to her female longing to relish the secret intimacy and pleasure of touching and exploring him whilst he slept.

Hastily Jaz dragged her thoughts onto more mundane things. She knew that Caid had been to college in Boston, where his family also had a store, and that his work as a financial consultant required a certain amount of travel.

'Fortunately I can work from any base, so long as I have a computer,' he had told her, adding jokingly, 'And my own plane.'

Did 'anywhere' mean that he was thinking of basing himself in her hometown, Cheltenham?

Or did he have somewhere else in mind? Jaz had been thrilled when his mother had sought her out privately to tell her how much she admired her work.

'It could well be that there are opportunities for you to branch out rather more after the takeover,' she had told Jaz, excitingly. 'Would you be interested? It could mean a change of scenery for you.'

'I'd be very interested,' Jaz had replied dizzily.

'Good,' Caid's mother had approved.

Had Caid perhaps hinted to his mother that Jaz might possibly work in one of their American stores?

He had told Jaz very comprehensively how well suited he thought they were, and she certainly felt the same way. She had deliberately refrained from saying too much to him about her job once she had realised who he was, not wanting him to think that she was trying to make a good impression on him out of some ulterior career-driven motive, but she had mentioned to him that she had known where her life lay from being a young girl.

The speed of their relationship and her own love for her parents had kept her from saying anything to him about the problems she had experienced as a child—as yet—but she knew that with his family background he would completely understand and sympathise with how she felt.

From the house's stately drawing room a corridor led to its other rooms, and from her end of the hallway Jaz could see the door that opened into Caid's bedroom was ajar. Instinctively, Jaz knew that Caid had reached the house ahead of her and was waiting for her. It was all she could do to stop herself from breaking into an undignified run and rushing into the bedroom to throw herself into his arms.

When she pushed open the bedroom door she saw that she had been right.

Caid was lying on the bed, a thin sheet pulled up to his waist, the rest of his body exposed as he lay back in the bed, his arms raised and his hands folded behind his head.

Hungrily Jaz's gaze feasted on him. There was, after all, no need for her to try and hide her feelings from him. After all, Caid understood her desire, her arousal…her love.

'Miss me?' he whispered as she hurried unsteadily towards the bed.

'Mmm…' Jaz admitted. 'But the warehouse was wonderful. I thought our buyers at home were good, but your mother is in a class of her own.'

'Tell me about it!' Caid agreed cynically, but the grimness in his voice was lost on Jaz, who was reliving the awe and excitement she had felt when she had toured the New Orleans store.

'I know that she personally approves everything that your buyers source.' Jaz shook her head. 'How on earth does she do it? She must be totally dedicated.'

'Totally,' Caid agreed tersely.

Frowning a little as she caught the sharpness of his voice, Jaz looked at him. 'What's wrong?' she asked him.

'Nothing,' Caid responded firmly, smiling at her as he added softly, 'Apart from the fact that you've got far too many clothes on and we're wasting too much time talking.'

'You said you wanted to talk,' Jaz reminded him. 'To talk and make plans,' she emphasised.

'Mmm…and so I do,' Caid agreed. 'But right now you're distracting the hell out of me and making me want you so damn much that the way I need to communicate with you has suddenly become much more personal and one on one. You haven't said hi to me yet,' he told her softly.

'Hi…' Jaz began, but Caid immediately shook his head.

'No. Not like that. Like this.' Swiftly he reached for her, his mouth starting to caress hers.

'Oh, *that* kind of hi.' Jaz managed to find the breath to tease him.

'That kind of hi,' Caid agreed, releasing her mouth to look into her eyes.

Jaz could feel the heat spreading through her body. She

started to quiver, and then to tremble openly. She could see from the look in Caid's eyes how much he was enjoying her helpless response to him.

Well, he would pay for that enjoyment later, when she tormented him the way he was tormenting her right now.

'I've never met anyone who shows her feelings so clearly and so openly,' Caid told her quietly. 'I love that honesty about you, Jaz. I don't have any time for people who cheat or lie.'

For a second he looked so formidable, so forbidding, that Jaz felt unsettled. To her he was the man she loved, but she could see that there was another side to him—a fiercely stubborn and unforgiving side, she suspected.

'I love the way you show me your feelings,' she heard Caid saying. 'The way you show me how much you want and love me. Show me that now, Jaz.'

Jaz didn't need a second invitation.

The heightened sound of Caid's breathing accompanied the speedy removal of her clothes, until her progress was interrupted by Caid's refusal to allow her to complete the task unaided, his hands hungrily tender against her body as they exchanged mutually passionate kisses and whispered words of love.

THE HEAT OF A NEW ORLEANS afternoon was surely made for lovers, Jaz reflected languorously a couple of hours later as she lay in Caid's arms, enjoying the blissful aftermath of their lovemaking. After all, where better to escape the heat than in the shadowy air-conditioned coolness they were enjoying?

'Time to get dressed,' Caid murmured as he leaned over to kiss her.

'Dressed? I thought we were going to talk,' Jaz reminded him.

A sexy smile crooked his mouth.

'We are!' he confirmed. 'Which is why we need to get dressed. If we stay here like this, talking isn't going to be what I feel like doing,' he added, in case Jaz had missed his point. 'I can't wait for us to be married, Jaz, or to take you home with me to Colorado—to the ranch. We can begin our lives together properly there. With your background, you'll love it, I'll get you your own horse, so that we can ride out together, and then, when the kids come along—'

'Your ranch?' Jaz stopped him in a shocked voice. 'What ranch? What are you talking about, Caid? You're a businessman—a financial consultant. The stores...'

'I am a financial consultant,' Caid agreed, starting to frown as he heard the note of shocked anxiety in Jaz's voice. 'But that's what I do to make enough money to finance the ranch until it can finance itself. And as for the stores...to be involved in the stores or anything connected with them is the last way I would ever want to live my life. To me they epitomise everything I most dislike and despise.' His mouth twisted bitterly. 'I could say that I have a hate-hate relationship with them. Personally, I can see nothing worthwhile in scouring the world for potential possessions for people who already have more than they need. That's not what life should be about.'

Jaz couldn't help herself—his angry words had resurrected too many painful memories for her.

'But living on a ranch, chasing round after cattle all day, presumably is?' she challenged him shakily.

With every word he had uttered Caid had knocked a larger and larger hole in her beliefs, her illusions about the kind of relationship and goals they shared. Jaz recognised in shocked bewilderment that Caid simply wasn't the man she had believed him to be.

'The stores aren't just about...about selling things, Caid,' she told him passionately. 'They're about opening people's eyes... their senses...to beauty; they're about... Surely you can understand what I'm trying to say?' Jaz pleaded.

Caid narrowed his eyes as he heard the agitation and the anger in Jaz's voice. From out of the past he could hear his mother's voice echoing in his six-year-old ears.

'No, Caid. I can't stay. I have to go. Think about all those people I would be disappointing if I didn't find them beautiful things to buy! Surely you can understand?'

No! I don't understand! Caid had wanted to cry, but he had

been too young to find the words he wanted to say, and already too proud, too aware of his male status, to let her see his pain.

But he certainly wasn't going to make the mistake of holding back on telling Jaz how he felt.

'I thought we were talking about us, Jaz! About our future—our lives together. So why in hell's name are we talking about the stores?'

'Because I work in one of them, and so far as I am concerned my work is a vitally important part of my life.'

'How vitally important?' Caid demanded ominously, his voice suddenly icily cold.

Jaz felt as though the ground that had seemed so safe and solid was suddenly threatening to give way beneath her, as though she was rushing headlong into danger. But it was a danger she had faced before, wasn't it? Listening to Caid was in many ways just like listening to her parents—although Caid's anger and bitterness was a frighteningly adult and dangerous version of parental emotion.

She felt intensely threatened by it—not in any physical sense, but in the sense that his attitude threatened her personal freedom to be herself.

As she looked at him, remembering the intimacy they had just shared, the love he had shown her, she was tempted to back down. But how could she and still be true to herself?

'My work is as important to me as it gets,' she told him determinedly. Though what she was saying was perhaps not strictly true. It was not so much her job that was important to her as the fact that it allowed her to express her creativity, and it was her creativity she would never compromise on or give up. 'As important,' she continued brittly, 'as you probably consider yours to be to you!'

'Nothing—no one on this earth—could ever make me give up the ranch!' Caid told her emphatically.

'And nothing—no one—could ever make me give up my... my...work,' Jaz replied, equally intensely.

Silently they looked at one another. The hostility in Caid's eyes made Jaz want to run to him and bury her head against his chest so that she wouldn't have to see it.

'I can't believe this is happening.' Caid's voice was terse, his jaw tight with anger.

'If I had known—'

'You did know,' Jaz interrupted him fiercely. 'I have never made any secret of how much my...my creative my work means to me. If I had thought for one minute that you might not understand...that you were a...a farmer...there is no way that—'

'That what? That you'd have jumped so eagerly into bed with me?'

'I was brought up on a farm.' Jaz struggled to explain. 'I know that it isn't the kind of life I can live.'

'And I was brought up by a mother who thought more of her precious stores than she did of either my father or me. I know there is no way I want a woman—a wife—who shares that kind of obsession. I want a wife who will be there for my kids in a way that my mother never was for me. I want a wife who will put them and me first, who will—'

'Give up her own life, her own dreams, her own personality simply because you say so?' Jaz stormed furiously at him. 'I don't believe I'm hearing this. Just what kind of man are you?'

'The kind who was fool enough to think you were the right woman for him,' Caid told her bitingly. 'But obviously I was wrong.'

'Obviously,' Jaz agreed chokily, then emphasised, 'Very obviously!' And then added for good measure, 'I hate farming. I loathe and detest everything about it. I would never ever commit myself or my children to...to a man as...as selfish and narrow-minded as you certainly are. My creativity is a special gift. It means—'

'A special gift? More special than our love?' Caid demanded savagely. 'More special than the life we could have shared together? The children I would have given you?'

'You don't understand,' Jaz protested, her voice thickening with tears as she forced herself not to be weakened by the emotional pressure he was placing her under. If she gave in to him now she would never stop giving in to him, and she would spend the rest of her life regretting her weakness. Not just for herself but for her children as well.

But still she tried one last attempt to make Caid see reason, telling him huskily, 'When I was growing up I knew how important it was for me to fulfil the creative, artistic side of my nature, but my parents didn't want to accept that I was different from them. If it hadn't been for Uncle John I don't know what would have happened. I had to fight far too hard for my right to be me, Caid, ever to be able to give it up for anyone...even you.'

What he hadn't understood as a child Caid certainly understood now, he acknowledged bitterly. Once again, the most important person in his world was telling him that he wasn't enough for her, that she didn't love him enough to want to be with him for himself.

'I thought after what I'd been through with my mother I'd be able to recognise another woman of her type a mile away,' he growled angrily. 'And perhaps I would have done too, if I hadn't heard your precious Uncle John talking about you and saying that your family expected you to return to your roots and settle down to the life they'd raised you in.'

The accusation implicit in his words that somehow she had actively deceived him infuriated Jaz, severing the last fragile thread tugging on her heartstrings.

'My parents might want that, but it certainly isn't what I want, or what I ever intend to do. And if you misinterpreted a conversation you overheard, that's hardly my fault. If marrying a farmer's daughter is so important to you, why didn't you say so?'

'Because I believed that what is important to me was equally important to you,' Caid told her bitingly. 'I thought that you were the kind of woman strong enough to find her fulfilment in—'

'Her husband and her children? Staying home baking cakes whilst her big strong husband rides his acres and rules his home?' Jaz interrupted him scathingly. 'My God. If your father was anything like you, no wonder your mother left him! You aren't just old-fashioned, Caid, you're criminally guilty of wanting to deny my sex its human rights! We are living in a new world now. Modern couples share their responsibilities—to each other and to their children—and—'

'Do they? Well, my mother certainly didn't do much sharing when she was travelling all over the world buying "beautiful" things,' he underlined cynically. 'She left my dad to bring me up as best he could. And as for her leaving him—believe me, he felt he was well rid of her. And so did I.'

Caid started to shake his head, his eyes dark with a pain that Jaz misinterpreted as anger.

'My mother was like—'

'Like me?' She jumped in, hot-cheeked. 'Do you feel you'd be well rid of me, Caid?'

Broodingly Caid looked at her. Right now he ached to take her in his arms and punish her for the pain she was causing them both, by kissing her until she admitted that all she wanted was him and their love, that nothing else mattered. But if he did he knew he would be committing himself to a life of misery. After all, a leopardess never changed her spots—look at his mother!

The look he was giving her said more than any amount of words, Jaz decided with a painful sharp twisting of her heart that made it feel as though it was being pulled apart.

'Fine,' she lied. 'Because I certainly think that I will be well rid of you!!'

She could feel the burning acid sting of unshed tears. As angry with herself for her weakness as she was with Caid for being the cause of it, she blinked them away determinedly.

'I'm a woman with needs and ambitions of my own, Caid, not some…some docile brood mare you can corral and keep snugly at home.'

'You—' Infuriated, Caid took a stride towards her.

Immediately Jaz panicked. If he touched her now, held her… kissed her…

'Don't come any closer,' she warned him, her eyes glittering with emotion. 'And don't even think about trying to touch me, Caid. I don't want to be touched by you ever again!'

Without giving him any chance to retaliate she turned on her heel and fled, almost running the length of the house and not stopping until she was halfway down the street, when the heat of the New Orleans late afternoon forced her to do so.

It was over. Over. And it should never have happened in the first place. Would never have happened if she had for one minute realised, recognised, just what kind of man Caid was.

She had been out of her depth, Jaz acknowledged miserably, in more ways than one.

The only consolation was that, thanks to Caid's practicality and insistence on protecting her, there was no chance there would be any repercussions from their affair. And for that she was profoundly thankful! Wasn't she?

CHAPTER THREE

'YOU WANT ME TO GO to England and find out what's happening?' Caid stared at his mother in angry disbelief. 'Oh, no…no way. No way at all!' he told her, shaking his head.

'Caid, please. I know how you feel about the stores, and I know I'm to blame for that but you are my son, and who else can I turn to if I can't rely on you? And besides,' she continued coaxingly, 'it would hardly be in your own financial interests for the stores to start losing money—especially not right now, when you've invested so much in modernising the ranch and buying more land.'

'All right, Mother, I understand what you're saying.' Caid stopped her grimly. 'But I fail to see why a couple of personnel leaving the Cheltenham store should be such a problem.'

'Caid, they're going to work for our competitors.'

'So we recruit better and more loyal employees,' Caid responded wryly. 'Which departments are we talking about anyway?' he asked, as casually as he could. So far as he was concerned, he told himself, if one of the people who had left was Jaz then so much the better!

It was over four months since Jaz had walked out on him after their fight. Over four months? It was four months, three weeks, five days and, by his last reckoning, seven and a half hours—not that he was keeping count for any other reason than to remind himself how fortunate he'd been to discover how unsuited they were before he had become any more involved.

Any more involved? How much more involved was it possible for him to have been? Hell, he'd been as deep in love as it was possible for a man to be!

Irascibly, Caid started to frown. He was growing a mite tired of being forced to listen to the mocking taunts of his unwanted inner voice. An inner voice, moreover, that knew nothing whatsoever about the realities of the situation!

So what if it was true that there had been occasions when he had found himself perilously close to reaching for the phone and punching in the English store's number? At least he had been strong enough to stop himself. After all, there was no real point in him speaking to Jaz, was there? Other than to torment and torture himself—and he was doing one hell of a good job of that without hearing the sound of her voice.

His frown deepened. By now surely he should be thinking about her less, missing and wanting her less—especially late at night…

'Caid…come back… You're miles away…'

His mother's voice cut into his private thoughts, mercifully rescuing him from having to acknowledge just what was on his mind late at night when he should have been sleeping.

'The employees who have left are both key people, Caid: loyal personnel who had worked for the store for a long time. I'm concerned that their decision to leave will reflect badly on us and on our ability to keep good staff. Not to mention our status as a premier store. The retail world is very small, and it only needs a whisper of gossip to start a rumour that we are in danger of losing our status as market leader…' She gave him a worried look. 'I don't need to tell you what that is likely to do to our stock.'

'So two people leave.' Caid shrugged. He knew his mother, and the last thing he needed right now was to have his time hijacked on behalf of her precious stores.

'Two have left so far, but there could be more. Jaz might be next, and we really can't afford to lose her, Caid. She has a unique talent—a talent I very much want. Not just for the Cheltenham store but for all our stores. It's in my mind to appoint Jaz as our head window and in-store designer once she has gained more experience. I'd like to have her spend time working at each of the individual stores first. Caid, we mustn't lose her, but I'm very much afraid we are going to do so. If it wasn't for this stupid embargo the doctors have put on me flying I'd go to Cheltenham myself!'

Caid watched as his mother moved restlessly around the room. It had come as just as much of a shock to him as it had to his mother to learn that a routine health check-up had revealed a potentially life threatening series of small blood clots were developing in her lower leg. The scare had brought home to him the fact that despite everything she was still his mother, Caid recognised grimly. The clots had been medically dispersed with drugs, but his mother had been given strict instructions that she was on no account to fly until her doctor was sure she was clear of any threat of the clots returning.

When she saw that he was watching her she told him emotionally, 'You say that you've forgiven me for…for your childhood, Caid, but sometimes, I wonder…I feel…' When she stopped and bit her lip, looking away from him, Caid suppressed a small sigh.

'What are you trying to say?' he asked her cynically. 'That you want me to prove I've forgiven you once more by going to Cheltenham?'

'Oh, Caid, it would mean so much to me if you would,' she breathed.

'I don't—' Caid began, but immediately she interrupted.

'Please, Caid,' she begged urgently. 'There isn't anyone else I can trust. Not when I suspect that the root cause of the problem over there is the fact that your uncle Donny has appointed his own stepson as chief executive of the store,' she told him darkly. 'I mean, what right does Donny have to make that kind of decision? Just because he's the eldest that doesn't mean he can overrule everyone else. And as for that dreadful stepson of his… Jerry knows nothing whatsoever about the specialised nature of our business—'

'I thought he was running a chain of supermarkets—' Caid interrupted.

The constant and relentless internecine war of attrition waged between his mother and her male siblings was a familiar ongoing saga, and one he normally paid scant attention to.

'Yes, he was. But honestly, Caid—supermarkets! There just isn't any comparison between them and stores like ours. Of course, Donny has done it to appease that appalling new wife of his... Why on earth he marries them, I don't know. She's his fifth. And as for Jerry... There's no way he would have ever got his appointment past the board if I hadn't been in hospital! There's nothing Donny would like better than to get me completely off the board, but he'll never be able to do that...'

'Mother, aren't you letting your imagination rather run away with you?' Caid intervened. 'After all, it is as much in Uncle Donny's interest as it is in yours to have the business thrive. And if Jerry is as bad as you are implying—'

'As bad! Caid, he's worse, believe me. And as for Donny! Well, certainly you'd think with four ex-wives to support he'd be going down on his knees to thank me for everything that I've done for the stores. But all he wants is to score off me. He's always been like that...right from when I was born...they all were. You can't imagine how I used to long to have a sister instead of five brothers... You'd think after all I learned about the male sex from them I'd have had more sense than to get married myself. You were lucky to be an only child, Caid—'

She stopped abruptly when she saw his expression. 'Caid, please,' she begged him, returning to her request. 'We can't afford to have this happen. We desperately need Jaz's skill. Do you know that her window displays for the Christmas season are so innovative that people go to the store just to see them? She has a talent that is really unique, Caid. When I think about how lucky we are to have her... We mustn't lose her. I've got such plans for her...'

'Mother—' Caid began resolutely.

'Caid, don't turn me down.'

Grimly he watched as his mother's eyes filled with tears. He had never seen her cry...never.

'This means so much to me...'

'You don't have to tell me that!' Caid responded dryly, and

yet he knew that despite his own feelings he would give in. After all, as his mother had just pointed out, he couldn't afford to see the value of his trust fund stock in the business go down—not now, when he had so much tied up in his ranch. And that, of course, was the only reason he was going, he reminded himself firmly.

'JAZ, I'D LIKE TO HAVE A WORD with you, please.'

Jaz's heart sank as she saw the store's new chief executive bearing down on her. Since returning from New Orleans things had been far from easy for her. She knew that she had been fully justified in everything she'd said to Caid, and that there was no way there could have been a relationship between them, but that still didn't stop her missing what they had shared, or dreaming about him, or waking up with her face wet with tears because she ached for him so much. The last thing she had needed to compound her misery had been the unwanted interference in her work of someone like Jerry Brockmann.

After meeting Caid's mother, and listening to her enthuse about the Cheltenham store and her objectives for it, she had never expected that they would be saddled with a chief executive who seemed to epitomise the exact opposite of what Jaz believed the store was all about. Already the changes he had insisted on making were beginning to affect not just the staff, but their customers as well.

Jaz had lost count of the number of long-standing customers who had commented unfavourably about the fact that the store was no longer perfumed with the specially made room fragrance she herself had chosen as part of the store's exclusive signature.

'What the hell is this stuff made of?' Jerry had complained, as he'd chaired the first departmental heads meeting after his arrival. He'd thrust the bill from the manufacturers beneath Jaz's nose. 'Gold dust? It sure costs enough. Why the hell do we have to scent the damn place anyway? Are the drains bad or something?'

'It creates the right kind of ambience. It's what our customers expect and it encourages them to buy designer fragrances for their own home,' Jaz had replied quietly, trying to ignore his rudeness.

It had been soon after that, and before Jerry had chaired his next meeting, that the chief buyer for their exclusive Designer Fashion Room had announced that she intended to leave.

'He says that he plans to cut my budget by half!' she fumed furiously to Jaz. 'Can you believe that? After what you said about the New Orleans store and its management I'd been putting out feelers to a couple of new up-and-coming designers to see if I could tempt them to let us stock their stuff—and now this! If I stay here now I'm going to totally lose my credibility.'

Jaz felt acutely guilty as she listened to her, and tried to smooth things over, but Lucinda refused to be appeased. She had already handed in her notice she informed Jaz angrily.

Even worse was Jaz's discovery that her closest friend on the staff was also planning to leave.

'But, Kyra, you've always said how much you loved working here,' Jaz protested.

'I *did*,' Krya emphasised. 'But not any more, Jaz. Jerry called me in to his office the other day to inform me that he thinks we should go more downmarket with our bed and bath linens. He said that we were catering for too small a market.'

'Didn't you explain to him that the mass market is so well covered by the multiples that we couldn't possibly compete with them, that it's because we supply only the best that we've got our Royal Warrant?'

'Of course I did,' Kyra had responded indignantly. 'But the man's obsessed by mass sales. He just can't seem to see that this isn't what we're all about. Anyway, the upshot of our "discussion" was that I completely lost it with him and told him what he could do with his mass market bedding *and* his job!'

'Oh, Kyra,' Jaz sympathised.

'Well, as it turns out I've done myself a favour, because I've got a friend who works at Dubai airport—that represents the real luxury end of the market—and she says there's a job for me there if I want it.'

'I'm going to miss you.' Jaz sighed.

'Well, you could always leave yourself,' Kyra pointed out. 'In fact,' she added, 'I don't know why you don't. It can't be for any lack of offers. Oh, I can understand that whilst John still owned the store you must have felt bound by loyalty to him. But now...'

'Perhaps I *should* think about leaving,' Jaz agreed huskily. 'But not yet. Not until—'

'After the Christmas windows?' Kyra supplied ruefully, shaking her head.

Jaz's devotion to her Christmas windows was well known throughout the store.

'It wouldn't be fair,' Jaz told her gently.

'You should think more about being fair to yourself than being fair to other people,' Krya chided. 'Which reminds me. I haven't liked to say anything before, but you haven't been your normal happy self since you came back from New Orleans, Jaz. I don't want to pry, but if you need someone to talk to...?'

'There isn't anything to talk about,' Jaz told her firmly.

'Or anyone?' Kyra persisted gently.

Jaz couldn't help it; she felt the tears stinging her eyes, the emotion blocking her throat, but she managed to deny it to Kyra.

And it was true—in a way. After all, what was the point in talking about Caid?

'Excuse me if I'm coming between you and your private thoughts, Jaz,' she heard Jerry saying sarcastically to her. 'But am I right in thinking that you are supposed to be working?'

Pink-cheeked, Jaz apologised.

'I've been going through John's files and I can't seem to find any budget forecasts for your department.'

Jaz forced herself to ignore the hectoring tone of his voice.

'Traditionally, my department doesn't work to a budget—' she began to explain, but before she could continue Jerry interrupted sharply.

'Well, in future it damn well does. And by in future, Jaz, I mean as of now. I want those forecasts on my desk by close of business tomorrow afternoon.'

He had gone before Jaz could either object or explain, leaving her hot-faced and resentful, her only small consolation the knowledge that it wasn't just her who was suffering.

Since Jerry's arrival the whole atmosphere of the store had changed—and in Jaz's opinion not for the better!

'Jaz, I thought you said the American stores were wonderful, very much on our wavelength. How can they be when Jerry's so obviously trying to turn the store into some kind of dreadful pile-it-high-sell-it-cheap place?' one of the department heads had complained.

'I don't understand what's happening any more than you do,' Jaz had been forced to admit.

'Can't you speak to John?' another of the buyers had urged her.

Jaz had shaken her head. 'No. He isn't very well…his angina is getting worse.'

So much worse, in fact, that on his doctor's advice John had had to move out of the pretty three-storey townhouse adjacent to the store, where he had lived virtually all his life.

For security reasons the Dubois family had insisted on buying the house, along with the store, but John had been granted a long lease on it which allowed him to rent it from them at a peppercorn rental. Jaz knew how upset he had been when his doctor had told him that the house's steep stairs were not suitable for a person with his heart condition.

Luckily he also owned a ground-floor apartment in a renovated Victorian mansion several miles away from her parents, and he was now living there under the watchful eye of his housekeeper.

To Jaz's delight, John had offered her the use of the townhouse in his absence, knowing that Jaz was in between properties herself, having sold the flat she had previously owned and not as yet being able to find somewhere she wanted to buy.

'Are you sure the Dubois family won't mind?' she'd asked John uncertainly when he'd made her his generous offer.

'Why should they?' he had demanded. 'And besides, even though it's not strictly mine any longer, I would feel much happier knowing that the house is occupied by someone I know and trust, Jaz.'

Her new home certainly couldn't be more convenient for her work, Jaz acknowledged; even if right now that work was becoming less and less appealing. But there was no way she could allow herself to leave. Not until after Christmas!

She had started planning this year's windows right after last Christmas, and had come back from New Orleans fired up on a mixture of heartbreak and pride that had made her promise herself that this year's windows would be her swansong—proof that she was getting on with her life as well as a way to show every single member of the Dubois family just how damned good she was. And then she would stand up and announce to them that there was nothing on this earth that would persuade her to go on working for a family of which Caid was a member.

At first she hadn't been sure just what angle to go for—she'd already done fantasy and fairytale, and she'd done modern and punk only the previous year. But then it had happened. Her idea to end all ideas. And the miracle of it was that it was so simple, so workable, so timeless and so…so right.

The theme of her windows this Christmas was going to be Modern Womanhood, in all its many guises. And her modern Christmas woman, in defiance of everything that Caid had thrown at her, was going to be the hub of her family and yet her own independent and individual person as well! Each of the store's windows would reflect a different aspect of her role as a modern woman—and each window would be packed with delectable, irresistible gifts appropriate to that role. Right down to the final one, where she would be shepherding her assembled family to view a traditional Nativity play, complete with every emotion-tugging detail apart from a real live donkey.

Everyone thought that the high point of her year were those few short weeks before Christmas, when her windows went on display, but in fact it was actually those weeks she spent working on the ideas and designs that she loved best.

This year she had spent even more of her time plotting and planning, drawing out window plans and then changing them.

Because she needed to prove to herself that she had made the right decision…because she needed to find in the success of achieving her own targets and goals something satisfying enough to replace what she had lost?

No. She simply wanted to do a good job, that was all…of course it was!

Now her ideas and her plans were almost all in place; there was only one vital piece of research she still needed to do, and her arrangements for that were all in hand.

Jaz was a stickler for detail, for getting things just right. She needed a real-life role model for her 'modern woman'. A role model who successfully combined all the elements of her fictional creation: a woman who was loved and valued by her partner and yet someone who had her own independent life. She needed a woman who acknowledged and enjoyed fulfilling her own personal goals, but still loved her children and her family above all else. A woman, in short, Jaz had dreamed of being herself—until Caid had destroyed those dreams.

Luckily, though, there was someone she could model her 'modern woman' on.

Jamie, her cousin, was in her thirties, ran her own business, and lived in a wonderful country mansion with her adoring husband and their three children.

In fact, if there was anyone Jaz might have been tempted to tell, about Caid and his unreasonable, appalling attitude, it would have been Jamie. But she had sternly refused to allow herself to be so pathetically self-indulgent.

However, what she had done was invite herself to spend a couple of days with Jamie and her family, so that she could observe them at close quarters and reaffirm to her own satisfaction that she had caught the mood of her 'model family'.

And soon when the whole of the retailing world was gasping over her genius, she would have the satisfaction of knowing she had made the right decision—that she had been true to herself.

CHAPTER FOUR

SUNSHINE IN ENGLAND, in autumn! Caid scowled. Right now there was no way that sunshine fitted in with his mood. It was all very well—and no doubt would earn him Brownie points in the cashbook of life—to have impulsively decided to give up his first-class aircraft seat to a worn-out young mother carrying a fractious baby and travelling economy, but right now he was paying the price for his generosity and suffering the after effects of having spent the night with his six foot tall, broad-chested body stuffed into the confines of a too-small economy class seat.

Not that the blame for his current black mood could be laid totally at the feet of a lost night's sleep...

As he got into his hire car, ready for the drive from the airport to Cheltenham, he tried not to think about the last time he and Jaz had been together...the way they had made love so passionately before the awfulness of their ensuing row drove her out of his life...

IT WAS ALMOST LUNCHTIME when Caid arrived in Cheltenham, and he had been wandering around the store, studying its workforce and its customers, for over an hour before anyone realised who he was. And that had only been when, to his own surprise, he had been tempted to buy a pretty antique fan for his great-aunt, who collected them, and had paid the bill with his credit card.

By chance it was the head of the department who had served him, and immediately recognised his name, discreetly and excitedly sending one of the juniors to alert Jerry to the fact that Caid was in the store.

JAZ PAUSED ON HER WAY UP the wonderful Gothic staircase that led from the ground floor of the store to the Designer Fashion Room, trying not to dwell on her latest altercation with Jerry. She concentrated instead on the pleasure and pride that looking down into the heart of the store always gave her.

Caid's mother had told her that she had been so very impressed with the unique layout Jaz had designed for the store that she wanted to adapt it for the American stores.

On the fashion floor clothes were displayed flung over antique brocade-covered sofas and hung on screens, and the cosmetics department, which sold only the most exclusive brands, was housed in a 'boudoir'. The building's original dining room had been redecorated in Georgian red, and was home to a display of the upmarket china, stemware and silver the store sold. It was these details that made the Cheltenham store so unique— a uniqueness that Jerry seemed for some unfathomable reason determined to destroy, Jaz reflected unhappily.

From her vantage point she looked automatically over the ground floor, and then tensed, as she recognised the man walking across it.

Caid. It couldn't be, but it was. Caid was here...in Cheltenham. He had come to tell her that he was sorry, that he realised how wrong he had been.

No firework display on earth could have come anywhere near matching the glorious exultant shock of brilliant explosive joy she was experiencing right now, Jaz acknowledged as she started to hurry down the stairs towards him, her eyes shining with a mixture of love and emotional tears.

'Caid!' As she cried his name he looked at her, his expression unreadable and controlled. How could she have forgotten just how dangerously and excitingly male he was? Her heart started to do frantic back-flips in reaction to her feelings.

'Caid!' She had almost reached him now! 'Caid,' she repeated. Her fingers brushed the sleeve of his suit jacket as she reached out to him, waiting for his arms to open and gather her close. There would just be time for her to look eagerly at his mouth before it covered hers, and then...

'Caid—hi. Why didn't you come straight up to the office? Donny said you were flying in today.'

Jaz froze as she saw Caid looking past her, through her, to Jerry, who was holding out his hand to greet him. Who was saying that *he* had been expecting him. Who had *known* that Caid was due to arrive. Which meant, she told herself nauseously, that Caid had not come here to see her at all, as she had so stupidly thought.

'What are *you* doing down here? Shouldn't you be working?'

Locked in the painful realisation of the truth, it was several seconds before Jaz realised that Jerry's loud-voiced criticism was directed at her.

Her face flaming, she saw that Caid was now looking directly at her. And it certainly wasn't love she could see in his eyes, she acknowledged miserably.

'Gee, Caid, you just wouldn't believe what I have to put up with from these people. I hate to be critical of your mom, but I have to say that Donny was right to question the buying of this store. I mean, the overheads! And the administration!' Jerry had started to shake his head. 'They don't have the faintest idea. And as for time-wasting!' He raised his voice pointedly as he flared up at Jaz. 'I thought I told you to go and work on your budgets. Have you done them, or is this your way of telling me that you don't know how to draw up a budget?'

Jaz could feel her face starting to burn with anger as well as pain and embarrassment as she was forced to stand and listen to Jerry insulting her.

'You said that the budgets had to be on your desk tomorrow afternoon,' she reminded him.

For some reason Caid had moved, was now standing closer to her. She could feel the bitter little tug of pain on her heart as she reflected that not so very long ago she would have automatically assumed he had moved closer to her in order to protect her. But after the way he had just looked at her—and then through her—she was under no such illusion! No doubt he was relishing hearing Jerry criticise and humiliate her.

'See what I mean?' Jerry appealed to Caid, totally ignoring

Jaz. 'Back home I would have had those budgets by now—no question. These people haven't a clue, Caid. And if you ask me the whole place is overstaffed anyway. If this store is going to turn in a profit one hell of a lot of changes need to be made—starting with getting rid of unproductive staff. Anyway, welcome on board. It will be good to have some decent down-home support here. Come on up to the office…'

'I'll be with you in a minute,' Jaz heard Caid saying to Jerry.

Jerry frowned as his mobile phone started to ring. 'It's Donny,' he told Caid.

'That's fine. You come on up to the office when you're ready.'

Caid waited until Jerry was out of earshot before turning back to Jaz, but the moment he did so she wheeled round on her heel and started to walk away from him.

'Just a minute!' he cautioned her, automatically reaching out to grab her arm and stop her leaving.

She was so fine-boned that his fingers closed easily around her arm.

Eyes glittering with pride and anger, she turned on him, demanding furiously, 'Let go of me at once.'

'Not yet,' Caid refused. 'Is Jerry always like that?' he asked frowning.

'In general, do you mean, or just with me?' Jaz challenged him.

'Does it make any difference?' Caid shot back.

'I don't know—you tell me.' Jaz gave an angry little shrug. 'And whilst you're about it perhaps you can tell me why you want to know! Is it out of concern for the morale of the staff? Or perhaps because it would give you some kind of pleasure to know that it was just directed at me? After all, we both know that it would give you a great deal of satisfaction to see me being punished, don't we? A man like you could never tolerate knowing that a woman would prefer to be on her own and have her career rather than live in the middle of nowhere as your possession.'

Jaz had no idea why she was behaving like this, other than a hazy recognition that it had something to do with her reaction to seeing him here in the store—that coupled with the knowledge that she had been about to make a complete and total fool of herself before she'd realised he had not come here to see her. But, whatever the reason for her verbal attack on him, she couldn't afford to back down now—and what was more she had no intention of doing so!

'Or is your concern on another level altogether? Motivated by a fear that the Dubois Corporation could be sued for condoning the harassment of its employees?' she continued.

'Now, look here—'

As he inhaled savagely above her, Jaz felt Caid jerk on her arm, drawing her closer to his body. Frantic to break free—not because she was afraid of him, but because she was afraid of herself and what the proximity between them might do to her—Jaz reached out with her free hand and clawed the exposed wrist of the hand gripping her arm.

'Why, you little she-cat,' Caid breathed in disbelief as they both stared at the red weals her nails had left against his skin.

Against his will he could feel himself reacting to her—and to her anger. Earlier, listening to Jerry verbally abusing her, it had been all he could do to stop himself from grabbing the other man by his jacket lapels and demanding that he leave Jaz alone. But now...

Now it was Jaz he felt like grabbing and holding—until he silenced her venom with his mouth.

Instinctively Jaz jerked back from him. He mustn't touch her, mustn't breach her defences. But the heat she could see shimmering in his eyes wasn't caused by desire, she recognised; it was caused by fury.

'Let go of me, Caid.' she demanded in a low voice. 'People are staring. And besides, I've got work to do...remember?'

As he turned his head to glance round Jaz seized her moment and took advantage of his slackened grip on her arm to pull away from him.

Grim-lipped, Caid watched as she made her escape. His eyes felt gritty and sore, but the adrenalin was pumping round his veins.

For a minute, when he had first seen her, his urge…his need to go to her and claim her, to beg her to give him—them—a second chance, had been fiercely intense! In fact if Jerry hadn't been there he doubted he would have been able to stop himself from taking hold of her! Why couldn't she see that they were made to be together? Why couldn't she realise that he was right? If she had loved him enough she would have done, he reminded himself bitterly. And there was no way he intended to allow himself to give a single damn about a woman who didn't love him one hundred per cent…no, one hundred and fifty per cent. Because that sure as hell was the way he had been prepared to love her!

It was almost an hour since she'd walked away from Caid, but she still hadn't stopped starting up nervously every time she heard footsteps in the corridor outside her workroom.

The budgets she had come here expressly to work on had not progressed beyond a few mere notes. Right now it was a battle to think of something as mundane as what she was going to have for her supper this evening, never mind anything more demanding. Right now her every single thought was occupied by one Caid Dubois!

Not that he deserved or merited the exclusive attention of her thoughts any more than he deserved her love. Anyway, what love? she challenged herself, her body stiffening. She didn't love Caid. She was over him. How could she not after the way he had behaved towards her? After he had shown her how overbearing and selfish he was—after he had made it plain to her how unimportant he considered *her* dreams and ambitions to be.

No way could she ever ever love a man like that.

No, she told herself firmly, what she was feeling now was anger against herself because of the stupid way she had reacted when she'd first seen him. Thank goodness she'd come to her senses and had been able to show him exactly how she did feel about him!

How could she possibly have thought he'd come to see her

when it was so obvious that he had not? But what *was* he doing here?

Had Jerry been sent here to do a clean sweep of the store's original personnel in such a way as to avoid any claims against the Dubois Corporation? Surely that was a far-fetched, indeed almost paranoid suggestion?

Jerry had made it very clear Caid was here to back him up. And, given Caid's reaction towards her, it seemed obvious to Jaz that he would enjoy making life as difficult and unpleasant for her as he could!

Well, she certainly wasn't going to give way…to allow herself to be pushed out of a job she loved. When she left the store—*if* she left it—it would be on her own terms and in her own time. Not because she was running scared from anyone, and most especially not from Caid Dubois.

She looked at her watch. Today was supposed to be her half-day, but it was almost halfway through the afternoon now.

At times of crisis in her life she had always sought and found solace and escape in her work. So stuffing the pieces of paper on her desk into a drawer, she got up. She would go next door, to the privacy of her temporary home, and work there—safely away from Caid and any temptation…

Temptation? What temptation? No way was she in danger of any kind of temptation, she assured herself firmly. Unless it was the temptation to tell Caid Dubois just how lucky she considered herself to be in having found out what an unbearable, unappealing, stubborn, selfish, sexy, impossible and arrogant specimen of the male sex he was!

JAZ GRIMACED ANGRILY to herself. Not even a long soak in the bath, whilst listening to the soothing sound of her special relaxation tape had managed to calm the turbulent effect on her senses of seeing Caid.

Pulling on her bathrobe, she went into the spare bedroom.

She hoped that working would keep Caid out of her head and her thoughts. And out of her heart?

Angrily she pushed the taunting little question away. He

wasn't in her heart. She had locked him out of it and she intended to keep him locked out!

She had work to do, she reminded herself, and working was very definitely a far healthier and more constructive thing to do than brooding on what had happened at the store.

Jaz opened the portfolio containing the sketches she'd made for the Christmas window displays.

The first window would depict the woman in her home as she studied her Christmas present list. She would be surrounded by gifts she had heaped up on the floor, along with wrapping paper and ribbons. After all, what better way to display the range of gift wrappings available in the store? On a small table in prominent view would be a photograph of her family, so that those looking into the window could see whom she had bought the gifts for.

Jaz smiled as she studied her drawings. So far so good. As yet she had merely outlined where the pile of gifts was to go—the textbooks, the laptop computer and the student pass, the golfing equipment and a cookbook of quick meals for one—but these gifts were not traditional. No, in her desire to show the complexities of this 'modern family' and its life Jaz had chosen to be slightly controversial. The student gifts were for the woman's mother-in-law, who had always secretly yearned to finish her education, and the cookbook was for her father-in-law—a hint that with his wife back studying he would need to learn to be more self-sufficient. The golf paraphernalia was destined not for the woman's husband, or her father, but for the second of her sons, whose dreams were of becoming a world-class golf pro.

To facilitate the onlookers' ability to recognise all this, Jaz had come up with the idea of depicting in other windows a member of her 'family' with two thought bubbles—one showing what he or she expected traditionally to receive and the other showing what they really longed for—as they gazed at their private dream surroundings, designed to echo their true desires.

It was a complex and ambitious scheme, but Jaz knew it was going to work. She knew too that it would be thought-provoking and cause interest, which would be good for the store and—she hoped—good for their customers, who would hopefully be tempted to be more adventurous in their choice of gifts!

In the final window she was giving in to sentimentality, she knew, in having her family viewing the traditional Nativity scene. But she hoped that this would show their customers that her modern woman, depicted in each window trying to balance her career, family life and home responsibilities, was still in touch with the realities of life. And that was why in her Nativity scene Jaz intended to highlight the presence of the infant Jesus's mother.

It was only where the woman's gifts *from* her family were concerned that she was having a problem. So far she had been toying with the idea of having the 'family' present her with beautiful antique and modern boxes, each of which would contain that member's feelings—'joy', 'love', 'happiness'—but ruefully she admitted to herself that she still needed to work on this concept.

Discarded drawings and notes covered the spare bedroom's bed, and in one corner of the room was a small mock-up of her first window. Only the staff who worked directly with her were allowed to know the content of the windows before they were opened to public view, and that was another reason why Jaz had been so pleased to be invited to make use of John's house, so conveniently situated right next to the store...

STILL FUMING AFTER HIS argument with JAZ, Caid left the store and headed for his temporary home, determined to rest and *not* think about her.

At such short notice it had proved impossible for him to find suitable accommodation in Cheltenham, but when he had pointed this out to his mother she had accused him of looking for excuses to back out of going.

'You can stay with John—like I would have done,' she had told him firmly.

'He told me when he was over here that his house has two large bedrooms, each with its own bathroom, and that he'd be delighted to have any of us stay whenever we choose. All we have to do is ring and let him know.'

'Okay.' Caid had capitulated, knowing when he was beaten.

He had only been in the store a couple of hours, but it was already obvious to him that Jerry was causing a good deal of unrest and unhappiness amongst the staff. And as for the way he had spoken to Jaz...

Caid frowned at he mounted the three stone steps that led to the front door of John's house. Why couldn't he stop thinking about Jaz? She was clearly not what he wanted. Jaz was a committed career woman, in no need of his championship or support.

Career women. He reached for the door-knocker. Why did his life have to be plagued by them?

Jaz made a small exasperated sound as she heard someone knocking on the front door. She wasn't expecting anyone and she was hardly dressed for visitors.

Ignoring the knocking, she concentrated on what she was doing.

Outside in the street, Caid grimaced in irritation, and then reminded himself that John was an elderly man with a heart condition—who surely should not, he recognised frowningly, be living in a three-storey building!

He reached for the knocker again, and this time banged it just a little bit louder and longer.

Jaz gave a small feline growl of resentment as she heard the door-knocker a second time. The visitor—whoever he or she was—plainly wasn't going to go away.

Getting to her feet, she opened the bedroom door and headed for the stairs.

Caid was just beginning to question whether his mother might have given John the wrong date for his arrival, when the house door was suddenly pulled open.

Only it wasn't John who was standing in the hallway glaring belligerently at him; it was Jaz.

'You!'

'You!'

CHAPTER FIVE

CAID WAS THE FIRST TO RECOVER and break the tense atmosphere of spiky silence. 'I'd like to see John,' he announced in a clipped voice.

'John?' Jaz let her breath escape in a small, secret, leaky sigh of relief. For a moment she'd thought that Caid had actually come to the house to continue the argument they'd been having in the store.

'Yes, John,' Caid agreed sardonically. 'He lives here—remember? And so for the next few weeks shall I be. Now, if you would kindly tell him that I'm here?'

'What? No!' Jaz started to shake her head in fierce denial. 'No!' she repeated. 'You can't stay here.'

Caid had had enough. He told himself it was jet lag that was making him feel the way he was feeling right now, and nothing at all to do with Jaz. 'Give me one good reason why not.' he demanded ominously.

Jaz reminded herself that it was anger that was making her shake inside, and absolutely nothing else. 'Because *I* am living here,' she told him. 'John invited me to,' she hurried on as she saw the way Caid's eyes were narrowing as he looked at her. 'When his angina got worse he moved away—and he didn't say anything to me about *you* staying here,' she informed him defiantly.

'Well, he sure as hell didn't mention anything to me about *your* presence,' Caid retaliated grittily.

'No—you can't come in,' Jaz protested angrily as Caid picked up his bag and shouldered open the front door, making his way inside before turning round in the confines of the long narrow hallway and closing it firmly.

'No?' he challenged Jaz in a deliberately exaggerated drawl. 'So who's gonna make me leave, honey? You?'

'Don't you dare call me that,' Jaz protested in a suffocating voice.

'Why not?' Caid taunted her. 'I don't remember hearing you complain before. Far from it. In fact, as I remember, you seemed to kinda like it—leastways that was the impression you gave me!' he told her with a deliberately insolent look that made Jaz burn with fury.

'If there's one thing I loathe and detest more than a man who believes that a woman should be subordinate to him, it's a man who behaves like a boorish, insensitive male brute, so desperate to prove just how wonderful he is that he tries to boast about…about imaginary sexual conquests! All it does is prove how *un*sexy he is!' Jaz burst out.

'Imaginary? Oh, no.' Caid told her softly. 'There's no way what happened between us—the way you gave yourself to me— was "imaginary". And as for me being unsexy…you know, honey, some men…might just be ungallant enough to think that that's a kinda come-on…an encouragement…a challenge thrown at them so that they feel they have to prove their sexuality.'

'How dare you say that?' Jaz breathed. 'No way would I give any man—and most especially you—any kind of come-on. I don't want anything from you, Caid, other than to have nothing more to do with you. You can't stay here!'

Was it really possible than he had grown taller, broader, more…more of everything male than she remembered?

'I don't have any option,' Caid told her shortly. 'There isn't anywhere else.'

Jaz frowned. She knew how busy the town was at certain times of the year. But there was no way she was going to allow Caid to force her into giving up the house to him—at least not until she had spoken with John.

'Why don't you go and share with Jerry?' she suggested

nastily. 'I've heard that he's taken a whole suite at the Grand Hotel—'

'Room with Jerry? I'd as soon move in with a polecat,' Caid drawled and then stopped and subjected her to a look that made Jaz's whole body burn from the top of her head right down to the toes she was currently curling into the carpet.

'Is it a British custom for a woman to answer the door in her bathrobe? Funny… Back home we also consider that to be kind of giving a man a come-on…'

'I wasn't expecting anyone to call,' Jaz defended herself, adding hotly, 'And I wouldn't have answered the door if—'

'If you had known it was me?' Caid supplied for her. 'And yet somehow or other I got the impression a little earlier on today that you were all too ready to give me a warm welcome.'

Jaz gasped in furious indignation.

So he *had* noticed!

Well, now it was time he was made to notice something else.

'That was a mistake,' she told him haughtily. 'I thought…'

'You thought what?' Caid encouraged her.

'I thought you'd come to your senses and wanted to apologise to me,' Jaz told him, revealing her pretty teeth in a nasty smile.

'Me, apologise to you?' Dark flags of angry male pride burned against Caid's taut cheekbones. 'Now, let's get one thing straight,' he told her savagely, 'there's only one reason I'm here and it has nothing to do with apologising to anyone for anything…'

'I see. So why exactly are you here?' Jaz challenged him.

Caid looked briefly away, guarding his expression from her. He could scarcely tell her right now what his mother wanted him to do. The mood she was in she was more than likely to hand in her notice right here and now…

'I can't say,' he told her coolly. 'It's family business…'

Jaz's heart jumped. So she had been right!

Feigning a casual attitude she was far from feeling, she shrugged and started to turn away from him, saying, 'There's no need to be secretive, Caid. I've already worked out for myself why you're here—and I might as well tell you right now that you're wasting your time! We've got laws about that kind of thing in this country!' she threw at him wildly. She wasn't sure if what she was saying was strictly true, but she was determined to show him that she was not going to be intimidated.

Grimly Caid listened to her. After hearing the way Jerry had spoken to her he couldn't pretend to be surprised that she was determined to leave, but he knew his mother. She would expect him to do far more than simply passively accept Jaz's decision without making any attempt to persuade her to change her mind.

He just never learned, did he? Caid reflected in self-disgust. From the moment he'd been born his mother had relentlessly turned his life upside down. If he'd listened to his own instincts he would never have agreed to come to Cheltenham in the first place. But now that he was here there was no way he was going to give up a comfortable bed on Jaz's say-so.

'Where are you going?' Jaz demanded sharply as Caid picked up his bag and headed for the stairs.

'To bed,' he drawled promptly.

'Oh, no, you aren't. Not here!' Jaz denied.

One foot on the first stair, Caid turned round, breathing in rather pointedly as he told her with exquisitely polite steeliness, 'I thought I'd already made myself plain on this one, Jaz. Where you choose to sleep is your affair, and likewise where I choose to sleep is mine. Right now I choose to sleep here. If you don't like that, then don't let me stop you finding yourself a bed somewhere else.'

Somewhere else! Jaz glared at him.

'John offered this house to me, and I am not moving out unless he asks me to,' Jaz told him, incensed.

How dared Caid expect her to give up the house for him? Let *him* find somewhere else to stay.

Caid put down his case, folded his arms across his chest and looked at her. 'I have just flown across the Atlantic, and I am in no mood for an argument. I need a bed and eight hours' sleep, and I fully intend to have both.'

'Maybe you do, but you are not going to have them in this house,' Jaz told him furiously.

'Oh, yes, I am!' Caid corrected her flatly. 'In this house and right now.'

'There's no way I am moving out of here until John tells me to,' Jaz repeated. Her colour was high and so was her temper. He was trying to bully her. Well, he wasn't going to. No way. And besides, she had nowhere else she could go at such short notice, other than her parents' home.

'My God, but you like to live dangerously, don't you?' Caid grated savagely. 'Don't push me too hard, Jaz. Because if you do you might get far more than you bargained for. Right now it wouldn't take very much for me to—'

'To what?' Jaz challenged him recklessly. 'To treat me the way you did in New Orleans?' Bitterly she started to shake her head. 'No way. No—'

'I don't seem to remember you doing any objecting at the time,' Caid interrupted her grimly. She might be claiming that she didn't want him now, but she hadn't faked her sexual response to him when they had been lovers. And if she continued to push him hard enough, he might be sorely tempted to prove that to her.

'Why don't you take a walk into the town?' Jaz threw at him. 'You might find it's a good way of easing your temper as well as finding yourself a hotel room.'

That was it! Caid had had enough. More than enough!

Advancing on her, he told Jaz through gritted teeth, 'Don't push your luck. Because right now the only way I'd like to ease my temper is by taking hold of you and—'

Caid knew how dangerously volatile the situation had become. He was also aware just how much of his anger was being fuelled by emotions he should not be feeling. Jaz was deliberately trying to incite him.

Things were going too far. Jaz knew that, and suddenly she felt very vulnerable. The sex between them had been so potent, so overpowering. Would she really be strong enough to resist him if he should…?

'You wouldn't dare,' Jaz breathed.

Somewhere at the back of her mind a cautionary little voice

was warning her that the mood had shifted from anger to excitement and arousal. Why couldn't she control her feelings around Caid?

'No?'

The very softness of his voice was enough to send alarm scudding through her. He had closed the distance between them, was already reaching for her, imprisoning her with arms that bound her to him whilst his mouth plundered hers with a furious refusal to be denied.

A hot, raw agony of longing seethed through her, enveloping her in mind-blowing waves of aching need. She was so hungry for him, for his touch, his mouth, for the feel of his body. With a little whimper Jaz reached out to touch him—and then stopped, her body freezing in self-disgust and horror.

'No!'

Her choked denial pulled Caid up short and reminded him of just what the situation between them was. But he couldn't shake the red-hot image branded into his mind of the two of them together, her naked body held fast against his, whilst he punished her for each inflammable word that she'd spoken. For refusing to see things his way, refusing to be the woman he needed and wanted her to be.

'You're right, Jaz. You can't be the woman I want. The woman I thought you were.'

The bitterness in Caid's voice shocked Jaz. Somehow it was far more painful for her to hear than his anger. The feeling of desolation and loss that suddenly rushed over her from out of nowhere, swamping her with its intensity, frightened her. Instinctively she struggled against it. There was no way she was going to allow herself to be dragged back into the black hole of despair and heartache she had suffered on her return from New Orleans. The very thought made her shake from head to foot with fear. She now realised she'd never really admitted just how deep the pain had been.

Caid was the first man she had truly loved, trusted and believed in. She'd committed herself to him heart and soul. Every now and again, in her darkest moments, the thought tormented her that he would be the only man she would feel all those things for. But Jaz prided herself on her own inner strength. She had needed that strength when she was growing up, and now she needed it again.

Love at first sight, a meeting of hearts, souls and minds, a sharing of goals in a love that would last a lifetime. That was what she had believed she had found with Caid. But she had been so very, very wrong.

No MATTER HOW FRAGILE and appealing Jaz might look in her bathrobe, with her hair casually tied back and her face flushed and free of make-up, he knew what she really was, Caid told himself angrily. A more stubborn, wrong-thinking, argumentative, independently sassy woman he had yet to meet. Why the hell had nature decided to give her such a tempting, sensual body? The kind of body that made him ache in a hundred different ways... She had the tiniest waist, wonderfully curving hips, and long, long slim legs. And as for her breasts... Couldn't she have also been given a personality he would have found equally irresistible, equally in tune with his?

Giving in just wasn't something that existed in Caid's emotional vocabulary—after all, his mother had never given in to his pleas for her to stay with him, had she? Compromise wasn't a word he normally recognised either, but right now...

Caid closed his eyes.

The thoughts he was having at this moment were as unique to him as they were dangerous.

Instinctively he fought to eject them, in the same way he had fought all his life to maintain his hard-won emotional independence.

If there was anywhere else at all where he could spend the night he knew he would be high-tailing it out of the house right now. Just being weak enough to admit to the thoughts he was having made him furiously angry with Jaz, for being the cause of them, and even more frustrated with himself. But there wasn't anywhere else. He already knew that.

WHY ON EARTH DIDN'T SHE SIMPLY WALK past him and leave? Jaz asked herself miserably.

All right, so it would take her a couple of hours to drive to her parents' farm...and a couple of hours to drive back again for work every day, she reminded herself grimly. But at least at home with her parents she would be safe...

Safe from what? she challenged herself. Safe from her own thoughts? Mentally she derided herself. What was she going to do? Leave them behind her here in the house?

Anyway why should she give in to Caid? Why should she be bullied by him? Uncle John had given *her* the use of the house.

'You can say and do what you like. I'm not leaving,' she told Caid flatly.

'Don't tempt me,' Caid growled.

Jaz flashed him a bitter look, but before she could say anything to her horror she felt her eyes suddenly began to sting with tears.

From what felt like another lifetime she could hear the echo of Caid's voice, whispering throatily to her, 'You tempt and torment me in a thousand ways, each of them uniquely pleasurable, each of them uniquely you.'

That had been the first night they had met...the first time he had kissed her...

'I'm going down to my car now, to get the rest of my stuff,' Caid warned her grimly. 'And when I come back...'

'You'll do what?' Jaz challenged him, grateful for the reviving surge of fury that had obliterated her earlier misery. 'Throw me out bodily? If you dare to lay so much as one finger on me—'

She stopped as she saw the way he was looking at her.

'Funny how things change,' he drawled, but Jaz could see the hot anger banked down in his eyes and wasn't deceived by the slow softness of his voice. 'Not so very long ago you were begging me to lay one hell of a lot more than a finger on you, honey, and when I did I don't recall you objecting—unless it was to tell me that you wanted even more.'

His smug, sure male confidence made Jaz want to physically

tear it from him and jump up and down on it until it was as damaged and battered as her own pride.

If she hadn't been convinced before of just how much better off she was without him she should be now, and she told herself grimly. Only the most callous and uncaring of men could say something like that.

'Nothing to say?' he mocked her.

Fiercely Jaz blinked away the threatening tears. To cry now, in front of him, would be her final humiliation. But she couldn't bear the way he was destroying the bittersweet memories which only now she was being forced to acknowledge she had foolishly clung on to.

'If you think you can bully me into giving in and doing what you want, Caid, you're wrong,' she told him quietly, before turning her back on him and heading towards the master bedroom.

Furiously Caid watched her. She had a way of getting under his skin and making him itch that no medical team in the world could possibly find a cure for.

SHE HAD MEANT WHAT SHE SAID to Caid about not being bullied into leaving, Jaz decided as she heard the front door close behind him. No matter how much pain it might cause her to stay here, under the same roof as him. From a practical point of view the house had two bedrooms, after all.

Deep down inside Jaz knew that her decision, her obstinacy and her pride, had nothing whatsoever to do with the house at all, but one hell of a lot to do with that idiotic way she had reacted when she had first seen him in the store earlier.

How could she have been stupid enough to think he had come to see her? To have wanted him to have come to see her!

How could she possibly love a man who was just…just a…a hatchet man, who had both supported and enjoyed the floor show Jerry had given as he'd tried to manoeuvre her into leaving?

He had shown her just how little she meant to him. Now he was going to be shown that he meant nothing whatsoever to her! Less than nothing! Less than less than nothing!

Furiously, she pulled open the doors of the wardrobe she was using and started to remove her clothes, knowing that it would be far easier to transfer them to the other bedroom, which she was using as a workroom, than to move and re-set up her work. Both bedrooms were the same size. It was simply that the spare bedroom had a good strong northern light which was much better for her work.

There was one thing that did concern her, though, and that was the fact that Uncle John had made no mention of his invitation to Caid to her. She knew how concerned her parents had been earlier in the year, when the stress of the sale of the business had caused John to become a little bit forgetful on occasions, and the last thing Jaz wanted to do was to upset her godfather. But her forehead started to pucker into an anxious little frown.

SILENTLY JAZ LOOKED AT HER bedside clock. Four o'clock in the morning! She had been awake since one, and prior to that she had hardly slept, her mind too full of painful, angry thoughts to allow her to relax.

Her heart was thumping in heavy anxious thuds whilst her head seethed with frantic, desperate thoughts.

No way was she going to be forced to leave the job she loved and had put so much into. Her windows for this year were going to be her best ever! But she knew that there was equally no way she could do her best work, give of her best, for a concern that did not value or appreciate her.

It hurt to recognise that the praise Caid's mother had given her, the interest she had shown in her, had not been genuine. Perhaps she just wasn't up to the world of big business, she acknowledged unhappily.

She turned over onto her side and tried to summon sleep, but it was totally impossible.

Perhaps if she got up and made herself a soothing hot drink that would help.

Quietly Jaz made her way to the kitchen and switched on the kettle.

In New Orleans Caid had teased her about how deeply she slept, tucked up against his side, burrowing into his warmth and staying there until he kissed her awake in the morning.

He had laughed too, at her shyness the first morning he had shared a shower with her, whispering that he couldn't believe she was being so prim when the previous night she had so passionately abandoned herself to him. But then, when she had reluctantly explained that he was the first man she had shared so much intimacy with, and that the total sum of her previous experience had been nothing more than a fumbled rite of passage with an equally virginal fellow student, something she had felt she had to do rather than something she'd overwhelmingly wanted to do, his laughter had died. And the tenderness with which he had treated her had brought emotional tears to her eyes.

And now tears were suddenly stinging her eyes again, at the memory of that tenderness.

Her hands trembling, Jaz reached for the cup of herbal tea she had made for herself, and then gasped in shock as it slid through her shaking fingers, spilling hot tea on her bare skin before crashing to the floor and breaking.

Almost boiling, the tea had been hot enough to cause serious burns, and the shock of her pain made her cry out sharply.

Caid heard Jaz cry out as he lay motionless and wide awake in his bed.

By rights he ought to have been asleep, and he had determinedly been putting the fact that he was not down to jet lag rather than admit that it could in any possible way be because of Jaz. But the minute he heard her cry he was out of bed and on his feet, reaching for his robe and pulling it on.

Two minutes later Jaz was shakily trying to insist to him that she was perfectly all right as he knelt at her feet, commanding her tersely not to move as he picked up the broken shards of crockery.

'Look, I can do that myself,' Jaz protested.

She wished he would not kneel so close to her, nor block her exit from the kitchen with his male bulk. His hair was shiny and tousled, and for some reason as she looked down at the top of his head she ached to reach out and stroke her fingers through it.

His body had that clean soap smell she still remembered, and his bare feet were so much larger than her own, his skin so much browner... As he stood up to dispose of the broken cup she gave an involuntary shiver, which he immediately registered and reacted to with a frown.

'Please go back to bed,' Jaz begged him stiffly. 'I can clean up the rest myself.'

Her fingers were covering her arm where the burn was beginning to throb painfully.

'It's four o'clock in the morning.' Caid told her, ignoring her to reach for a cloth to mop up the spilled tea. 'Just what exactly were you doing making tea?'

'Perhaps I happen to like a cup of tea at four in the morning,' Jaz told him sharply. 'Not that it's any business of yours!'

'Not unless you spill it all over the place and wake me up,' Caid agreed dryly, conveniently ignoring the fact that he had been very far from asleep.

'I'm sorry if I disturbed you,' Jaz apologised insincerely.

'You don't disturb me, Jaz!' Caid told her silkily. 'Not any more. But something obviously disturbs *you*, if you need to be making yourself cups of tea in the early hours. The Jaz I remember slept like— Something bothering you?' he taunted unkindly, as Jaz suddenly tried to push past him, and his hand reached for her arm to stop her.

The moment his fingers closed over her burned skin Jaz let out a whimper of pain, and her face paled so quickly that Caid's frown deepened.

Removing his hand, but still blocking her exit from the kitchen, he studied her arm. He could see that her skin had been badly burned and looked very sore, with a blister already starting to form where the hot tea had scalded her.

'That needs some attention,' he told Jaz firmly.

'Yes, I do know,' Jaz agreed angrily. 'It is after all my arm.

And if you will just get out of my way that is exactly what I am going to give it.'

She just hoped that John had something in his bathroom cupboard she could put on the burn. It was now beginning to feel very uncomfortable.

'You can't manage to dress it by yourself,' said Caid. 'You'd better let me deal with it.'

Him? Touch her? No way! Jaz opened her mouth to tell him as much and then closed it again, her objections forgotten as her glance inadvertently dropped to his body. His robe had come open whilst he had been cleaning up the mess, exposing the hair-roughened warmth of his chest.

A dizzying wave of sensation swamped her. It must be the pain of her arm that was making her feel like this, she said to herself, as she tried to drag her gaze from his torso and discovered that she couldn't. She could still remember how wonderful it had felt—he had felt—that first time she had touched his naked body...

Caid's family had taken her and John out for dinner, and John had stayed on at the restaurant to continue talking business whilst she had opted to walk back to their hotel. Caid had offered to escort her, insisting that she ought not to walk through the streets of the French Quarter on her own.

The evening had been hot and sultry. They had walked slowly through the streets, talking to one another. She had known by then just how she felt about him, and, although he had been discreet about it, Caid had shown her by his attentiveness towards her that he shared her desire.

They had come to a quiet shadowy corner and Caid had drawn her to him, telling her thickly, 'If I don't kiss you soon I am going to go crazy.'

And then he had covered her lips with his and kissed her with such urgency and intensity that Jaz had been oblivious to anything and anyone but him. When he had kissed her exposed throat and shoulder she had shuddered in hot response, unable to resist slipping her hand inside the unfastened neck of his shirt. And then somehow one thing had led to another.

Before they had finally broken apart his shirt had been unbuttoned right down to the waist and her breasts had been aching so much for the touch of his hands that when they had finally reached her room, and Caid had pushed her up against the bedroom door the moment he had closed it, she had actually helped him to tug down the top of her dress…

'Jaz—you aren't going to faint on me, are you?'

Abruptly she dragged herself back to the present, fiercely swallowing against the tears of self-pity she could feel filling her eyes.

In the bathroom, Caid dealt quickly and efficiently with her burn—dressing it and then bandaging it in a far more effective way than she could have managed herself, she was forced to acknowledge.

As a rancher he was, of course, very self-sufficient—would be well used to dealing with minor medical crises. She, on the other hand, was not used to dealing with the touch of the man she had thought loved her but who she had discovered did not. And the effect it was having on her was thoroughly unsettling.

JAZ HAD JUST GOT BACK into bed, and was about to switch off her bedside lamp, when the door opened and Caid stood in the doorway.

Her heart leapt, then skidded to a frantic halt before slamming against her breastbone.

Caid had come to her room. What…?

'I've made you a fresh cup of tea.'

Wordlessly Jaz stared at him, wondering why on earth so prosaic an action should make her want to cry so badly.

GRIMLY CAID STRODE THROUGH the store. He had barely slept at all the previous night, knowing that Jaz was so close to him, that only a mere wall separated them, and that there was nothing apart from his own will-power to stop him from going to her and—

He was here to work, he reminded himself angrily, not to waste his time thinking about Jaz. He had been so furious with her when she had refused to quit the house, his fury partially driven by shock and partially by jet lag-induced exhaustion. Just seeing her had made him ache to take hold of her, show her just what her stubborn refusal had destroyed. But somehow he had made himself keep his distance from her, had gone down to his car to collect his bags.

He had returned to find Jaz standing in the middle of the bedroom floor, the bed in front of her stacked with clothes and other personal possessions she was in the process of removing from its cupboard and wardrobes.

At first he had thought that she'd given in and she was going to move out, and his heart had slammed against his ribs before doing a very slow and uncomfortable somersault that in no way could he pretend to himself constituted a victory roll.

The thought that she was leaving had created a good many complex feelings inside him, but not one of them had come anywhere near approximating triumph!

As he had stood there watching her she had looked antagonistically at him and grabbed a handful of underwear from the drawer she had just pulled open, telling him belligerently, 'I can't stop you from staying here, if you're going to be ungentlemanly enough to insist on doing so, but there is no way I am going to move out, and no way you can make me! Anyway, it just so happens that the house has two bedrooms.'

'And you, being the altruistic human being that you are, are moving your stuff out of this one for me?'

Desperate to ignore the relief seeping like venom through his veins, Caid had made his voice as deliberately cynical as he could.

'Not for you,' Jaz had corrected him immediately. 'But *because* of you. And my work is in the other room.' She had given a small dismissive shrug as she had told him, 'It makes more sense to move my clothes rather than my work.'

As she had spoken she had made her way forward to the door, carrying the huge pile of clothes she had picked up off the bed.

Unable to stop himself, Caid had responded bitterly and unchivalrously. 'Yeah, after all—as I have good cause to know—

removing your clothes is something that comes easily and unimportantly to you. You sure enough removed them pretty fast for me.'

Jaz had gasped and gone white, her voice a whispery thin flicker of raw sound as she'd responded, 'Thank you, Caid. You've just confirmed everything I already know about you. How lucky I am to have you out of my life.'

And she had walked past him with her head held high, for the entire world as though she were the innocent party!

When she had left Caid had glanced down at the floor and seen the delicate lacy garment she had dropped. Bending down, he had picked it up. It was a tiny fragile cream lacy thong he'd last seen adorning Jaz's body. There were women who could wear thongs and women who could not, and when it came to Jaz—well, Jaz's delicious derriÈre would stop the traffic. Fully clothed!

Following her through the door, Caid had crossed the corridor and pushed open the half-closed door of the other bedroom. When she had seen that he had followed her, her mouth had compressed, her eyes widening and then darkening with anger.

Her eyes really were the most extraordinary colour, Caid acknowledged now, shimmering through a thousand different shades with each of her emotions. When she was aroused they turned the colour of molasses; when she was complete and satisfied they glowed pure gold...

What the hell was he thinking about? he derided himself, dragging his renegade thoughts away from the treacherous quicksands of Jaz's sensuality and his own reaction to it.

'What are you doing in here?' Jaz had demanded sharply, glowering at him.

'You dropped this,' Caid had replied, dangling the tiny scrap of cream lace from his finger.

If he was honest, there was a part of him that had taken a grim sort of pleasure in her reaction. Her skin had flushed the colour of a Colorado sunset in winter. She had given a small, sharp gasp and then reached out to snatch the thong from him.

'Give it to me. It's mine,' she insisted, when Caid had stepped back from her, his a hand closing round the lace.

'Funny how little it takes to turn a man into a fool,' Caid had responded as he'd tossed the lace to her.

Caid had known as he spoke that he was being ungallant, that he was delivering a low blow and descending to the kind of depths he would never normally have stooped to, but just holding that intimate scrap of female apparel, remembering how good things had been between them, how good they still could have been between them if only Jaz would see sense, had filled him with such a burning sense of outrage and anguish that he hadn't been able to stop himself.

Somehow the memory of Jaz in his bedroom, wearing that same lacy nothing, her breasts bare as she leaned over him whilst he lay on the bed watching her, desire and what he had so foolishly believed was love darkening her eyes, had driven him to do it.

He had heard quite plainly the hiss of her indrawn breath, and the sound that accompanied it. Her face had gone paper-white, as though she had been dealt a mortal blow, and he had had to battle against the urge to tell her that he hadn't meant it, that it was only his pain that was driving him to say such things, only the ache of his need for her tormenting his body that was sending him crazy.

Unable to trust himself to stay in her bedroom any longer, he had turned on his heel without waiting for her to make any response and quickly headed back to his own room.

TIREDLY JAZ PUSHED HER HAIR off her face, mentally acknowledging that the monthly heads of department meeting, fraught though it had been, was not the real cause of her low spirits.

When she had refused to give up the house to Caid she had not fully realised what the stress of sharing living accommodation was going to do to her. It was bad enough that she was spending hours when she should have been asleep lying awake, knowing that he was there in the next room to her, but what was even worse was the destruction of her self-respect, the impact of their unwanted physical proximity.

It was barely three days since he had arrived, and every morning she promised herself she would tell him that she did not wish to have her breakfast in the same room as a half-naked man, that if he had to wander around the kitchen wearing nothing other than a towel draped carelessly around his hips, then he should do so when she was not there. And every morning she had found that she just could not bring herself to end the silence between them, or to betray her real feelings with an unwanted stammer or, even worse, a vivid blush.

She had become so on edge that she was starting at every sound, tensing her body with anxiety, and she knew that she was already perilously close to breaking point without the added pressure of the problems she was facing at work.

Jerry had taken an aggressive stance right from the start of the meeting—which, to Jaz's relief, Caid had not attended—humiliating one of their most senior departmental heads by querying his monthly sales figures and then boastfully comparing their turnover to that of the supermarket chain he had run in America.

Then it had been Jaz's turn to be denigrated and criticised.

'These supposed budget figures you've given me,' Jerry began. 'This is what I think of them.'

And then he ripped them up and threw them in his wastepaper bin.

'Trash. Which is what I'm going to say when I report back to my stepfather. Your department is trash, unless you come up with something to prove me wrong and change my mind. Hey we all know you were John's blue-eyed girl—his *god-daughter*,' he emphasised, 'but John isn't here any more.'

His implication that she had been accorded special privileges because of her relationship with John infuriated Jaz, but not as much as his unsubtle suggestion that she just wasn't up to her job.

'My job is to make sure that the store draws in the maximum

amount of customers,' she started to say, just as the door opened and Caid walked in.

It was obvious to Jaz from the hard-eyed look Caid gave her that he supported Jerry's antagonistic stance towards her, but then what else had she expected?

'I detest the stores,' he had told her in New Orleans, but obviously he didn't detest them enough to pass up the opportunity to witness her public humiliation.

'You wouldn't be trying to tell me how to do my job, would you?' Jerry demanded ominously. 'I hope not, since it's obvious to me that you aren't that good at doing your own.'

It took all Jaz's will-power not to look at Caid or react to Jerry's inflammatory and unfair criticism in the way she suspected he wanted her to.

To Jaz's relief the store's manager came to her rescue, saying quietly, and very bravely, 'Jaz's Christmas window displays in particular bring an enormous amount of extra business to the store—past sales figures from all departments prove that—and in fact they've become something of a local cult and get us a lot of free publicity.'

'Well, that's as may be,' Jerry blustered, 'but there's still the little matter of her budgets. And, speaking of window displays, I'd like to know just what her plans *are* for these supposedly wonderful Christmas windows. I would hate our customers to discover that they can't buy anything they see in the windows because it's merely some arty display piece and we don't have it in stock.'

Jaz's face stung at this slur on her professionalism. It was true that she liked to keep her windows a secret—it helped to build up a sense of Christmas excitement—but of course she checked beforehand that they would have in a large stock of whatever she featured, and she was scrupulous about only using store stock.

Jerry's attack on her was both unprofessional and unfair, and after the meeting ended she edged her way out of the room—past Caid, who was standing by the wall. His stance was that of a man expecting and ready for trouble, and she couldn't stop herself letting off steam by hissing furiously to him, 'You're really enjoying this, aren't you, Caid?'

Jaz tensed now as, almost as though she had conjured them up by her thoughts, she saw Caid and Jerry walking towards her. She quickly turned on her heel and headed for the lift to take her down to the basement and the cubbyhole that was her workroom.

Caid frowned as he watched her go. He'd just spent the best part of an hour on the phone to his mother, who had rung to demand an up-to-date report on what was happening.

As Jerry complained about the store Caid listened in silence. He hadn't cared much for Jerry when he had first been introduced to him, and now he liked him even less. Right now he wasn't sure if the man was just plain unfit to be in charge of the store, or if he was deliberately trying to cause anxiety and mayhem amongst the staff.

As he had said to his mother, in answer to her anxious question, 'What's happening? I wish I knew! The jury's still out on just what Jerry is trying to do here, Mom, but whatever it is isn't doing the store any good.'

'What do you mean, the jury is still out?' She responded indignantly. 'Caid, it's perfectly obvious what he's trying to do. This is Donny's way of attempting to discredit me. Oh, I know him so well. This has his trademark all over it… Oh, I just wish I could be over there.'

Caid heard the energy and frustration humming in her voice.

'Quit being a control freak, Mom,' he told her wryly. 'It isn't good for your blood pressure.'

'Me a control freak?' She responded immediately. 'That's good coming from you, Caid. And at least I'm not so judgemental that I can only see everything and *everyone* in black and white. You remind me so much of your grandfather. He was just like you…stubborn! That man would never admit he could possibly be wrong about a single thing. I can still remember how he was when I told him that your father and I should never have married.

'"You're a female, Annette," he told me, "and it's a female's job to make her marriage work." Just like you, Caid, he thought I should stay home and play house, defer to your father in everything—just so long as your father deferred to *him*, of course.'

Caid listened in silence. He already knew the sorry saga of his parents' marriage, and the fact that his grandfather had put pressure on them to marry because there was a distant family relationship. As well as having the family name, his father had also had a handful of family shares.

Familiar though the story was, it still irked him to be told he was like a man who by all accounts had been an unpleasantly dictatorial and narrow-minded patriarch to his family.

'It's good to know we share such a high opinion of one another, Mom,' he told her warningly.

He heard her sigh travelling along the miles separating them.

'Oh, Caid,' she protested. 'I know what personal unhappiness can do to a person, and I don't want that to happen to you. You are my son, after all…'

When he made no response she sighed again, before asking him, 'Have you spoken to Jaz yet? Have you told her how much we need her to stay?'

Caid cursed under his breath as he heard the anxiety and the persistence in his mother's voice.

'No. Not yet,' he told her curtly. Though talking about Jaz reminded him of something he needed to discuss with his mother. 'You did check with John that it was okay for me to use his spare bedroom, didn't you?'

'Yes, of course I did. He said it would be fine,' she responded promptly.

'Uh-huh. And did he happen to mention that he'd been told by his doctor that his heart condition means that it isn't wise for him to live there at the moment? And that because of that he'd offered the house to Jaz?'

There was a small telling pause before his mother acknowledged the truth. 'Well, yes, he did say something about it, now that you mention it.'

'And you didn't think to tell me?'

'Well, no.' Caid was quite plainly able to hear the defensiveness his mother's voice. 'I mean, neither of us thought that the pair of you would mind sharing… As John said, the house has two bedrooms.'

'You thought we wouldn't mind, but you didn't think we ought to be offered the chance to make up our own minds?'

'Caid, you said yourself that you couldn't get a hotel room— and like John said he could hardly ask Jaz to move out. The last thing I wanted was—'

'To give me an excuse to refuse to come here?' Caid guessed. 'Well, let me tell you—' He stopped abruptly, realising what he'd been about to say was too personal.

And as for his mother's comment about not thinking he and Jaz would mind sharing! If she believed that then she should see the look Jaz gave him every morning when he walked into the kitchen after his shower. It was a look that said quite plainly just how infuriated she felt about having him there. But he was sure she felt nowhere near as infuriated as he did about having to share his living accommodation with her.

And he wasn't just infuriated, if he was honest—and Caid prided himself on his honesty. It irked him more than he wanted to admit to be forced to admit that physically he still reacted to her, still wanted her!

'Caid, please be nice to Jaz.'

'Be nice to her?' Caid exploded. 'Have you any idea—?' He began, and then stopped, slowly mentally counting to ten before telling his mother grimly, 'What I intend to do is find out what Jerry is doing, and deliver your message to Jaz. And then I'm getting on the first flight home. And nothing and no one is going to stop me!'

CHAPTER SIX

JAZ TENSED AS SHE HEARD Caid let himself into the house early the following afternoon. Involuntarily her glance was drawn to the sketch she had just done, supposedly of the male partner for her windows woman. Her husband, the father of her children, her lover and her best friend—a man who was genuinely her partner in every single way. The kind of man a woman could trust and rely on and yet know at the same time that he cherished her individuality and her independence. The kind of man who was fully prepared to take his share of the chores and the child rearing. The kind of man who was still macho and male enough to allow himself to resort to a few sensual caveman type tactics when the mood allowed. In short he was the kind of man that every woman secretly wanted.

So why, why, why had she sketched him with Caid's familiar features?

'Jaz?'

As Caid rapped on her door, she snatched up the drawing, hiding it behind her back.

'There's something I want to talk to you about,' Caid announced brusquely as he pushed open Jaz's bedroom door.

Out of the corner of his eye he could see the piece of paper she was screwing up behind her back and then letting fall in a small ball to the floor.

'You're wasting your time,' she told him fiercely, then frowned as they both heard someone knocking on the front door.

Caid cursed mentally under his breath at the interruption. So far as he was concerned, the sooner he said what had to be said to Jaz the better. As he'd said to his mother, he couldn't wait to be on a plane back home.

When Jaz hurried away to answer the door Caid absently put the ball of paper he had retrieved into his pocket before following her.

As she went downstairs Jaz was acutely conscious of Caid's more leisurely pace behind her. They reached the narrow hallway virtually together, and Jaz fought to ignore the effect Caid's proximity was having on her body.

The door-lock was slightly stiff, and as she tussled with it Caid reached out to help her. Jaz exhaled sharply as their fingers touched, recoiling from the contact.

'Leave me alone. I can manage,' she told Caid fiercely.

But it took Caid's stronger, surer fingers to release the mechanism that for some reason her fingers had been too tense to manage.

Silently they stared at one another, Jaz's expression mutinous, Caid's mocking, until Caid pulled open the door.

'Jaz—I thought you'd be here.'

As Jaz stepped back into the hallway Jamie, her cousin, accompanied by her two younger children, swept inside like a warm and busy whirlwind, dispensing hugs and kisses to Jaz at the same time as instructions to her children, her chatter only coming to a breathless halt when she saw Caid.

One eyebrow rose speculatively she looked from Jaz to Caid and then back again.

'This is Caid Dubois,' Jaz introduced him weakly. 'He's here to—'

As Jaz floundered for an explanation Caid quickly stepped in, smiling at Jamie with a warmth that immediately made Jaz want to stand between Caid and her cousin. How dared Caid look at Jamie like that in front of her? How dared he look at another woman like that? Ever?

As she battled with the shock of her own searing jealousy she heard Caid explaining pleasantly to Jamie, 'I'm here on family business.'

'Family business?' Jamie frowned, then her face cleared as

she exclaimed, 'Oh, Dubois, of course! It's your family who have bought the store. How do you like Cheltenham? Where are you staying?'

In typical Jamie fashion she was firing off her questions without waiting for any answers.

'I haven't had time to see much of the town as yet,' Caid responded easily. 'And I'm staying here. John was kind enough—'

'Here?' Jamie exclaimed. 'With Jaz?'

'Jamie…' Jaz pleaded in a slightly choked voice.

'Jaz and I are co-tenants,' Caid interjected smoothly. 'John seemed to think that neither of us would mind sharing the house.' He gave a small shrug.

There was a telling pause whilst Jamie looked from Caid's impenetrable and very dominant alpha-male face to Jaz's slightly flushed and much more vulnerable one.

Please, Jamie, don't say anything, Jaz was mentally begging her cousin, knowing how outspoken, not to say outrageous her cousin could be at times.

To Jaz's relief, when Jamie did speak it was only to say easily, 'I expect John was pleased to think that Jaz would have the protection of a male presence in the house. He's very sweetly old-fashioned like that.

'I hope we aren't disturbing you, Jaz,' she continued with a smile, after Caid had asked to be introduced her two children. 'We're here on a mission to book our Christmas trip to Aspen,' she informed them both, 'and to try to persuade Jaz to come with us this year,' she added with a meaningful look in Jaz's direction.

'My husband, Marsh, is a very keen skier,' she explained to Caid, 'and once he discovered just how good American snow is we couldn't keep him away. Last year for the first time we spent the whole of Christmas and the New Year staying at a marvellous lodge complex not far from Aspen. I desperately wanted Jaz to come with us—she's much more of an outdoorsy type than I am—but there was no way I could drag her away from her precious windows.'

'I'd love to come, but you know how it is,' Jaz told Jamie with a shake of her head. 'As soon as Christmas is over the windows have to be prepared for the sales. It seems unfair to go off and leave others to do it.'

'That's so typical of you, Jaz.' Jamie sighed ruefully. 'You are far too conscientious. I know how important your work is to you, but there are other things in life, you know! Caid, do you ski?' Jamie asked.

'I do—weather conditions and livestock permitting,' Caid responded laconically.

'Caid owns a ranch in Colorado.' Jaz explained reluctantly to her cousin.

'Oh, you farm!' Jamie exclaimed beaming. 'Then you'll have a lot in common with my husband, and with Jaz's father. Have you taken Caid home with you yet, Jaz?'

Jaz shook her head. Her exuberant cousin, in her normal way seemed about to adopt Caid into their family circle. Jaz mentally cursed the fact that she had not taken the opportunity to explain the situation before Jamie had met Caid.

'You must go,' she was now telling Caid enthusiastically. 'Jaz's father breeds world-famous cows—doesn't he, Jaz?'

'My father owns two very highly rated Holstein breeding bulls,' Jaz explained quietly.

'You'd never think that Jaz comes from a farming background, would you?' Jamie laughed as she gave Jaz a teasing look.

'No, I wouldn't,' Caid agreed with a coldness Jaz prayed her too-curious cousin would not pick up on and question.

'Remember when you used to help clean out the bull-pens to earn enough money to pay for your art materials, Jaz?' Jamie was asking with a rueful and reminiscent shake of her head.

'I remember,' Jaz agreed, her own voice now nearly as terse as Caid's had been.

But luckily Jamie's suspicions weren't aroused.

'Is there any chance that you can come down to the Soda Fountain with us?' she asked Jaz. 'It's been half-term, and I promised the kids a treat.' She turned to Caid. 'My husband, being a farmer, works from home, and devoted though he is he likes his own space every now and again. Allied to that we've got our family elders living with us, and after five days of two boisterous children they're ready for a break too.'

'You've got three generations living under the same roof?' Caid asked, looking impressed.

'Three generations and a few add-ons,' Jamie agreed, laughing. 'Jaz thinks I'm crazy. She says she'd hate to live my life.'

'Yes, I'm sure she would,' Caid agreed grimly, giving Jaz a cold look as he smiled warmly at Jamie, announcing, 'Personally, I think you re to be admired, and your husband and family envied.'

'We want the Soda Fountain,' Jamie's children began chanting, bringing a halt to the adult conversation. And as Jaz absorbed Caid's praise of her cousin she angrily tried to deny the sharp twist of pain in her heart.

Why should she be jealous of Caid praising Jamie? She didn't want to love a man who felt and thought as Caid did!

Angrily Caid watched as Jaz turned her back on him to talk to her cousin's children. What kind of fool was he for noticing how much such a cherishing role suited her, when he already knew that Jaz was just too stubborn to admit that she might be making the wrong choice?

The Soda Fountain, like the caviar and smoked salmon bar in the store, was famous in its own right. Generations of children had enjoyed its sodas and ice creams, and it had been at Jaz's suggestion that it had been updated and redecorated just prior to the Millennium celebrations.

'I should be working——' Jaz began, but to her surprise Caid cut across her.

'I thought it was your half-day?' he said simply.

'Yes, it is but——' Jaz agreed, caught off-guard.

'Why don't you come with us too?' Jamie invited Caid.

On the point of refusing, Caid saw Jaz's anxious expression. 'I'd love to,' he accepted, ignoring the mutinous look of angry resentment Jaz was giving him. 'I've been wanting to have some lime ice cream ever since I arrived—it's always been one of my favourites!'

As THEY ALL MADE THEIR WAY to the store Caid watched the speed with which Jamie's children left their mother's side to be with Jaz. It was plain that they adored her from the way they vied for her attention, but what surprised him even more was how natural and loving she was with them. Narrow-eyed he watched the three of them together. After the declarations she had made to him about her plans for the way she wanted to live, he had imagined that she would find it difficult to relate easily to children. And yet here she was, cuddling and teasing these two youngsters in a way that was totally uninhibited and relaxed. A way that made him feel...

'Jaz will be a wonderful mother.'

Jamie's affectionate comment, thankfully bringing his dangerous thoughts to a halt, prompted Caid to say bitterly, 'Do you think so? In my experience career women do not make wonderful mothers. At least not so far as their children are concerned.'

Jaz and the children had already reached the Soda Fountain, but Jamie stopped and frowned a little as she studied Caid.

'Do I sense a man who believes that a woman's place is in the home?' she challenged him, with a small smile.

'I'm certainly a man who believes that a child—children—need a mother like you. One who is there for them one hundred per cent of the time,' Caid acknowledged curtly.

'Like me?' Jamie raised her eyebrows and shook her head. 'One hundred per cent of the time? No way could I ever do that. In fact Jaz is far more of an ideal mother than I could ever be. My children have virtually had to bring themselves up—with a little help from their grandparents and their father. Oh, yes, I've done my bit, but—as I explained to Marsh when I agreed to marry him—there is no way I could live without my own space and the freedom to do those things that are important to me.

'I ran my own business and, like Jaz's mother, I'm a keen rider,' she explained. 'I demand a husband who is prepared to accept that there are times when his needs have to come second to my own. And that's what modern marriage should be all about, in my view. Both partners respecting and accommodating one another's needs. Despite what they say, love is not always enough. Mind you, it certainly helps. If I didn't love Marsh as much as I do, there's no way I'd ever have agreed to having his parents living with us—and yet as it happens it's turned out to be one of the best decisions we ever made.'

Caid listened to her grimly. This wasn't what he had expected or wanted to hear at all.

'Jaz!' Jamie called out to her as they reached the Soda Fountain. 'I've just had a great idea. Why don't you and Caid come over to us for dinner, I know that Marsh would really enjoy meeting you,' she told Caid warmly.

Appalled by her cousin's suggestion, Jaz immediately shook her head in denial, protesting, 'I don't think—'

Immediately Caid cut her off. 'Thank you I'd like that,' he accepted, giving Jaz a grim look as he did so.

'Wonderful! How about the end of next month?' Jamie beamed. 'My in-laws will be away then which will give us more room for guests.'

'That's fine by me,' Caid concurred.

'Good. You could drive down together on a Friday evening, stay over for dinner on Saturday, and travel back on Sunday.'

'I'll be looking forward to it,' Caid assured her politely, whilst Jaz looked on in furious disbelief.

What on earth did Caid think he was doing? Her cousin's home was virtually her only retreat—somewhere she could be totally herself and allow both sides of her nature to emerge without fearing that someone was going to use one of them against her.

Even now, whenever she went home, her parents still took the slightest indication of any enjoyment on her part of anything remotely connected with their lifestyle to mean that they had been right all along. Why couldn't the people who claimed to love her best simply accept that it was possible for her to enjoy some aspects of a country lifestyle and yet at the same time need to fulfil herself artistically?

Unlike her visits home, her visits to Jamie had never made her feel on edge and defensive, or anxious and conscious of a sense of pain and loss because she could not be the daughter she knew her parents had really wanted her to be.

Which was why it was so very important to her that the man she loved—the man who loved her—

Jaz swallowed hard. She mustn't start thinking like that now, when Caid was only a few feet away from her. Only she knew just what it had cost her to walk away from him in New Orleans, and only she would ever know!

Somehow, from somewhere, she would find the strength to deal with Caid's presence in her cousin's home. But she still couldn't help feeling angrily resentful that Caid had accepted Jamie's impromptu invitation primarily to spite her!

Out of the corner of his eye Caid watched Jaz. Whilst he and Jamie had made their way to the circular champagne and smoked salmon bar in the centre of the food hall, which was situated in the original basement kitchen of the building, Jaz had elected to remain at the Soda Fountain with Jamie's two sons—where she was quite plainly enjoying herself, Caid noted.

How the hell was it possible for one small woman to be two so very different people? Caid wondered savagely. Jamie was right, Jaz was a natural-born mother and just the sight of her right now with Jamie's two boys was stirring instincts, desires in him, which had nothing to do with logic or reality and one hell of a lot to do with a much more basic male instinct—like picking her up and kissing the breath out of her and then… Why the hell was he tormenting himself with impossible images of Jaz with his child in her arms?

'YOU CAN'T PUT THAT IN THERE!' Jaz almost shrieked.

'Oh, I think you'll find that I can,' Caid corrected her with soft menace as he glanced from her face to the very large piece of fresh meat he had just placed on the empty central shelf of the fridge. 'There are two of us living in this house, Jaz,' He reminded her. 'And if I want to put my food in this fridge…'

The look he was giving her was both implacable and intimidating, Jaz acknowledged, but she had her own weapons for dealing with a man who couldn't take advice and believed he always knew best.

'Anyway,' he continued contemptuously, 'There's plenty of room left for that rabbit food you eat.'

Jaz could feel her temper starting to rise.

'That's typical of you, Caid, to start criticising me, blaming me for your own pigheadedness. And as for my "rabbit food" as you choose to call it, I shall hardly be able to eat it once your meat has dripped blood all over it—which is why for health reasons it is normally considered safest to put meat on the lowest possible shelf in a fridge. That's all I was going to say to you. But of course no one can tell you anything, can they, Caid? No one apart from *you* can possibly have a valid opinion about anything—'

'If you're trying to pick a fight with me,' Caid interrupted her coldly. 'let me warn you—'

'No,' Jaz broke in sharply. 'Let me warn *you*, Caid. Let me warn you that you had no business accepting Jamie's invitation.'

'No business?'

Jaz tensed as she saw his thunderous expression, but she wasn't going to back down. As he slammed the fridge door shut and came towards her she tried to make herself stand her ground, but to her chagrin she realised she was retreating from him, backing away until the feel of the wall behind her told her that she couldn't go any further.

'This is what marriage to you would have been like, isn't it, Caid? You giving the orders, making the rules. You expecting everything to be done your way. You demanding that your needs always come first. It isn't because of any children you might have that you want your wife at home under your thumb all the time,' she told him with biting scorn, 'it's because you can't bear the thought of not being in control. Because you're so selfish and stubborn that you can't allow anyone other than yourself to be right about anything. Well, go ahead and give yourself food poisoning, then. I don't care. Why should I? I feel very sorry for the woman who does eventually make the mistake of marrying you. Thank goodness it won't be me.'

'Have you finished?' Caid demanded with ominous anger.

When Jaz turned away from him without making any response she heard him saying savagely under his breath, 'My God, but you know how to wind me up! Does it give you a kick?' he taunted her. 'Pressing all the wrong buttons because you can't press the right ones any more?'

Jaz gave a small furious gasp of female outrage. 'How can you say that?' she breathed indignantly. 'When you…when you—?' To her chagrin her voice had developed a small betraying hesitation, and she knew too that her face had begun to burn. Taking a deep gulp of breath, she said quickly, 'When you touched me—'

'Touched you?' Caid threw back his head and laughed. 'My, but you are naïve, aren't you? You might know where to put meat in a fridge, Jaz, but when it comes to knowing about the male sex… Shall I spell it out for you? I'm a man and I simply have a man's needs!'

It wasn't the indifference in the small shrug he gave as he turned away from her that hurt, Jaz told herself fiercely. And it certainly wasn't hearing him spell out the fact that he didn't love her any more. After all, she didn't love him, did she?

No! It was just… It was just…

Pinning a bright smile on her face, she told him in the most dismissive voice she could manage, 'Your needs are of no interest to me, Caid, and neither are you!'

There! That should reassure him that there was no danger of her making a lovesick fool of herself over him.

But Caid's reaction was anything but one of gratitude, Jaz acknowledged apprehensively, as he suddenly closed the distance between them and demanded, 'No? Then what does this mean?'

Struck dumb with horrified embarrassment, Jaz stared at the sketch he had thrust under her nose. The one she herself had drawn and discarded! The one depicting him in the role of her windows husband and father, complete with winsomely adorable children carrying his unmistakable likeness and an even more doting wife.

Bitterly Jaz wondered what could possibly have possessed her to put down on paper such a potentially betraying and feeble-minded set of images.

'Nothing to say?' Caid taunted her.

Hot-cheeked with discomfort, Jaz demanded huskily, 'Where did you get that? It's mine. Give it to me.'

As she made it to snatch the paper from him, Caid held it up out of her reach.

'So you did draw it,' he commented with satisfaction.

'It means nothing,' Jaz denied passionately. 'You don't mean anything to me now, Caid. You never really did,' Jaz lied wildly, desperate to protect herself.

Caid's expression hardened, making her heart miss a couple of beats and her body shake apprehensively. Unable to move, Jaz watched as Caid stood menacingly over her. Why had she said that? She had pushed him too far, but pride was refusing to let her back down.

'Oh, didn't I?' Caid demanded savagely.

Her words had raked his pride, exposed the raw nerve endings of the emotions he had been fighting to bury. They goaded him beyond the already overstretched limits of a self-control worn thin by night after night of knowing how close she was, of knowing just how much he still wanted her and knowing too, that he must destroy his feelings for her. Rationality was replaced by primitive male instinct.

'Well, let's just put that to the test, shall we?' Caid suggested in a voice so soft Jaz couldn't believe it had the power to savage her.

Trapped between Caid and the wall, she tensed her muscles defensively, pride flaring in her eyes as she silently dared him to touch her. But Caid was beyond recognising such subtle signals. His hands grasped her wrists, pinioning her arms on the wall, whilst he lowered his head towards her.

Jaz could feel his hot breath on her skin, could smell its scent of mint. It was heart-searingly familiar. Helplessly Jaz turned her head one way and then the other as she fought to avoid the unwanted domination of his mouth. But she already knew it was a lost fight.

The weight of his body imprisoning hers against the wall

felt like a merciless physical brand. Instinctively she closed her eyes, wanting to blot out the sight of him. But instead by some dangerous alchemy her senses were suddenly sweeping her back to when they had first met, when she had wanted him beyond reason and sanity, when just to be within sight of him had been enough to melt the flesh from her bones and make her body respond to him on a thousand different levels.

Like ice cracking under immense pressure, her emotions forced a fissure in her self-control. Every sense she possessed reacted to him, reached for him, ached despairingly for him. Her whole body was acting as though it was outside her own control, her emotions overwhelming her.

Feverishly she waited for the taste of Caid's kiss, knowing with a sense of helpless desperation just how much she wanted it. How much she wanted him. His mouth touched hers—hot, angry, demanding—and fiercely she responded to it, her anger against herself as well as against him. They kissed with fury and pain, with disillusionment and destruction, until the room was filled with the charged sound of their breathing.

Jaz shuddered as she felt Caid's arousal. Her own body was equally vulnerable. Her breasts ached for his touch, and that sensation deep down inside her that only he could arouse was a slow throbbing torment.

She wanted him to pick her up and carry her to his bed, to remove the restriction of their clothes as speedily as he could—in any way he chose. She didn't care how he did it, just as long as she could feel his flesh against her own. She was so hungry for him, so much in need of him that her whole body shook with it. It was as though she had a fever that only he could cool—a wound that only he could heal.

Tormentedly she pressed her lips against his throat, his jaw, his mouth, desperately prising the hard lines of his mouth apart with her tongue-tip.

Beneath his hand her breast swelled and ached. She couldn't wait for him to remove her top, to touch her the way he had done in New Orleans when she had shivered convulsively, her body arcing in hot, shocked delight at the feel of his work-hardened fingertips caressing the wanton sensitivity of her nipples.

'Admit it, Jaz,' Caid was groaning against her skin. 'Right now you're as hungry for me— For us—as I am for you.'

His words shocked her back to reality—and self-loathing.

'No!' she denied in panic, pulling away from Caid. 'No. No, I'm not.'

Silently Caid let her go. But she could imagine what he must be thinking. How much he must be enjoying his triumph and her own humiliation!

HALF AN HOUR LATER, as she stood in the bathroom of the house, her fingers pressed to her kiss-swollen mouth, she wondered how on earth she was going to survive what was happening to her.

She couldn't still love Caid. It just wasn't possible. She *mustn't* love him.

A small sob of panicky despair closed her throat.

GRIMLY CAID WONDERED WHAT the hell he was doing and why he didn't just make good his earlier threat and get on the first flight home. Surely it wasn't because his body was aching for a woman he knew it would be crazy for him to still love?

The air in the room still held her scent, accentuated by the heat of their shared sexual urgency. No matter what Jaz had tried to say, she had wanted him as much as he had done her; been as hungry for him as he for her. Oh, yes, Jaz had wanted him… His nerve-endings felt exposed, raw, a restless urgency burning through him.

He took a step towards the kitchen door and then stopped. So he had proved that sexually Jaz wasn't averse to him—what did that mean? Turning round, he walked over to the fridge and opened the door.

Removing his steak, he started to clean the shelf he had placed it on, and then meticulously washed Jaz's salad and fruit before packing them back in the salad crisper and returning his meat to the fridge—on the lowest shelf.

CHAPTER SEVEN

'AND YOU'VE WRITTEN HERE under Special Effects an amount of £5,000. But so far as I can see there is no breakdown of just what these "special effects" are going to be—nor any past receipt evidence to support this expenditure.'

Caid compressed his mouth as he listened to Jerry hectoring Jaz about the budget she had produced for him. It was plain from the angry flags of colour flying in Jaz's cheeks and the hostile atmosphere in the office just what her own and Jerry's feelings were.

Even now Caid wasn't sure just why he had insisted at the last minute on being included in the one-to-one meeting between Jerry and Jaz. It certainly didn't have anything to do with any protective male concern for Jaz. Why should he feel either protective or concerned for a woman who cared more about her career than she did about him?

'Where exactly is this money going to go? Or can I guess?' Jerry sneered openly.

Jaz gasped in outrage as she correctly interpreted his accusation. 'If you are trying to suggest that I would do something underhand or dishonest—' she began immediately.

'All I'm asking for is proof of what the money is to be spent on,' Jerry told her smoothly. 'If you don't like or can't comply with my request—'

'Jerry, that's enough.'

The sharp incisive interruption of Caid's angry voice caused Jerry's face to burn an unpleasantly angry colour.

'Hey, Caid. I'm the one in charge here,' he began, but immediately Caid overruled him.

'My uncle may have appointed you, Jerry, but in my book—and I'm sure in the family's as well,' he told him meaningfully, 'I think we both know that my authority ranks way above yours. If, historically, Jaz has not been asked to provide budgets for her department, then so far as I am concerned she certainly doesn't need to now.'

Reaching across the desk, Caid picked up the folder Jaz had brought in with her. 'Thank you, Jaz. You can go,' he told her as he handed it back to her.

'Now, wait a minute!'

Jaz could hear Jerry blustering furiously as Caid opened the office door for her. But no matter how angry Jerry was at Caid's interference he couldn't be anywhere near as angry as she was herself, she decided as she blinked away the tears of fury and humiliation that were burning her eyes.

How dared Caid belittle her like that? How dared he interfere? And for what purpose, when she already knew that he wanted to see her leaving his family's employment every bit as much as Jerry did?

Downstairs in her workroom, she flung the folder into a drawer, her face still burning.

What Jerry had just tried to imply was an insult—an insult that hadn't just infuriated her but had hurt her as well, and all the more so because Caid had witnessed it.

Reluctantly she acknowledged that her resolution was beginning to waver, that she was beginning to ask herself if the price of staying on at the store was one she was going to be able to pay. Wouldn't it be much easier to give in; to hand in her notice and leave? It wasn't as though she wouldn't be able to find another job.

But she liked this job. She reminded herself stubbornly and she wasn't going to be pushed out of it just to suit the Dubois family! And she certainly wasn't going to be patronised by a certain arrogant member of it who, for reasons best known to himself, had suddenly decided to act as her defender!

Her angry resentment was still bubbling hotly inside her half an hour later when Caid pushed open the door to her small domain.

'Why did you do that?' she challenged him. Her workroom felt cramped at the best of times, but now, with Caid in it, it was unbearably claustrophobic. How was it possible for a man she knew hadn't been anywhere near the great outdoors within the last twenty-four hours to smell somehow of huge open spaces, cool, clean air, and that indefinable something which her senses recognised as being uniquely Caid?

'Why did I do what?' Caid responded. 'I came down here to talk to you about something, Jaz—'

'Something?' Jaz interrupted him wildly. 'What kind of something? If you're expecting me to shower you with gratitude because of the way you belittled me upstairs in front of Jerry—'

'I *belittled* you? Now, just a minute—!'

'Yes, belittled me,' Jaz insisted. 'I don't need you to protect me or come to my rescue, Caid. I'm perfectly capable of dealing with Jerry on my own. You had no right to interfere.'

'No right?' Caid stared at her. 'Do you really think that I'm the kind of man who just stands to one side and allows a person—any person—to be bullied like that? Just because you…'

'Just because I what?' Jaz demanded. Colour burned in her face and her hands were clenched into two tight, defensive little balls. 'Don't think I don't know what you're trying to do with all this pseudo-sympathy and protection.'

Jaz could hear the emotion shaking her body beginning to infect her voice. 'I've been there before, Caid, with my parents. But at least I knew when they tried to undermine me that they were motivated by love. But you! You just can't wait to see me fall, can you, Caid? You'd do anything and everything within your power to bring me down and humiliate me. To have me down on my knees begging you to take me back just for the satisfaction it would give you. Well, it's never going to happen. I could never, ever commit myself to a man who can't accept me as I am. You wouldn't expect me to change the colour of my eyes because you preferred blue to brown, would you? Or dye my hair, cut off an arm? But you obviously think it quite acceptable to expect me to deny part of my personality, part of my most sacred inner self.'

'Don't be ridiculous. You're overreacting,' Caid told her curtly.

'I am not being ridiculous,' Jaz stormed. 'In wanting me to give up my career to conform to your idea of what a woman should be you are every bit as guilty of trying to bully me as Jerry is. But you can't see that, can you? You're too stubborn to *want* to see it! You want me to be less of the person I am, less of the woman I am, and I can never ever do that. Oh, why, *why* did you have to come over here?' Jaz demanded.

Bleakly Caid looked at her down bent head. The angry explosion of words she had hurled at him felt as though they had embedded themselves in his pride, like so many pieces of shrapnel, tearing him to pieces.

He had come down to Jaz's workroom anticipating that she would be in need of some comfort and reassurance—wanting to let her know that no matter what might lie between them she was assured of someone on her side, to take her part, and that she need have no fears of Jerry whilst he was there.

The reality of her reaction could hardly have been more different.

Bitterly he told her, 'As to my reasons for coming here...' Shaking his head, he added coldly, 'I doubt that they are something you would be able to understand.'

AS HE FINISHED THE SOLITARY meal he had just eaten in a nearby restaurant Caid glanced at his watch. It was ten p.m. now. If he found himself a quiet bar and had a drink he need not return to the house until gone eleven, by which time hopefully Jaz would have gone to bed. And tomorrow he would be driving down to stay with John.

He and Jaz had been studiously ignoring one another since their argument in Jaz's workroom, and this morning Caid had telephoned John—ostensibly to thank him for allowing him the use of his spare room and to invite himself down to spend a couple of days at John's apartment so he could take him out for a thank-you dinner, but in reality simply so that he could get away from Jaz. Because if he didn't he didn't think he would be answerable for what might happen.

JAZ FORCED HER LIPS INTO WHAT she hoped would pass as a natural and genuine smile as she slowed her car down ready to turn into the drive that led to her parents' property. She had said nothing to Caid about her visit to her parents, but after all why should she?

The land on which her father raised his pedigree stock had been in his family for many generations, and Jaz felt she wouldn't have been the person she hoped she was had she not felt a small rush of pride and belonging as she drove towards the pretty manor house.

As she continued down the drive she glanced over at the stable block. Jaz enjoyed riding—but as a relaxing hobby, that was all. She had never shared the competitive instinct which had taken her mother to the top of her chosen career, but that did not stop her loving and admiring her mother for all that she had achieved and for the determination and dedication she gave to training and teaching her young hopefuls.

At least here she would be spared having to see Caid, she reminded herself. She usually took pride in her strength of mind, her resilience and her self-control—but right now...

The atmosphere between them had become so dangerously hostile and tense that Jaz was actually starting to feel physically sick with nerves at the thought of having to come face to face with Caid. The way he was making her feel was even beginning to affect her work.

Right now, she acknowledged shakily, each and every one of her defences had become frighteningly weak. He made her say and do things that were totally the opposite of the way she normally behaved. It frightened her to know she was so out of control. But what frightened her even more was the way she couldn't stop herself from thinking about him, from obsessively going over and over everything he had said to her.

It was obvious he didn't love her any more. Her face burned as she remembered the way he had taunted her about using her for his sexual satisfaction.

She needed to put some distance between them and this was the perfect way of doing it because there was no way Caid would turn up at her parents', as he had done at the store, standing there, and filling her with foolish hope and delight, when all the time…

No, here with her parents she was totally safe!

CAID FROWNED AS HE LISTENED to John explaining that he had organised a small treat for him.

'I couldn't help feeling that you would be bored stuck in my small apartment, so I rang Helena and asked if we might stay with them for the weekend.'

Caid checked him. 'Helena?'

'Yes. Helena and Chris—Jaz's parents. They only live a few miles away, and you'll be much more comfortable there than here.'

John was suggesting that they spend the weekend with Jaz's parents? In Jaz's home?

She hadn't been in the house when he had returned from the store to pack his bag, so he had left her a curt note, explaining that he was going away for a couple of days.

His immediate response to John's suggestion was to refuse to go, but he argued with himself. To do that would be unfair to John—and bad manners as well. After all, it wasn't as though he was afraid of going, was it?

An hour later, as he stowed John's overnight case away in the boot of his hired car and made sure the older man was comfortably installed in the passenger seat, Caid acknowledged that it didn't matter where he was, just so long as he was away from Jaz.

If he were to come face to face with her right now he didn't think he could be responsible for his reaction. But then he wasn't going to come face to face with her, was he?

CHAPTER EIGHT

'Darling...you've made good time! You look pale, though. You need some fresh air,' Jaz's mother reproved. 'It's almost time for lunch. John's here, by the way. He's staying for the weekend.'

As she followed her mother into the kitchen Jaz tried to relax.

Coming home always put her on the defensive, but she knew now that the determination not to be undermined she felt with her parents was nothing when compared to the fierce need to defend her independence that gripped her when she was with Caid.

Caid! As she walked it the kitchen she closed her eyes for a second. She had come here to escape him, hadn't she? So why was she letting him dominate her thoughts?

'Darling, why don't you do through to the sitting room?' her mother suggested. 'The others are in there, and you know what Dorothy's like about serving meals on time. You might warn your father that she's on the warpath.'

Dorothy was the linchpin of the household, the person who held everything together, acting as cook-cum-housekeeper-cum-secretary to her parents, running the household and devoted to them.

Leaving her mother to remove the outdoor clothes she was wearing, Jaz made her way along the hall to the sitting room. As she pushed open the door she could see her father and John.

'You run cattle yourself, then, do you, Caid.' Jaz heard him asking interestedly.

Freezing in disbelief, she stood in the open doorway. This couldn't possibly be happening. She was imagining it. She must be. She had to be. Caid could not possibly be here. He *must* not be here!

'Jaz…come on in. Don't just stand there. I don't know!' Jaz could see her father shaking his head wryly. 'Are you sure she's as good at this job of hers as you're always telling us she is, John?' he asked John as he turned towards him. 'Only she's always been such a daydreamer…'

'She's exceptionally good at her job—and exceptionally gifted as well.'

Jaz heard John defending her gently. But for once all her attention was not focused with painful intensity on the usual underlying parental criticism. How could it be when Caid was standing less that five feet away from her, his expression shuttered and austere, only the grim tension of his jaw giving away the fact that she was as unwelcome a sight to him as he to her?

'Mother said to warn you that Dorothy is about to serve lunch,' Jaz told her father, managing from somewhere to summon a brightly false smile for him before deliberately ignoring Caid and stepping past him to give John a warm hug.

She could almost feel Caid's cold, concentrated gaze turning her spine to ice.

'Jaz—I didn't realise you were going to be here.' John greeted her with warm enthusiasm.

'Oh, you know what Jaz is like,' her father broke in jovially. 'Head always in the clouds. But then that's these arty types for you. Can't really understand what it's all about myself.'

'What what is all about, dear?' Jaz's mother enquired, coming in to shepherd them all into the dining room.

'This arty thing of Jaz's,' Chris Cavendish replied, shaking his head. 'She had every opportunity to join a farming life. But all she wanted was this art business.'

Jaz could see the way Caid was frowning as he looked from her to her parents, and her face started to burn with a mixture of angry pride and embarrassment.

'Caid's family own the store that Jaz works for,' Jaz's mother reminded her husband as she ladled soup into everyone's bowls.

'Maybe so, but Caid's like us—he's a rancher,' Chris informed her approvingly.

'Well, I have to admit we were disappointed when Jaz told us what she wanted to do,' she sighed. 'We tried to talk her out of it—for her own sake, of course—but she can be amazingly stubborn.'

Jaz tensed, her spoon clattering against the plate as she put it down with a small bang.

'I don't think that Caid is interested in hearing about my failings,' she said grittily to her mother.

'I think Caid already knows how gifted you are, Jaz,' John intervened quietly. 'I know for a fact how impressed his mother was with your work.'

It was on the tip of Jaz's tongue to demand to know why, if that was the case, she was now being bullied into handing in her notice? But mercifully she managed to restrain herself.

She couldn't bring herself to look at Caid, but she knew how much he must be enjoying hearing her parents criticising her. A childish desire to claim that she wasn't hungry any more and get up and run away threatened to turn her into the child her parents always treated her as. Fiercely she resisted it.

Dipping her head, she concentrated on drinking her soup.

Grimly Caid surveyed Jaz's downbent head. An unfamiliar and discomfiting insight was challenging him to take note of what was happening. Logically he knew he should be applauding and supporting the opinions he had just heard Jaz's parents voice, but instead…

Jaz realised that her father had started to engage Caid in a discussion about livestock. Relieved not to have to defend herself any further, she lifted her head—only to realise her mistake.

Caid might be listening to her father, but he was staring right across the table at her. And the look in his eyes was one which…

A brilliant surge of colour seared Jaz's skin. What was Caid doing? He had no right to look at her like that. As though…as though…

'Goodness, Jaz, you look flushed,' her mother commented solicitously. 'I do hope you aren't coming down with something…'

Something? Did dying dreams, shattered illusions and a breaking heart count as 'something'?

Caid's gaze had locked with hers, refusing to let it go. Desperately Jaz struggled to escape from its searching intensity; from the ignominy of what she was having to endure.

Just as soon as lunch was over she made her escape, heading for the barn which housed her mother's free-range poultry. She carried Dorothy's egg basket over her arm.

An hour later, with the basket almost full, she put it down. It was warm inside the barn, and she took off the jacket she was wearing, putting it on top of the basket before going to climb the ladder that led to the barn's hayloft.

As a girl this had always been one of her favourite retreats. Her special sanctuary where she had come when she'd felt as though life and its problems were becoming too much for her to bear. From its windows she could see right across the fields to the hills. It was the place she'd come to think her private thoughts, dream her private dreams.

She had certainly never needed its sanctuary more than she needed it now, Jaz acknowledged as she headed for a small window, curling up beneath it on the soft hay.

'You look angry, Caid.'

Caid started as John spoke to him. They had finished lunch and the older man had announced that he was going upstairs to rest. Caid had offered to carry his bag up for him and the two of them were now standing outside the room John was going to occupy.

'I hadn't realised that Jaz's parents—' he began tersely, then stopped when John sighed.

'They love her, of course—very, very much. And I don't mean to gossip, but it's no secret that in their eyes Jaz doesn't fit their idea of what a child of theirs should be. That made life very hard for Jaz when she was growing up. I can remember her as a little girl.' He smiled ruefully. 'She desperately wanted to please them, to be what they wanted her to be, but whenever she could she would try to show them how important it was to her to follow her artistic urge. They couldn't understand...

'That hurt her. Badly. And she had to fight very hard for the right to fulfil her own destiny. Too hard I sometimes think, for a person of her loving temperament. Her parents taught her that a temperament like hers could be used against her. She wanted to please them because she loved them, and I'm afraid that they tended to use that love to try and make her do as they wanted— but for the best of motives, you understand. They genuinely believed that she would be much happier living the same kind of life as them. They couldn't understand how it might make her feel trapped and cheated, how it would deprive her of a part of herself that was so very important to her. Of course that's all in the past now, and naturally they are very proud of her.'

'They treat her as though she were still a child,' Caid objected grimly. 'Patronising and without respect.'

Leaving John to have his rest, Caid went back downstairs. He was finding his own reaction to what John had said even more disturbing than John's actual disclosures.

But the fact that he had suddenly discovered there might be a valid reason for Jaz's attitude didn't mean that he had changed the way he felt about it!

'YES, I'M VERY PLEASED with the results of our breeding programme,' Jaz's father confirmed to Caid an hour later as they walked towards the kitchen.

Naturally, in view of their shared interest, Jaz's father had offered to show Caid his stock—an offer that Caid had been unable to resist accepting. During the course of their conversation it had become plain to Caid that Chris Cavendish did love his daughter, though it was equally plain that he could not understand her.

'Of course,' he'd confided to Caid, 'her mother and I haven't given up hope that she'll come back to her roots. You should have seen her when she was young. She loved feeding the calves...' He'd shaken his head and sighed.

'Look, I've got a couple of phone calls I need to make,' he

said now. 'Please, make yourself at home and feel free to have a look around if you wish.'

Thanking him, Caid watched as he walked back to the house before turning to study the vista in front of him.

This land so unlike his own fascinated him, and he walked over to the fence to study it better. Hens scratched busily in the dust of the yard, beyond which lay an old timber-framed barn. There was a date carved over the opening and he walked over to inspect it more closely.

As he entered the barn he saw the basket on the floor beside the ladder, and Jaz's jacket folded neatly over it. Broodingly he studied it. He knew it was Jaz's because he recognised it. Picking it up, he let the fabric slide through his fingers. It felt soft and warm, like Jaz herself—sensuous, perfumed. He eyed the ladder, then came to a decision.

He might have come here to get away from her, but now that they were here together perhaps it would be as good an opportunity as any for him to deliver his mother's message to her and make a plea on her behalf.

Determinedly he started to climb the ladder, frowning as it creaked beneath his weight. Jaz had apparently climbed it safely enough, he reminded himself.

He was well over three quarters of the way up when he heard an ominous cracking sound. Caid held his breath and waited, hoping that he was wrong and that it didn't mean what he feared it did. But then, as he held firmly onto the ladder and tried to make up his mind what to do, he heard the wood crack again, and this time he felt the ladder start to buckle and slide away as it broke beneath his weight.

Grimly he reached up and managed to grip hold of the loft floor above him, intending to haul himself up...

JAZ WOKE UP WITH A START. She didn't know how long she'd been asleep but what she did know was that she'd been dreaming about Caid. Dreaming about the time they had shared in New Orleans, the way things had been between them before...

Her eyes dark with remembered emotions, she turned her

head and then blinked dazedly as she saw Caid's head and shoulders framed in the opening to the loft.

'Caid…'

Her eyes widened. It was almost as though she was still locked in her dream. Caid was here… She could feel herself beginning to tremble with longing and need…

'Jaz, the ladder's snapped,' she heard Caid telling her abruptly, and his words brought her shockingly back to reality.

Immediately she was her parents' daughter, brought up from birth to deal with this kind of emergency. Getting up, she hurried across to him, quickly recognising the danger he was in. There was no way he could go back down the broken ladder, and the floor was too far below for him to jump down safely. The only thing he could do was haul himself up to safety in the loft. But to do that he would need her help.

Determinedly she braced her body and instructed him briskly, 'Give me your hand. If I hold on to this beam, and you hold onto me, you should be able to lever yourself up here.'

Jaz hoped she sounded more confident than she felt. She weighed just under eight stone, and Caid, she suspected, weighed over half as much again—at least. If she lost her grip on the beam they could both end up falling and injuring themselves. The floor of the stable was flagged in Cotswold stone, and Jaz hated to think what a fall from such a height might do to the human body.

Clenching her teeth, she wrapped her free arm around the beam whilst Caid gripped her wrist. Closing her eyes, she prayed silently, her whole body flinching when she heard the sound of the broken ladder crashing to the floor and felt the sharp pull of Caid's weight on her body.

'Jaz, it's okay. You can open your eyes.'

Her whole body went limp with relief as Caid released her wrist. When she opened her eyes he was kneeling on the floor of the loft in front of her.

Caid had made it! He was safe!

Yes, he was safe, but *they* were trapped up here together in the hay loft until someone realised they were missing and came to look for them, Jaz recognised distractedly. And that wouldn't be until at least dinner-time!

'YOU'VE GOT HAY IN your hair.'

Jaz made to pull back as Caid reached towards her.

'Hold still,' he commanded matter-of-factly, securing her arm with one hand whilst he reached out to pluck the pieces of hay from her hair.

Jaz could feel the warmth of his breath on her skin. She could see the tanned hollow of his throat. Her chest felt dangerously tight, constricting her breathing and depriving her of oxygen— which must be why her thoughts had become a dislocated hap-hazard muddle and why her heartbeat was echoing noisily in her own ears.

'Caid...'

She had meant her voice to sound strong and distancing, dis-missive, but instead it was a soft, shaken sound that had exactly the opposite effect from the one she had wanted.

Instead of releasing her Caid moved closer to her, looking down at her mouth.

'No, don't!' Jaz whispered, reaching up with her free hand to push him away.

'No, don't what?' Caid murmured, capturing her hand and holding it within his own, rubbing his thumb lightly against the softness of her palm so that she shuddered violently.

Don't kiss me! she had wanted to say. But it was already too late. Already his mouth was feathering hers in the lightest and most tempting of kisses.

It's just sex, she tried to remind herself. That's all he wants you for. He doesn't love you. You must not... But her body was swaying into his, curving to meet its hardness, her muscles soft-ening, her body yearning, opening.

'Jaz...'

Just the way he breathed her name was enough to make her moan achingly.

His hands cupped her face.

'Look at me.' She heard him demand roughly. 'Look at me, Jaz, and tell me that you don't want me.'

'I can't… I can't…' Jaz told him in anguish.

His nose rubbed tenderly against her own and his thumb tip stroked the softness of her lips.

Automatically she parted them, flicking her tongue softly against his skin, feeling him shudder in response against her.

'Why do we fight when we could be doing this?' Caid groaned hoarsely as he gathered her up against him.

'I don't know,' Jaz admitted dizzily. And right now it was the truth—she didn't! She didn't know anything apart from the fact that she had just been dreaming the most wonderful dream about him and now he was here, and she was here, and the way he was holding her, touching her, kissing her, was melting away all the bad times and taking her back to when they had first met. Right now that was the only place she wanted to be, she acknowledged.

'Don't deny me,' Caid was begging her. 'Don't deny this… don't deny us, Jaz.'

And then he was touching her mouth with his, capturing it in a kiss of searing domination and demand.

Jaz felt her whole body go limp as her desire to reject him was overwhelmed by a far stronger and more elemental need. Her heart smashed against her chest wall and her legs went so weak she was forced to lean on Caid for support. Her lips parted eagerly, greedily, whilst her poor embattled mind fought and lost its lonely fight for resistance.

This was what she hungered for, longed for, ached for, in that secret part of her heart she had refused to acknowledge existed. Caid's touch, his warmth, his kiss. His body…

Mindlessly Jaz clung to him, returning his kiss, oblivious to everything but the feelings driving her.

She could feel his excitement as she pressed herself against him, as hungry for him as she could feel he was for her. She opened her mouth to the searching probe of his tongue, wrapping her arms around him as though she would never let him go.

Her head swimming, her heart pounding, her whole body a

delirious mixture of longing and excitement, Jaz marvelled that she had been able to live so long without him.

Greedily she pressed tiny kisses against his jaw and then his throat, almost high on the taste and the feel of him. This was her lover, her man, her destiny… And her body, her senses, her heart flatly refused to listen to any pathetic whining from her head. This was love; this was now; this was Caid.

In the heat of the hay-sweet privacy of the barn they tugged impatiently at one another's clothes in between increasingly passionate kisses, two equals in their longing and love for one another.

Jaz felt Caid shudder as he released her breasts from confinement, cupping them with his hands whilst he gazed down at them in absorbed wonder.

She had never felt so proud of her body, her womanhood, never felt so strong and empowered by its desirability.

She could feel the fine tremble of Caid's fingers as he touched her, circling and then tugging gently on her taut nipples whilst her breasts swelled eagerly against his hands. Daringly she leaned forward and brushed her lips against his own body, flicking her tongue against one hard flat nipple in both a caress and a subtle invitation. The hard male body, which it now seemed to her she had known and loved for a thousand hidden and shadowy past lifetimes, trembled with heart-aching vulnerability beneath her touch. How she loved to see him like this. Reduced in his need for her to the same level of intoxicated adoration as she was by him.

There was, she reflected dreamily, no pleasure on earth greater than the liberty to enjoy the body of one's beloved. To reach out and touch it…him…to stroke and kiss him as she was doing now, running her fingertips hotly down the line of silky dark hair that disappeared beneath his belt and following that journey with her lips.

She heard Caid groan and then suddenly she was lying on her back against the hay, with Caid leaning over her, looking down at her, his blue eyes so dark with passion they were almost black.

His gaze locked with hers, he began to unfasten his jeans. Jaz could feel herself starting to tremble slightly and then to shake. The pain of the months without him overwhelmed her, and there were tears in her eyes as she leaned forward to touch him in all the intimate ways they had so fleetingly shared.

'No—wait!' she heard him say, his voice thick, slurred and distorted by his desire for her.

He had just begun to pull down her jeans, burying his face in the smooth swell of her stomach as he kissed her skin, his breath hot with passion, his kisses sending exquisite needle-sharp darts of fiery pleasure through, her.

'Are you sure you can live without this?' he was demanding thickly.

'Without us? Because—'

'Jaz—?'

Abruptly Jaz came to her senses, the betraying response she had been about to make freezing on her lips as she heard her father's voice calling her name.

What was she *doing*? Her face stung with shame and anger. She knew that Caid didn't love her any more. So why on earth had she behaved so—so...?

Her face burned even more hotly as Caid handed her her clothes and called out to her father, 'We're up here, Chris!'

Whilst he was speaking Caid was quickly dressing himself. Miserably Jaz looked away from him.

The shock of hearing her father's voice had brought her very sharply back to reality, Her hands were trembling as she fastened the last of her shirt buttons. She felt so angry with herself, so ashamed. What could she have been thinking of?

'Jaz...Caid...' Jaz could hear the relief in her father's voice. 'Your mother was just about to insist I sent out a search party. She was convinced that you must have had an accident.'

'Well, we have, in a manner of speaking,' Caid answered her father ruefully before Jaz could speak. 'I'm afraid I've damaged your loft ladder beyond repair.'

'The loft ladder? Oh...' Jaz could hear the consternation in his voice. 'Dammit! I should have warned you. We've got a new one on order. It's fortunate that neither of you were hurt. Hang on a minute whilst I go and get another ladder.'

As she watched him hurrying away and out of sight Jaz knew there must be a hundred different things she should say to Caid. But the stifling silence of the barn and the weight of her own misery made it totally impossible for her to speak.

'Jaz?'

She froze when she heard Caid say her name. How dared he sound so tender, so dangerously warm, so much as though he actually cared about her, when she knew that he did not? When he himself had proved to her that he no longer loved her!

'Whatever it is you're planning to say, don't. Because I don't want to hear it,' she told him grittily, each word hurting her as though it was a piece of sharp glass being ripped across her throat.

To her relief her father had returned, bringing with him a set of long ladders.

Caid went down first, waiting halfway down for her and reaching out with his hands to steady her. Immediately Jaz recoiled from him, telling him stiffly, 'I can manage by myself, thank you.'

The coldness in his eyes as he turned away from her closed her throat with painful emotion.

Why was life punishing her like this? What on earth had she ever done to deserve what she was suffering now?

'I'M AFRAID JASMINE won't be down for dinner,' Jaz's mother apologised several hours later, when Caid and John joined her in the drawing room. 'She sends her apologies. She's got a migraine.'

CHAPTER NINE

'Is that all you're having to eat?'

Jaz could feel the tiny hairs on her skin prickling antagonistically in response to Caid's sternly autocratic question as he looked at the salad she had prepared for her evening meal.

'Yes, it is,' she agreed, adding belligerently, 'Not that it's any business of yours.'

Ignoring her warning, Caid pointed out disapprovingly, 'All you had for breakfast was a cup of coffee. It's a proven fact that in order to operate at maximum capacity the human body needs a proper protein breakfast—and, since you work for a company in which I have a financial interest, I can legitimately insist that I have every right to—'

'Will you stop behaving as though you're my father?' yelled Jaz. 'When will you all realise that not only am I capable of making my own decisions but also that it is my right to do so. How would any of you like it if I denied you that right?'

'I am not behaving like your parents,' Caid insisted, his voice harsh with his own immediate response to her accusation. 'Just because they refused to allow you to be yourself when you were growing up, Jaz, it doesn't mean you have to hang on to some paranoid belief that no one else will either.'

'No?' Jaz challenged him. 'I don't know how you have the gall to make a statement like that,' she told him witheringly. 'At least my parents were motivated by love. Unlike you! I know exactly what you're trying to do, Caid, and why you're so determined to wrongfoot and undermine me! It's obvious that this is yet another attempt to coerce me into handing in my notice!'

Caid stopped her. 'What the hell are you talking about?'

'Oh, come on, Caid,' Jaz derided. 'You know full well what I mean.'

'No!' Caid corrected her, placing his palms flat on the table as he looked at her. 'I don't know what you mean at all.'

'Of course you do,' Jaz insisted, refusing to be intimidated. 'You've made that clear. And I've told you that there is no way I am going to be bullied into handing in my notice just because it suits the Dubois family to get rid of some of this store's existing personnel. Jerry has made it more than plain what he's been sent here to do. Well, let me tell you—'

'Now, just a minute—' Caid began ominously.

'It's no good, Caid.' Jaz stopped him sharply. 'I realise how very…satisfying it must be from your point of view, to be here not just witnessing but also being instrumental in putting me in my place—seeing me get my comeuppance as it were. And I can see how from your blinkered point of view you must be looking forward to gloating over the fact that the career I chose over being with you is about to come to an abrupt end. But it isn't quite like that. For one thing I can get another job. In no way am I dependent on the Dubois family. Yes, foolishly I did perhaps assume that your mother meant what she said when she hinted that there might be the potential for promotion for me within the business. But it wasn't my career that came between us…it was your attitude.'

'Now, see here—' Caid began sharply.

Jaz could see the fury smouldering in his eyes, turning them a dangerously dark shade of blue, but she wasn't going to allow herself to be intimidated. 'No, Caid!' she told him determinedly. 'It's time you listened to *me*. Before you start relishing the taste of the revenge you obviously think you are getting at my expense, there are one or two things you ought to know! The first is that I have no intention of handing in my notice until I am ready to do so. The second is that I'm glad you have done what you are doing. Because it totally confirms to me how right I was to end our relationship.'

'To end it? You mean like you were doing in your parents' barn?' Caid interrupted stingingly.

Jaz met the look he was giving her with pride and defiance.

Shrugging as nonchalantly as she could, she told him, 'So I felt like having sex? What's wrong with that?'

'One hell of a lot, if you want to convince a man that what you were doing was purely sex,' Caid told her softly.

Jaz didn't like the way he was watching her. It made her feel as though he was just waiting for her to betray herself so that he could pounce like a cat on a mouse. And no doubt when he did he would toy with her and torment her as cruelly as any hunter with its prey, inflicting wound after wound on her emotions until she was incapable of protecting herself any longer.

'That isn't something I feel any need to talk about,' she told him, assuming an expression of haughty disdain. 'It happened, but it doesn't have any real relevance in my life.'

'You mean like I don't?' Caid suggested.

'Exactly,' Jaz agreed in triumph.

'But you told me you loved me and you wanted to spend the rest of your life with me,' Caid reminded her softly. 'You cried out to me that you had never known such pleasure could exist; you begged me...'

White-faced, Jaz tried to blot out what he was saying and the images he was conjuring up—shockingly intimate and private images that now turned her face as hotly red as it had been tormentedly pale.

'That was before I knew what you were really like...before I realised that you would never allow me to truly be myself,' she burst out. 'I can't live like that. I've already tried for my parents and I can't do it—I won't do it. And I won't give in and resign from my job either, Caid, no matter what kind of pressure you and Jerry put on me.'

'Can I have that in writing?'

Jaz stared at him. What kind of Machiavellian sleight of hand was he trying to work on her now?

'Excuse me?' she asked.

'You heard me, Jaz. I want it in writing that you don't intend to leave. Or rather my mother does.'

'Your mother?' Now Jaz was confused.

'Yes, my mother,' Caid confirmed grimly. 'Contrary to what you obviously believe, I did not come over here either to try and get you to resign or to gloat over any potential loss of your job.'

Jaz shook her head. 'I don't believe you,' she told him flatly. 'Why else would you be here?'

An unfamiliar hesitancy held Caid silent for a second before he made any response. But Jaz was too wrought up to be aware of its significance, or to question it as he told her shortly, 'Filial duty and financial prudence, I guess.'

Something in the slightly hoarse sound of his voice and the way he looked away from her alerted Jaz's intuition to the fact that he wasn't being totally honest with her.

'No,' she repeated firmly. 'Although I don't know what you think you can achieve by lying to me at this stage of things!'

'Lying to you?'

Jaz flinched as she saw the fury in his eyes.

'Now let me tell you—' He stopped; cursing under his breath as his mobile suddenly rang.

Taking advantage of the interruption Jaz hurriedly left the kitchen.

'Tell me what, Caid?'

Caid heard his mother's voice enquiring in bemusement as she caught his muttered imprecation against Jaz and her departure, across the transatlantic telephone line.

'Nothing, Mom.'

'I've got some wonderful news, Caid. You'll never guess what! Donny and Number Five are getting a divorce, and he's as good as admitted that she was pushing him to try to get me off the board. Anyway, to cut a long story short, Donny is ringing Jerry right now to tell him to pack his bags and go join his mother. There is one small problem, though…'

'Whatever it is, I don't want to hear about it,' Caid told her. 'The minute this call is over I'm calling the airline.'

'Well, yes, I can understand how much you must want to get back to your ranch, Caid. But surely it won't hurt to stay there just a little while longer, say a week or so? Only it's going to take a few days to appoint a replacement for Jerry. We've got someone in mind, of course—the current assistant chief executive of the Boston store. Oh—and have you spoken to Jaz yet, by the way?'

'Yes. I have,' Caid told her tersely. 'You can stop worrying. It seems that Jaz has no intention of leaving, nor of being coerced into leaving.'

'Coerced into leaving? What on earth do you mean?'

Caid cursed inwardly as he realised he had let his feelings get the better of him. 'It's nothing,' he denied brusquely. 'Just that Jaz thought because of the way Jerry has been treating her that the family wanted to get rid of her.'

'What? Oh, Caid! You told her how much I want her to stay, I hope?'

'I did,' Caid confirmed.

'I think I'd better speak with her myself,' he heard his mother saying. 'I'll give her a ring now. You will stay there until we can sort out the new appointment, won't you, Caid?'

'You've got ten days,' Caid told her firmly.

Ten days would take him just to the other side of their dinner engagement with Jamie and Marsh. Caid knew that he should have cancelled—and of course the only reason he was not doing so was out of good manners. It had nothing whatsoever to do with Jaz!

IMPATIENTLY, JAZ STARED at the sketch she was working on. Why was it that when she tried to alter the features of her woman's partner, and make him as physically unlike Caid as she could, the image staring back at her from her drawing board simply did not convey the emotions she wanted to project?

She had just ripped the sheet from the board when the phone rang.

The shock of hearing Caid's mother's voice on the other end of the line made her voice crack slightly as she responded to her greeting.

'I've just been speaking to Caid,' she said, and that made Jaz's heart lift and then drop with anxiety. 'Jaz, I'm so sorry about what's being happening,' Annette Dubois apologised.

'The very last thing we want is to lose you. In fact…'

As she listened to what she was being told Jaz's anxiety gave way to surprise, and then bemused relief as Annette explained briefly what was going to happen.

'Caid will be delighted to be able to get back to his ranch.' She laughed. 'He's probably been acting a bit like a grizzly with a sore paw, but there just wasn't anyone else I could trust in the way I trust him who could take my place and sort out all the problems in the UK store. I specifically asked him to persuade you not to leave. No doubt he'll be counting the days now until he gets on that flight. Now, tell me about your plans for the Christmas windows, Jaz.'

Forcing herself to focus, Jaz did so, but it was hard to talk about her work when she was still trying to absorb the fact that she had got it wrong about Caid's purpose in coming to the store. So she had made a mistake—got things wrong! Well, that was hardly surprising, was it, given Caid's own attitude towards her? If she had misjudged him he had brought that on himself, hadn't he? And for her to be thinking of apologising… No way was she going to do that!

'I TAKE IT THAT YOU HAVE spoken with my mother?'

'Yes,' Jaz responded to Caid's worryingly smooth voice and calm question.

'And of course you now realise that at no time was I in any way looking to "gloat" over—'

'All right, Caid,' Jaz interrupted him defensively. 'So I got that wrong—but it was hardly all down to me, was it? I mean you made it plain enough in New Orleans how you regarded…' Jaz pressed her lips together firmly and shook her head.

'I don't want to discuss this any further. There just isn't any point,' she burst out when he remained silent.

She could see the condemnation in his eyes…the contempt. Remembering what he had been saying to her before his mobile had rung she lifted her head and admitted, 'I can't pretend that… that sexually there isn't…that I don't…' Biting her lip to stop it from trembling, she shook her head.

'Look, the kind of life I want to share with my…with some-one…is about much more than just sexual desire. I want…I need to feel that the person closest to me understands my emotional needs as well as my physical ones, Caid, even if he can't share them. I need to feel that he supports me, that he is strong enough to allow me to be me, that when he can't agree with me he can at least attempt to compromise.'

'Compromise? You mean like you do?' Caid demanded harshly.

Jaz looked away from him. Why was it that they couldn't be together without verbally ripping into one another? Or physi-cally ripping one another's clothes off?

'Your mother said that you'd be flying home just as soon as you could arrange it,' she told him in a clipped voice, changing the subject.

'That's right,' Caid agreed in an equally distant tone. 'I've already booked my flight. I leave on the Tuesday after your cousin's dinner party.'

Jaz's heart did a double-flip.

'You still intend to go to that?'

'It would be bad manners not to do so,' Caid told her coldly.

CHAPTER TEN

ANXIOUSLY, JAZ STUDIED the clothes she had put out to pack for the weekend visit to her cousin's.

When Jamie had rung earlier in the week to check on the arrangements she had informed Jaz that she'd invited some of their neighbours to join them for dinner on the Saturday evening.

'Alan will be there,' she had told Jaz. 'He's bringing his new girlfriend. She's not really our type, but apparently his mother approves of her. Alan asked to be remembered to you, by the way. If you ask me he's got quite a thing about you, Jaz,' she had teased.

Alan Taylor-Smith was one of Jamie and Marsh's closest neighbours and Jaz knew him quite well. Although she liked him as a person, she had never been particularly attracted to him.

'What about your other guests?' she had asked, ignoring Jamie's comment.

'Newcomers to the area, from London. He's a musician and she's a TV producer. A very glamorous couple—think cool and Notting Hill. Oh, and get as glammed up as you like. I thought we'd make a really special occasion of it.'

As glammed up as she liked! Well, the dress she had decided to wear for the dinner party was certainly glamorous, Jaz acknowledged as she studied it uncertainly. She had happened to be there when the fashion buyer had been overseeing the unpacking of an order.

'Jaz, you have to see this!' she had called out. 'These clothes are from a new designer and I think they'll be a sell out over Christmas. Just look at this dress.'

The dress in question was a mere sliver of damson-coloured silk velvet, cut on the bias and dipping right down at the back almost to the point of indecency!

'Try it on,' the buyer had urged her. 'It's the perfect colour for you and you've got the figure to wear it.'

Even now Jaz wasn't entirely sure just why she had ended up buying it. It was far more daring that anything she would normally have worn. Of course the fact that the dinner party would be the final time she and Caid would be together had nothing whatsoever to do with it…

Despite the buyer's amusement, Jaz had refused to follow her recommendation and not wear anything beneath the dress.

'But you can see for yourself that briefs spoil the gown's line,' the buyer had complained.

'No way am I going anywhere without my knickers—VPL or no VPL!' Jaz had retorted sturdily.

As a compromise she had bought for herself a couple of pairs of ridiculously expensive pieces of silk nothings which barely showed through—and the pedicure in the store's beauty salon she had just managed to squeeze into her busy schedule meant that her toenails were now painted in one of the season's hottest new shades, which just happened to tone perfectly with her gown.

For the rest of the visit Jaz had packed a spare pair of jeans and a couple of tops. Her cousin might be able to muster a dinner table of guests any hostess would envy, but she was still a countrywoman at heart.

It was four o'clock, and they were due to leave at six. She hadn't seen Caid all day, and half of her was hoping that he would change his mind and not go to her cousin's. But the other half…the other half was rebelliously determined to overrule Jaz's stern disapproval and show him on this final time they would spend together just what his stubbornness was costing him!

When he walked away from her she wanted him to carry an image of her that would torment him every bit as much as her memories of him were going to torment her.

Quickly showering, she hesitated before getting redressed. With time in hand before they were due to leave, Jaz succumbed to the nervous impulse dictating that she try the dress on one more time before she packed it—just to make sure it looked alright...

CAID CHECKED THE TIME as he let himself into the house. The door to Jaz's bedroom was half open, and he could hear Jaz moving about inside the room. He had sourced half a dozen bottles of a particularly rare red wine he hoped Marsh would enjoy, to take with them, but he needed to check with Jaz to find out if Jamie preferred chocolates or flowers.

In her bedroom, Jaz slipped into the minute piece of underwear she had bought to wear under her dress. It would show through the fine silk velvet, she knew, but there was no way she intended not to wear it. Frowningly, she went to lift the dress off its hanger.

Caid knocked briefly on Jaz's bedroom door, pushing it open as he called out, 'Jaz—I want to—'

Freezing as she heard his voice, Jaz turned towards the now open door, glancing wildly from it to the dress that was still out of reach, a couple of feet away. She could feel her face turning a deep shade of hot, self-conscious pink as Caid looked at her.

'I just wanted to try on my dress for tomorrow night,' she heard herself explain defensively. 'I wasn't sure...'

With the delectably sexy sight of Jaz's virtually naked body in front of him, stirring up as it did all manner of erotic and demanding memories and longings, Caid was not really able to focus on what she was actually saying—nor make an immediate connection between her alluring state of semi-undress and the slither of silk velvet hanging up behind her on the wardrobe door!

Somehow, instinctively, deep down inside, Jaz could almost feel what Caid was thinking. What he was wanting!

Without moving, she watched and waited as he looked at her. No, there was no mistaking that hot, dangerous look of male arousal she had glimpsed in his eyes before he had managed to tamp it down.

Recklessly, she wanted him to do more than just look at her. Much, much more. Perhaps her own feelings were so acutely intense because she knew how soon they would be parting for ever! Whatever the reason, she was immediately aware of her own sharp thrill of tension, and of the highly sensually charged effect on her of having him standing there looking at her. Her body was trembling in the grip of a dangerous surge of longing so immediate that it shocked her.

Quickly she tried to counter-balance what she was feeling. Taking a step back from him whilst holding up her hand, she denied huskily, 'Caid! Don't! Stop!'

Even as she spoke Jaz could hear her own words repeated inside her head. But this time in a remembered soft, broken litany of love and helpless desire, as she had lain beneath him in the shadowy privacy of her hotel room, begging him achingly, as he loved her, 'Caid! Don't stop… Please don't stop!'

It was like being swamped by the uncontrollable forces of nature; thrown into a maelstrom over which she had absolutely no control.

As Caid came towards her, her body quivered in helpless arousal. His eyes were the deepest, darkest most passionate colour she had ever seen them, and as their gazes locked Jaz felt totally unable to drag hers away.

Dizzily she acknowledged that there was something volatile and erotically alluring about the visual impact of his dark business-suit-clad body contrasting with her virtual nakedness. She believed in total equality between the sexes, in total honesty and trust, and yet here she was being hotly turned on by the knowledge of her own vulnerability to Caid through her semi-nakedness.

His hands felt cool and powerful as they closed around her upper arms, drawing her to him, but when Jaz opened her mouth it wasn't to deny him, but to take as eagerly and hungrily as he was giving the bittersweet physical passion of his kiss.

She made him feel more angry that any other human being

he had ever met. The sheer stubbornness of her refusal to see what she was denying them infuriated him to the point where…

Beneath his hands Caid felt Jaz quiver, as though she could sense what he was thinking.

That small betraying gesture shattered his self-control. Unable to stop himself, he ground his mouth hotly and urgently against hers, driven by a deep, gut-tearing need to absorb every bit of her as deeply into himself as he could.

Wrapped tightly in Caid's arms, her mouth fused hotly to his, Jaz had to grit her teeth against the low, moaning sob of pleasure and need burning in her throat. His hand touched her breast, cupping it, and she cried out in an urgent frenzy of pleasure. The savage burn of her own inner anguish engulfed her in pain. She wanted him so much. Just this one last time…just to give her something to cling to for comfort…even if it was only a memory.…

'No!' Caid denied them both fiercely, thrusting her away from him.

As he stared at her, torn between his hungry need of her and his pride, Caid fought to control his breathing. He was dangerously close to the edge and it would take very little to push him over. What he wanted, with an intensity he could only just hold at bay, was to take Jaz and lay her on the bed so temptingly close at hand, to allow himself the sweetly savage pleasure of tasting every inch of her exposed skin, to caress her until she was crying out to him in need, until nothing could stop her from wrapping those slim, sexy legs around him as she urged him deeper and deeper within the moist intimacy of her body.

But most of all what he wanted was not only to have her body, but to have the infinitely more precious gift of her heart. For her to tell him that nothing else, nothing in this universe or beyond, was more important to her than him, that her love for him was so powerful, so comprehensive that he and it came before everything else in her life.

What he wanted, Caid recognised, was to receive from Jaz the totality of a love that would eradicate for ever that cold, hurting place in his heart where a young boy's fear of not being loved still tormented him. What he needed from Jaz was not just her love, but proof of her love. And she could not give him that...

JAZ TOOK A DEEP BREATH as she saw Caid walking towards her. She had just finished stowing her luggage in the boot of her car, and she was fiercely determined that not so much as by the smallest quiver of a single eyelash was she going to betray to Caid just how much what had happened between them in her bedroom earlier was still affecting her.

They were in the car, and she had driven several hundred yards down the road, when she suddenly remembered that she had left her big coat behind on her bed. Well, she wasn't going to go back for it now and invite Caid's criticism of her for forgetting it in the first place.

After all, it was Caid's fault. If she hadn't been so busy torturing herself about what had happened between them...

She had tried frantically to convince herself that he was totally responsible, totally to blame, that she herself had done nothing to encourage his unwanted touch and his equally unwanted kiss, but her conscience would not allow her to do so. Shamingly she had to acknowledge that she had been within a few pulse-beats of ignoring the fact that he simply wanted her for sex. Another second of that fiercely demanding kiss, of his touch on her skin, and she would have been all melting compliance, begging him to go on.

Only her pride was keeping her going now—her pride and her determination to show him that he meant as little to her emotionally as she did to him!

Coolly ignoring Caid, Jaz gradually increased the speed of her little compact car. She had saved up for it herself, refusing her father's offer to buy her something larger. Now, though, seeing the way Caid had to hunch himself up into the passenger seat, she acknowledged that it was perhaps a little on the small side. Certainly this enforced intimacy was making her far too acutely aware of Caid sitting alongside her.

Being familiar with the country route to her cousin's, Jaz had chosen to use that rather than the motorway. Her cousin lived to the west of the ancient town of Ludlow, right in the heart of the Welsh marches, and good manners obliged her to turn to Caid as they approached the town, and tell him stiltedly, 'Jamie won't be serving supper until late this evening—I normally stop here in Ludlow on my way to see her; you might like to see the town—it's very old.'

It was the first time she had spoken directly to him since they had set off.

'Good idea,' Caid agreed coolly, 'I'd like to stretch my legs.'

'I'm sorry if my car isn't up to American standards,' Jaz answered back with immediate defensiveness.

They had had a sunny day, but the evening air was crisp and sharp, hinting at an overnight frost. As she got out of her car Jaz could smell the familiar scent of winter in the air and huddled deeper into her jacket.

By the time they had walked out of the car park and up the hill past the castle Jaz was shivering, wishing that she had turned back for her thicker coat.

Refusing to check to see whether or not Caid was following her, she hurried through the market square and down a little side street to her favourite Ludlow coffee-shop-cum-wine-bar.

An hour later, when they left, having had a coffee during which they had barely spoken to one another at all, Jaz shivered in the cold night air.

It was a good twenty-minute walk back to where she had parked the car. Frost had already started to rime the ground, sparkling in the light from the clear sky. It was beautiful to look at but far too cold to be out in without the protection of a warm coat.

Within seconds of stepping outside Jaz felt her teeth start to chatter. Automatically she started to walk faster, gasping out loud as they turned a corner and she was exposed to the icy air being channelled up the hill they had to walk down to reach her car.

It was too late to try to conceal the open shivering of her body. Caid had seen it.

'Wait,' he told her cursorily.

At first Jaz thought that he was going to offer to give her his jacket, and she had the words of self-denial and refusal all ready to say. But to her consternation instead he closed the small gap between their bodies, reaching out with one arm to tug her firmly against his side, inside the jacket he had unfastened, so that she was pressed up close against his heart whilst the warmth of his body soaked blissfully into her chilled flesh.

However, when she realised that he intended them to walk back to the car like that, with her body pressed up close against his, just like the love-drugged pair of teenagers she had just seen crossing the grass in front of the castle, pausing every few steps to exchange passionate kisses, Jaz struggled to pull herself free. Caid refused to let her go.

The young lovers had disappeared into the protective shadows of the castle's mighty walls, but Jaz was oblivious to their disappearance. Pain had snatched her up in its grim claws, squeezing the love out of her heart until it dripped like lifeblood into the vast emptiness of the dark despair she was fighting to deny.

The walk to the car felt like hours. With each step they took Jaz was more and more aware of Caid's body next to her own.

Yes, she said to herself as they finally reached the car and he let her go. So far as she was concerned Tuesday could not come fast enough. Surely once the Atlantic Ocean was safely between them she would be able to get on with her own life?

'WELL, ARE YOU GOING TO tell me what's wrong or am I just going to have to guess?'

Mutinously Jaz turned away from Jamie, whom she had offered to help with dinner preparations.

'Nothing's wrong.' she insisted, and then to her horror she promptly burst into tears.

'It's Caid, isn't it?' Jamie guessed, coming over to her.

'No. It's got nothing to do with him. Why should it have?' Jaz fibbed defensively, before whispering, 'Oh, Jamie!'

Jamie simply stood and looked at her. 'Tell me about it?' she invited.

Half an hour later, when she had finally stopped speaking, Jaz looked at her imploringly. 'You do understand, don't you?'

'Yes, I do,' Jamie acknowledged sadly.

'THESE LOGS ARE JUST ABOUT the last of the trees we lost in the year before last's bad gales,' Marsh informed Caid as they stood in front of the drawing room fire, waiting for the other dinner guests to arrive.

Caid had barely seen Jaz since their arrival the previous evening; both of them had been keeping an equally determined distance from one another.

Marsh handed him a bourbon, and saw his look of appreciative surprise. 'Jaz told us it was your drink,' he told Caid with a smile.

The newspaper he most liked to read and a whole pot of coffee, strong enough to stand a spoon up in and boiling hot, had also been brought to his room this morning by one of Jamie and Marsh's children. It was exactly what he most enjoyed early in the day, and now he'd been given his favourite drink. They were not fortuitous coincidences, as he had assumed, but the result of Jaz's observations.

For Caid, that kind of detailed knowledge about a person's tastes equated not just with caring about them but with caring *for* them as well. It certainly wasn't the kind of thing he expected from a woman who prized her own freedom and independence above all.

He started to frown.

'Speaking of Jaz, I hear that you got to see her father's Holsteins. I have to tell you that that is a real compliment. He's very protective of them and pretty choosy about who he shows them to.'

'Fine beasts,' Caid responded enthusiastically, and before too long the two men were deep in a discussion about livestock. But although outwardly he was listening to what Marsh was saying, inwardly Caid was thinking about Jaz.

JAZ TENSED AS SHE HEARD the soft rap on her bedroom door, but when she went to answer it was only her cousin standing out-

side, her eyes widening appreciatively as she saw what Jaz was
wearing.

'Wow!' she exclaimed approvingly. 'You look stunning.'

'You don't think it's too much, do you?' Jaz asked anxiously
as Jamie studied her.

'It will certainly be too much for the men.' Jamie laughed.
'If I'd known you were going to be wearing something like that
I wouldn't have gone to so much trouble with the food. They'll
scarcely notice what's on their plates with you in front of them!
What do you wear underneath it, by the way?' Jamie teased.
'That fabric is so fine...'

'The briefest little thong I could find,' Jaz admitted ruefully.
'And our buyer didn't even want me to wear that. You can actually see it,' she added, pointing out the faint line in the fall of
her gown to her cousin.

'Only just!' Jamie assured her. 'Are you ready to come down?
The others are just about due to arrive.'

'Give me five minutes,' Jaz told her.

As luck would have it she was halfway down the stairs when
the other dinner guests arrived—and, as Jamie had predicted,
the arrested and approving gazes of both male guests went immediately to her as she stood poised there.

Their female partners' glances were equally immediate, but
assessing rather than admiring.

'Jaz, come down and meet everyone,' Jamie instructed, explaining to her guests, 'Jaz is my cousin.'

'Jaz!' Alan enthused, stepping forward and kissing her for
just a little bit longer than was really necessary.

'Aren't you going to introduce me, Alan?'

'Jaz—Sara,' Alan introduced obediently.

Everything about Alan's new girlfriend was sharp, Jaz reflected as Alan introduced them. Her voice, her nose; her chin,
her fashionably thin body, and even her cold china-blue eyes.

No, you don't like me, do you? Jaz reflected as she correctly interpreted the look she was being given, and the determinedly proprietorial way in which Alan's girlfriend was
gripping his arm.

To Jaz's relief the television producer and her husband were much more sociable—a pair of thirty-somethings confidently at ease with themselves and, Jaz guessed, very socially aware.

'Do you work? Are you here with a partner, or on your own?' Myla Byfleet, the TV producer, quizzed Jaz with open interest.

'You'll have to forgive my wife,' Rory Byfleet apologised with a grin. 'She used to be a reporter.'

'Jaz is the window and display designer for Cheltenham's largest department store—you may have heard of it,' Jamie explained with a smile. 'She's here with Caid Dubois, whose family have bought the store,' she added diplomatically, ignoring the look that Jaz gave her.

'I should have guessed you're artistic,' Myla complimented Jaz warmly as they all went through to the drawing room, adding, 'I love your dress! You look stunning.'

'Doesn't she just?' Alan agreed enthusiastically. As he spoke he reached past her, ostensibly to push the drawing room door open wider for her, but as he did so his hand brushed her hip and lingered there briefly.

Ruefully aware of Sara's sour glare in her direction, Jaz moved away from him. If this was the kind of reaction her dress was going to provoke, she knew she was going to regret buying it.

One man was obviously immune to its allure, though, she recognised as she saw the way that Caid was frowning at her.

Deliberately she kept her distance from him as Jamie reintroduced everyone. With a speed and obviousness that Jaz would have thought out of character, Sara began flirting openly with Caid, her voice girlishly high as she exclaimed that she adored American men. Watching them together, Jaz felt an immediate pang of angry jealousy.

BARELY LISTENING TO WHAT the woman just introduced to him was saying, Caid continued to glower at the man who had ushered Jaz into the room.

Caid had seen the way he'd touched Jaz, his hand lingering on her hip. Did she have any idea just what she looked like in that dress? It clung to her skin as fluidly as water, rippling provocatively with every movement she made. It was, Caid suspected, impossible for her to be wearing the slightest thing underneath it. But then she turned towards Marsh, accepting the aperitif he was handing her, and Caid saw the discreet line that just marked the fabric—and remembered what she had said to him about trying on her dress.

Heat shot through him—a fierce, elemental surge of possessiveness and knowledge. Without the slightest effort he could see her as she had been in the house, her body naked apart from the tiny scrap of fabric that had tantalised and tormented him so much.

He was barely aware of finishing his drink or sitting down at the table. All he could think about was Jaz. He wanted to take her somewhere very private and slide that sexy, distracting and dangerous dress from her even more distracting and dangerous body. Then he wanted to hold her, touch her, kiss every single inch of her until her voice was a paper-thin whispering sob of pleasure, begging him to satisfy her need.

Jamie had seated Alan on Jaz's right, whilst Caid sat opposite her. Despite the presence of his girlfriend, Alan was making full use of his proximity to flirt openly and fulsomely with Jaz.

Since Jaz knew him, she refrained from treating him as coolly as she would have done had he been a stranger to her. The truth was that she felt slightly sorry for him. His bossy mother was itching for him to get married and produce grandchildren, so she could dominate them in the same way she had done him, but she was equally determined to choose her own daughter-in-law. And poor Alan had a penchant for exactly the type of woman his domineering mother least wanted as her son's wife. To judge from the fact that he was dating Sara, Jaz guessed that his mother now had the upper hand.

Generously she made allowances for Alan's heavy flirting, telling herself that the poor man was probably trying to make a last desperate bid for freedom.

Beneath the table Alan had started to stroke her leg.

Immediately she moved out of his way, shaking her head at

him in discreet admonition. Across from her, Sara was shooting Jaz a bitterly resentful look, at the same time moving closer to Caid, her hand fixed firmly on his arm as she turned to smile at him.

The Byfleets were recounting a mildly ribald anecdote about a minor media personality. Politely Jaz listened and smiled though out of the corner of her eye she could see Sara whispering something to Caid. Sara's glass was already empty, and so was Alan's. To judge from the looks they were exchanging, Jaz guessed that angry words had been exchanged between them prior to their arrival.

'So you work in a store? Oh. Yes, of course—Alan's mother has mentioned you,' Sara informed Jaz dubiously, making it abundantly plain that whatever Alan's mother had had to say about her, it had not been complimentary. 'And *your* family now owns the store,' she whispered to Caid in a false 'little girly' voice.

How could any man be taken in by that kind of thing? That kind of woman? Jaz wondered irritably.

'Actually, Sara, Caid is a rancher,' she told the other girl coolly.

But if she had been hoping to deflect Sara's interest away from Caid with her statement it had backfired on her—and badly, Jaz recognised, as Sara's eyelash-batting went into double time.

'A rancher? You mean like in cowboy films? Oh, how exciting…and…and romantic! Sort of noble.'

'I think you must have got the cowboys mixed up with the Indians,' Myla Byfleet told Sara, laughing. 'You know—the noble savage sort of thing,' she explained carefully, exchanging an ironic glance with her husband.

Obviously Sara appealed to Myla as little as she did to her, Jaz recognised, but, whatever the other women around the table thought about her, Caid quite obviously thought she was wonderful.

In her own way, Sara certainly seemed determined to dominate the dinner table conversation, and to demand all the available male attention for herself—especially Caid's!

Forcing herself to ignore Caid's rapt concentration on Sara, Jaz joined in the conversation going on between the Byfleets.

She laughed when Rory Byfleet told her admiringly that she had a wonderfully musical voice, and it was the sound of that low husky laughter that drew Caid's fixed gaze to her.

'Oh, I do wish I was more like Jaz.' Sara sighed helplessly at his side. 'I do so envy women like her...'

'You do? Why?' Caid felt obliged to ask.

'Well, she's a career woman, isn't she? Men like that type of woman, don't they? They find them dangerous and exciting. All I've ever wanted to do is fall in love and have babies—stay at home and look after them and my husband.' She gave another soft sigh. 'I'm boring, I know, but that's just how I feel. Of course, Alan's always had a thing about Jaz,' she added, less softly, both her voice and her gaze sharpening as she looked across the table to where Alan was still trying to engage Jaz's attention.

'I suppose it gives her a bit of a kick to encourage him. She's that kind of woman, isn't she? It's so hard for someone like me to compete with someone like her. But Alan's mother says I would make him a good wife, and I think that in his heart Alan knows that as well. I know it's old-fashioned of me, but I believe that a woman's role is to love and support her husband and her children.'

Catching this artless declaration from the other side of the table, Jaz could feel her ears starting to burn.

Sara couldn't have found a better way to gain Caid's attention and approval! Well, she was welcome to him! Very welcome!

To Jaz's relief the evening finally came to an end. She had barely eaten or drunk anything, and now she was feeling so on edge that her head had actually begun to pound with tension.

As everyone began to exchange goodnights, Alan made a lunge towards her, obviously intent on kissing her. Immediately Jaz moved slightly to one side, so that his kiss landed against her cheek, rather than on her mouth, but she was still too late to stop him from enveloping her in a tight and embarrassingly sexual embrace.

Firmly disentangling herself, she stepped back from him just in time to see the lingering kiss that Sara was sharing with Caid.

The sickening wave of jealousy and pain that struck her was so strong that it actually physically rocked her on her feet.

Jamie, witnessing that small betraying movement, reached out and put a hand on her arm, saying quietly, 'You look exhausted. Why don't you go up to bed?'

'And leave you to clean up? No way.' Jaz shook her head, turning her back on Caid as Marsh finally closed the front door on the departing dinner guests.

Normally this was the part of Jamie's dinner parties that Jaz relished—the relaxing winding down after the event, when she and her cousin could talk intimately about the party and the guests whilst they worked companionably and efficiently together to clear everything away. But tonight…! No way did she want to discuss the intimacy that Caid and Sara had shared with anyone!

IN THE END ALL FOUR OF THEM cleaned up from the dinner party together—Jaz and Jamie hand-washing the expensive dinner service Jamie and Marsh had been given as a wedding present, whilst the two men did everything else.

'I've got a favour to ask you tomorrow,' Jamie confessed when the four of them had finally finished. 'You know the cottage we let out on the edge of the estate?' she asked Jaz. 'You pass it when you drive back.'

'Yes, I know the one,' Jaz confirmed.

Running an estate the size of Marsh's was an expensive business, Jaz knew, and her cousin and her husband did everything they could to find ways to maximise the estate's revenue. Letting out empty estate cottages to holidaymakers was one of them. This particular cottage, which had originally, in Victorian times, been the home of one of the estate's many gamekeepers, was very isolated, and a favourite location for people wanting a romantic hideaway.

Jamie had focused on this aspect of the cottage when she had refurnished it for visitors. The main bedroom possessed an enormous four-poster bed, complete with gorgeous bedlinen. And real fires burned in both the bedroom and sitting room grates—backed up by modern central heating. As part of the package she sold to visitors Jamie ensured that on their arrival they would find the fridge stocked with all manner of foodie luxuries, specially chosen with both their preferences and their status as lovers in mind.

'I've promised to take Chester over to see a friend of his to-morrow afternoon,' Jamie told her, 'and I was wondering if on your way back to Cheltenham you could possibly stop off at the cottage with the food for the guests who are due to arrive on Monday evening.'

'No problem,' Jaz assured her, only too happy to be able to help.

She had studiously ignored Caid whilst they had all been cleaning up and now, as she kissed her cousin and Marsh good-night, she deliberately kept her back to him.

Her head still ached—even more painfully, if anything—though fortunately she had some painkillers with her that she could take. They would put an end to her headache, but what about the pain in her heart? No medication on earth could ease that...

'SORRY WE HAD TO SEAT you with Sara,' Marsh apologised to Caid as he offered him a final nightcap. 'Dreadful woman. I fought like hell against Jamie when she told me that no way was she going to be a stay-at-home wife—I'd envisaged her playing the same supportive role Sara seems to favour—but Jamie made it clear that she had other ideas.

'No career, no relationship. That's what she told me. At the time I thought I was being quite the hero to give in to her, but every time I come across a woman like Sara I realise what a narrow escape I had.

'Imagine having to live with a woman like that, who has no identity of her own, no thoughts, ideas, no personality, and who spends most of her time working out how best to manipulate you and everyone else into doing what she wants whilst maintaining her chosen role of doting subservience?'

'What's that you're saying?' Jamie enquired, as she caught the tail end of Marsh's comment.

'I was just saying how lucky I am that you saved me from a fate worse than Sara,' Marsh teased her.

'Worse than Sara? Is that possible?' Jamie grimaced. 'Poor Alan. I do feel sorry for him—especially knowing what a thing he's got for Jaz.'

'A "thing"? What "thing"?' Marsh began in bewilderment, but behind Caid's back Jamie shook her head, warning him, and like the observant and intuitive husband he was Marsh recognised her silent message.

Oblivious to the looks that Jamie and Marsh were exchanging, Caid put down the drink he had been holding unfinished.

'I think I'll go up, if you don't mind,' he announced abruptly.

'What was all that about?' Marsh enquired plaintively, once he had gone. 'What did you mean, Alan has a "thing" for Jaz?'

'Well, perhaps I exaggerated a little.'

'Hmm!'

JAZ HAD JUST SWALLOWED down the second of her painkillers when she heard the knock on her bedroom door.

Going to open it, she saw Caid standing outside.

'Can I have a word?'

He looked and sounded so formidable that she automatically stood back from the door.

As she did so the light from the room fell across her body, revealing the sheer delicacy of her dress.

'I must say you looked very impressive this evening,' Caid told her coldly. 'But then of course you don't need me to tell you that, do you? Who exactly were you dressing for, Jaz, or can I guess?'

'Well, it wasn't for you!' Jaz lied.

'No, I think I managed to work that out for myself. Have you no compassion for others? No respect for their feelings?'

Jaz raised her hand to massage the pain in her temple. This was the last thing she needed right now.

'Whatever it is you want to say, Caid, I don't want to hear it!' she told him stonily.

'No. I'm damn sure you don't! But you sure as hell are going to!' Caid responded grimly.

Jaz could see how furiously angry he was, but for some reason, instead of alarming her, her recognition of his anger only served to add to the savagery of her own righteous sense of betrayal.

'Have you any idea of the damage you were causing back there during dinner?' Caid challenged her. 'The hurt you might have been inflicting?'

'What?' Jaz exclaimed, her voice taut with disbelief and incredulity. 'On who?'

Caid's mouth compressed.

'On Sara, of course,' he told her tersely. 'She's desperately in love with that—with Alan. God knows why. And she's equally desperately afraid that she will lose him. Personally I think she'd be better off if she did. Why on earth a woman like her wants a man like that, who doesn't respect her, doesn't realise how lucky he is—'

'Well, Alan might not but you obviously do,' Jaz interrupted him. 'But then of course she is your type, isn't she? Your perfect woman! Did you tell her that? You should have done. From the way she was behaving my guess is that she'd be only too delighted to ditch poor Alan if she thought you would be willing to take his place.'

'What the hell are you talking about?'

Jaz stared at him. She took a deep breath as she tried to control the fury rushing through her in a dangerous riptide.

'Isn't it obvious?' she threw at him savagely. 'I mean, Sara was hardly behaving like a loving and faithful girlfriend, was she?'

'She was very distressed,' Caid countered. 'Naturally for pride's sake she didn't want Alan to see how upset she was.'

'Which was no doubt why she gave you such a lingering goodnight kiss—even though Alan was nowhere in sight,' Jaz shot back.

Her head was pounding so badly now she was afraid she might actually be physically sick. Just thinking about the passionate kiss she had seen Sara give Caid was threatening to shatter what was left of her composure.

'Lingering? You call that a lingering kiss?' Caid derided.

'Well, it certainly looked that way from where I was standing,' Jaz countered.

'I don't care how it looked,' Caid denied. 'And besides, the best way to judge a kiss in my book is to experience it—feel it. Like this…'

Jaz realised just too late what he intended to do, and by then she couldn't evade the fierce pressure of his mouth as it came down on hers. But the punishment, the harshness she'd automatically steeled herself to resist never came. Instead Caid was softly stroking her lips with his—caressing them, teasing them, making her feel…making her want…

Helplessly she swayed closer to him, unable to stop her lips from parting as he ran his tongue-tip along them, easing them open, dipping into the soft, moist warmth of her mouth, slowly caressing her tongue, biting gently at her lips and then running his tongue over their kiss-bitten sensitivity.

Over and over again Caid brushed her mouth with his own, stroking her lips with his tongue, one hand cupping her face whilst he drew her closer to him with the other.

Mindlessly Jaz gave in to her emotions.

'Now that,' Caid told her rawly when he finally lifted his mouth from hers, 'is a lingering kiss!'

White-faced, Jaz pulled back from him.

Reaching for the bedroom door, she slammed it shut, leaving Caid standing on the other side.

Taking a deep breath, Jaz leaned against the door she had just closed whilst the tears she could no longer control filled her eyes and rolled painfully down her face.

Frowning, Caid stared at Jaz's door. The savagery of his own pain and jealousy shocked him. After one last look at the firmly closed bedroom door he made his way back to his own room.

CHAPTER ELEVEN

'AND YOU'RE SURE YOU don't mind calling at the cottage with the food?' Jamie checked, having looked from Caid's set face to her cousin's shockingly pale one.

'Not in the least,' Jaz confirmed in a brittle, too bright voice that matched her equally forced smile.

They had all just finished Sunday lunch, although Jaz had barely been able to eat more than a mouthful or so of her own. Her headache might have gone, but it had left in its place the deepest, blackest sense of despair and anguish that she had ever known.

She and Caid had totally ignored one another during the meal, and she suspected that he must feel the same abhorrence at the thought of sharing the car journey back to Cheltenham as she did.

An hour later, with Jamie's delicious home-cooked gourmet meals and other food packed into cool bags in the back of her car, Jaz paused to give her cousin a final hug, before heading towards her car.

Silently, his face drawn into grim lines, Caid followed her.

JAZ FROWNED AS SHE SAW the way the wind was beginning to whip the bare branches of the trees into a fierce frenzy, its unforecast strength scooping up piles of dead leaves and flattening the grassy pastures on either side of the road.

The morning's weather forecast had given slight a gale warning, but this looked as though it was going to be far more severe than the forecast had threatened. Automatically she switched on her car radio, to try to get an update, but all she could hear was the crackle of static.

Sensing her concern, Caid broke the silence which had lain bitterly between them since the start of their journey to demand, 'Is something wrong?'

'Not really. It's just that the wind seems to be getting very strong,' Jaz responded stiffly.

Out of the corner of her eye she could see the sudden quirk of Caid's eyebrows, and heard the slight amusement in his voice as he drawled, 'If you think this is strong you should see some of the twisters we get back home. And in the winter the wind can blow up one hell of a snowstorm.'

Jaz didn't bother to make any response; she was too busy gritting her teeth against the way the wind was now buffeting her small car as she took the turn-off into the long and winding unmade-up road that led to the cottage.

Right at the furthermost boundary of the estate, it was nestled in the heart of a small pretty wood, overlooking a good-sized natural pond which was the habitat of a variety of wildlife.

Skilfully, Jamie had utilised this charming setting to create an artlessly wild garden for the cottage—which in actual fact was really more of a small four-square Victorian house than a mere cottage.

As she parked her car outside Jaz was disturbed to see how increasingly wild the wind had become, causing the branches of the trees around the cottage to thrash frantically. She could feel the car rocking, and was unable to suppress the small gasp of alarm that rose to her lips.

Jaz could see the frowning look Caid gave her as he thrust open the passenger door, but unlike her he did not have seared into his memory pictures of the destruction caused by a certain other gale, which had shocked the whole country with the devastation it had caused.

A little nervously she too got out of the car, flinching as the branches of the trees beat frantically against the sky. Caid was already opening the boot of the car, and, reminding herself of

just why they were here, Jaz reached in her pocket for the spare
set of keys to the cottage and hurried up to the front door.

As she opened it the scent of Jamie's home-made pot-pourri
soothed and enveloped her. The cottage felt warm, thanks to its
central heating.

As she looked back towards the car she saw that Caid was
starting to remove the food carriers.

In view of the weather Jaz was glad that they wouldn't need
to spend very much time there. No longer, in fact, than it would
take to put the food safely in the fridge and leave a welcome note
and a bowl of fruit for the incoming guests. The truth was that
the sooner they were on their way the happier she would be—
and not just because of the storm that was threatening outside.
No, the real danger was within herself: the fear of what even the
smallest degree of physical intimacy with Caid might do to her
self-control.

Even as her thoughts formed, Jaz could hear how the gale
was increasing in intensity. As she crossed the hallway, leaving
Caid to follow her inside, she tensed at the sudden and breath-
catchingly eerie silence that made the tiny hairs on her skin lift
in atavistic warning.

Instinctively she turned towards Caid, who was now standing on the other side of the hallway, listening as intently as she
was herself.

The storm wasn't over, she knew that, but even though she
was prepared for it, the sudden high-pitched whistling of the
wind as it picked up again at a terrifyingly high speed, made
her flinch.

From outside they could hear the sharp cracking noise of
wood splintering whilst rain spat viciously at the windows.

'What the hell is happening out there?' Caid demanded, strid-
ing towards the door.

Jaz went to follow him, but as she did so she heard a door
banging somewhere upstairs, as though a window had been left
open.

As Caid disappeared through the open front door, Jaz headed
for the stairs.

The cottage had two smaller bedrooms in addition to the large master bedroom suite, and a huge bathroom, with a sensually luxurious spa bath. It was in one of the two smaller rooms that Jaz found the window which had been left slightly open and quickly closed it before turning to hurry back downstairs.

She was just about to step into the hall when she heard it—a horrible renting, a savage cacophony of sounds, that had her running for the front door and tugging it open, her heart leaping in frantic panic and hammering against her chest wall as her worst fears were confirmed.

The storm had brought down a huge tree which had fallen right across the lane, completely blocking it—and crushing her car.

For a few seconds shock froze her into immobility. She could see the bright patch of colour that was her car beneath the tree's heavy branches, just as she could see the huge hole in the earth where the tree's roots had once rested. But the whole scene seemed to be being relayed to her with her senses in slow motion, so that though she saw it, she somehow could not quite comprehend it.

Her gaze panned the whole scene slowly, several times, and then abruptly focused on the dark blur that was Caid's jacket, just visible on the ground between her crushed car and the heaviest part of the uprooted tree. Caid's jacket! The jacket which Caid had been wearing when he had walked out of the hall a few minutes ago! Caid's jacket… The jacket he had been wearing. The jacket with his body inside it…

Jaz started to run, brushing aside the branches that tore at her clothes and hair, pushing them back as she fought to get to Caid, sobs tearing at her throat as her fear for him shook her whole body. Ignoring the cold wet sting of the small whippy branches as she climbed through them, she cried out Caid's name in frantic panic.

Only now, when the fear of losing him had stripped bare her emotions, could she truly see how much she loved him. As she focused on his jacket she knew with a sudden blinding flash of insight, in a way she had refused to recognise before, that he was quite simply the only man she could ever love.

She had almost reached him, but the branches were thicker now, and more tangled, too heavy for her to move. She would have to—

'Jaz!'

Disbelievingly, Jaz stood still. She could hear Caid calling her name. But the sound was coming from behind her, not from the frighteningly still dark mass of the jacket she had been working her way towards!

'Jaz!'

Stronger now, and more urgent, the commanding tone of Caid's voice forced her to turn round.

The sight of him standing just outside the open front door of the cottage filled her with a feeling that was at once both so joyous and so humbling that she found it impossible to give it a name. More than relief, it was a sense of profound gratitude so intense that it blurred her eyes with tears.

Slowly at first, and then more quickly, she made her way back, his name a shaky tear-stained gasp, blown away on the gusting wind. 'Caid—you're alive. You're safe...'

It was Caid who was walking towards her now, reaching out to extricate her from the final tangle of branches until she finally she stood beside him, trying to push the damp hair off her face with numb fingers, unaware that the moisture on her face was not rain but her own tears.

'Oh, Caid... Caid...'

Unable to stop herself, she threw herself into his arms, shaking from head to foot as he opened them to enclose her. 'I thought you were hurt...dead...' she whispered chokily as her body shook with the ferocity of her emotions. 'I saw your jacket...'

'It caught on a branch whilst I was collecting some extra logs for the fires—I noticed that they needed some. I took it off, and then the wind must have blown it into the tree,' Caid said, his voice as thick with emotion as her own.

Her emotions overwhelmed her. To her own shame and disgust tears filled her eyes once again.

'Jaz—' Caid began, but she shook her head.

'It's nothing—I'm not crying,' she denied shakily. 'Not really.' She made to pull away from him, but Caid refused to let her go.

'You're in shock,' he told her curtly. 'I saw what had happened. That's why I went back inside—to tell you and ring Jamie. You nearly gave me heart failure when I came back and saw you crawling through those branches.'

Suddenly Jaz was trembling so violently that her teeth were chattering; the trembling turned into a deep intense shaking as shock and relief fought for control of her emotions.

'Come on—let's get back inside,' she heard Caid telling her.

Was it her imagination, or had his arms tightened just that little bit more around her?

As she started to move away from him, to walk back to the cottage, she felt the resistance of his hold. A brief silent questioning look into his face brought an answering equally silent shake of his head. Gratefully Jaz sank back against him, allowing him to guide her back to the house and revelling in the sensation of being so close to him.

With the door closed against the still howling gale, the warmth of the cottage embraced her, permeating the numbness of her shocked body.

'I'd better warn you that we're here for the night,' Caid told her ruefully. 'When I spoke to Marsh he said that he doesn't feel it's safe enough to send anyone out tonight to lift the tree. He reckons it would be dark before he could get anyone here...'

Listening to him, Jaz closed her eyes, and then wished she hadn't as behind her closed eyelids she saw the mental image she had recorded of the moment she'd looked across at her car and seen what she had believed to be Caid's trapped, broken body beneath the full weight of the tree.

Tears filled her eyes and splashed down her face.

'I thought you were there...under the tree,' she whispered, pulling herself free of Caid's arms to look up into his eyes, her own huge and dark with emotion. 'I thought… Oh, Caid… Caid…'

'Shush…it's all right,' Caid comforted her, and he drew her back into his arms, holding her as carefully as though she were a small hurt child.

The intensity of her emotion made him ache with love for her, and at the same time the raw nakedness of her pain made him want to hold her and protect her for ever.

'What happened to us, Caid?' Jaz asked him chokily. 'Why did it all have to go so wrong?'

Her fears had stripped away from her any desire to pretend any longer that she didn't care.

'I don't know,' Caid admitted sombrely. 'But what I do know is how much I want to make it all right, Jaz. How very, very much I want to start again…to tell you and show you just how much I still love you.'

'You love me?'

She had said it with all the shining joy and hope of a child discovering that there was a Father Christmas after all, Caid recognised, looking down into her eyes and seeing there the love and bemusement he could hear in her voice. But before he could reassure her she suddenly reached up and pulled his head down towards her own, kissing him with frantic anguished passion, her face wet with tears.

Fiercely Caid struggled between logic and love. Logic told him that they should be talking through their problems, but with Jaz's mouth pressed so hungrily and so sexily against his, how the hell was he supposed to think about logic?

'Hold me, Caid! Love me!' Jaz demanded in between feverish kisses. 'I need to know that this isn't a dream, that this is real, that *you* are real, not…'

As she started to shudder, unable to put into words the fears that had filled her earlier, Caid knew there was no way he wanted to resist her.

'I've never stopped loving you,' he told her rawly, cupping her face in his hands and looking down deep into her eyes as he kissed each word into her mouth, spacing them slowly apart so that the kisses between them grew longer and more intense. 'And as for holding you...' He went on in a husky dangerously male voice, 'Jaz, no way can I hold you right now and not make love to you,' he admitted thickly.

For a second Jaz hesitated, but she knew that if she were to close her eyes she would see again his jacket lying beneath the fallen tree, feel again the agonising sensation of believing he was dead.

'Then make love to me,' she answered him softly. 'Make love with me, Caid.'

Silently they looked at one another. Even the air around them seemed to be holding its breath, as though something beyond it was waiting, hoping...

'Jaz...'

As he moaned her name Jaz took Caid's breath into her own lungs, digging her fingers into the hard muscles of his shoulders and then the back of his neck as they kissed one another with passionate abandon. She couldn't stop touching him, running her hands over his flesh, his body. A tiny gasp of tormented longing locked in her throat as their need for one another burned out of control.

Blindly she tugged at the fabric of Caid's shirt, its buttons, anything that was stopping her from reaching her longed-for goal of feeling his skin beneath her touch. She was heedless of the impatient help that Caid himself was giving her as he ruthlessly wrenched buttons from fastenings, ignoring the tearing sounds of destruction he was causing to his shirt.

Even more than Jaz wanted to touch him, he wanted to be touched by her. To be kissed by her, welcomed by her into the soft, sweet mystery of her wholly womanly and beloved body.

His hands cupped her breasts, tugging at her own clothes. White streaks of heat shot through her, and Jaz gave a small, thin cry of desperate longing, burying her face against his throat as her body convulsed into his touch.

On the floor she could see Caid's shirt, and her own top, although she had no knowledge of just how it had got there. She moaned as Caid bent his head, easing her breast free of her bra to caress it with the hot sweetness of his mouth.

'Not here,' Jaz heard Caid protesting huskily, lifting his mouth from hers only to rub his thumb against her softly swollen lips whilst he watched her aching reaction to his touch with a look that said he simply could not bear not to be touching her. 'Let's go upstairs—so that I can really enjoy you. So that we can really enjoy one another,' Caid begged her.

As she listened to him a long, slow shudder of response passed through Jaz. Silently, she nodded her head.

It was Caid who picked up the clothes they had discarded, and Caid who halfway up the stairs turned to Jaz and held her against his body, devouring her mouth in a kiss of such intimate passion that its intensity and promise made Jaz's eyes sting with emotion.

Like her, Caid seemed reluctant to speak—perhaps because he was afraid of damaging or destroying what was happening between them, Jaz reflected, as Caid led her to the door of the main bedroom and then opened it.

They kissed with hungry, biting little kisses, unable to get enough of one another, unable to control their shared longing to touch and taste every belovedly familiar, ached-for part of one another.

A stream of discarded clothes marked their progress to the huge four-poster bed, and now they stood body to body at the foot of it, Jaz naked apart from her silky briefs.

'I love you. I have always loved you. I shall always love you,' Caid told Jaz as he kissed her closed eyelids, the curve of her jaw, the soft readiness of her mouth, and then the pulsing hollow at the base of her throat, whilst his hands moulded and shaped her willing nakedness for their shared pleasure.

His own body, taut and naked, virile, visibly mirrored the desire beating through Jaz. Achingly she reached out to touch him, but Caid stopped her, and instead dropped to his knees in front of her, sliding his hands beneath the silky fineness of her briefs and slowly removing them, whilst his lips tormented her with hotly erotic kisses placed with hungry sensuality against her naked flesh.

He had loved her intimately and sensually in the past, but this, Jaz knew, was something else—something richer. This was a total giving of himself, a revelation of his need and vulnerability, almost a worship of all that she meant to him, a form of loving that somehow went way beyond even the wildest shores of desire.

When his tongue finally stroked against the innermost places of her sex, for a heartbeat of time both of them went still, sharing a special communion, a special bonding in a place that was totally their own.

Tenderly Jaz reached out and touched his downbent head, catching her breath as her own sensual response to his intimacy suddenly crashed through her. Her fingers slid to his shoulder, sweat-slick with the heat of his arousal, and her sob of pleasure was sharp and high.

She had to touch him, taste him, feel him again where he belonged—deep, deep inside her.

As the words of love and longing poured from her Caid responded to them, gathering her up and placing her on the bed, his own moan of raw triumphant pleasure when she reached for him, stroking the length of his erection whilst she studied him with eager hungry eyes, joining the soft aching words of praise she was whispering against the pulsing fullness of him.

'I want you inside me, Caid. Now! Please, please now!'

'ARE YOU AWAKE?'

Instinctively Jaz burrowed tightly into the warmth of Caid's body before answering him.

'Yes, I am,' she admitted.

It was too early yet for dawn to have begun lightening the sky, but plenty late enough for the fire Caid had lit to have burned down to mere ashes. Jaz gave a small shiver at the metaphorical parallels her thoughts were drawing. She didn't want to acknowledge them any more than she wanted to acknowledge the purpose she could hear behind Caid's question.

'Last night was wonderful,' she whispered to him, stroking her fingertips along his chest, ruffling the soft hair lying there. '*You* were wonderful,' she added.

'Wonderful? But not wonderful enough for you to change your mind and come back to America with me? Is that what you're saying?' Caid guessed.

Jaz could feel the happiness seeping out of her. She didn't want to have this discussion. All she wanted was to lie here with Caid and keep them both enclosed in their own special world, here beneath the bedclothes.

Their special world? A world as fragile as a glass Christmas tree bauble, as ephemeral as a soap bubble? That was their world. In the real world their world could not survive. Like their love?

Tears pricked her eyes. She so much wanted things to be different. For Caid to be different…? Jaz closed her eyes. She loved so many, many things about him. His strength, his warmth, his honesty. But she could not live the life he wanted her to live with him.

'I love you more than I can find words to tell you, Jaz. There is nothing I want more than for you to be my wife and the mother of my children. What we have between is just so good.' Caid groaned, kissing the top of her head and tightening his hold on her. 'So very, very good. Come back with me when I fly home. At least give the ranch a chance. If I can't persuade you that you'll love living there with me and our kids in oh, say ten years, then you can come back.'

His voice was warm and teasing, but Jaz did not make the mistake of forgetting that the issue he was raising was very serious.

'Caid, I can't,' she interrupted him firmly. 'No matter how much I might want to, I couldn't go anywhere until after Christmas.'

When he started to frown, she reminded him, 'My windows, Caid. They're the focal point of my working year. There's no way I can walk away and leave them. No way at all. Not for anyone.'

'You could fly out for a few days. For Christmas and New Year at least,' Caid argued crisply.

Jaz shook her head.

'No, Caid.' Her voice was equally crisp. 'Not even for Christmas. I shall be working right up until the last minute on Christmas Eve, and then even before the store opens again I shall be going in to help the others get ready for the sale—and that includes redressing the windows. You know what you're asking is impossible, Caid. Not even my parents…'

Caid looked at her.

'Your parents? Yes, I can see how hard it must have been for you growing up, Jaz, and how…how hurt you must have felt at times, how alone. But surely that makes what we have even more special? I know it does for me, which is why— Look, Jaz can't you see?'

Jaz could hear the frustration and the stubbornness in his voice and her heart went cold—cold but unfortunately not numb, so that she could still feel every sharp agonising vibration of the pain she knew was lying in wait for her.

The temptation to give in, to tell him that she could be what he wanted, was frighteningly strong. But Jaz knew that she could not give in to it.

Taking a deep breath, she answered unevenly, 'No, Caid. Can't *you* see? Can't you see that this issue goes much further than just you and I?'

'No. I can't see that. What do you mean?' Caid challenged her. He had already shifted his body, so that now there was a chilly little distance between them in the bed, and now he removed his arms from her. Ostensibly so that the could prop his head up and look at her, but to Jaz the withdrawal of the warmth of his body and his arms was very symbolic.

'What I mean,' Jaz told him, hesitating as she tried to choose her words extra carefully, 'is that I am not just thinking of this as an issue that involves you and I. I have to think about the lessons I learned as a child, Caid—just as much as you have to think about yours. My parents love me dearly, I know that, but I also know how it feels to be a child who is not allowed to be their own person and to follow their own life path. I don't want that for my children—our children.'

She could see the way Caid was frowning at her as he absorbed what she was trying to say.

'But I would never do that to my kids. Never.'

'Caid, you can't say that,' Jaz argued quietly. 'What if we had daughters? What if they wanted to be high-flying career women? How would that make you feel? How would it make them feel if the father they loved disapproved of their ambitions? And even if you didn't…if you were able to give them the right to be themselves that you could not give me…what kind of effect do you think it would have on any child to witness a relationship between his or her parents which sent out a clear message that it was not acceptable for a woman to be anything other than a wife and a mother? I can't marry you and not have children, Caid. But neither can I give my children a father who could not accept and respect them and me as individual human beings.'

'Jaz, please…' Caid implored her. 'I can't change the way I am. The way I feel.'

'No, Caid,' Jaz agreed quietly. 'I don't suppose you can.'

'You know my flight is booked for tomorrow morning?' Caid warned her. 'This is our last chance, Jaz.'

'Yes, I know that,' Jaz agreed woodenly. 'I can't do it, Caid,' she burst out, when she saw the way he was looking at her. 'I can't mortgage my—our children's future happiness to buy my own. I can't. And I don't think that you'd be able to either. This problem isn't going to go away…ever. It would always be there, confronting us. Separating us. I can't live like that—and, more importantly, I can't love like that.'

'Where are you going?' Caid demanded sharply as she moved away from him and got out of bed.

'It's morning,' she told him flatly, directing his gaze towards the window. 'The storm has gone now. It's blown itself out, Caid. It's time for us to move on. To go our separate ways.'

She could cry later, Jaz told herself. After all, she would have the rest of her life to cry for Caid and their love!

CHAPTER TWELVE

'I WISH YOU WOULD CHANGE your mind and join the rest of us in Aspen for Christmas, Caid.'

'I can't. It's a busy time at the ranch,' Caid answered his mother brusquely.

'Besides, Christmas is a time for kids, and I don't have any.'

'Kids and families,' his mother corrected him gently. 'And you do have one of those.' She smiled ruefully as she got up from the chair she had been sitting on in the large kitchen of his ranch. 'I can still remember the Christmas you were four. We'd got you a toy car, but you ignored it and spent most of the day playing with the box it came in instead.'

Caid gave her a bleak look.

It was just over two weeks since he had left England—and Jaz—and there hadn't been an hour, a minute, a single second during those weeks when he hadn't been thinking about her... wanting her.

That last night they had shared together would stay in his memory for ever. No other woman could or would ever take her place, but he couldn't go back on what he had said to her, nor alter his feelings. But knowing that didn't stop him longing for her.

'The Christmases I most remember,' he told her curtly, 'are the ones when you weren't there. Remember them, Mom? There was the one you spent in Australia—you sent me photographs of yourself and a koala bear—and then there was the time you were in India, sourcing embroidered fabrics, and then China, and—'

He stopped and shook his head, bitterness drawing deep grooves either side of his mouth.

He only had to access those memories to know how right he was to feel the way he did about his own marriage.

'Caid, listen to me!'

As Annette Dubois turned her head towards him Caid saw the pain in her eyes.

'When you were a child—'

'You had your work and that was way, way more important to you than I was. Your need to express yourself came first. You—'

'Along with the koala bear I sent airline tickets for your father to bring you to me,' Annette interrupted him. 'It was all supposed to be arranged. I'd organised a special barbecue on the beach with some other kids for you... But your father changed his mind at the last minute. That's how it was between us.

'When I was in India I tried to get back, but I was hospitalised with dysentery. In China...well, by the time I went to China I'd begun to give up. But I did send you a video of myself, telling you how much I loved you and how much I wished I could be with you. I guess you never saw it! You see, Caid, by then I'd realised that no matter what I did, how much I tried to be conciliatory, to find ways to persuade your father to allow me to have you with me, it was just never going to happen.'

'Dad allow you? Oh, come on, Ma. I was there. I heard him on the phone to you, pleading with you to come home. "Don't worry, son," he used to promise me. "I'll speak to your mom and tell her how much we need her here."'

'Oh, Caid... I promised myself I would never do this, but... your father and I should never have married—'

'I've heard it all before, Mom.'

'Some of it...but, no, you haven't heard all of it, Caid. By the time you were born we both knew that our marriage was all washed up. I would have gone for a divorce before you were born—raised you on my own. But my father persuaded me not to. Afterwards... Well, I guess I was so desperate to prove that I could support the both of us, and to show big brother Donny that I wasn't going to be sidelined out of the business, that I overcompensated.

'My plan was that I would take you with me when I travelled, but the family were horrified at the idea of me taking a new baby into some of the remote areas I was going to, and I guess they frightened me enough to think that perhaps you were safer at home. But then when I came home I found that I was being eased out of your life, that your father was making decisions that should have been made by both of us.

'Those phone calls you just mentioned, for instance—' she shook her head '—there never were any—not to me. Your father knew how much I loved you, Caid. How important you were to me. You see, after you were born the doctors told me that I couldn't have any more children, so he blackmailed me into letting him play the role of good father whilst I was forced into the position of bad mother!'

'You could always have given up your job,' Caid pointed out coldly.

'Yes, Caid, I could. But you see, I had inherited the fatal family stubbornness—just like you—and I thought I could make everything work out. By the time I was ready to admit that I was wrong it was too late. Had I been less stubborn, less determined to see everything as black or white, no doubt your father and I could have reached a compromise. And do you know what hurts me most, Caid? Not what I have lost, but what has been lost to you. I know we've mended our broken fences, and that we now share a good relationship, but whatever I do I can never give you back those lost years, that lost love. But you must never think that I didn't care, Caid, that you weren't in my mind every single second. You were my child. How could you not be?'

When Caid wouldn't meet her eyes, she changed the subject.

'I managed to persuade Jaz to tell me about her Christmas windows. She is very, very talented. She'd been interviewed on national TV the day I spoke to her—a contact she'd made through her cousin apparently. The final window is just so special! Did she discuss the theme she was using with you when you were over there?'

'No,' Caid replied curtly. He turned away from his mother to look out across the snow-covered land beyond the window, so that she wouldn't see his expression.

'Well, she took these photographs and sent them to me. Would you like to see them?'

As desperately as Caid wanted to refuse, he knew he couldn't without arousing his mother's suspicions.

'I loved this touch,' Annette chuckled a few minutes later, when the photographs were laid out in order on Caid's kitchen table. 'To have dressed the man—the husband and father of the family—in such very American clothes is a really unifying idea that subtly underlines our ownership of the store.'

Caid froze as he looked at the photograph his mother was pointing to. The window dummy was dressed in denim jeans and a white tee shirt underneath a designer label shirt. Just like the man Jaz had drawn in the sketch he had picked up off the floor—the man who had borne such a remarkable physical resemblance to himself.

'And look at these,' his mother was commanding excitedly. 'I mean in our modern consumer-driven world, when we're all so hungry for something meaningful, what could mean more than the gifts this woman is being given?'

Unwillingly Caid studied the photograph. Beautifully presented gifts were being handed to the window woman by her family.

Caid tensed as he read the handwritten notes, Jaz had placed in each of the open gift boxes.

Love… Joy… And there, tucked away in so small a box that he almost missed it, an extra gift that the man was handing over. Inside it, in writing so small he could barely read it, Jaz had written the word, *Acceptance.*

As she slipped unobtrusively into the crowd of Christmas shoppers admiring her windows, Jaz wondered why she didn't feel her normal sense of thrilled pride.

It was true, after all—as the local paper had reported—that this year she had outdone herself.

Annette Dubois had raved excitedly about Jaz's work, but all the praise and excitement in the world couldn't warm the cold despair from her heart. In her bleakest moments Jaz feared that nothing ever would.

'They look wonderful, Jaz.'

Startled, Jaz turned her head to see Jamie smiling at her.

'I've come to do some last-minute bits of shopping,' Jamie explained. 'We fly out to America tonight. I must admit, I'm not really that keen on going. I'd prefer to stay at home and then go somewhere lovely and hot in January. You know me, I hate the cold and I'm definitely no skier. But Marsh loves it, and so do the kids, so we agreed to compromise. Aspen this Christmas, but next year we're going to stay at home and Marsh is going to take me to the Caribbean in January.'

Nervously Jaz waited as her luggage was checked in. Her flight left in just under an hour, and she still wasn't sure she was doing the right thing. It had been the conversations she'd had with Jamie that had done it—that and the unendurable pain of longing for Caid.

Compromise. Could they do that? Would Caid even want to try? She hadn't warned him what she was doing. She had been too afraid that she might not have the courage to go through with it, that she might change her mind. And besides…

He might refuse to see her. He might tell her that he did not want to compromise…that he preferred to live his life without her rather than give even the smallest bit of ground.

Her whole body shook.

What was she doing here? She couldn't go through with it… She was a fool to even be thinking that anything could be different. But it was too late to change her mind now. Her luggage had been checked in!

Was he crazy for doing this? Caid had no idea. He only knew that it was something he had to do. And anyway, there was no going back now. Blizzard conditions had been forecast for the part of the state where his ranch was; there was no way he could get back.

His flight for Heathrow didn't leave for another four hours.

In his suitcase he had the Christmas gift he had carefully wrapped for Jaz.

Would she accept it? Would she accept him? Would she accept that he had come to realise there was a need for change within himself? That they had something so important, so precious to share with one another, that there had to be a way they could make it work? That listening to his mother had softened his iron-hard implacability? Given him the key to turn in the rusty lock of the prison wall he had constructed for himself out of stubbornness and the ghost of his childhood fear of losing the people he loved? And, even if she accepted the genuineness of his willingness to change, would that be enough?

GRITTY-EYED AND EXHAUSTED, Jaz stared at the desk clerk in disbelief.

'What do you mean,' she faltered, 'there are no flights to Freshsprings Creek? I'm booked on one…'

'I'm sorry, all flights to that part of the state have been cancelled due to weather conditions,' the clerk told Jaz politely. 'There's a blizzard out there. No planes can get in or out. Everything is grounded until the weather clears.'

'But I have to get there,' Jaz protested. 'Is there another way… train? Road…?'

The desk clerk was shaking her head, giving Jaz a pitying look.

'Honey, like I just said, there's a blizzard. That means nothing moves. Nothing.'

ABSENTLY, CAID GLANCED at his watch. Another half an hour and he would go through to wait for his flight. He glanced round the terminal building and then froze.

Over by the enquiry desk a familiar figure was speaking with the clerk. It looked like Jaz. But it couldn't be. Could it?

'Please, you don't understand. I have to get there,' Jaz was begging the clerk. 'You see—'

Helpless tears of frustration blurred her eyes as she recognised then the impossibility of explaining to this stranger just why she was so desperate to get to Caid.

'Perhaps I can help?'

'Caid?' Jaz stared up at him in disbelief. 'Caid! What—? How—?'

Colour tinged her face, drawing out its tired pallor, her eyes huge and dark with emotion.

Caid looked away from her and glanced towards the announcement boards.

'They've just called my flight,' he told her.

'Your flight?' Jaz went white.

'Listen,' Caid demanded.

Straining her ears, Jaz heard a voice announcing that the international flight for London, Heathrow, was now boarding.

'You're going home?' Jaz whispered in shock.

'No,' Caid told her softly, shaking his head as he relieved her of the bag she was clutching and took her in his arms. His voice was suddenly muffled as he whispered, 'I am home, Jaz. Now. *You* are my home. My heart. My love. My life. I was on my way to see you. To tell you…to ask you…to see if we could…'

'Compromise?' Jaz offered hesitantly.

Silently they looked at one another.

'There's a decent spa hotel a few miles from here. We could book in there—at least until the weather clears,' Caid suggested. 'Then we could…talk…'

As LAZILY AND SENSUALLY as a small cat, Jaz stretched out her naked body, revelling in the warmth of Caid's. She had no idea just how long they had been asleep, but it was dark outside now.

Contentedly she leaned over and kissed the top of his bare shoulder, grinning when he immediately wrapped his arm around her and turned to look at her.

'Still love me?' he asked her softly.

'What do you think?' Jaz teased back.

'What I think,' Caid told her, his expression suddenly serious, 'is that I don't know how I ever thought I could possibly live without you. I was an arrogant fool...'

'No.' Jaz corrected him tenderly. 'You were a wonderful, but very stubborn man.'

'We *will* make it work,' Caid promised her. 'I know it won't always be easy. But if we—'

'Compromise?' Jaz smiled.

During the long hours of the fading day, when they had talked everything through with one another, it had become their private buzzword.

'Jaz, I want you more than I want life itself. I love you totally and absolutely, without conditions or boundaries. And nothing—*nothing*,' Caid stressed emotionally, 'will ever change that. I love you for the woman you are. I love every bit of what you are. Every bit, Jaz,' he added emotionally. 'I will never come between you and your career, I promise.'

'And do you also promise that you won't regret any of this?' Jaz asked him, searching his gaze.

'The only thing I could ever regret now is being fool enough to let you go!' Caid answered rawly. 'I guess what my mom had to say made me see a lot of things in a very different light. But even without that I couldn't have gone on much longer without you.'

'Like me with my windows. They matter. They matter a lot. But every time I looked at that mannequin all I could see was you.'

'Well, I have to tell you that ranchers do not wear designer shirts.' Caid laughed.

'Will the blizzard stop in time for us to spend Christmas together at the ranch?' Jaz asked him eagerly.

'It might. But there's something important we have to do before I take you home with me,' Caid informed her.

Jaz frowned. 'What?'

'Well,' Caid murmured as he bent his head to kiss her, 'winter hereabouts lasts a good long time... Once the snow settles it could be well into March before it lifts, and that's a lot of cold dark nights when there won't be much to do except snuggle up in bed together. And if we do that…I want us to get married, Jaz,' he told her abruptly his voice suddenly becoming much more serious. 'Now. Not next year, or maybe some time, but now—just as soon as we can. Are you ready to make that kind of commitment to me? Do you trust me enough to believe what I've said about being willing to change?'

Jaz took a deep breath.

'Yes,' she told him softly. 'Yes, I do…'

EPILOGUE

'I DO...'

'Are they married yet, Mummy?'

Jaz could feel the ripple of amusement spreading through their guests as they all heard Jamie's youngest son's shrill-voiced question.

Pink-cheeked, she was glad that only she could hear Caid growling to her, 'Once we are I'm taking you away from this lot. Somewhere very, very private just as soon as I can.'

Their arrival in Aspen a few days earlier, followed by Caid's announcement that they were getting married, had been all it needed to have the focused determination of the Dubois family, plus some hefty input from Jamie, swinging into action.

So much so, and so effectively, that here she and Caid were on Christmas Eve, exchanging their vows in the fairytale setting of Aspen, surrounded by the love and approval of both their families.

Jaz's dress had been specially flown in from the Dubois store in Boston, a dozen junior members of the Dubois family had rushed to offer their services as her bridal attendants—and Caid had declared that he wished he had simply flown her to Las Vegas and married her in some drive-through wedding chapel.

'You may kiss the bride...'

'You wait,' Caid promised softly to Jaz as his lips brushed tenderly against hers. 'Once we're on our own I'm going to show you how a man really wants to kiss his bride.'

'Will it be a lingering kiss?' Jaz dulcetly teased him back.

And then they were finally alone, in a wonderfully private suite at the luxurious hotel Caid had booked for them.

'Come here,' Caid demanded throatily, reaching for her.

Willingly Jaz went to him, looking enquiringly up at him as he handed her a small, carefully wrapped gift.

'What's this?' she asked.

'Your Christmas present,' Caid told her. 'I was going to give it to you when I reached Cheltenham.'

A little uncertainly, Jaz unwrapped it. He had already given her the most beautiful engagement and wedding rings, and a pair of matching diamond earrings, but she could tell from the tense set of his shoulders that this gift was something special.

Very carefully she lifted the lid from the box and then removed the layers of tissue paper.

Right down in amongst them was a small scrap of paper.

Jaz's heart started to beat unsteadily.

Her fingers were shaking as she took out the paper.

'Read it,' Caid urged her.

Slowly, Jaz did so.

Written on the paper was one single word. *Acceptance.*

'Oh, Caid.' Tears blurred her eyes and trembled in her voice as she flung herself into his arms. 'That is the most wonderful, the most precious…the best present you could have given me,' she told him. 'I shall treasure it for ever.'

'And I shall treasure *you* for ever. You and our love,' Caid promised.

* * * * *

REQUEST YOUR
FREE BOOKS!

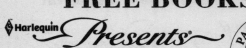

2 FREE NOVELS PLUS
2 FREE GIFTS!

YES! Please send me 2 FREE Harlequin Presents® novels and my 2 FREE gifts (gifts are worth about $10). After receiving them, if I don't wish to receive any more books, I can return the shipping statement marked "cancel." If I don't cancel, I will receive 6 brand-new novels every month and be billed just $4.30 per book in the U.S. or $4.99 per book in Canada. That's a saving of at least 14% off the cover price! It's quite a bargain! Shipping and handling is just 50¢ per book in the U.S. and 75¢ per book in Canada.* I understand that accepting the 2 free books and gifts places me under no obligation to buy anything. I can always return a shipment and cancel at any time. Even if I never buy another book, the two free books and gifts are mine to keep forever.

106/306 HDN FERQ

Name _____ (PLEASE PRINT)

Address _____ Apt. #

City _____ State/Prov. _____ Zip/Postal Code

Signature (if under 18, a parent or guardian must sign)

Mail to the **Reader Service:**
IN U.S.A.: P.O. Box 1867, Buffalo, NY 14240-1867
IN CANADA: P.O. Box 609, Fort Erie, Ontario L2A 5X3

Not valid for current subscribers to Harlequin Presents books.

**Are you a current subscriber to Harlequin Presents books
and want to receive the larger-print edition?
Call 1-800-873-8635 or visit www.ReaderService.com.**

* Terms and prices subject to change without notice. Prices do not include applicable taxes. Sales tax applicable in N.Y. Canadian residents will be charged applicable taxes. Offer not valid in Quebec. This offer is limited to one order per household. All orders subject to credit approval. Credit or debit balances in a customer's account(s) may be offset by any other outstanding balance owed by or to the customer. Please allow 4 to 6 weeks for delivery. Offer available while quantities last.

Your Privacy—The Reader Service is committed to protecting your privacy. Our Privacy Policy is available online at www.ReaderService.com or upon request from the Reader Service.

We make a portion of our mailing list available to reputable third parties that offer products we believe may interest you. If you prefer that we not exchange your name with third parties, or if you wish to clarify or modify your communication preferences, please visit us at www.ReaderService.com/consumerschoice or write to us at Reader Service Preference Service, P.O. Box 9062, Buffalo, NY 14269. Include your complete name and address.

HP11B

REQUEST YOUR FREE BOOKS!
2 FREE NOVELS PLUS 2 FREE GIFTS!

♠ Harlequin®
Super Romance®
Exciting, emotional, unexpected!

YES! Please send me 2 FREE Harlequin® Superromance® novels and my 2 FREE gifts (gifts are worth about $10). After receiving them, if I don't wish to receive any more books, I can return the shipping statement marked "cancel." If I don't cancel, I will receive 6 brand-new novels every month and be billed just $4.69 per book in the U.S. or $5.24 per book in Canada. That's a saving of at least 15% off the cover price! It's quite a bargain! Shipping and handling is just 50¢ per book in the U.S. and 75¢ per book in Canada.* I understand that accepting the 2 free books and gifts places me under no obligation to buy anything. I can always return a shipment and cancel at any time. Even if I never buy another book, the two free books and gifts are mine to keep forever.

135/336 HDN FC6T

Name	(PLEASE PRINT)	
Address		Apt. #
City	State/Prov.	Zip/Postal Code

Signature (if under 18, a parent or guardian must sign)

Mail to the **Reader Service:**
IN U.S.A.: P.O. Box 1867, Buffalo, NY 14240-1867
IN CANADA: P.O. Box 609, Fort Erie, Ontario L2A 5X3

Not valid for current subscribers to Harlequin Superromance books.

Are you a current subscriber to Harlequin Superromance books and want to receive the larger-print edition?
Call 1-800-873-8635 or visit www.ReaderService.com.

* Terms and prices subject to change without notice. Prices do not include applicable taxes. Sales tax applicable in N.Y. Canadian residents will be charged applicable taxes. Offer not valid in Quebec. This offer is limited to one order per household. All orders subject to credit approval. Credit or debit balances in a customer's account(s) may be offset by any other outstanding balance owed by or to the customer. Please allow 4 to 6 weeks for delivery. Offer available while quantities last.

Your Privacy—The Reader Service is committed to protecting your privacy. Our Privacy Policy is available online at www.ReaderService.com or upon request from the Reader Service.

We make a portion of our mailing list available to reputable third parties that offer products we believe may interest you. If you prefer that we not exchange your name with third parties, or if you wish to clarify or modify your communication preferences, please visit us at www.ReaderService.com/consumerschoice or write to us at Reader Service Preference Service, P.O. Box 9062, Buffalo, NY 14269. Include your complete name and address.

HSR11